THE LAST BATTLESHIP

JOSHUA T. CALVERT

FOREWORD

Dear Reader,

I don't normally address you with a preface, but in this case, I'm making an exception because I think it makes sense to explain how you should read this book: This is the first volume of at least one trilogy. I've been working for months on a large story arc with lots of little mosaic pieces all in place. As such, *The Last Battleship* is more in the tradition of a Peter F. Hamilton novel than current Kindle stories with continuous action. Yes, *The Last Battleship* is military science fiction, but it's also space opera with great world building. So, you can expect action, but a good half of the first book deals with politics, world building, positioning of chess pieces, and loose ends that don't fall into place until volume two or three. I deliberately chose intermediate chapters that repeatedly interrupt (in very short form) the main plot to give little glimpses of 'the bad guys.' So, a little patience is needed, just like 'before.' In return, I promise that when 'the bullets fly,' they will fly all the time, and over the next volumes they will have more impact, as you will hopefully know your way around the world by then and easily find your way. I've already prepared volumes two and three so you won't have to wait more than four weeks for the sequels.

Sincerely,
  Joshua T. Calvert

Portimao, Thursday, January 27, 2023

PROLOGUE

L udwig von Borningen climbed the seemingly endless steps of the Palace of Unity. He approached alone of his own volition. You could think what you wanted about Omega, but he didn't think the AI was an assassin. Not today, anyway. Not on this night.

The palace had been built on the highest point of Harthholm, a four-hundred-meter-high mountain with a flat top, around which the villas of the upper city were arranged with their neat red tile roofs and white facades. The planet's capital spread out like a shining sea under the moonlight and the palace rose like the Acropolis from the center. Not that there was anything antique about the monumental structure, even if the architects had suffered from some of the ancient Greek building pathos when they designed the thirty-story building with its many columns and frescoes.

Each spire of the octagon ended in a tower topped with bright flames, which could be seen over a hundred kilometers away, well into the countryside, announcing Harbingen's self-confidence and wealth. Of course, they were much more than that. Powerful fusion generators hummed inside them, permanently feeding the invisible force field that protected the palace.

Ludwig still remembered the first time he had climbed the 1,111 steps, from the triumphal hall below to the palace, on his second day as a young member of Parliament. The awe he felt then at the edifice he faced, that collective throne of the people that seemed more reminiscent of imperial than democratic times. It was precisely in this, however, that he had felt the importance of the palace: Democracy could show greatness, and it should, in order to illustrate and tangibly demonstrate the success of rule to the people.

Today would be his last visit to Parliament, and it was taking place under entirely different circumstances. He paused on the eight-hundredth step and turned to look at the city. In the upper city, lights glowed, fireworks rose into the air and dissolved into colorful, short-lived flowers in the night sky. The Harbingentag celebration had already been going for several hours, to mark the 80th anniversary of the founding of the colony—at least by most of the citizens. In the outer districts of the city, diabolical fires were flickering as whole houses burned down. In his mind's eye, he saw the crowds there, fighting street battles with police and riot-bots.

It was a strange sight, a city torn between joy and anger, and yet the most fitting the night could produce.

He mentally shook himself and continued on his way.

The main gate towered twenty meters high and featured elaborate carvings, a scene of the first colonists stepping out, close together, from a ship's hangar onto the New World. There stood six palace guards in medieval-style powered armor. Two of them came to attention while the others surveyed him with their visors closed, suspiciously he imagined. He nodded once to those on the right and once to the left, then passed through the gate and entered the palace.

The interior was cathedrallike, large enough to hold thousands of people. The ceiling was so high it was hard to make out the complex images that had been hand-painted there. In front of a standing desk and box was the semi-circular plenum with over a thousand gray seats on the rising tiers of brown marble. Balloon drones provided warm yellow light, almost homey and reminiscent of candlelight. Ludwig walked down the center aisle toward the lectern, where a lone figure waited for him. He was trailed by the echo of his own footsteps until he finally stopped, alone in the vast hall that completely shut out the noise of a capital in turmoil and created an unnatural silence.

I'm alone, he reminded himself, nodding to the figure standing in front of him at the lectern. It gazed at him out of lifeless eyes. It was slightly shorter than him, with smooth, gray limbs clad in composite instead of clothing.

"I greet you, High Lord of Borningen," said the robot, inclining his head. His expression was meaningless according to the laws and left no doubt about his mechanical nature.

"My family hasn't held that title for two generations," Ludwig replied stiffly.

"But you do intend to wear it again, don't you?"

"Shall I call you Sprecher or Omega?"

"Both are the same," the AI replied.

Ludwig tried not to think about the fact that the entire mountain they were standing on was a powerful computational core containing the data sphere the Harbingers called "Omega," in reference to their last greatest invention.

"I think you offered to talk to me in order to make peace?"

"That's right. According to my calculations, my assumption of office as the primary legislator will entail a consolidation period of several years, which our people—"

"*Civil war.* You mean that *my* people will be plunged into civil war."

"Is that the term you chose when you prepared your Separatists for this day?" Omega wanted to know.

If it had been human, Ludwig would have said it sounded

cynical and suspected a rhetorical sideswipe. As it was, he wondered what was really behind the robot's words, through which the AI was speaking to him.

"Does it matter?"

"Everything plays a role. Every word is data, and data is the baseline of the cosmos."

"We have different views on this, as you know. I came because you wanted to negotiate," Ludwig said seriously. "So, here I am."

"Your fleet at Artros is of concern to Parliament. According to my calculations, an armed conflict would result in the destruction of your three sleeper ships, along with the Separatist fleet under *your* command that has gathered around them."

Ludwig did not respond because he did not want to get into a discussion about figures with an AI. He stood by his convictions, but he would not be standing here if he had been a hothead.

"I don't want a conflict with my people. They are mistaken in their recent decisions, and they will eventually come to that painful realization," he said after a long pause, "but I am not willing to wait that long. We are Harbingers, and we would rather go down than submit to a fate we did not choose."

"But the people *have* voted. Are you willing to shed the blood of your own countrymen to impose your views?"

"If there is an armed conflict, it won't be because we start it. We've built sleeper ships; with the same resources, we could have produced warships in the last four years."

"That would have been more difficult than large civilian vessels because of regulatory oversight," Omega noted.

Ludwig remained silent.

"I have decided to let you go. There will be no violence under my rule. This is best for Harbingen."

"Is that what your *calculations* say?" Even he was not immune to a certain degree of cynicism.

"Yes."

"Good." Ludwig wanted to turn to go.

"But you must never return," said Omega. It almost sounded like there was some emphasis in its voice, but he was probably imagining it.

"We won't."

"You want to leave for another spiral arm. Stay there. Forever."

Ludwig froze and cleared his throat. He should have been aware that the AI knew more than it was supposed to.

"You also know our jump route there, I assume?"

"If your navigators' calculations and my own match, yes."

"Then I have a condition."

"A condition?" asked the Omega.

"The route. It remains a secret. Forever."

"No one has access to my computational core except the chancellor and the admiral. No one but you will ever have access. That is my offer."

Silence spread through the palace. Ludwig wondered if the factions knew about this meeting, and how much Omega had told the human representatives.

"I accept. We will leave the system in three days via the outer jump point. Jump point control must not be occupied."

"Acceptable."

"I have one more request, though I know full well that I have no way to force you to comply: Our sleeper ships do not have enough capacity for every loyalist. Do not persecute them for their beliefs. Let those go who wish to go."

"I will not prosecute anyone unless he or she threatens the safety and integrity of Harbingen."

"Like me?"

"Like you."

"No intelligence or purge actions," Ludwig demanded.

"Then, in a system-wide message, I will ask our loyalists not to take violent action against Harbingen, not to form a rival political faction, and not to undertake a political underground to educate the civilian population. Agreed?"

The robot paused briefly, then inclined its head. "That is acceptable."

Ludwig nodded and turned to leave again. After two steps, he paused and turned his head to look back at the robot.

"Why are you doing this? This conversation? You could have taken me out. Are you afraid I might endanger your rule?"

"Fear is an emotion that is not a possible outcome of my heuristics," the AI replied tonelessly. "But my job is to protect the Harbinger people from harm, and that has recently included you, High Lord. However, making you a martyr and letting blood flow in the streets was not an option."

"You are overlooking one thing in your calculations, that *you* are the disaster, conjured up by this Parliament." Ludwig spread his arms and shook his head before leaving the palace.

His shuttle was already waiting outside the force field at the three hundredth step to take him off the planet, to Artros, away from his home, to which he would never return.

1

"U nidentified hyperspace signatures!" shouted a specialist in front of Captain Orb. The control consoles were laid out in two dense semicircles on the large observation deck that sloped slightly forward. The transparent disk in front, now showing twinkling stars, was actually a gray wall of composite, heavily armored and buried deep in the Brown-III asteroid, Harbingen's last listening post that monitored the outer system jump point.

Orb's post was that of a sidelined officer, which was known not only to his superiors, who had transferred him here because he had inadvertently come under fire for his politics, but also to his subordinate crew and junior officers. Nothing happened out here, except the regular exits of interstellar traders, fleet ships, and private yachts. It was an administrative job that had nothing in common with the excitement of hunting pirates or even fighting humanity's archenemy, the Clicks.

Typically, a ship would jump into the system, extend its sensor beams and check its position while transmitting its transponder code. Captain Orb's job was to verify it and disable the eight automated defense platforms which surrounded the jump point like oversized plates staring at cutlery. It was all routine, and he had nothing to do with it. His specialists, most still in training by the chief, handled everything. He merely sat in his chair, bored for one shift, while he spent his other shift bored in his room or in the small, cramped mess hall where the recycled air smelled of sweaty feet.

So, when the call of his subordinate rang out, whom he could not make out among the two dozen uniformed sailors in their seats because no one turned around, he was far too irritated to say anything but, "What?"

"Multiple unidentified hyperspace signatures!" the voice in front of him repeated.

"Several? Only one exit after the next is allowed," he grumbled. He frowned and leaned forward in his chair. Several faces turned to him. He straightened and said loudly, "Identify! How many contacts, exactly?"

"I count thirty so far, but they are steadily increasing. One new contact every second!"

"Transponder codes?"

"Negative!"

"Clicks!" shouted another specialist, this one easily identifiable by the way he leaned forward at his console, a jumble of displays and input pads which surrounded him.

"Clicks," Orb repeated lamely, his eyes widening. "Here?"

"Ninety-four contacts!"

"Fire the defensive platforms!" he bellowed superfluously, as he saw several bright, short-lived explosions pierce the blackness of space through the virtual screen in front of them. The battle was already in full swing.

Ninety-four Click ships, he thought, quickly wiping the cold sweat from his brow. *Why Harbingen?*

"Platforms one through eight are already engaged," the specialist reported.

Not enough. Eight is not enough!

"Priority alert to Fleet base," Orb said. "Send along all signatures and determine current and projected flight vectors!"

The specialist, one back among many in their dark gray uniforms, didn't reply, which could be tolerated in the current threat situation.

The listening post was a shapeless lump of rock and loose regolith, compressed and hollowed out before it had been pushed into high orbit around the outer gas giant of the Harbingen System. The station was built inside the asteroid so it could withstand Bohr's harsh radiation. Long-range sensors with the ability to detect nearly the entire electromagnetic radiation spectrum had been placed on its surface, giving the listening post the appearance of a mud ball marred with cutlery. Since its orbit was located at the Lagrange point between Bohr and his largest moon Inn, it maintained its relative position with respect to the outer jump point at the center of the convergence point of Bohr's and Inn's gravitational funnels. Thus, they always had a clear view, and nothing escaped the complex sensor systems.

The Clicks' ships—elongated, teardrop-shaped structures about a hundred meters long with pearly hulls—flew in a wide, fanlike formation toward Harbingen, the only inhabited planet in the system of the same name. Apart from a few asteroid settlements and lunar habitats, the overwhelming majority of the two billion inhabitants lived on the pale blue dot so far away that its location had to be guessed rather than seen at the edge of the viewscreen in front of Captain Orb.

"Why are they still on course?" he asked angrily, despite knowing that it was a stupid question. *Ninety-four Clicks! Here!*

"They are flying at maximum thrust: seven Gs," the specialist reported. "Six of them have been destroyed by the platforms, but the others will soon be out of range."

"Not for the torpedoes! Each platform has a hundred of them loaded!"

9

"No torpedoes were fired, sir."

"What?" Orb leaned forward again. "What do you mean?"

"Malfunction in the weapons guidance systems," someone else explained.

"In *all of them* at the same time?"

"Yes, sir."

"You've got to be kidding me!"

The Priority Level One Alert Warning Signal, intended for the highest danger level—like an alien attack—took a little over ninety-one minutes to reach Harbingen, at the current distance of eleven astronomical units between Bohr and Harbingen. So, the Clicks' fleet would make quite a bit of progress by then, but it would still take them a week to reach the planet, if they could maintain their insane acceleration. A highly dubious notion, considering the enormous physical strain it would put on the crews of the ships.

The battle took place five million kilometers from Harbingen. The Harbinger fleet used the week to prepare and position itself in a fan formation as ordered by the commander aboard the *Oberon*. The Click attack fleet had adopted a tight wedge-shaped formation during its flight, as if it were a pearly arrow-head targeting the human world.

As the attack fleet came within range of long-range defenses, several thousand torpedoes exited the launch bays of three hundred ships of Harbinger's fleet and sped toward the invaders like a swarm of accelerated fireflies. But before the torpedoes reached their targets, the attackers dissolved in a torrent of violent explosions that, for a few seconds, created a second, flickering sun. Hard radiation raced up and down the spectrum, blasting the approaching wall of torpedoes.

Then it was over. What remained was a dense, massive

cloud of debris that had somehow survived the inferno without turning into volatile gas molecules.

Sarah Mantell's hands tightened in the cushions of her gimbaled acceleration seat as the braking phase neared its end. *Ezekiel's Revenge* rode a propulsion flare of ultra-hot plasma, spreading like a mile-long spear in front of the independent minesweeper, about to incinerate the first debris of the annihilated Click fleet.

The spacecraft was a hulking structure made of a central sphere on which scarred deuterium tanks were stuck in a composite frame. The fusion reactor's drive nacelle was a fifteen-meter-diameter funnel that looked far too large and accounted for nearly half the ship's total length. In short, *Ezekiel's Revenge* was as ugly as its reputation; after all, the independent minesweepers were referred to by the fleet as "scavengers"—and that was considered flattering. Since many of the thirty ships that had pounced on the two-day-old debris of the Click fleet also hired themselves out as smugglers to make ends meet, they were notorious among the general population as pirates and almost never received permission to dock at the orbital stations of the Core Worlds.

Sarah Mantell, of course, had her own opinion. She was a starship captain at heart and loved her free life among the stars, belonging neither to Fleet nor to one of the big interstellar corporations. If that meant living in her own flying bowl and being confined to the underdeveloped outer worlds if she wanted to breathe fresh, unrecycled air, then so be it.

"Braking phase complete," reported Georg Breusken, her copilot and fusion engineer and the father of her eight-year-old son, who was currently sleeping in an acceleration cocoon in her cabin. "Activating radiators."

"Then the dirty work can begin," Karell Poikow said

cheerfully from the third seat on the bridge, diagonally behind Sarah's other shoulder.

The bulky sensor specialist tapped away on his old-fashioned keyboard, each stroke sounding like someone smashing saltines with a hammer. Six powerful sensor beams extended from the hull of *Ezekiel's Revenge* and soon began scanning the surrounding space.

The ship itself was over fifty years old and, despite good maintenance and many small improvements, could easily be described as a piece of junk. But the sensors had been upgraded only last year, after they had picked up a stray freighter from Okasaki. The Japanese-ethnic Core World made the best telescopes, radars, and lidars you could buy in the entire Terran Federation, and Sarah hadn't had to pay for them. That made them even more valuable.

The virtual display that developed as a patchy hologram on the wall in front of them showed the cloud of debris they were slowly and silently gliding toward. Dark shadows rotated in apparent slow motion around an invisible center and formed a stretched cylinder, through which hundreds of individual parts twinkling like stars could be seen again and again.

"My goodness, this is one huge, dense debris field," Georg said. "From the footage we've seen of the battle, there should be billions of little pieces of shrapnel flying around here, but there are some pretty massive chunks right there."

"The field has a cylindrical shape and is rotating around a point that I can't locate yet. Calculations are ongoing," Karell said intently. "It consists of eighty-six massive iron cones, eighty-one meters long. In between, there may very well be shrapnel: countless pieces from the size of a soccer ball to that of a rivet."

"Iron cones?" Sarah asked, irritated, imagining that the thousand sparkles between the powerful shadows filling the screen before them were tiny slivers of the destroyed enemy ships. In every direction, she saw plasma flares from other minesweepers approaching like scavengers to a carcass. *Like a flock of vultures,* she thought to herself and snorted laconically. Little by little, the flames died out and the blackness of space remained.

"Yeah," Karell replied. "I don't know what those things were loaded with, but what we're looking at is a dense cloud of massive pieces of metal bigger than the *Revenge*, and they're so tightly packed that we'd better get out there with our spacecraft."

Sarah snorted. "Forget it! With the sensors from the RFZ, we couldn't even see a cargo container if it was a kilometer away."

"May I remind you that Fleet pays us to look for mines before they send their people in?" Georg said. "The emphasis is on *search*, not *find*."

"I don't like this," she grumbled. "There should be a widely scattered debris field of tiny pieces that we scan from relative safety. What's out there is different, though. If the iron accumulations are really as large as they look, then yes, the damned Click ships would have had to be built with cast iron, which would have made them pretty heavy."

"And with no room for the crew," Georg added.

"But it would explain why they didn't return fire at the jump point or here. Maybe no one was on board," Karell said. "You guys saw it on the news feeds; a tight formation like that was absolute suicide. No captain would have done it precisely because a single hit on a sister ship could have led to a chain reaction of hyper-fast debris, like what we all observed."

"And what good is that going to do?"

"You're asking me?" The sensor expert snorted behind her. "Why would I know what those damned metal skulls are thinking?"

Sarah made a curt hand gesture. "It doesn't matter! We

have a job to do, and we want to earn our money honestly. We're not vultures, after all. I'm going out."

"Forget it, your son—"

"What about him? Have you ever seen me take a back seat just because I became a mother? The little one means everything to me, but Georg and I can't dump everything on you just because you don't have any offspring."

Karell sighed and shrugged. He knew when he couldn't win an argument with her and did not press her further.

"Be careful."

"I will." She unfastened the seat belts, which automatically retracted from her chest and hips like snakes, and floated out of her seat. She held onto the metal arch of the gimbal with her hands and pressed a kiss to Georg's mouth.

"You take care of yourself out there. And don't take any chances, all right?"

"Sure," she said truthfully, and said goodbye with a smile as she moved toward the living module of *Ezekiel's Revenge*, one of four back-to-back spheres of life support.

The shuttle was jammed under the second module, which contained the mess hall and supply rooms, by four retaining clamps. The small ion-field glider sat like a dark moth between the large deuterium tanks, attached by a short, thick umbilical cord to the lower airlock, above which was emblazoned a large red S. Twenty years ago, when she had bought *Ezekiel's Revenge* from an enthusiastic smuggler, Sarah had made sure relative directions had been marked on the ship to provide guidance for passengers and new crew members with little experience in zero gravity. In space, it was easy for up to become down and right to become left, and even practiced 0-G veterans like her often found themselves shifting gears a second too late in the heat of the moment.

After this job, Georg and Karell would be bugging her about how it was time for a newer ship with inertial compensation, but she still resisted. The Omega might spit out one technological marvel after another, not only making Harbingen rich but blessing the Federation with ever-new possibilities, but who understood exactly how it all worked? Hell no, she would continue to keep it as simple as possible. Make no mistakes and everything else as best as they could. *That* was the best motto for free ship crews like hers.

She passed through the airlock and slid nimbly into the ion-field glider, which had been ancient when she bought it ten years ago, and manually locked the hatch behind her. Then she strapped herself into the pilot's seat, which wasn't even gimbaled, and started the ship's systems. In front of her, the instruments came to life with an audible whir, followed by flashing lights that formed a colorful kaleidoscope before her.

"I'm in," she said after pulling on the headset, from which the ear pads were peeling away. The cable was plugged into the junction box above her head and wobbled as she flipped two toggle switches, releasing the retaining clips.

"Good hunting!" came Georg's reply. He couldn't quite keep his concern out of his voice, but she chose to ignore it. This wasn't her first mission as a minesweeper in a debris field of a past space battle.

It was always the same thing: The battle was fought—ideally, the Federation won—and then the free ships were paid to be cannon fodder to search out possible sources of danger for Fleet barges that would follow them. There were no mines, of course, since such things were not used, but occasionally there were unstable antimatter reactors that were ejected before the destruction of a ship. Just one malfunction with that, and the entire field would be obliterated. So, people like Sarah scanned everything, including distress signals from escape pods and other valuable relics that could be bagged without attracting attention. The Fleet weighed the risks and accepted the situation if they sent their own crews. Flying through a debris field was highly dangerous, and not everyone returned unscathed. Some debris was large, easy to dodge—

and some was tiny, deadly to the hull of an ion-field glider like the one she was currently sitting in, depending on her speed.

"Approaching entry point," she radioed, more to keep herself company than to report her status, and pushed the joystick forward to dive between two of the giant iron cylinders. "The connection is about to possibly..."

A roar in her ears told her she was already out of contact, so she shut it down to rid herself of the unpleasant noise.

The pitch-black formations that filled the window in front of her looked like eerie shadows writhing around an invisible center. Like bugs in the cosmos, they rapidly floated past in front of her, but Sarah recognized the parallax effect and didn't need an extra push to dive between the first cylinders. With rapid inputs on her control panel, she activated the multidirectional scanners that sat like bumps on the hull and scanned much of the electromagnetic spectrum. One by one, images from the ultrasonic scan appeared on the screens, followed by infrared images.

"The cylinders have already cooled, no residual heat, no radiation reflection at all. They're cold as ice, barely warmer than the surrounding vacuum," she said into the mission log she would later sign off on and send to Fleet. "They are not uniform, and they are not smooth. Ultrasound shows several indentations."

She had an idea and added a three-dimensional image of a Click cruiser as it had appeared during the battle. She stripped the image of detail until only a grid of false colors remained. Then she superimposed it over the processed ultrasound data. The results surprised her.

"Curious. According to the databases, the basic length, width, and height are consistent with a Type 004 STD cruiser. There are some clear indentations at the rear where the drive nacelles must have been, and on the upper forward section where the bridge should have been, according to the publicly available data. Those are the only systems that are essential for rudimentary flight capability. But the rest... I'm trying to scan and match some of the smaller debris. With a spectral analysis, I should be able to determine their composition."

She followed her own directive and pointed the dorsal sensor systems forward, where the darkness was repeatedly streaked with dense glittering patches. The high-powered spotlights under the bow of the ion-field glider flooded a cone-shaped area over a kilometer long, allowing the high-resolution cameras to piece together a complex picture along with data from the other spectra. It took five minutes of dodging large pieces of debris with short pulses from the steering thrusters for the dusty computer to spit out an answer to her most pressing questions.

"Well, if that's not an answer to whether or not the Clicks are really robots," she muttered. "The debris is ninety-five percent likely to be from drive pods and broken bridge cocoons. No biomarkers detected. Barring stray gas molecules, all pieces—regardless of size—consist of these two parts of the cruisers. Except for remnants of the composite shells and tanks, of course. If I had to guess, I'd say that the ships were cast in iron and had no crews aboard. But why? If no torpedoes from Bradley's fleet were responsible for their initial destruction, it could only have been caused by an initial collision followed by a chain reaction similar to Kessler syndrome."

Sarah hovered near one of the gigantic cylinders to her left, against which her glider must have looked like a moth next to a whale. After two collision warnings, she gave up, exasperated, and switched the autopilot to primary mode. Inside the debris cloud, the density of dangerous fragments was increasing, bouncing from one iron colossus to another and back again like a chaotic ping-pong match. When they hit each other, they shattered into smaller pieces and changed direction, making it impossible for her to steer manually even with the display aids. So, she aimed the sensors and expanded their arc to make a ten-minute recording of the movement of the debris. That should be enough data to predict their trajectories.

As the control software steered her through the madness of heavy metals, making unpredictable jerky movements, she cursed and vowed to buy a software update soon. When the motion data finally came up, she rechecked the fit of her harness, then looked at the simulation of flight vectors and velocities.

"They're not only rotating around some center, they're attracted to it like a magnet. The distance between the individual cylinders decreases in the direction of pull, and convection zones form between them into which the smaller debris is sucked."

With a few hasty inputs, she stretched the simulation over a time duration of an hour and blinked.

"In less than thirty minutes, everything will clump together. But why?" She snorted and increased the thrust from the ion thrusters and glided swiftly toward the gap between four iron giants, which were beginning to close in front of her like a giant rosette. At the last moment she flew through it and exhaled, cheeks puffed out, to get rid of her tension. For a moment she had thought that the wings, which were suitable for atmospheric flight, would collide and break off.

Outside her window, it abruptly became darker. The light from Harbingen's distant central star was mostly obscured by the closely rotating iron cylinders. This made the bow lights an intruder in the alien microcosm, and they seemed to increase in intensity.

A chill rushed down Sarah's spine and she suddenly felt both locked in and locked out at the same time. Every creak of the cabin and every whir of a computer seemed like a disturbance that could awaken alien powers.

Shh, she thought, then swallowed when an intrusive beep startled her.

"Collision Warning" flashed red on her primary display

and the navigation console showed a large, menacing dot five hundred meters ahead of her.

Sarah leaned forward and stared into the beam of the headlights, only to let out a curse. Right in the middle of the black nothingness, where multitudes of small, unseen pieces of debris were flying uniformly toward the center, was a sphere fifty meters in diameter swallowing the light she had brought with her. Her fuel gauge was now emitting an error message. The consumption did not match the thrust.

Irritated, she frowned and initiated a short burst of braking thrust that should have been enough to bring her to a stop. It worked for a moment, but then she suddenly accelerated again, even though the engines remained silent.

"What the hell...?" she breathed and initiated counterthrust. Sure enough, she slowed and then slid back, but again, the fuel input was many times more than expected. "A magnet! It's a giant freaking magnet!"

Hastily, she initiated a turn maneuver and started up the main engine to increase the still-closing distance to the dense, massive center of the debris field. The close-range scanners searched for gaps in the closing wall of iron without a separate prompt as the pilot software recognized her predicament and tried to plot a way out.

There were not many left.

Only one, in fact, and it was between two colliding shadows that crashed into each other in front of her like giant rams. The magnetic force relentlessly pulling them toward the center of the debris field was strong enough to prevent a cascade of uncontrolled collisions. Normally, that would have been good news for Sarah, because massive, erratic cylinders of compacted iron could pulverize her ship with a simple touch, or at least send it into a dangerous tailspin. But here, where the debris formed a closed sphere around the sinister cavity at its center, less movement meant more danger in the form of an impenetrable wall. The shuttle had no armament, except for a defunct maser cannon —not that she thought she could have done much with it against the black behemoths. So, her only option was to flee forward.

The autopilot applied 80 percent thrust to the ion engine, known more for efficiency than high acceleration, and propelled them forward at an uncomfortable but tolerable 3 Gs into a rising turn, anticipating the likely position changes of the obstacles. Sarah skimmed the data and noted that the AI planned to hold back 30 percent fuel after the maneuver as a safety margin to return to *Ezekiel's Revenge*.

"Fuck it!" she said, and unceremoniously shut down the pilot software. She took over the joystick and pushed the thrust control to the maximum, which gave her a meager 5 Gs that pressed her into the seat as if she had been hit by a wrecking ball. The fuel gauge knew only one direction from here on: Down. The glider rode its long, blue tail, which bathed the artificial debris sphere with a fluctuating glow, and illuminated a straight line toward a gap five meters high and twenty meters wide.

"Come on!" Sarah growled through clenched teeth, which she couldn't pry apart due to five times her body weight bearing down on her. Just before the narrow band of shimmering stars in the wall of darkness ahead, she began to scream.

A metallic screech rang out as the ion-field glider broke free of the sphere. A dozen flashing red alerts simultaneously flooded the central display in front of her, and a schematic representation of her craft highlighted so many damaged areas that her watering eyes lost track of them all. Everything wobbled and jerked, as if she were sailing through a hurricane on a fragile raft before going quiet again.

With a titanic effort, she pushed her right hand forward until her trembling fingers reached the thrust control and pulled it back to the default position. Suddenly, a pleasant 1 G of acceleration remained, and the wrecking ball on her chest instantly disappeared.

"We're not repeating that," she gasped, blinking the tears from the corners of her eyes so she could survey the damage report alarms that were bathing the cabin in red light. "All right. Communications system destroyed, right wing torn off —don't need it out here, anyway. Left retaining clips crushed and not responding. That's going to be a problem, but not yet. Loss of atmosphere. That's a hell of a problem."

She grumbled and raised her left arm, which felt like it was plagued by a severe muscle ache, to pull the breathing apparatus out of its holding loop above her head. Since the loss was slow, oxygen would have to do for now, as long as the temperature didn't drop too quickly.

By now, the debris field was heavily compacted, but there was still sharp-edged composite debris whizzing around that she had to avoid. But radar and lidar, even with their rather old technology, had no problem providing her with a safe course.

"Georg, Karell?" she tried over the course-range transmitter, only to find that the power supply for the small antenna on the bow had been interrupted. "Great."

The dorsal sensor beams had also been so damaged when she crashed through the sphere wall she could no longer target *Ezekiel's Revenge*. With her fuel down to 5 percent and because she'd had to shut down to drift out of the four-thousand-kilometer-diameter debris field, she held out no hope of returning to her ship. Her two crew members, whom she could well call her family, would hopefully be long gone by the time they registered the magnetic field building up. At least she prayed they would.

As the cloud of half-evaporated and fused remains from the Clicks' hulls thinned, she turned the autopilot back on and located the leak in the hull using a drinking tube. She squeezed the water out of it and watched as the drops moved, first leisurely and then faster, toward a spot below the air recycler in the ceiling. Using a mono-bonded, self-adhesive patch she had pulled from one of the emergency panels, she plugged the microscopic hole, invisible to the naked eye, then returned to her seat.

"What did I just see, huh?" she asked her glowing console. The sonorous hum of computer systems calmed her. She should have been scared, but instead she was just fixated on what she had just witnessed. It was like a nightmare that had passed so quickly she wasn't even sure she had really dreamed it. She called up the system data for Harbingen, with its ultra-hot rocky planets, the only habitable one being Harbingen of the same name, and its two gas giants, Bohr and Braun. Next she marked the position of the debris field, which she was still moving away from, although her acceleration, which should have remained the same in vacuum even after the engine shutdown, was gradually slowing. It was a million kilometers from Harbingen's densely industrialized twin moons of Kor and Kir, and five million kilometers from the inner gas giant Braun, in whose conjunction zone was the system's inner jump point, where the gravitational forces between Braun and Harbingen intersected in a unique configuration that allowed the space distortion fields of starships to rip open an entrance or exit into subspace. The only other similar point was far out between Braun's big brother Bohr and the ice giant Karl.

"What the hell were you trying to do with those poured-out ships?" she whispered. She looked at the diagram and frowned thoughtfully. "Tried..." Sarah tasted the word on her tongue and snorted. *What if they didn't just try, but actually achieved it?* What was their intention in performing such a maneuver? What was the point of pouring iron on a hundred ships and rendering them unfit for battle? Harbingen was an important strategic target, and with the newest Titan, the *Oberon*, and a powerful escort fleet, not an easy nut to crack.

This was no coincidence, since the most promising research project on true hyperspace gates with stable connections was taking place on the moon Kor under Omega's guidance. No one knew how far they really were. If the Federation succeeded, unlike the Clicks, they would no longer have to rely on jump points and could finally end this incessant conflict. That was the reason why most of the fleet had gathered around the moon after the battle for *Oberon*, although the enemy fleet had obviously moved in a direct line toward Harbingen.

"What a waste," she thought as she looked at the circular representation of the debris field on the display. Then she got an idea. She typed commands into the console in front of her in analog because the voice control had long since broken. The computer calculated the mass of the field based on her theory that each of the ninety-four ships had been pumped full of compacted iron atoms, and simulated a packed, rotating mass to put it in gravitational relation to the rest of the system.

It took her five minutes to see the result.

"Hm," she uttered, rubbing her lips, only to bump her fingers against the breathing mask. She pulled it away from her mouth. Her head buzzed as she looked at the numbers, and she switched back to the display of the conjunction zones with the two jump points, except there were now three. The third was between the new center of mass and the moon Kor until it suddenly disappeared again. A display error?

"What was that?" She ran the display back and there it was again.

Kor, a barren ball of regolith right between Harbingen, with its great green continents and deep blue oceans, and the debris field that now resembled a pitch-black ball of mass. Kor, just like its twin Kir, pulled elliptical orbits around their planet, to which they were bound, once every twenty hours. The data the onboard computer possessed was asynchronous due to an error in the data heuristics, so the AI had nineteen hours of latency.

Again, it rewound, and again the jump point appeared for

ten virtual minutes and then was gone as soon as Kor moved on. As the moon disappeared, so did the conjunction zone.

"Holy shit," she whispered and swallowed. "They created an artificial temporary jump point with a jump window every twenty hours!"

She hastily called up the current time from her forearm display and shuddered. In thirty minutes, Harbingen, Kor, and the debris field would slide into conjunction and allow a hole into subspace if enough energy was expended.

"The Clicks are coming back!"

Horrified, she hacked at the button for communication, only to find that the entire system was still offline.

"Shit!"

Frustrated, Sarah went through her options. She considered squeezing into one of the old spacesuits and going outside to manually repair the system, but even as an accomplished technician, that was not merely unrealistic, it was irresponsible.

She was struggling with the thought of never seeing her son and Georg again when a sudden jolt went through the small ship and, despite the now extremely low microgravity, she began to wiggle in her seat.

A loud hiss came from behind her, and as she turned, the hatch through which she normally floated into the airlock of *Ezekiel's Revenge*, was cut open.

"Hey!" said the figure in the spacesuit, who poked his head in a moment later. It was Georg. "Gotcha!"

"This is Sarah Mantell, captain of the free ship *Ezekiel's Revenge*," Sarah transmitted as she took her place in the pilot's seat on the bridge. George and Karell were extremely agitated, not only because they had violated their orders not to fly into the debris field, but also because they were horrified at the loss of the ion-field glider, which had drifted into space due to the lack of any holding clamps and been burned to cinders by the exhaust flare from their fusion engines. They did not understand why she had abandoned it so quickly, and she did not have time to explain it to them. If she was right, they only had eight minutes before it was time.

"This is Sarah Mantell, captain of the free ship *Ezekiel's Revenge*," she repeated. "I need to speak to Commander Konrad Bradley."

All she got was white noise from the speakers.

"Bloody hell! Those bloody Fleet asses. I've been using those frequencies for a lot of..." she continued her tirade until there was a loud *crack!*

"This is a scrambled priority channel!" a cold female voice rang out. "*Ezekiel's Revenge*, you are under arrest for—"

"I don't care! I just came from the debris field and the commander—"

"The commander *what?*"

Bradley. The voice belonged to Konrad Bradley. Inevitably, Sarah stiffened and gulped his commanding tone.

"Sir, I believe the Clicks are planning an attack on Kor in less than six minutes. The first one was merely—"

"You will report for arrest at Fleet Base Delta in orbit around Kir," Harbingen's senior Fleet officer interrupted her gruffly. "Then you will explain to our intelligence how you got this priority code. Fly there now and deactivate your jump nodes!"

"Commander! You don't understand! The Clicks are going to attack, why shouldn't I—"

"You are a pirate. Why should I trust a pirate who has tuned into my personal priority channel, whose data she could only have obtained by stealing?"

Smuggler, she thought defiantly and felt helpless rage rise inside her. Suddenly the connection was gone.

"Sarah!" Georg shouted, upset, and his tone made her gulp.

On the screens, she saw twelve large objects had jumped into the system, right at the third jump point the Clicks had created with their apparent suicide mission. She blinked once and there were over two dozen, and their numbers continued to increase steadily.

Twenty thousand kilometers away, a cosmic cat's leap, the Clicks' mighty battle cruisers materialized: long, teardrop-shaped objects with an elongated toroid under their bellies, weapons ready. Their emergence, as with every jump, was not preceded by any warning. For a fraction of a nanosecond, the universe itself was ripped open and expanded at its spherical edges into a rotating hole that unnaturally bent the lights of the stars behind it and set them into apparent rotation, then a ship was simply there, sending out concentric gravitational waves, not visible to the eye or high-resolution cameras but visible to the laser interferometers of nearby ships, like that of *Ezekiel's Revenge*. An automated gravity alarm blared, as it tended to do when the ship got too close to an active jump point.

Dozens, and then hundreds, of ships materialized closer and closer to her little nutshell, accelerating with glowing engines toward the moon Kor, where Omega was overseeing the Terran Federation's most important research project.

The current position of the defense fleet, with the giant *Oberon* at its center, like a whale lazily drifting above the cloud bands of Harbingen, was too far away as the moon's first orbital defense platforms launched their torpedo swarms and the first were squadrons launched to face the attacking superior force.

"Next to Omega!" Karell yelled behind her, his voice a shrill squeal. "What is it?"

"The Clicks," Sarah replied absently, activating the battle alert throughout the ship. She accelerated more than she would usually allow *Ezekiel's Revenge* to do under normal circumstances, but if the old lady couldn't take it, it was too late anyway. The Clicks, unlike the Federation, didn't use automated short-range defenses, which probably saved their lives when they swerved in a breakneck turn at 7 Gs acceleration.

The aliens accelerated with glowing fusion flares toward Kor, which was visible as a barely perceptible gray glint against the blue dot of Harbingen. More and more Click ships emerged from hyperspace, releasing short-lived flashes of hard radiation into the battered space around their respective event horizons.

The arrival of the first Click fleet caused astonishment and uncertainty among Harbingen's fleet leadership. Fleet headquarters on Terra had also been concerned with the courier's report. Ultimately, however, they followed Omega's assessment as the system's top political authority and agreed to let expendable free ship owners conduct a more thorough investigation before putting military personnel at risk. For Fleet, it was a win-win situation. On the one hand, they outsourced the dangerous and thus costly work, on the other, every loss of a "free ship" was one less potential pirate.

Omega ordered the *Oberon* and its homeland defense fleet to Lagrange Point 1 between Harbingen and its satellite Kor to conserve fuel while the two hundred ships held their position. The system held several potentially vulnerable and important targets for the aggressive aliens: A colonist fleet orbiting the richest of the Core Worlds as it waited for its six missing sister ships being completed in the orbital shipyards, the planet itself with its nearly two billion inhabitants, and, of course, Kor, where Omega was researching jump gate technology with the assistance of humanity's best scientists and building an experi-

27

mental gate that was already well advanced, if speculation from various news feeds was to be believed.

The course of the attacking Click fleet, which so far numbered more than three hundred ships, and more were continuing to appear at the improvised jump point, did not provide any clues to their target. Along the long tangent, they could have targeted Kor, as well as Harbingen, or the civilian fleet.

The battle began with torpedo volleys from Harbingen and Kor's numerous orbital defense platforms, armed and automated space stations, and the defenders' ships frantically rushing into a protective formation, propulsion nacelles blazing. Defense was aimed primarily at the planet.

When the two fleets were still two hundred thousand kilometers apart, their respective salvos of thousands of projectiles clashed. Sophisticated computer systems made nanosecond decisions and launched submunitions in the form of miniaturized nuclear warheads. Sharp clouds of shrapnel filled space with a kinetic hellfire that pulverized everything in its path and turned it into smaller and more dangerous shards. A cloud of short-lived plasma, ionizing gases, and debris flared in the photon storm of explosions as they spread out, and shortly thereafter was penetrated by the attackers hurtling forward at a brutal 11 Gs, their nose armor lighting up from a burst far too rapid for the human eye to discern, as if they were thundering through a swarm of fireflies.

Over four hundred ships of humanity's worst enemy fired their medium-range weapons while the defenders struggled to intercept the torpedoes with their close defenses. Mass catapults hurled kinetic cones the size of a hand, propelling a hail of ultra-high accelerated iron in front of them. Impossible to locate and far too fast to dodge, the defenders responded with barrages from their anti-aircraft guns at a rate of one thousand shells per second and blanketed the space around their fleet with flickering explosions and dense shrapnel, hoping to catch as many attacking projectiles as possible.

But it was a simple game of numbers, and the Clicks were sending as many ships as they could through the jump point before the conjunction ended.

Sarah watched the brutal skirmish on her screens as she continued to accelerate away from the battle at a half-tolerable 4 Gs. The colored symbols were like a digital mockery to the forces raging out there, reducing them to cold data. It didn't take any special military knowledge to see that the defenders were not merely caught off guard but grossly outnumbered. The Clicks must have assembled several fleets to launch this attack.

The *Oberon* had retreated with most of its escort ships to the orbital shipyards where the already loaded colonist ships had fled. This allowed the aliens to continue their attack on Kor with their entire force. First, they pulverized the remaining active defense platforms in the orbit around the moon, while the installations around Harbingen continued firing at them. But the Clicks seemed to accept the losses and soon began bombarding the fully industrialized surface of Harbingen with thousands of kinetic missiles.

"Sarah!" Karell shouted, "I've got something on the screen here!"

"Me too," she whispered, shaking her head. Why hadn't Bradley listened to her? How narrow-minded did these Fleet assholes have to be?

"No, I mean before us, not the battle!"

She frowned and gave him a wave that took a lot of strength from her arm and hand. Six blinking white symbols appeared on the overview map her close-range scanners had created. As if pulled on a string of pearls, six ships were coming toward them, which, according to initial scans, were sleeper ships. Torpor capsules were often used to save fuel while transiting from the outer system to the interior, to bridge the sometimes several months-long flights with cheap spaceships that utilized ion drives.

The transponder codes indicated the ferries belonged to the Harbingen Science Corporation, which transferred key personnel from the Bentheim research station that orbited the gas giant Bohr to Kor.

"Great, a large-scale shift change," she said. "Why didn't the control software shut it down? They've got sensors, and Fleet alerts have been buzzing through the entire system for an hour!"

"Maybe their communications equipment is broken, or the Clicks' jamming fire is affecting them more than it is us. They could also be in the slipstream of the battle's radio emissions," George suggested.

"This is Sarah Mantell, captain of *Ezekiel's Revenge*," she sent to the forward ship. She used one of the message lasers, figuring she had a better chance with the directional beam. "You must turn back immediately! You're approaching a freaking space battle!"

"No response," Karell said. "They can't hear us."

"What a bummer!"

"The Clicks haven't been interested in any civilian ship so far. Not even the rescue ferries that left Kor and escaped the bombardment and the debris fields in orbit," Georg pointed out, and once again she would have liked to yell at him for his misplaced optimism. He seemed to notice. "Look; there are twelve civilian fleets fleeing in panic to the jump points, and none of them are being attacked by the—"

"Guys!" Karell interrupted them, and his tone made Sarah freeze, which she already was due to the unyielding G forces pressing her into her seat.

"What?" she hissed more harshly than she intended.

"A Click cruiser has turned around and is heading full thrust toward the explorers' ferries."

"That can't be..." Sarah checked the sensor image. Sure enough, a ship that had been blanketing the surface with bombs and kinetic weapons broke away from the cloud circling Kor. The vector data was two minutes old because of the distances involved, but the onboard computer showed that in less than half an hour, the forward shuttle would collide with the ship if it wasn't shot down first. The resulting debris would shred the five trailing civilian spacecraft right along with it. "They're going after the explorers! They're going after our hyperspace technology."

"It sure looks like it. But without—"

"I don't care about the damn research," she snapped at him. "But I do care that a few hundred sleeping scientists are about to be blown to kingdom come by these damned aliens without even realizing it."

"There's nothing we can do. They just won't respond—"

"Yes, we can." Sarah checked her idea with the help of a short simulation on the display in front of her after she entered several navigation and acceleration data.

"No!" Georg protested. "No!"

"Yes, you are! Get Karell and our boy out of here. I'll drop you off on course for Bohr. There are enough habitats and stations there capable of locating and recovering your rescue pod, and it's a long way from this madness here."

"Sarah, please, there has to be another way."

"I love you, but this is my decision and my ship! Now, get out!"

She slowed *Ezekiel's Revenge* to a comfortable G and sighed with relief, though her heart was hammering in her chest. Fortunately, Georg did not come to say goodbye. After so many years, he knew how much she hated goodbyes and understood when there was nothing to gain by it. Karell and her husband quietly disappeared. She wiped furiously at the tears in her eyes. She watched on the internal cameras as they retrieved her son from the acceleration cocoon and took him to the ship's only rescue pod. Without hesitation she pressed the launch button and catapulted the pod at 0.5 G toward the distant gas giant, which they would reach in three weeks.

"I won't let you do this, you damned metal heads," she growled as she entered the data corresponding to her plan into the navigation computer and switched to full acceleration. The three fusion thrusters roared back to life, pressing her into the seat with the force of a giant fist.

Reinforced membranes and capillaries in her body fought vascular occlusions to circulate blood kept fluid by anticoagulants and amphetamines as the brutal 11 Gs brought her close to fainting. After five minutes, she had to shut down the engines and drift. It took her five minutes to come back to her senses and ignore the headaches and aching limbs that nearly took her mind away.

Like an arrow, *Ezekiel's Revenge* shot toward the alien ship's flight path. Sarah glanced at one of the left displays and blinked away the tears in her eyes. The high-resolution telescope under the bow of her ship had reformed the complex image of the battle near Kor that arrived after a delay but was as close to a live shot as it got.

What she saw made her cry out in despair. The massive bombardment of the moon had caused it to break up into six gigantic pieces of debris; the edges glowed like lava. The surface's regolith, melted to glass, shone in the reflections of the ongoing battle, as the *Oberon*'s escort fleet continued to offer desperate but ultimately futile resistance. Measuring hundreds of kilometers, the chunks of Harbingen's satellite were inevitably drawn by the gravitational pull of their giant neighbor and hurtled toward the surface of the green-blue sphere. There was nothing that could stop them. Not even when the defense fleet *had* existed, would it have been able to neutralize or deflect such massive objects fast enough. Death came from above, and it was inevitable.

Sarah had been born on New Manhattan, not German American ethnic Harbingen, and yet the shock ran deep as she watched the inevitable fate of the world and all its two billion inhabitants.

"Where's the damn *Oberon*?" she asked in a trembling voice as she jabbed at the sensor controls like an eagle at its prey. She finally found the Titan twenty million kilometers away amid the fleeing colonist fleet heading for the inner jump point. She stared in disbelief at the screen for nearly a minute.

"They're escaping," she breathed in horror. "They're just running away! Damn Bradley!"

A red warning message appeared on her main screen, cutting through her horror. The Click ship had ejected a swarm of kinetic missiles which accelerated at 50 Gs and hurtled madly toward *Ezekiel's Revenge*. The faint glow of their exhaust flares was a sure sign of her death. They had responded sooner than she had hoped, but with any luck she would at least force them to correct course or destroy them with their cloud of debris.

One last time, she checked the course of the rescue barge holding her family as they flew toward safety. She managed a smile before the end came. It happened so quickly that not even a single calming impulse managed to reach her brain.

The ship and its captain dissolved in a steaming cloud of gas that drifted among the chopped-up remains of *Ezekiel's Revenge*.

2

TWENTY YEARS LATER

Captain Konrad Bradley stood with his arms folded behind his back in front of the huge window of the observation deck and gazed at the gas giant Artros. The opening was large enough to allow several cargo tugs to park directly in front of it and be inspected. The retracted armored doors were dark gray bulges that made up the edges. He always felt a little lost and small standing by himself, like a tiny stick figure, in front of the mono-bound glass. But that was exactly the feeling he actively sought when he came here before the crew ranks changed shifts, to be alone for fifteen minutes.

He commanded over eight thousand sailors aboard the Federation's largest ship, far more than anyone else of his rank, and yet was envied by no one for it. The reasons were obvious, but they were not *his* reasons. His had to do with the fact that there were several tempting traps in responsibility. Overconfidence, for example, but also too much self-expectation. The many eyes, the expectant stares that weighed on him every day, they were what made him come here to collect himself and remember that even the mighty *Oberon* was but a tiny speck of dust before the grandeur of this epic scene he contemplated on the other side of the armored glass.

Once powerful, he recalled, pushing the thought aside with a sour grimace.

Artros filled nearly half the window through which as many as one thousand sailors normally relaxed at the end of their shifts on more than fifty tiers, admiring the beauty of the stars. The system's only gas giant sparkled like a pseudo-sun when it was in conjunction with the distant central star Lagunias. Its edges were fringed with optical illusions like the prominences of a coronal mass ejection. Bands of brown and burgundy clouds passed almost lazily in changing layers and shades over the gigantic ball of raging gases. In the convection zones between the individual bands, circular patches formed and were dragged along behind.

Konrad was fascinated by the power of perspective. As an observer from half a million kilometers away, Artros lay virtually still, and he had to look for a long time with a steady breath and a patient eye to see the movements in the outermost layers of gas. In truth, however, superstorms raged on the huge planet, with wind speeds of many thousands of kilometers per hour. Only one of the spots he saw was as large as Lagunia, the system's namesake oceanic planet. These were whirlwinds of unimaginable proportions that could sweep away even the Federation's most advanced atmospheric probes.

"Admiral?" said a familiar voice behind him. It sounded distant and created a soft echo. No wonder, the room was huge, and the voice came from the central access point behind him.

"Don't call me that, Silly," he said, not turning away from the cosmic spectacle that would have cooked him with its harsh radiation if not for the protective armored disk.

Instead of a response, he heard footsteps echo off the two-dozen-meter-high ceiling. It was an agonizingly slow rhythm, but Konrad had all the time in the world.

Still.

Commander Silvea "Silly" Thurnau was half a head taller than him, her straw-blond hair was tied in a short ponytail that violated Fleet regulations so was hidden beneath her blue beret. She was slender and would have been attractive even with her high cheekbones and slanted eyes, had it not been for the thin-lipped mouth that belied an ascetic implacability.

She joined him, jutting her chin out and placing her booted feet a little more than shoulder-width apart, hands clasped behind her back, just as he did.

"You haven't come to keep me company, have you?" he asked, his gaze still fixed on the glowing gas giant, watching the asteroid settlement Taurus, a tiny black dot, as it crossed the surface.

"No," his XO replied in her usual direct manner. "We just received the *Caesar*'s crew manifest via courier. I thought you should know that Jason will be part of the admiral's entourage."

Konrad nodded and felt the muscles in his neck tense.

"Anything else?"

"No." Commander Thurnau already wanted to turn around and leave.

"It's beautiful, isn't it?" he asked, and she stiffened a little.

"I guess so."

A hint of a smile stole onto his wrinkled face.

"I'm seventy years old, Silly. Thanks to the genetic tweaks of my ancestors, I may have another fifty or sixty years ahead of me. The gray in my hair is not a fashion statement, but proof that we are dying out. It probably sounds like an old man's swan song, but I can feel it." He gestured in front of them. "That will still be there when we're decommissioned and discharged, even a million years from now, when everything we do here is long forgotten. All the smoke and mirrors and antics of distant masters."

"Is that a quote?"

"No."

"Oh." The XO quietly cleared her throat. "I don't think it's that durable. But durable enough to end this war."

Konrad frowned and was about to ask her what she meant when he finally understood. The reason for their journey to the outer gas giant of the Lagunia System sat around the terminator of Artros: A nearly perfect ring two kilometers in diameter with small indentations on the outside. Hundreds of tiny dots buzzed around the construct, flashing repeatedly: Construction bots completing the final pieces on humanity's greatest project—at least one of fifty parts.

"End the war?" He raised an eyebrow and shook his head slightly. "Even if we actually defeat the Clicks with the help of *that*, no war has ever been ended."

"Sir?"

Konrad smiled thinly. She only ever called him sir in private when she wanted to dig at him in her own way. It did not surprise him.

"Mankind sustains itself through coitus and manslaughter."

"A quote." This time it was not a question.

"Shakespeare."

"Ah. Quite pessimistic."

"Quite apt. Today we call them Clicks, tomorrow maybe dissidents, the day after that, bugs."

"The COB wants to know exactly what protocol to prepare the old lady for," said the XO, changing the subject.

"Of course, he does." Konrad sighed without taking his eyes off the nearly complete hyperspace gate, which was getting closer and closer, no longer ten kilometers away. It rotated with Lagunia's outer jump point, on which it sat like a gravitational plug.

"Sir?"

"First things first, they're boarding at 1800, which means we won't make it to the bridge for the daily shift briefing."

Konrad saw her sour expression as she realized he was right. "So, XO?"

"The lieutenant is expecting you," was all she said. "If that's all...?"

"Dismissed."

She nodded, turned, and walked up the center aisle stairs with the same jagged yet hollow step she had entered with.

She'll understand, he thought, and took one last long look out at the silhouette of the ring structure. The *Oberon* had already moved into a correlative position opposite the hyperspace gate, and now it was as if neither of them would budge. Only a glance at the eternal storms of the gas giant revealed that they were both moving parallel to each other. *Are you really bringing us to the end?*

Konrad Bradley took a deep breath and then also climbed the sixty-six steps to the middle entrance. Behind him, the mighty armored bulkheads closed with a low rumble, leaving before him a bright sliver of light that became ever narrower.

The corridor led to the ship's largest room, after to the hangar, at its bow. Fifty meters in it was bifurcated and formed two arcs through the *Oberon*'s belly until they rejoined, forward of the stern section and its powerful antimatter annihilators. The huge coils and magnetic containment chambers he had admired back in Harbingen's orbit during the ship's launch were off-limits to most of the crew, and he always knew his way around. Knowing the magnetic fields in the chambers were filled with enough positron-enveloped antiprotons and antineutrons to annihilate half the system still made him uneasy.

The tapering walls of corridors were interrupted every ten meters by open emergency bulkheads, identifiable by angular steel frames on the right and left. Uniformed sailors saluted by lifting a hand to the crown of their head as if lifting an imaginary hat; an old Harbinger tradition. He had long since given up trying to beat it out of them. Perhaps it was nostalgia and those very traditions that still held this ship and its crew together.

After several minutes, he arrived at the first cluster of multidirectional elevators. There he met a group of ensigns who had come aboard only a week before. Young men and women who had been born on Harbingen but too young to witness its destruction. A new generation that would look at the universe differently than the current crew, still largely made up of veterans. Standing before them was an older senior chief petty officer who was part of the inner circle of his COB Walter Borowski.

Daniel Hofer, Konrad remembered, and stood next to a sergeant, who was currently engrossed in an explanation about the elevator system and had not yet noticed him, in contrast to the young officers, who visibly stiffened.

"There are one hundred and forty elevators in all, with twice as many cabs. In *Oberon*'s dorsal rings are maintenance caverns where the cabins can pass each other or be replaced should a problem occur. Six tubes run lengthwise through the old lady, from stern to bow; they are quite close together. Thirty much shorter shafts intersect those shafts and lead to the inner hull of the ship, where the electron matrix cells for the jump engines are spread out like a net. You know all this shit from the Academy, but trust me, you don't want to get out there with metal on your body. So, it's best not to get off at stop twenty at all, unless one of the engies told you to and briefed you accordingly. Got it?" Hofer said.

"Yes, Senior Chief!" the ensigns replied in chorus, most of them squinting at Konrad. The senior chief didn't seem to notice either.

It was normal for young officers new to the ship to spend about six standard months receiving more training and getting to know the entire ship with all its areas of responsibility. Their teachers were the NCOs of the respective departments, who had experience and were familiar with the details of daily operations. This was not only common on warships but also Konrad's personal preference because only those officers who understood what was going on in the ship and what their subordinates had to deal with every day could be good commanders and take responsibility. He did not tolerate a division between the command and crew sections and certainly did not tolerate aloof and arrogant officers at his side.

Anyone who couldn't handle being ordered around and briefed for half a year by a hierarchical subordinate who had more knowledge and experience than them left the *Oberon* faster than he'd arrived.

"If you've been paying attention, you will have noticed that there are twenty-two stops, but you don't have access to the last two. Those are only for the engineering corps, hence the DNA scanners for the corresponding stations. These are located between the hulls and house the maintenance accesses to the outer superconductors, the electron matrix cells for energizing the armor, and the molecular bond nodes. The engies are crawling around there with flashlights and sweating through their chins, so be respectful of them, all right?"

"Yes, Senior Chief!" the ensigns replied again, and Konrad was sure they were only tense because of him. They were being briefed by Hofer, but they didn't really need to stand at attention in front of him, nor did they need to act like sailors during basic training.

"Next, we're going to the starboard flaks. You may have been told at the Academy that the *Oberon* belongs in a museum. Too heavy, too old, no hyperspace weapons, no drones, too big, too slow. You can forget that snot right now. Once you've seen two thousand flak rounds in action at a rate of fire of one thousand shells per minute, and you see a damn wall of shrapnel filling the vacuum fifty kilometers away, you don't care about all that newfangled stuff. The *Oberon* is a Titan, not one of those self-flying paper ships. So, prick up your ears, because the boys in weapons engineering are about to give you—" Hofer frowned when he finally became aware of his junior officers' stares and looked to the side. He noticed Konrad, came to attention, and saluted. Briefly disconcerted, his charges followed suit.

"At ease," Konrad said, carelessly returning the salute. "Good speech, Hofer."

"Thank you, Admiral!"

"Captain," he corrected the senior chief petty officer, not too sternly, a fight against windmills on this ship. Hofer merely stuck out his chin and gave a small nod.

"How are the new guys doing?"

"They listen."

"Good." He turned to the assembled men and women. "That's all you need to do for the next few months. Only those who learn to listen can eventually get others to listen to them."

One of the three elevator doors opened with a whir. Another thing the engineers would have to fix. The list was long.

Hofer stepped aside to make room for Konrad.

"We'll take the next one, sir."

"Good job. Carry on." He stepped into the low-ceilinged cabin, turned, folded his arms behind his back, and gave the ensigns a final nod. Whether they adored him or despised him, he didn't know, only that they would be one kind or the other. And that had several consequences at once, of which he was all too aware. "Welcome to the *Oberon*."

The doors closed, and with a gentle jerk the elevator started moving through the vacuum tube destined for the port hangar, one of two on his ship. A huge space that spanned eight decks, it was large enough to hold fifty *Barracuda*-class fighters at a time for maintenance or repair. On the right and left sides were elevators leading to the catapults, and the outward side was the slot where the hangar doors interlocked. Each door was half the size of a soccer field, made of hardened carbotanium, and so matte black that they absorbed the surrounding cold, white light.

At least two dozen fighters were arranged on the hangar deck, covered with colorful lines and complex markings, and a hundred technicians and engineers in orange ship overalls buzzed around them. The sounds of tools and machinery mingled with the typically gruff tone of the crew in an ebb and flow of unpleasant sounds that hurt the ears of someone who didn't come here often.

The fact that Konrad didn't appear here often was evident from the looks from his subordinates, who looked up from their work, first in confusion, then in fright before coming to attention. Each time, he held out his hand for them to move or not to stand up at all.

"Admiral," said a lieutenant junior grade with four yellow circles on his shoulder who had just climbed down from an extension ladder leading to the cockpit of one of the Barracudas. The pilot inside was busy with the controls and did not notice him.

"At ease," Konrad said as the lieutenant saluted.

"Don't get many visits from you down here."

"I know, and hopefully that will change soon. Although, I don't know how you put up with it every day." He sucked in the smell of ozone and sealant but put on an appreciative look so the man wouldn't misunderstand him.

"These help." The lieutenant tugged at the soundproof headphones hanging around his neck and shrugged. "You'll want to talk to the chief, won't you?"

"Yes, but first gather the current shift. I want to say a few words. He'll see me then."

"Of course, sir." The young man, wearing smudged coveralls, raised his left arm, which had a flexible display strapped to it, and briefly typed on it. Then his voice boomed through the hangar's speakers like thunder, even drowning out what sounded like a particularly nasty buzz saw in the distance.

"Attention on deck! The commander is here. Everyone, come to C22."

Konrad smiled at the simple and direct manner that prevailed among the Corps of Engineers, which was a kind of self-contained microcosm on each ship. Gradually, men and women in orange coveralls converged among the parked Barracudas, forming a dense semicircle around him as he stood directly in front of a large C22 marker drawn on the deck. Some pulled protective masks from their sweaty faces and rested them on the tops of their heads. Others casually wiped their hands on towels that were so filthy that he couldn't imagine they did anything but make them dirtier.

"Everybody here?" he asked the chief, Lieutenant Commander Karl Murphy, who was angrily pushing his way through the ranks because of the interruption in work. Only when he saw Konrad did he halt his muttered tirade, which was drowned out by the roar of the air recyclers. His brow remained furrowed, however, as he nodded.

"Good evening. I would say that it's nice to be with you again, but I've always been a bad liar. You should vent!" Konrad shouted in his deep bass voice, earning some laughs. "I am aware that you are all concerned about the future of the *Oberon* when that gate out there opens to let our visitor in. I am here to assure you that I have no intention of giving up without a fight. Our old lady was once the pride of the Terran Fleet, and if I have my way, she still will be."

Shouts and applause echoed through the hangar.

"The new frigates may be faster, more maneuverable, more efficient because of me, and flyable by fewer personnel," Konrad continued, changing his voice to a rumble, "but we are a *Titan*! We don't need to be faster than the enemy, nor more maneuverable. Our *enemies* need to be all that, so they can run from our firepower faster."

Now real cheers erupted, and some technicians whistled loudly.

"We don't need drones, we don't need hyperspace torpedoes, we don't need a cut-down crew. I wouldn't want to do without any of our Barracudas, and I wouldn't want to do without a single member of our crew. Our *family*!"

Thunderous applause and stomping boots echoed across the deck like a force of nature. Some chanted: "O-be-ron! O-be-ron! O-be-ron!"

"We may be the last Titan, a relic of an *obsolete* doctrine. We may be derided as refugees and outcasts, as fringe worldlings, but we are *Harbingers*, the last of the only Core World left with a Titan, and we have earned our place in the ranks of the Fleet." Konrad paused to allow for the renewed cheers. After a few minutes he raised his hands to stop the seemingly endless cheering. "And I don't need to be an expert on Fleet statutes to know that the Titans were created for a single purpose: To be the backbone of an entire Fleet, one of fifty flagships. And that's exactly what I'm going to make clear to the admiral when he arrives. You can count on that."

When the chief saw Konrad's brief nod, he clapped his hands loudly and blew a small whistle dangling from his chest.

"Come on, you lazy asses! Get back to work! These birds aren't going to maintain themselves!"

The deck crew gradually dispersed in all directions, talking loudly, and Murphy approached and clipped a stained towel to his belt.

"Evening, Admiral."

"Captain."

"For some, maybe." Murphy shrugged impassively. It looked like a bear bristling its fur. The lieutenant commander was at least a head taller than Konrad and nearly twice as wide with a belly that could earn him a dismissal on any other ship.

Konrad ignored the obvious disregard for rules by his chief engineer, whom he had known for over forty years. One could say that he had years of practice.

"How's she doing?" he asked in a low voice.

"Like an ancient battleship. We start plugging the holes in the front and by the time we get to the back we can start over in the front." Murphy scratched his furrowed brow, leaving a black line. "But all in all, we're doing a good job."

"Has the shipment arrived?"

"Yes. Four hundred Predator drones. Next to last generation, all still in their original packaging." The chief pointed to several large black cubes standing behind two Barracudas in front of the hangar doors being loaded into two cargo shuttles. "They'll be packed and on their way in an hour. You should send a couple guys from the fighter squadron along, just to be safe."

"No, too flashy."

Murphy scratched his close-cropped beard. "If you say so, boss. But that must be five hundred million credits in there."

"And if I send an escort along, every pirate in the system will know it. There are a lot of them in Lagunia."

"All right."

"You're flying yourself, don't forget that."

"As long as the hundred Marines cover my ass like you promised."

"Meyer is already on his way."

The engineer looked surprised. "Meyer's coming?"

"He volunteered when he found out what it was all about," Konrad said. "Are you ready?"

"Of course. We'll fly to the station, make the drop, then dress the old lady out with the hottest stuff in the Federation so she looks pretty."

"Good man! Good luck!"

INNER ASTEROID BELT, ATTILA SYSTEM

The TFS *Sphinx* slid out of the inner asteroid belt of the Attila System like one of the many varied chunks of rock that were regularly flung away from their seemingly inert orbit around the central star. The two-year journey would soon come to an end for the crew of the *Sphinx*.

She was not the only spy ship the Federation had sent out. Four sister ships also sheered away, seemingly at random during a 24-hour window, from the herd of dark asteroids, following the *Sphinx*.

Captain Firtan Mahorai licked his lips. He watched the five chunks of regolith and ice on the passive scanners as they set off on their journey to the center of Attila, at the end of which their fate would be to burn up in the prominences of the central star. Most of them would become comets much sooner, when their frozen water content evaporated under the increasing heat and turned into long tails.

If Mahorai was lucky, he and his *Sphinx* would not be one of them. Instead, they would crash in a controlled manner on the second moon of Attila-62, the Clicks' home world, which went by the Fleet-sounding name of P3X-888. P3X-888 was the target of many asteroids because it was the planet's most massive satellite and acted as a natural defensive shield for the Clicks. Their home system had four asteroid belts, the innermost of which was unusually close to the central star and almost touched the orbit of the third planet, Attila-62, as it circled their sun. The gravitational effects of this peculiarity caused Attila-62 to be pulled out of its orbit, like a vacuum cleaner, by asteroids which had too little velocity of their own to resist the gravitational funnel.

Federation scientists attributed the fact that life had been able to develop and exist on the Clicks' home world at all was because Attila-62 had six satellites, which caused violent tidal storms on the surface, but also formed a natural shield, with P3X-888 at the center. With over six thousand impact events per orbital period, which equaled about one and a half Earth years, P3X-888 was uninhabited and had no surface activity with the exception of an observation station and what was thought to be a research base. However, we could get a good overview of the nearer system around the Click homeworld from there due to a lack of atmospheric disturbance and, more importantly, no defense systems or war fleets.

They rarely wasted ammunition on asteroids, which fell upon the moon anyway, thereby fulfilling its task. The situation was different with the sister rocks that were in danger of hitting one of the other satellites, all of which were inhabited or used for military purposes. They were destroyed by an efficient defense system long before they could become dangerous, as the Federation had been forced to discover painfully early on.

But the loss of all his predecessors only made Firtan Mahorai realize how important his mission was. After thirty years of spying, they had finally found a way to learn more about the Clicks and their home world. The solution was as simple as it was complicated. Simple in its basic structure: You send spy ships into the asteroid belt undetected—not easy and very time consuming if you didn't want to be detected, but doable. Let one of these ships, with deceptively genuine rock signatures and without active sensors, with adapted speed, drift along among the asteroids and monitor via passive scans until some fellow travelers released themselves from their inertia and crashed, according to some rapid computations, on P3X-888. Then it was just a matter of delivering a short boost from the thrusters and joining the shower heading straight for the moon. The hard part, however, was waiting and timing it for the right moment.

He had lived in the belt for two years, eating dry food and drinking his own piss, watched all the holofilms in his collection ten times, and more than once toyed with the idea of opening an airlock, just to relieve the yawning boredom and psychic degeneration. In the end he realized, as he so often did, that he'd bitten off more than he could chew—which was probably why he'd been chosen for the mission—to ensure his family back home on Panjas would collect a princely bonus.

His flight toward P3X-888, disguised as one of eight asteroids, four of which had the same dimensions as him and were too small for telescopes, were only recognizable as such on the radar and lidar screens, lasted another nineteen days, most of which he spent in the cockpit throwing balls at the wall. Once an hour, which was much more often than necessary, he checked the results of the passive scanners, which reported a total of eighteen radar scans.

On the fifteenth day, three asteroids were apparently classified as too large by the system defenses or their trajectories too difficult to calculate and shot down. Stupidly, two of them were not asteroids at all, but his sister ships, *Uluru* and *Berchtesgaden*.

At this point he should have been frustrated, angry, worried, depressed, but he was none of those things. Two years of silent waiting between dark, ugly boulders ranging from a few meters to many kilometers in diameter without any contact with the outside world had deadened him. He was as aware of this as he was indifferent to it, an instinctive protective mechanism that had formed like calluses on the soles of his feet. Mahorai had stopped trying to fight his body's natural defenses early on. If he needed to cry, he cried. If he wanted to scream, he did. If he felt nothing at all, so be it. Who was he to think his mind was smarter than his body and its natural processes? After all, that same mind had convinced him it was a good idea to sail blindly around in a cramped spy ship in the heart of enemy territory and wait for a chance to crash on a moon—if he wasn't shot down first.

As it turned out, he was not shot down. The plan had apparently worked and ensured that *Sphinx* was thought to be a harmless asteroid that would merely add another crater to P3X-888. To maintain this appearance, he did not allow himself to apply the braking thrusters until just before impact, which would hopefully become a landing. The swirling regolith kicked up by the landing would make it look like an impact rather than the plasma flare of an engine at maximum power.

Flights similar to this one had already provided the Federation with important, if sparse, information about the Clicks. It had been known for some years that their planet consisted of 80 percent greenish oceans, apparently covered by dense algal carpets. So, except for its color, it was not entirely dissimilar to Earth, nor was it dissimilar in mass, providing 1.1 G. Near constant storms raged on the surface, with winds reaching several hundred kilometers an hour, often with numerous hurricanes at the same time, which then combined into superclusters and picked up even more speed. This was why Fleet researchers thought there were no cities of any kind on the three continents. Instead, all known settlements were located on the moons, where asteroids needed to be shot down from time to time, but no storms ravaged as the local central star was too stable and calm for that.

Mahorai let the onboard computer handle the landing, as

protocol dictated. It didn't even feel strange to give up control so freely. He simply waited, while he shook in his seat and closed his eyes until the vibrations subsided. Since he was still breathing, he opened them again and initiated a system check by pressing a button.

Everything was nominal.

"So far, so good," he said. It was strange to hear his own voice. It was also a little unpleasant, but so be it.

The next phase of the mission required deploying the telescopes and listening equipment, which was also handled by the onboard computer. The *Sphinx* was basically a simple cylinder, due to its stealth capabilities, with a small section in the middle with three rooms. In his case there was one for life support and the cockpit, one in the front with deployable telescopes, and one in the back with gravity sensors. After such a long, sluggish time in space, everything was suddenly happening very quickly. There were no windows in his thirty-meter-long, three-meter-wide sardine can, so he watched the control screens as the AI took over what was the exciting part of the job. It opened the flaps and extended the entire linkage with the spheres, cold eyes, and laser interferometers and then remained still.

Now Firtan Mahorai's job was to simply wait for the computer to spit out the data to him, interpret it—which usually meant agreeing with the AI—and verify it—to satisfy Fleet authority. He still had a few hours before then, however, and the *Sphinx* had an airlock, in case he needed to EVA to repair minor damage, which he had never had to use.

So why not now? He unbuckled his seatbelt, squeezed into the bionic pressure suit that tightened around his skin to maintain pressure, and then put on the helmet until it clicked into place on the neck ring.

Outside, the first thing he noticed was the low gravity, which was somewhere around a fifth of Earth's gravity and which, oddly enough, he had barely registered in the ship. This was probably due to his long time in weightlessness and the shaky ride down to the surface. The amount of energy required for artificial gravity had made it a no-go in the stealth ship, so despite his training his body was atrophied enough to find the meager 0.2 G slightly uncomfortable. But he wasn't about to complain; after all, he could finally see a real horizon again. While no stars twinkled above the small crater his engine had bored into the regolith, there was a beautiful, flawless darkness, with a head-sized dark green planet hanging in the center like a faux-painted sun. If he put his hands together, he could just about cover Attila-62.

It's strange that on this beautiful spot, this oasis in the noth-ingness, the archenemy of mankind has arisen, he thought. *How sad it is that we have nothing better to do to each other than bash each other's heads in.*

The white bands of clouds on Attila-62 could have come from Earth, as pure and cotton-soft as they looked. From this distance, unclouded by dancing gas molecules of an atmosphere, even the massive storm eyes looked like a work of art in the best resolution.

His forearm display sent a signal to his helmet, interrupting his musings. Annoyed, he was about to suppress it when he saw that the ship was already proposing a relay transmission to Fleet.

That was fast.

Mahorai reluctantly pulled his gaze away from the alien world and the surrounding gray of the moon and skimmed the data. The telescopes were still scanning the Clicks' military installations, which were numerous in orbit around Attila-62, and the gravity wave detectors were still powering up. The onboard computer had completed its analysis of the captured passive data from its eighteen-day flight here from the asteroid belt and thought it had found something of importance.

He stared at it for five minutes and frowned. He had to agree with it and immediately sent out an undirected radio signal that would be picked up by any of the eighty remaining spy ships in the belt. Some might have been found by the Clicks' ever-searching fighters, but Fleet had ensured that the number of remaining ships always remained high. While they were not efficient or at all valuable while flying blind among the boulders, they could become so at any time.

The data had to get to Fleet, and as quickly as possible. He may have just discovered a way to end a war that had been raging for far too long. Well, the computer had actually found it, but without him, Firtan Mahorai, the silicon box wouldn't have gotten here in the first place. So at least he could grace the cherry on the cake with his name.

It took ten seconds to send the message. Only encrypted text, no attachment.

It took fifteen seconds for a directed microwave laser somewhere in orbit around the moon to pick up the bearing of his signal and vaporize Firtan Mahorai into a cloud of volatile gas. For those remaining twenty-five seconds of his life, he smiled at the beautiful green planet and let out a long sigh.

How beautiful it was here. And how ugly it would become.

3

The *Quantum Bitch* materialized in complete silence. The jump point flashed briefly, bathing the surrounding space in false colors, so briefly that no human eye could perceive it. A corona of radiation glistened over its curved hull and quickly faded away. Sensor beams and radiators extended from the ring-shaped segment around the elongated toroid with the downward-curved snout at its prow.

In it sat captain and owner Devlin Myers, known in his circles simply as Dev. In the seats behind him, his crew members ridded themselves of the "spring frost" by rubbing their arms and shaking their heads as if to remove water from their ears.

"Everyone awake?" Dev asked as his hands sank into the soft gel of the neural controls, blue nubs at the end of his armrests that glowed intrinsically. With micro-movements of his fingertips that looked more like twitches, he steered the entire ship.

"These fucking pills are driving me crazy!" grumbled Willy, his flight engineer, whose real name was Brun Gronski and who was a fifty-five-year-old scumbag. Ever since he lost his family to collateral damage in a Click attack on the

Aurora habitat, he must have blown a fuse. Dev had known him only as a cynical, grumpy augment addict who had not only replaced his arms and legs with metal, but most of his organs and vascular system as well. This made him an excellent spaceman, but with each procedure that took away some of his flesh and replaced it with metal and circuitry, he seemed to lose more of his empathy and humanity. Dev would have promoted him out the airlock long ago if he wasn't such a darn good tinkerer and he didn't like Willy so much.

"You don't need pills for that, do you?" Aura snorted. The *Bitch*'s energy node specialist sat in the seat directly behind him. "Just grow some balls. Or better yet, screw them on."

"Easy, kids," Dev intervened, grinning. On the holoscreens in front of him, a clear picture of their surroundings was slowly coming together. They had arrived centrally at Jump Point 2 from the Lagunia System, a comfortable distance from the gas giant Artros and not quite as comfortable a distance from the next largest object, barring the numerous moons.

The *Oberon* looked like a gigantic eyeless whale on the telescope images. The bow section was a little thicker than the bulky body. The matte black hull with its many nicks and dimples looked as if someone had beaten a seal with a hammer, and the dormant drive nacelles resembled the suction cups of a sea monster. Only through multiple optical zooms could he make out the gun ports, which stretched from the stern to the bow like a deep crevice along the port side, facing them.

"A real Titan, I'll be damned," Willy grunted. "I can't believe I still get to see one of those."

"Can't be long before they recycle the old tin can for its parts and raw materials. How many cruisers of the new pattern could you carve out of that thing?" Jezzy, their fusion engineer, asked.

"Ten?" the augmented man estimated. "It's hard to believe how much has changed in just twenty years. Back then, you'd go out on a limb and really hit the shit and demolish asteroid after asteroid and bust everything out for these things."

"All that destruction already looks like pure wastefulness," she agreed with her comrade in a sour voice.

"The *Oberon* is more than a relic," Dev objected. "It is a sign of double standards."

He instructed the navigation computer to plot a direct course to Lagunia, the fringe world that gave the system its name and was barely visible as a dim blue dot.

"Don't you start crying, boss," Willy grumbled. "We got ourselves into our Core World ban all by ourselves."

"Speaking of which," Aura said from behind, "our transponder code has been retrieved."

Dev, who was busy with the sensors searching for ionizing gas molecules, heard her but not her words. His mind was focused on the holodisplay in front of him. The emission spectrum of volatile atoms captured by the sensor array indicated two medium-sized fusion engines operating on deuterium. Somewhat aged, probably still a ship without artificial gravity.

That must be it, he thought.

"I've got it!" he exclaimed triumphantly, pulling his right hand out of the neural control's gel pad with a smack. He clenched his fist and let a loud, "Ha-ha!"

"Ready, boss?" Aura asked.

"A little more enthusiasm, please! We've been chasing this barge for four jumps. Now we're in a system that doesn't even seem to have enough money for jump point control, and except for one old barge about to be retired, the place looks pretty quiet."

"We should throttle back on the thrusters now."

"What?" Dev frowned and was about to reply angrily when it occurred to him that she had been trying to tell him something all along. "What's wrong?"

"I said," she repeated, growling, "that our fucking transponder code has been interrogated and that I very much hope the broker's tip is worth the money because otherwise we're going to get blown out of the damn vacuum."

"It'll hold!" He had an uneasy feeling in his stomach that didn't match his encouraging words at all. He looked at the transponder log and found that a hunter had scanned them as they flew by.

A hunter! He should work on that damn proximity alarm.

"We'll see." Something about Aura's answer displeased him.

"What's wrong?"

"Wait a minute." Jezzy threw an image onto the holoscreen, a boxy spaceship that was little more than a tiny dot against the great corona of its exhaust tail. The perspective could only mean that the thing was coming toward them.

"What am I looking at, Jezzy?"

The fusion engineer grunted at the same time a loud beep sounded through the cockpit, announcing an incoming directional beam link. Reluctantly, he placed his right hand back into the neural gel and accepted the connection. The ship's computer identified it as military coding, which meant that unknown subroutines, mandatory for every Federation ship, ensured it could not be rejected or shut down. When push came to shove, no matter what, Fleet could force their civilian counterparts to shut down their engines.

At least for normal ships. Not with the *Quantum Bitch.*

"*Quantum Bitch,*" a cool voice said, for once not conveying any particular derogatory emphasis as it uttered the name. Dev didn't know whether to be pleased or alarmed by that. "This is Commander Nicholas Bradley of System Fleet; you have been selected for inspection. Shut down your thrusters and prepare to be boarded."

"Bradley?" Willy rumbled as the message ended, and Dev reluctantly complied with the order. Calling his bluff now would only cause more trouble and get them no closer to their goal. Besides, there was still a chance that it was indeed a routine check, they hadn't been caught out. "This can't be..."

"Yes, I think that's Captain Bradley's son," Jezzy replied. "What other Bradley would hold the rank of commander in Lagunia, huh?"

Aura snorted. "System Fleet, don't make me laugh. Are they even allowed to call themselves that?"

"I don't know what Fleet guys are allowed to say or not," Willy said. "I don't give a shit, either. They're coming aboard in five minutes!"

"Then you'd best go down to Dozer's and make sure there's nothing to discover on the sleeping deck," Dev ordered sullenly.

"I'm supposed to be ready in just five minutes—"

"No, in four."

"Ihatethisfucking..." the flight engineer growled angrily to himself, unbuckling his seatbelt with a loud *click!* before trudging to the access bulkhead, emitting a metallic *clonk!* with each step.

Dev, meanwhile, disengaged from his own seat after sending a standard acknowledgment to the *Oberon*'s boarding shuttle and instructing the onboard computer to hold position. Aura and Jezzy remained in their seats to the left and right, surrounded by the claustrophobic confines of the cockpit's solid gray walls.

He turned to his fusion engineer from the Kent Core World, who always looked like an angst-ridden dog with its tail between its legs, expecting a slap from its master.

"Jezzy, make sure we gather enough potential in the pattern cells to get up to top speed quickly without setting off the energy surge warning messages on those Fleet ass monitors. You got it?"

"I'll try," she said, letting out a long, drawn-out sigh before fixing her blonde hair and leaving the cockpit.

Once she was gone, he addressed Aura.

"Let me guess," the downright criminally attractive technician snorted and rolled her eyes. Her cinnamon brow furrowed and the look she gave him was downright scathing. "You're gonna need some hot ass and white teeth to get us out of this shit."

"Sorry." He struggled to keep an innocent expression on his face.

"I don't care. I'll wiggle my tits too if it helps, but next time don't send the little princess out first. You're just coddling her. If you keep pretending the world is better than it is, it's only going to get worse with her. Hell."

Dev wanted to laugh at the contrast between Aura's mouth and her appearance, but that would probably have earned him a slap in the face. But she was right, Jezzy did act like a princess with a lot of airs and graces, while Aura, who could have passed for a holomodel, acted like a Dunkelheim military mechanic.

"You're right," he started to explain, but she merely raised her hand and an eyebrow and tapped her wrist.

"Save your sermon, we should be heading for the airlock to receive our visitor." She snorted again. "And shake your ass."

"I'm serious, Aura. We need to take advantage wherever we can here. You know about the liners that are disappearing more frequently in Lagunia?"

"I've heard of it. Eighty-four StarVans in twelve years. That's a respectable rate, but also not unusual with the Jump Control here. It's just amateurs working there, and the damned StarVans are ancient pieces of junk that shouldn't even be licensed anymore."

"Maybe. But if it's not just Jump Control—and I don't believe in that much incompetence in a system inhabited by Harbingers—then there's something else behind it, and I bet it's that shady Captain Bradley hogging ships."

"Civilian clunkers? Oh, come on."

"Just keep your eyes open and make an effort, okay?" he asked, not waiting for her to agree.

The airlock was on the relative underside of the ship and could be reached via the short central corridor and a ladder that ended in the exterior operations vestibule. Along the walls were six lockers on the left and on the right, six spacesuits hanging in their holders like limp coveralls. The empty helmets with closed visors looked like the mummified faces of alien insects.

Dev hoped that Willy and Dozer had cleaned up their area and didn't get into such a tizzy that they ruined everything. *I should have sent Jezzy,* he thought, when a loud *clunk!* followed by a yellow light above the inner door of the airlock announced that the boarding shuttle had docked. The pressurization was initiated when he pressed the appropriate button, and then they waited side by side, Dev a little behind Aura.

Two Black Legion Marines came through first. They wore massive, powered armor that made them resemble superhuman Space Marines from a comic book. Their helmets had no visors, but a sensor band where the eyes would be that stretched three hundred and sixty degrees around their heads, and a small round breathing hole in the shape of an air filter where their mouths should have been. They carried short Gauss rifles for use on starships, and their magnetic boots, which let them operate inside and outside ships alike, were audible, even though the inner airlock was still closed. Behind them was a uniformed officer in Fleet blue with all sorts of insignia on his chest and shoulders. He was not particularly tall, had blond hair that was combed back, and no more than thirty-five years old. His features were unmistakably those of the Bradley's, with the long, slightly downturned nose and large dark eyes. Nicholas, if Dev was not mistaken, the younger son of arguably the most famous Federation captain, had a hard, or perhaps merely aloof, look that seemed to pierce him even through the porthole separating them.

"Good morning, uh, sir," he greeted the officer as the inner airlock opened and the two Marines exited right and left like golems, the muzzles of their rifles casually pointed down. "Good morning, Captain Myers," Nicholas Bradley said, returning the greeting. "A military salutation is not required for a civilian."

So much for casual politeness.

"It's an honor to have you on board. How exactly can we help you?"

"By cooperating," came the curt reply.

Bradley looked around the cramped area, then turned back to Dev. "According to the transponder check, as the ship's owner, you have ninety-eight transit permits for hyperspace jumps, every one of them from a fringe world."

"We care about the less privileged colonies, and we haven't had a reason to visit any of the Core Worlds yet." He shrugged and smiled. "The crew is from Gotha and Dunkelheim, so we probably wouldn't be very welcome there anyway."

If he had hoped for a reaction from the commander to his cynical, hinting comment, he was immediately disappointed.

"There are a lot of pirates and smugglers who rely on mass-market models like this one," Bradley explained as two uniformed men carrying cases came out of the airlock behind him and walked past them to the ladder.

Damn snoopers!

"Transponder codes are easily spoofed but Jump Control can use their sensors to create clear hull profiles that can't be forged," the commander continued as Dev fought the impulse to turn and look after the snoopers. "Using a frequently sold civilian ship is helpful, of course, but it makes for an inevitable check every time you transit to a Core World."

You think you're pretty smart, don't you?

"After all, each of the fifty Core Worlds has enough sensors and defense platforms, including space control personnel, to keep a close eye. Unlike the fringe worlds."

He's clever, Dev grumbled inwardly, without letting his outward smile waver. *Fucking scumbag!*

"The ship was convenient. As you can imagine, we don't have many resources out here to be picky," Aura finally said, pursing her lips sweetly, such an inappropriate facial expression for her that he would have laughed out loud if he hadn't been so annoyed with this arrogant Fleet fop who seemed about as easy to work on as a security bulkhead.

"We'll see," Bradley said impassively, not even casting a sideways glance at Aura's uniform, which was tight across the chest area and which she deliberately strained against. Which was probably why she looked at Dev questioningly. Or helplessly, which was not a particularly common occurrence with her either. "Please show me the bridge and cabins for inspection."

"Cabins? I didn't know Fleet was interested in our underwear," Aura tried to joke and winked at the commander charmingly. The look in her eyes alone would have been enough for Dev to plant a rose bush for her in his cabin. Nicholas Bradley, on the other hand, merely frowned briefly and shook his head.

"It doesn't. We're interested in contraband and hidden or altered log files."

"We're not pirates!" Dev protested.

"Then you have nothing to worry about," Bradley said humorlessly. He gestured to the ladder. "After you."

On the way to the "bridge"—he hated that word, it reeked of military—they passed Willy, who was standing in the corridor wearing a sour expression, as if someone had tied him there. Behind him, he heard the threatening footsteps as he tried to filter information from his engineer's gaze.

In vain.

In the cockpit, Bradley instructed the two Marines to take up positions on either side of the access door and approached the holoconsole. He pressed his right index finger into the

63

corresponding neural pad and looked down at his forearm display.

"Commander Nicholas Bradley, Federation Fleet. Service designator H-H-2233488."

"Priority code accepted," confirmed the smooth voice of the ship's computer, and Dev felt as if he had been cheated when his own ship obeyed this boulder of a human so willingly.

Like a dog that changes masters without loyalty in exchange for a treat, he thought, wishing he could have a serious word with the algorithm afterward. *Damn computers.*

For the next few minutes, Bradley scrolled through the doctored log files with precise, error-free gestures, trying to retrace the ship's course over its last fifty jumps, including the *Quantum Bitch*'s changing total mass and her respective noted cargo, which made Dev increasingly uneasy.

He had done a good job, but during Fleet inspections so far—there were few in the marginal systems—no officer had ever come aboard, certainly not one boasting the rank of commander. Whether it was due to his better training—if that was even the case—he didn't know, but this guy wasn't stupid, and more than that, he was hardworking, almost motivated. Nothing like the usual bored inspectors who always seemed like punitive transfers to him. He had been able to distract them with Dunkelheimer Starkbier or get them to have a boisterous chat with Aura rather than go through the logs very carefully.

It wasn't long before Aura gave him a startled look and he glanced at the holo-display. Bradley had arrived at the current load: twenty-two Tauron coffins in the crew compartment.

"What are these for?"

"We've heard that accidents are more common here at Taurus Station," Dev said in a playfully relaxed manner, shrugging his shoulders. He could tell from Bradley's deadpan expression that he wasn't going to settle for something half-baked. So, he followed it up with, "When a courier in Dunkelheim told us there was a mining accident, we wanted to play a part in returning the deceased to their home systems."

"The Core Worlds may not be particularly religious, but we fringeworlders know that you don't just throw the deceased into the recycler," Aura said, trying a little outsider patriotism. The commander's reaction was about as productive as a sip of water.

Unmoved, he eyed them both.

Don't tell me you're checking to see if there really was an accident or when!

"When is this accident supposed to have occurred?"

Dev sighed inwardly. Aloud he lied, "The courier came two days ago."

"So, a time frame of three to four days between the alleged incident and now."

Dev didn't like it at all, as Bradley conveniently pointed out, "I'm going to check to see if there really was an accident."

What the fuck kind of day is it today?

"Of course," he said trying to stay calm. Aura gave him a "what-do-we-do-now" look.

"Commander, sir?" one of the uniforms said, poking his head through the door past the Marines flanking them like robots out of a horror movie.

"Yes, Seaman?"

"A message from the pilot."

"I didn't want to be disturbed." Dev could tell from his tone that he was displeased, and the young soldier visibly swallowed.

"He said your father is ordering you back."

"Like this?" Bradley looked surprised, but immediately tensed and pulled his finger out of the neural pad. After a few quick inputs on his forearm display, he looked at Dev. "Report directly to space control. I have entered the appropriate notation into your onboard computer. The officers there will delete it as soon as you have complied."

Son of a bitch! Without the release we can no longer jump away!

"Of course," he said, clenching his teeth so hard it hurt.

"Good." Bradley nodded to them in turn, as if none of this was personal—which it may not have been to him and made it worse—then left the cockpit, followed by his Marines.

Fifteen minutes later, they were back in their seats—except for Dozer, who remained in the crew compartment. There was no room for his massive frame, anyway.

"That was damn close, boss!" Willy was unusually relieved.

"I know. We got lucky." Dev turned to Aura and snapped his fingers. "Do you have the sensor data yet?"

"Yes. They are fifteen million kilometers ahead of us."

"Let's not catch up," Jezzy said. She sounded like her usual mournful self, as if she had just crossed the end of humanity.

"Oh, yes we will. You still have to go through the asteroid belt. We have twenty-two coffins to fill, remember?"

"We have an ocean to cover," Willy corrected him.

"First things first. For salvage rights we need money, and unless you've been shitting ducats lately that I don't know about, well, we have to do A before we can think about B."

FLEET HEADQUARTERS, TERRA

Fleet Admiral Hannibal von Solheim stood in front of the panoramic window of his office on the two hundredth floor of the star-scratcher, which bore the typically bulky Fleet name AZ-001. The space station, from which the star-scratcher stood out as one of twelve dagger-like extensions, formed a massive ring around the orbital end of the Space Elevator East. This connected the highest peak of the Himalayas, the Earthbound part of Fleet Headquarters, to them. The twenty elevator cars shot like fireflies along cable structures that looked as thin as spider webs from his window, shuttling ceaselessly between the barren brown slopes of Earth's highest mountain and the most powerful space structure in human history, to what was supposed to be its most luxurious location, where he now found himself as head of Fleet.

He remembered too well how, as a young adjutant to Commander Brighton, he had anxiously wandered through the winding corridors of the hallowed mountain, always looking for a way to accelerate his own climb up the ladder. Back then, he and his colleagues—he hadn't had time for friends—had cracked jokes about the office-chair bigwigs of the sky fortress at the other end of the cables and behaved as if it were something special to hurry through dark mountain tunnels like wizened dwarves. Today, he enjoyed the tranquility that the view offered him. There was no real difference between the eternal elevator rides and the corridors in the Himalayas, except that the former ended with panoramic views like this one. Together with Earth, he spun through space, watching the lights of the sprawling megacities below him merge with the darkness of space on the ball of stone and gas that was so unique and yet so broken. He liked to boast that he had visited all the Core, and many fringe worlds, and the sight of these fresh, unspent oases in the vastness of nothingness had reminded him each time of how much Earth had suffered at the hands of humanity. Today, it was battered by violent superstorms, possessed hardly any forests, and was largely devastated by and at the mercy of constant fires. The hardy inhabitants lived in their megacities behind high protective walls and the blatant effects of ubiquitous geoengineering, which was provided by over eighteen thousand state-of-the-art satellites to redirect extreme weather events away from the urban centers.

Earth had become a monument to both foresight and ignorance, and thus always worth a look whenever he found the time, which was not often.

A gentle hum alerted him that his guests had arrived, and he sighed.

"Yes, Samuel?"

"Admirals Saunders, Legutke, and Hachiro have arrived," his aide replied over the speaker.

"Have them come in. In two minutes."

He took a deep breath and contemplated the glint of orbital defense platforms that formed their dense network of automated weaponized satellites in higher orbits, as large as corvettes, their never-sleeping eyes fixed on the darkness of space where the enemy lurked. But there were others in much lower orbits, and their eyes, like their weapons, were fixed on targets below. Seventy sorties a week, and with them as many microwave and X-ray laser beams, kept dissidents, insurgents, terrorists, and other subversive elements from destroying from the rear what Fleet was building in front.

Humanity had grown weary of war after so many decades of states of emergency, lost sons and daughters, and continuous casualty reports. No wonder, then, that the frequency of deployment of the platforms increased. One more reason why this war had to end as soon as possible before they were forced to fight on two fronts at once.

The door opened with a whir, and he turned around. His office was a large, lavish space fifty meters square, with a marbled floor and walls. At first, he wanted to reject this part of the "privileges" of his new office, but instead he had all the bric-a-brac removed except for the oil portraits of his predecessors and left the rest of the myopic ostentation as a reminder of what he wanted to do differently. Frills and gold had never won wars, but what they could buy had.

Fleet Admirals Saunders, Legutke, and Hachiro came in, dressed in simple ship overalls adorned with nothing except their rank insignia on their shoulders and their names on their chests. Fleet Headquarters was separate from political institutions, a military facility, not a peacock enclosure. They had quickly realized that after he took office and left the parade uniforms in their cabins.

Saunders was a short stocky man in his midseventies with the leathery face of a hard worker, which he was indeed. Legutke was a Franco-French Alsatian, tall and scrawny with narrow cheeks and an intellectual look. They sometimes exchanged a few words in German without the man imagining he was earning bonus points because of it. Bonus point. Shinto Hachiro was still a blank slate for him since he had only been appointed head of espionage a week prior and they had not had any interactions with each other so far.

"Come in." Von Solheim waved toward the three prepared chairs in front of his simple aluminum desk, which was clear except for a datapad and a family photo showing his wife and son Hannes on a vacation in the mountains on Ruhr. Once they sat down, he did the same and folded his hands on the desk.

He tapped the datapad. "I read the report. Before I say what I think of it, I want to hear your opinions, so you don't take biased positions. Please speak freely."

Admiral Saunders was the first to speak. "We need to attack, and we need to attack as soon as possible. Not only is this anomaly unique in its own right, but it's also a once-in-a-lifetime opportunity to cut off all the Hydra's heads."

Von Solheim saw a sour expression flit across Admiral Hachiro's face. He knew it was customary on Japanese worlds to let the elder among equals speak first, something Saunders either didn't know or didn't care about. Either would suit him. Still, he decided to follow up.

"Hachiro. Do you disagree?"

"Yes, sir." Hachiro straightened and nodded. "This anomaly we discovered thanks to the *Sphinx*'s records is highly... *delicate*. For all we know, it could be that the exact mass ratio of the celestial bodies involved at the same point is necessary to achieve the same effect again."

"Maybe," Saunders said, agreeing with the Japanese man and leaning forward in his chair. "But even if we do, we have to do everything we can to make sure we strike under exactly the same circumstances."

"That would mean sending the same number of asteroids with exactly the same mass on exactly the same trajectory at exactly the same speed toward the satellite."

"So?" Saunders shrugged. "Then we make that happen. We'll give our spy ships in the belt plenty of time to select the right asteroids and get them into position. In the meantime, the eggheads here in the sky fortress can do the calculations for how big a push we need to give them."

"Michael," Hachiro said, pausing briefly. "That would cause us to lose all the spy ships—and their pilots. Because something like that doesn't go undetected."

"That's why it has to happen quickly."

"That's not what I mean. The Clicks' hunters will shoot them down."

Saunders waved it off. "Losses we have to accept. This is about ending a war!"

"Maybe."

Von Solheim turned to Legutke, who had remained conspicuously silent until now and looked up as if startled out of a dream. "Romain?"

"*Oui?*"

"What's going on in your head?" Von Solheim spread his hands. "Let us in on it."

The admiral squirmed in his chair as if uncomfortable. "I think Michael is right in this case. Losing our spy capability in the inner belt will be a bitter loss and will ensure that we can never play that trump card again once they see how many ships we had hidden so close to their homeworld. But the pilots knew what they were getting into, and if we see an opportunity but don't want to use our resources on the ground, those resources aren't particularly valuable, are they?"

His colleagues were silent and von Solheim gestured impatiently for him to continue.

"*D'accord.* Even if we deploy our spy ships, however, we still have a timing problem. Project Tartarus has not yet gone through its critical testing phase. We don't even know if the various sections of a gate can jump, and if so, how quickly they can be assembled. We'd have to send a substantial force through one of the first gates to protect the assembly of the

71

mobile counterpart until a solid connection could be established."

"That's the next problem," Hachiro countered. "How do we hide such a large fleet from the Clicks in such a way that they won't guess its function?"

"We collect them at the furthest, least important point in the Federation," Saunders suggested.

"With the Harbingers? That's not going to go well. Either they'll insist on participating in Operation Iron Hammer, or else their nationalism will make them feel threatened and want to expel Fleet. Anything is possible with those fanatics."

"Maybe, but the Clicks know that too, if their intelligence is even half as good as ours. Even without having decoded our language, they know for sure that Lagunia is a conflict system hanging by a thread."

"We could kill two birds with one stone," Legutke said, rubbing the tip of his nose thoughtfully. "Just tie in Captain Bradley's fleet. A Titan in a defensive battle defending a point long enough is just what we need, isn't it? And as far as I can remember, the *Oberon* is our last one."

"The *Oberon*?" Saunders snorted contemptuously. "I'd rather send the child squadron from Dunkelheim than those cowards and traitors!"

"Romain is right." They all looked at von Solheim. "The situation of the *Oberon*, and the Harbingers in general, is extremely... *special*. But we must not deprive ourselves of important resources and possible courses of action due to a political issue. We are paid for results, not political sensitivities. Send someone with the necessary tact. Bradley must be convinced to participate in the first strike. If he declines, there will be consequences, but only if there is no other way to convince him."

"And what consequences would those be?"

"An honorable discharge."

"Honorable?" asked Admiral Saunders incredulously.

"Yes. That would get rid of him without giving his people a reason to think about armed insurrection. And without Bradley, even the Titan is no good. I'm sure much of the military council, and especially the damn Senate, would be pleased if they were finally rid of him. But that's only if it's absolutely necessary. The priority is his inclusion in Operation Iron Hammer."

"I can take care of that. I have a couple rear admirals who are eligible," Hachiro suggested.

Saunders sighed. "No, I'll do it. I've got just the man I was going to propose for the first strike at the anomaly, too."

"Who?"

"Vice Admiral Augustus Bretoni, one of my best, and hopefully at some point the one who will succeed me in this chair. He has the tactical skills for the job and is also a shrewd politician. If anyone can impose his will on a stubborn man like Bradley, it's him."

"I'll look at his record. If I agree with his command, you'd better make sure he delivers." Von Solheim looked Saunders in the eye. "I know you don't have anything left for Bradley and the Harbingers, Michael, so I'm trusting you to impress upon your man that his priority is to get the *Oberon* for the operation and not to behead Bradley on behalf of the Senate when we need him. Do I make myself clear?"

"Crystal."

"Good." He turned to Hachiro. "You will work out a detailed schedule and send it to me before we give instructions to our spy fleet. Report back to me tomorrow."

They all nodded.

"Gentlemen, remember that we are about to deploy a new technology that will allow us to use jump points not merely one ship at a time, but to simultaneously transit entire fleets. That will fundamentally change this and every other future war. We *have* to make sure that the first engagement is a complete success, and that the enemy can't respond."

More nods and their expressions were even more serious than before.

"That's it. Romain, remain behind, please. We need to discuss how to best inform the public about the upcoming strike against the Clicks."

4

The *StarVan*-class liner with the sober designation NM—for New Manhattan—98-03 was turning toward the last jump point on her targeting system when she received clearance from Pilgrim jump point control. The ship contained six hundred men, women, and children on two decks, which offered no cabins, but rows of seats packed tightly together.

Sirion sat in one of the last seats and thought the passengers looked like chickens roosting in a coop with long rows, particularly since every single seat was occupied. The background noise, the crying of many children and complaints from unnerved parents, evoked thoughts of escape in him, not to mention the potpourri of ugly smells: sweat, unwashed skin, and greasy hair produced their own disgusting note after a week and was probably the reason why the cheap StarVan connections between worlds like Christian Pilgrim and the fringe worlds were simply waved through by space control. Who wanted to examine the IDs of six hundred smelly and annoyed Federation citizens?

"Are you scared?" asked the woman next to him, who had been struggling to keep up with her four small children ever since they boarded at Pilgrim's Orbital Liner Station. She wore a simple black dress that revealed nothing of her figure, a white hood on her head, and a silver cross around her neck. Her children looked like something out of a period film.

Sirion eyed her. *According to her ID she was thirty-three years old, weighed about sixty-five kilograms, her left leg slightly longer than her right. The corner of her mouth twitches in a repetitive pattern. Damage to facial nerve, possibly from abuse of corticosteroids. Convert. Street life, end in a reception mission, move to Pilgrim.*

"Scared?" he asked, trying hard not to sound too dismissive, even though he wanted to just walk away.

"Before the jump," she said, smiling kindly at him. Her motherhood seemed to extend beyond her children. When he didn't answer and turned away, she continued, "It's not so bad. You took the Hyper, so you won't accidentally fall asleep in transit."

"I'm not afraid," he said, realizing she was probably looking for a distraction from her children and wouldn't leave him in peace. "I only sleep two hours a day and only at the times I set."

"They implanted a cerebral computer." The woman wrinkled her nose, but then waved her hand and smiled again. "You may think I'm judging you because we banned all implants on Pilgrim, but the nurse always said, 'God's zoo is big.'"

"Uh-huh."

"Besides, only about two thousand citizens now die from transit sleep each standard year. If you ask me, they're probably drug addicts or smugglers fleeing Fleet and oversleeping."

"You're probably right." He accepted one of the pills being handed out by the only flight attendant on their deck, who wore a bored expression. In his gray suit and patched cap, he probably looked like a discarded robot.

A message from the onboard computer popped up on Sirion's forearm display. *"Dear passenger, please be advised that taking the drug with the trade name 'Hyper' is mandatory on this flight. Refusal may result in exclusion from future flights and, in the worst case, death. Place the tablet under your tongue and wait ten seconds. Keep your eyes open and do not blink before the end of the transit countdown."*

He shook his head and immediately swallowed the pill. The active ingredient would be neutralized by his blood filter anyway.

"What are you planning to do on Lagunia?" asked the woman, who apparently couldn't bear to sit there in silence. Presumably, it was she who was afraid of the hyperspace jump. There were enough Federation citizens who constantly watched gimmicky documentaries about the horrors of hyperspace sleep and then wondered why they suffered from anxiety disorders and never left their system.

"I want to kill someone," he said, and for a few seconds she eyed him, startled, as she studied his serious expression. Then she began to giggle and put a hand over her mouth. Somewhere a baby cried for attention and a man wetly cleared his throat.

"Ha-ha," she chortled. "I know the feeling."

Sirion merely nodded and tried to remember the video footage and photos of Franc and Valeska Bellinger. Simple targets, but in the right place at the right time. His real targets, however, were not them. He easily visualized their faces, having never seen such tanned, weather-beaten countenances before. Their aquamarine eyes gazed out of deep sockets and their hair was bleached and brittle from all the salt water, and they looked pleased every single time.

"You know, I used to be angry a lot, too, until the Lord showed me that I was really just angry at myself. Maybe your anger doesn't have anything to do with them and you wringing their necks," the woman went on, looking at the chronometer on the front bulkhead above the door to the stairs counting down sixty seconds.

I will not wring their necks. Probably a shot in the head, above the root of the nose, he thought, smiling noncommittally at the woman. His seatmate was getting more nervous as the transit drew closer, and her voice quickened accordingly.

"If you get angry at others, you're only getting angry at yourself."

What a profound calendar saying.

"After all, you wouldn't even notice the stick in your neighbor's eye if you didn't know what a stick was. 'Why do you see the stick in your brother's eye, but the beam in your own eye you do not see?'" she quoted the Bible.

Whoever wants to believe should be able to learn by heart. Bravo.

"Hey!" she shouted, suddenly so upset that he looked at her. She had grabbed her infant from the seat next to her and was cradling him rather ungently in her arms. "Don't fall asleep, Abraham. No, no, no."

The baby seemed to nod off again and again. The countdown showed only a few seconds left.

"Give it to me," he said.

"What?" she asked, frowning.

"It must not sleep." Sirion held out his hands to her. She placed Abraham, swaddled in white cloth, in them after hesitantly glancing at the countdown. It was deathly quiet on the deck. He took the child, held him before him, and looked him straight in the green eyes when they opened briefly.

The baby began to cry.

The transit began, and he felt like he was immersed in liquid nitrogen for a fraction of a second, a dizziness so brief that a normal brain wouldn't even register it, then it was all over. The cold slowly fell away from him, as did the heaviness in his limbs.

He returned the screaming child to his mother, who practically snatched it from him and gave him a reproachful look.

You're welcome.

"TT jump complete," came the announcement from the speakers and a collective sigh went through the ship. Sirion's seatmate had lost all interest in further conversation now that they had arrived at their destination system.

Which was fine with him. He got up and went to the toilet. A small queue was already forming, and he joined it.

"An overpass, too?" asked one of the miners who made up about half the passengers. He was a stocky man with a short torso and long limbs. His forearms ended in two six-fingered metal hands. Miners were the only civilians who had extensive augmentations that were not sanctioned or were excluded by most occupations since the fall of Omega. By necessity, any taboo was apparently quite fine with the policy.

"Overpass?"

"Yeah. Most of us are Harbingers, bringing downed colleagues back to Lagunia to be turned over to the sea as they would have wished," the man explained, pursing his lips. "It's a shame how many of us still get killed in the asteroid mines."

"I don't suppose you'd rather have robots do your job," he said.

The worker waved off his comment. "Ha! No! But at least under Omega there was better pay and good health and safety when we worked with the tin buckets."

"These bodies you spoke of, you're personally bringing them back to your home system from their place of work?" Sirion asked, his interest piqued.

"Yes. We put you on hold until the interval change. The work goes for six months, then the new workforce comes in and we have six months off, and we can fly back to our families. Most of the mates come from the edge worlds, work in the asteroids further out that haven't been pushed into orbit around a Core World, and industrially hollowed out there. Nobody wants to die and rot in a Core system." The brawny little man raised his arms and rotated his wrists like saw blades. "We're cheap labor for the Core Worlders, we know that, but as long as the pay is right, we don't care. Still, we don't forget where we came from."

"But Harbingen was a Core World. You must have been born there."

The line moved slowly toward the door with the stylized man above it, and they shuffled forward in sync.

"Yeah. But if you're honest, we were already a fringe world back then. The only one ruled by an AI rather than a Parliament. Rich, but outsiders, ridiculed for our traditions."

Sirion nodded. "I understand. The fringe worlds meet the same criteria, except for the wealth."

"That's it. Poor, outsiders, bound by traditions, and dependent on talking yourself up." The worker let out a booming laugh. "How better to do that than to badmouth the more privileged? Fucking Core Worldlings!"

Sirion smiled politely and nodded as the man, rigged for zero gravity work, winked at him and disappeared into the restroom when it was his turn.

"Dear passengers, this is your pilot speaking. You are requested to return to your seats and fasten your seat belt. Thank you." The announcement ended with a short crackle from the speakers and the rest of the waiting passengers looked at each other in surprise before, for the most part, shrugging their shoulders but not moving otherwise.

Sirion, however, went straight back. Not to his seat, but to a free one at the very front of the stairs, whose owner was probably still in line. The other passengers to the left and right didn't seem to mind because they were engrossed in whispered conversations. The engines vigorously picked up thrust, which his upgraded ears effortlessly picked out from the background noise. But liners, with their ion engines, were not known for being able to muster much acceleration, nor were they known to do anything about it while underway. StarVans were all about cheap production and cheap use, which meant long flight times. Presumably, the pilot would be fired before he would be allowed to use up expensive fuel to reach their destination faster. So, the announcement coupled with the increased thrust could only mean that something was wrong. Sirion didn't like it when that happened.

Using his forearm display, he activated an aggressive routine from the hidden memory and accessed the ship's computer. The firewalls were a joke, as cheap and stodgy as the ship.

They were in the middle of the asteroid belt, which separated the inner system from the outer and still had many hundreds of millions of kilometers to go until they reached their destination. Unlike what most people imagined, who had little idea of cosmic relationships, "asteroid belt" did not mean that large chunks of rock rotated close together around the sun, but that they rotated close together in relative relation to the sun. The distances were measured in tens of thousands to hundreds of thousands of kilometers, and so only the glimmer of reflective objects could be seen through the aging telescopes. But a single reflection was brighter and possessed a frayed rim, as if on fire.

Exhaust flare, he recognized immediately and rolled his eyes. *Pirates.*

He had wondered how long it would be before he had his first fringe-world experience, which the authorities always warned about. He quickly reviewed Lagunia's system data and then nodded as he understood. Using his implanted throat microphone, he recorded a voice message, "I'm coming in earlier than expected and changing my route."

He sent it off in the direction of Artros, fully encoded and compressed strongly enough that even the antenna of NM 98-03 needed only a millisecond for the transmission, which could also pass for interference.

One last look at the telescope images showed him that the attacking spacecraft was already decelerating. Through the bridge's camera feed, he saw personnel frantically engaged in a panicked discussion. A woman in a run-down operator's uniform spoke incessantly into her microphone, but radio was all but useless this deep in the asteroid belt. The signal would make it out, but it would hardly be targeted. The ship had no directional beam, so they could only hope that the system fleet had patrols in and around the belt, which was unlikely. After all, fringe worlds had no fleets worth mentioning. Lagunia, while special because the *Oberon* was there, did not have even a fraction the number of ships a Core system did.

Quickly, Sirion went through the cargo and analyzed the blueprint of the passenger liner until he found what he was looking for. Then he stood and tapped into the speakers on all three decks.

"Dear passengers, we are being hijacked by pirates. Stay calm and do not panic. There is no reason—"

He didn't need to say anymore because the effect he desired began with "pirates" and reached its hysterical climax with "panic." Passengers jumped out of their seats to join family and relatives in other rows, others flocked to the stairs or the toilets hoping to find somewhere to hide. Sirion calmly mingled with them and made his way to the lower deck, whose stairwell was completely jammed. Some passengers were trampled and begged for help, but this was lost in the general tumult of shouting and screaming.

He reached his destination near the entrance to the bridge in the bow section, where the only two security guards had drawn their cortical destroyers and were guarding the door while issuing angry threats at the angry passengers, who alternately pleaded for help from Fleet or blamed the pilots for not reaching their destination long ago.

Sirion used the confusion as cover, noticed but ignored by bystanders. He knelt in front of a maintenance bay hatch normally reserved for robots. The fingertip of his right middle finger flipped open, and a pin of programmable silicon formed into a screwdriver that fit precisely into the screw heads in the corners of the hatch. After loosening it, he slipped into the shaft and switched his retinal implants to ultrasound, so they provided him with a real-time image of his surroundings.

After crawling toward his target for a few minutes, he heard the diminishing yelp of an alarm.

Power failure. ECM harpoon, he thought, and instantly there was weightlessness. Screams swelled behind him. Sirion continued moving, pushing off and sliding through the shaft until he came to a fork and turned downward—at least to what had been down before.

Before he reached his destination, a violent jolt went through the liner followed by a noise that sounded like the tearing of paper, abruptly ending the ship's flight.

He didn't have much time left. He extended a tiny fission cutter from another fingertip and began to cut precisely along the edges of the grid. The thin yellow beam melted the composite, and he was finally able to pull it toward him in one piece. The lack of gravity worked in his favor. He didn't fall but was able to stay suspended in position without any effort while he watched the scene below him.

The cargo bay of the liner was quite small and tapered off on the sides to match the underside, reminiscent of the belly of a classic ship that would have sailed across an ocean centuries ago. Toward the bow were the magnetically affixed supply containers with scannable codes on them so the crew could identify the appropriate contents as they were unpacked. Further aft, he found what he was looking for, and presumably not just him. Four heavy-duty shelves held long, trapezoidal containers that were transparent on the surface and appeared to be iced over on the inside. In all, he counted twenty-two of them.

Four figures floated among them, whispering excitedly. Two of them were tugging the first coffin out of its holder and a third was tapping away on the side control panel until the Tauron pod popped open and they pulled out a black body bag and let it sail toward the fourth figure. The fourth one jammed its feet into a handhold on a circular cutout section of the starboard wall, and passed the bag into a long, retractable airlock.

Sirion silently slipped from his hiding place and between the first containers before deftly pulling and pushing his way through the rows like a fish until he finally reached the shelves. The pirates proceeded purposefully but frantically and had already stolen the fourth body. Two of them were obviously augmented. One was tall and had metallic joints at the elbows and knees that could be rotated one hundred and eighty degrees. His massive frame matched the hulking face and scowling expression. He seemed to be in charge of passing the wrapped bodies to a petite woman, with blond hair and fearful wandering eyes waiting at the doorway to the airlock, and another person Sirion could not see. The third figure was at least six feet tall and as wide as a closet with bulging artificial muscles and a bull's neck. Thick tubes grew from his upper arms and connected to his forearms just below the elbow. This giant hadn't bothered to hide his implant eyes and their chrome reflected like two small suns even in the sparse light. In any case, these people would not be able to show themselves in Core Worlds. The second woman in this strange foursome was extremely attractive, even if Sirion wasn't interested, and looked completely out of place with her elfin elegance.

"A lucrative business, smuggling augments that no one misses," he said, floating out from between the containers into the small space between them and the shelves. About four and a half feet separated him from the airlock and he was a little more than five from the three engaged in the actual theft.

All eyes were instantly fixed on him, and handguns were drawn. He could tell from the gas valves behind the grips that they were zero-G-capable pistols that had no recoil. Sirion didn't care.

"No one is looking for the bodies of twenty-two miners as

84

expendable as this ship," he continued. The augmented giant with the dead chrome eyes wanted to float toward him, but the elf held him back by his arm.

"Since you've already gone to the trouble of sneaking up on me: What do you want?" she asked.

"You have upset my schedule," Sirion replied. "If I kill you now, your bodies will be found, and I will be questioned by Fleet personnel. I don't have that kind of time. If I let you go, the ship will have a leak in the hold and the crew will try to seal it before we move on. I don't have that time."

"If you *kill* us?" laughed the smaller of the two giants. But the woman remained serious and studied him.

"Yes," he said. "You have two choices. The first: I come aboard, and you fly me to Lagunia. The second: I kill you and take your spaceship."

"And the third is that I'm going to give you a new parting of the hair with my knife, so I don't have to see your smug face anymore," the loudmouth said angrily.

"Willy," the pretty woman admonished her comrade, "I think you'd better—"

"Listen to your girlfriend," Sirion finished the sentence for her, looking at his forearm display. "You have ten seconds."

"What do you really want?" asked the woman. Her strained swallow was almost audible.

"Nine."

"Coal?" Willy asked.

"Eight."

"I've had enough," growled the augmented giant and threw himself toward Sirion with surprising speed by pushing off a post of the heavy-duty shelving. His agility almost caught Sirion off guard. Almost.

He waited a second, then quickly turned to the side and activated his reflex booster. Immediately, his arms and legs shook as if they were under high voltage. Five million credits did their job and brought him next to his opponent. He struck the man's back, near the right kidney, but the reaction was small.

The giant spun around and parried the next blow. As he tried to bring his carbotanium-covered fist down onto Sirion's forehead, Sirion dodged it by jamming his foot into an open holding loop on the floor and dove under the blow, only to have the giant land blows against his ribcage and larynx. The tip of his left index finger flipped open, and he sank the tiny needle into the augmented's artery, and he immediately went limp.

"Seven."

"Shit!" Willy cursed and drew his pistol.

Sirion was faster, as the world around him suddenly felt as if it was spinning in slow motion. He snatched the gun from the unconscious man and using retina targeting shot directly into the muzzle of the pistol being aimed at him. It exploded and Willy cried out as several splinters pierced his arm.

"Six," Sirion said impassively.

"Fuck!" The woman looked helplessly at Willy.

"Five."

"Stop!" she cried, looking in horror at the unconscious drifting giant.

"Four."

"I'm telling you; you can fly with me!"

"Smart."

Sirion let the weapon slip lazily from his hand and gave the pile of metal and flesh beside him a push toward the airlock.

5

J ason Bradley steered the small shuttle in a tight turn after it was catapulted out of the hangar, along the vector lines that marked his course on the HUD projected on the huge screen. The actual pilot and his copilot sat behind him in the two luxurious passenger seats and were probably scowling at him. At least he thought he felt a tickle on the back of his neck that matched two frustrated pilots who had been ordered by a superior to watch, even though *they* were supposed to be driving *him*.

At least they had the somewhat dubious pleasure of sitting on the lavish armchairs that only a fleet that was criminally confident of victory could install in its ferries.

And I finally get to grab a joystick and control the power of a spaceship myself, he thought cheerfully.

The trajectory took him past the Eden Halo, a narrow band of habitat that circled humanity's oldest colony like a life preserver. In addition to the massive orbital defenses that reflected, as on every other Core World, that they had been in a state of war for many decades, the Eden Halo housed space industry, homes for the system's wealthiest citizens, and the second largest Fleet Headquarters of humanity apart from Terra.

Eden itself had not unjustly received its name from the first sleeper ship to arrive after its hundred-year voyage. From a distance it was a lush green sphere, larger than Earth and with slightly less water, which stretched across the planet's surface, not in the form of oceans but wide, endless branching rivers that covered the landmass. Under the white clouds, it looked like a complex vascular system. Despite how paradisiacal Eden had been in the early days of colonization, there was not much of it left now. The rapid development of industry and subsequent poisoning of the biosphere over nearly two hundred years had resulted in toxic rain, poisoned rivers, and acidic soil. Once-extensive agriculture eventually collapsed, and with the advent of superstorms, aided by massive deforestation—Eden oaks were still the most sought-after timber among those who could afford it—the inhabitants had to retreat to large domed cities. About five hundred million people still lived in them today. However, as so often in the history of their species, humans had survived and adapted even under difficult conditions.

Jason's destination was not Eden, but a point on the relative starboard side. Through the forward viewport he could see what looked like a particularly dense cluster of stars in the endless black of the universe, crowded together below the Milky Way band like a flock of twinkling sheep. The Terran Federation's Second, Third, and Seventh Fleets were one hundred eighty thousand kilometers away in the shadow of the giant moon Freya, which was a pitch-black disk conspicuous only by its lack of stars. Freya was completely hollowed out and crisscrossed by a network of vacuum tubes and ledges for warships to dock without gravity, a cold, nondescript anthill that teemed with life.

The three fleets that had been gathering here for the last two months, where they could not be seen by a Click spy ship from any of the jump points, were in a sort of dormant state. A large number of the ships were connected to each other by tether clamps and airlocks, forming clusters. Those that were still "free" had arranged themselves around the Lagrange point between Eden and Freya to make as few corrective maneuvers as possible. Emissions were avoided whenever possible.

For Jason, who was steering the shuttle toward his target ship with a little more thrust than allowed, it was a strange sight. Visually, the nine hundred or so ships reflected only the little light radiating off Eden's surface and appeared downright nondescript. On the HUD, however, which assigned a name and identifier to each point, the display exploded with information. The concentrated power of so many ships, even the most advanced in the Federation, was awe-inspiring. It showed not only how determined Fleet leadership was about the next step in this war, but also that the time was almost right.

His fingers tingled as he swung the shuttle into the final turn around the TFS *Gloine* and headed for his target, the TFS *Caesar*. The newly launched generation battlecruiser was a two-hundred-meter arrow of a ship with a thickened engine section from which protruded six nacelles with the latest phase engines, capable of providing up to 40 Gs of acceleration. Launch pads for Predator drones were tiny holes in the flanks, and the port hangar no longer needed armored doors because it was protected by a force field that shimmered faintly. Jason turned off the flight aids and accelerated, pushed the joystick forward just before the hangar, and dove through the field at maximum braking thrust.

Behind him, he heard a relieved yip.

"Sorry, Lieutenants," he said grinning as the hangar systems took control and maneuvered him inside the small metal cavern to one of the six parking clamps.

The two junior officers merely nodded and struggled to maintain polite expressions as he turned his seat around to face them and stood. He retrieved his duffel bag from a holding net and slung it over his shoulder.

"Why are you in such a good mood, sir?" the copilot asked, adjusting her hat. "If you don't mind me asking?"

"I've been transferred to the *Caesar*," he replied lightly. "That means Admiral Augustus has assigned me to Strike Group 2 as a staff officer. In two days, I'll be at the spearhead of the assault and will be able to see it through."

"Do you really think this will be the end?" The pilot sounded hopeful, but restrained, like someone who didn't dare to be disappointed by his own optimism.

"I don't just believe it, I know it!" Jason nodded one last time to the two, whereupon they saluted, and he exited the shuttle via the opening ramp. Since the hangar was fully automated, he encountered only a few loading bots rolling past him until he disappeared into one of the corridors, where two Marines came to attention, and an ensign with red hair and a perfectly pressed uniform did the same, but with considerably more precision.

"Nice outfit, Ensign," Jason joked, smirking, but the young man merely nodded gravely, eyeing him just sardonically enough that it didn't pass for an insult.

"Welcome aboard, Lieutenant Commander. I am to take you directly to the admiral."

"Well then, after you."

The ensign nodded, turned briskly, and was about to leave when Jason dropped his duffel bag. He turned back around.

"Thank you for the offer, *Ensign*. You are welcome to carry my luggage," Jason said, looking the ensign directly in the eye. His jaw muscles tightened visibly before he nodded and passed a hand through the loops.

"Of course, Lieutenant Commander."

Vain young fellow, he thought disgustedly as they walked down the narrow corridor. *If he doesn't become a greasy political officer, I don't know who would.*

They made their way to the top deck where the commander's quarters and the officers' cabins were located, as he knew from his preparation. They didn't encounter even a dozen crew members, but those they did wore scrupulously clean and pressed uniforms, so he felt like a foreign body in his usual blue ship's overalls. Dress uniforms usually had no place on board, except for special occasions, so he wondered what he might have missed. Since there were no elevators—the *Caesar* was probably too small for them—they had to use ladders several times, until they finally arrived in front of a bulkhead with golden ornaments, on which a holosign read Vice Admiral Augustus Bretoni, Commander.

The ensign set Jason's duffel bag next to the door, saluted, and walked away without further comment.

Jason waited patiently until the bulkhead in front of him opened and an adjutant with gray temples and the insignia of a commander appeared. Jason saluted briskly.

"Come in, Lieutenant Commander. The admiral is expecting you."

"Thank you, sir." He entered the anteroom, where two data secretaries were working at holoscreens, so engrossed in their work that they didn't seem to notice him. They looked like fortune tellers at their crystal balls, sitting in their chairs where they faced holographic data whirling around in a column that distorted the light. The adjutant's desk was next to another door, which appeared to be wood and apparently led to the admiral's quarters and office.

"You can go right through." The commander gestured to the mahogany door, and Jason nodded his thanks.

Like in a castle, he thought. *And you are Alfred?*

The admiral's quarters were almost lavish for a warship. There was a large lounge adjoined by a door to a bathroom, a row of protein synthesizers, sofa seating with a holoscreen in the center, and a low display case with several expensive whiskeys inside. The wide desk was on a pedestal by the only window, which presumably worked by means of live projections and was in fact not a window at all, since warships did not usually tolerate such weak points.

Admiral Augustus was still extremely young at forty, a tall, slender man with a finely coiffed short haircut, shaved exactly at the edge of what was permissible. His features were soft, like those of a rejuvenated man, but his hawkish, slanted eyes warned any onlooker against hasty misjudgment. Augustus had climbed the military career ladder at record speed, establishing himself not only as an able politician within Fleet, said to have the best connections to Terra, but also as an effective leader. His victory at the Battle of T-39 four years ago was legendary at every fleet academy. Whether the admiral's skill in front of the press and the training cadre had paid off in spreading it, it was at least open to conjecture.

"Ah, Bradley." Augustus waved him closer without looking up from the papers before him. Behind him was green Eden with its deceptive freshness displayed in the window. The passive ships of the three fleets looked like the dead skeletons of imaginative space creatures.

Jason stood, guarded, in front of the desk and waited. He couldn't help but shake his head inwardly at the sight of the handwritten papers. Fleet was notorious for its outdated traditions, but the preferences of some of the upper ranks of officers were simply absurd. All that was missing was for the admiral to press the thick gold ring shining on his right little finger into hot sealing wax.

After what felt like an eternity, Augustus closed the folder. It was only then that Jason realized how quiet it was in the cabin. On the *Zarathustra*, the ten-year-old frigate on which he had served up to that point, the hum of machinery and wiring had been omnipresent. Here, he could have heard a pin drop.

"So, here he is at last, the lieutenant commander of my wishes," the admiral gloated. His thin mouth twisted into a smile, but his eyes seemed to be exploring every emotion on Jason's face.

"Reporting for duty, sir."

"I'm sure you're wondering why I called *you* here, of all people, so close to Operation Iron Hammer."

"Indeed, I am, sir."

"At ease, Commander." Augustus waved casually and Jason placed his feet a little wider apart. It hadn't escaped his notice that there were no chairs for visitors. Surely that meant something.

"In any case, I am honored to participate in the operation aboard the *Caesar.*"

Augustus's face parted into a sly smile.

"Very good, very good. She's a beauty, the *Caesar.*" Another terse wave. "You know, Bradley, it's about time you stepped out from your father's shadow. You graduated from the Academy on Terra with top marks, even though it was rumored in the media that you were just a ward of Fleet leadership. Every one of your superiors was full of praise. You're a hotshot who's in control, if I interpreted all the analyses correctly, and that's rare. But you know better than I that you're still fighting in the shadows while everyone else is enjoying the sun."

"If you're alluding to the *Zarathustra,* sir, I can assure you that the Fringe World patrols taught me a lot, and I think that—"

Augustus snorted and sat back in his chair. "A bit of fringe-world play and banter with pirates, that's not work for a high-profile officer like you. We need you where it really counts. You can't help what your father did or didn't do. After all, the Federation isn't even sure how to evaluate it."

"The public *is* safe, sir," Jason corrected his superior, clenching his teeth. "It's just the military justice system that couldn't find any specific wrongdoing."

"Ah, that's how it is, politics. You can do the wrong thing

and still be within the law. Who knows in advance how history will judge one's actions?" Augustus folded his hands in front of him. "I don't blame your father legally."

Legally, Jason repeated in his mind. "I understand."

"Maybe he actually got the appropriate orders, maybe not. After Omega's destruction, we will never know. In any case, the fact is that you are *not* your father, and you chose to serve in the Core Worlds, unlike your brother. That's why I need you here on board."

"Why are we talking about my father, if I may ask, sir?"

"You get straight to the point; I like that." Augustus leaned forward. Jason didn't think he liked it; the man liked to talk too much. "Strike Group 2 will be on its way to Lagunia in two hours."

"Excuse me?" he asked in horror, hastily adding a "sir" after it. The admiral's right eyebrow twitched disapprovingly. "I mean, I don't understand, Admiral."

"We will personally supervise the activation of the hyperspace portal there and honor your father with a high visit."

"Fleet leadership wants to *honor* him?"

"Yes. You look disappointed."

"Permission to speak freely, sir?"

Augustus gave him a small nod.

"My father is a coward and hides behind his Titan. Just because he commands the last battleship in the Fleet, he should not be given de facto control of a system. He belongs in a court-martial, not on a bridge. Even a place as insignificant as Lagunia deserves someone with decency and honor."

"Harsh words toward one's own father," the admiral said, pursing his lips. "He was one of the most up-and-coming commanders in the entire fleet before the destruction of Harbingen. And Lagunia is no longer insignificant since it was assigned the fifty-first hyperspace gate. The only fringe world."

"But that's only because it's farther from Click territory than any other." Jason struggled to keep his anger in check. He had begun to fear that this time, once again, he had received orders related to his name and origin rather than his abilities.

"Right, but that's not all. Captain Konrad Bradley will not be participating in Operation Iron Hammer. He will be released from duty upon our arrival. *Honorably*," Augustus added when he noticed Jason's pleased expression, which immediately evaporated. "I want you to assist me in making this change as peaceful and orderly as possible. The loyalty of his crew is not infamous without reason."

"That's also why the Admiralty was so lenient with him, isn't it? Don't risk a secessionist war with the ex-Harbingers."

"I'll let you get away with that informality, Lieutenant Commander."

Jason swallowed.

"I understand your frustration, but the decision has been made and we will implement it. Once that is done, Strike Group 2, under my command, will launch an attack on AT-66 from Lagunia. Do you understand what that means?"

AT-66, he thought and thought for a moment.

"That's the second moon of Attila-62, the Clicks' home planet," he finally said.

"Right. We are preparing the final strike against the enemy, Bradley. We will jump into the system and engage the aliens in battle. That will give the main body of the fleet time to bring in the individual components of the super gate and assemble it so we can take all forty Strike Groups into the heart of the enemy."

Forty Strike Groups. Jason's head spun. That meant eighty fleets. Over twenty-four thousand ships. That left only twenty fleets in reserve in case the strike failed. The entire power of the Federation united on one target.

"So, our task is essential to the success of the operation, sir."

"That it is. I want you on the bridge as a tactical officer, Bradley. And when this thing is over, and you've proven yourself..." Augustus paused. "Then I'm going to need a new XO because Carla is retiring."

"I understand, sir. Thank you, sir." Jason got the impression the conversation had ended and was getting ready to salute and leave the admiral's quarters, when Augustus suddenly stood and came around the desk. He gestured toward the seating area.

"Do you appreciate a good scotch, Bradley?" came the casual question, as if they had known each other for some time.

"I must confess that I've only had one chance to taste a real whiskey in my life, and it was... very resinous," Jason said cautiously and followed the admiral to the sofa.

At the admiral's urging, he sat somewhat stiffly and watched as Augustus filled two bulbous glasses with the amber liquid from one of ornately shaped bottles. He held one of them out to Jason and sketched a toast before sitting gracefully.

"*Peaty*, we'll say to that. But don't feel bad about it. I hated my first scotch. Now I enjoy a glass at least twice a week. It helps relax the mind."

Jason looked into the brownish liquid that barely covered the bottom of the glass and inhaled the scent, which was slightly acrid. Then he sipped it and nodded appreciatively. It tasted awful.

"Thank you, sir."

"Don't thank me for a few sips of scotch that are more expensive than some apartments in Eden Halo." Augustus laughed and gestured to the window, where the distant ring was visible as a shimmering ribbon. "You'd better thank me for serving on the *Caesar*."

"A beauty," he nodded with honest enthusiasm. "The acceleration figures are impressive. Is it true the combat speed doesn't have to be throttled back to accommodate the Predators?"

"Mm-hm," the admiral confirmed with a smile. "We may not be as heavily armored as the old models, but we are faster, more maneuverable, and more heavily armed."

"Sir..."

"Feel free to ask questions. I encourage all my officers to ask questions. There are no stupid, wrong, or improper questions with me on board. The answers are my responsibility."

"Did we load hyperspace torpedoes?" he asked the question that had been burning in the back of his mind. He had heard about the top-secret development, but as yet the bulk of the officer corps were not sure if they really existed, and if they did exist whether they had been delivered yet.

"Yes. We were allotted twenty."

"Twenty?"

"If I couldn't pull strings to get them for something like this, I'd make a lousy commander," Augustus said, not without pride. "You're on a *real* warship now, Bradley. You'll get used to it all right."

Jason thought back to his service on the *Zarathustra* and became a little wistful. His two-year stint dealing with pirates had been largely one of boredom and mind-numbing routine, but hardly anyone had teased him about his background.

"No one will be unpleasant to you here, I promise you that. For me, performance and loyalty count, everything else is old news. Everyone here has earned the seat they're sitting on. Not because of their origins, but because of the gray matter in their heads. Anyone who can't acknowledge that will be rigorously disciplined and replaced by me," Augustus said sternly and sipped his scotch. "I'm a breeder, did you know that?"

Jason shook his head in surprise.

"That's right. I was born in vitro. Exo-uteri fertilization in Sicilia, before they joined the Christian Council and banned children from multiple donor parents. I was an outcast from the day I was born without knowing it. Later, my classmates and fellow students made sure I didn't forget."

"I'm sorry about that, sir."

"No!" the Admiral said so quickly that Jason was startled. "Don't mistake my past for weakness. Some people come into the world with many resources: rich parents, good genes, few hurdles. Others come into the world with a starting disadvantage like a discredited father or as the result of a brief cultural aberration and have to fight for every single resource. What do you think makes a person better able to take care of themselves, rise above, work hard, and find creative solutions?"

Jason nodded and smiled. He hadn't thought of it that way at all. "I understand, sir."

"Don't forget it." Augustus drained his glass and Jason quickly did the same, understanding that *this* was the end of their conversation. After they stood and saluted they shook hands, and the admiral held his for a moment longer. "I know you dislike the next part of our mission, Bradley, but remember that I am aware of it and appreciate it. Loyalty is all they need here. I already know your capabilities from your record."

"Of course, sir!"

"Remember that when the time comes. And the moment will come."

QUARTERS OF ADMIRAL AUGUSTUS BRETONI, TFS CAESAR

Vice Admiral Augustus Bretoni's gaze lingered on the door after it closed behind young Bradley. An observant officer. Inexperienced, yes, but only where politics were concerned, and that was a good thing. He had to admit that Saunders had probably been right, and his strategy might actually pay off.

When the door opened again, his aide came through. Like a well-dressed skeleton, he stalked across the marble floor and stood beside him near the sofa.

"Have a seat, please."

Pyrgorates submitted to his offer, but looked as if he was being forced to sit on a pincushion.

"Well?" Augustus asked. "What is your impression?"

"Poorly dressed."

The admiral smirked and nodded in amusement. "He's new. Give him some time. Maybe he'll realize on his own why we have slightly different rules on board. In the meantime, let's let him think that we're vain political officers who know our way around the corridors of the solar Senate better than we do between the stars."

"What good will that do?" his aide asked.

"It will allow us to learn a lot about him." Augustus waved

it off. "Surely you had other impressions of him beside his overalls, which absolutely do not violate Fleet statutes?"

"He has the gait of an impatient man, the habitus of an upright man, and the look of an angry man," Pyrgorates summarized, looking at the door as if the lieutenant commander were standing there. "He is young."

"Not the youngest of his rank. Ongoing casualties and hard-to-find officer replacements make it possible. Look at me; I think I may be the youngest vice admiral in Fleet history."

"You earned it."

"Bradley did, too."

"By hunting pirates?" His aide's raised brow made it clear what he thought.

"Let's not forget that he was previously deployed on the front lines for five years. Pirate hunting is part of any good training and reminds junior officers that Fleet fights and must fight on multiple fronts."

"Pirate hunting." Pyrgorates said shaking his head. "Pacifist hunting, that's what it actually is, isn't it?"

"The Senate doesn't like that word," Augustus reminded him.

"But this isn't the Senate, and I really hope Bradley understands that when we get to his father's system."

"The enemies of war are a thorn in our flesh, but no more than that, and Captain Konrad Bradley is certainly many things, but not an enemy of war. We can be assured of that."

"He's sitting in this backwater system with his fleet and he's not moving. Not toward the front—"

"—but not away from it, either."

"How could they? Lagunia is farther from the contested rim worlds than any other system. The nearest ocean world, ironically, is the farthest inhabited world known to us from Lagunia, Attila."

"We are not here to nurse our justified reservations about

Konrad Bradley," Augustus admonished his aide with a hint of sternness in his voice.

Pyrgorates bowed his head. "Of course. How do you intend to use Bradley's son?"

"As little as possible," Augustus said thoughtfully. "My hope is that his mere presence will be enough to keep things running smoothly. If not, we will force them to make a mistake and use it as a dilemma. Don't underestimate the family ties of a dynasty."

"Regarding *that* matter, is there any news from Harbingen?"

"No, but we don't need it. We have our orders, and we know what to do." He gestured at Pyrgorates. The adjutant rose stiffly and turned to go.

"Do you ever wonder if it was a mistake?"

"If *what* was a mistake?"

"You know what I mean."

The admiral's expression remained stony as always, but there was a thoughtful look in his eyes. When he stirred, he spoke with more emphasis than usual. "The life of a Fleet officer is one of duty and privation. The greatest dilemma of this war is that Fleet officers cannot raise families because they are away between the stars, and more and more offspring are being bred in tanks. Entire generations are growing up without their genetic parents, and the social conflicts this brings about are ignored by the Senate and it may be too late. The paci—*pirates*"—he corrected himself—"are merely a logical consequence of this. They are degenerates, and we have the senators to thank for their short-sightedness. Since when has any politician ever thought further than his next election?"

Augustus considered stopping the conversation there, but decided against it. Pyrgorates was not a man of many words, so it was especially important for him to vent every now and then about what made him so tight-lipped.

"They pretend to be social and progressive in their starscratchers over Terra and Jupiter, talk about miracle babies being much healthier than natural-born ones, and try to tell us about the societal duty of inclusion to curb hatred of exos. But that's easy to say at campaign rallies and interviews in industrial centers where no one has to deal with hidden bombs, sabotage in enemy territory, and the desertion of entire ship crews. If these parasites saw their friends lying next to them on a stretcher with burned skin and burst eyes, they might come down from their ivory tower." Pyrgorates noticed Augustus was surprised by his emotional outburst—his eyelash twitched —and tensed. "To answer your question, sir, I don't like what we're doing any more than you do—at least, I assume you don't. But there is no alternative. I'd rather walk through fire and know that not everyone will emerge on the other side than see us rot from the inside out."

"Our hearts will be broken, Commander," Augustus said gravely, setting his empty glass down. "But after that, we will move on, and we will make sure that it has not been in vain and that old mistakes will never be repeated."

6

Lagunia was a deep blue ball in front of the cockpit window, which was divided into equal segments by the composite struts in the transparent metal. Bands of white and dark gray clouds stretched from one terminator to the other, providing a pretty to ugly contrast of the endless water that could have made the world a major exporter of seafood had it not been so far out. The Lagunia System was almost as far from Terra as the home of the Clicks—only in the opposite direction. Even the most advanced cruisers in the Fleet, which could travel incredibly fast between the jump points of the respective transit systems, needed at least three days from the nearest inhabited star system. And that was already a fringe world. It was over fifty jumps to Terra. So, if you wanted to know how it felt to arrive at the end of the universe, Lagunia was the closest you could get.

The reasons why a small colony with little more than one million inhabitants could still survive were, ironically, two famous demises. That of the *Lagoon*, as the former alien inhabitants were called, who had died out about a hundred years ago, and that of the Harbingers. The annihilation of

Harbingen by fragments of the moon Kor shattered by the Clicks had burned itself into the memory of the Terran Federation as a collective trauma. But it also did something else: The colonization of a planet that was uninviting and should have been abandoned. There were no continents, only isolated volcanic islands and so-called flogs, carpets of algae so dense and deep that structures could be built on them. They changed position by moving with the great ocean currents. One flog held the capital city of Atlantis, which Dev headed toward with the *Quantum Bitch*. It was already recognizable as a small green spot in the endless blue, if he looked closely.

Seventy years ago, when a fleet of prospector ships discovered Lagunia, the crew immediately noticed that the planet had a strange ring. At first, they thought it was a moon destroyed long ago by an asteroid, the remains of which were circling the equator, but they soon learned it was a debris belt. Melted metal, corrugated composite, and sharp-edged pieces of machinery testified to a past battle they dated to only twenty years earlier. Whatever had happened, it had taken place just two decades before Lagunia's discovery by humans. At that time, the excitement in the Federation was great, as they hoped for a peaceful first contact with aliens, after the one with the Clicks had not gone well.

But with the arrival of whole swarms of xenologists in the system it quickly became clear that there was no one to meet. The Lagoon had disappeared, destroyed by the Clicks, to whom much of the debris in orbit could clearly be attributed. They were in the early days of the war at that time, the news had not merely caused horror, but a real surge of support for the political hardliners on Terra and the Solar Congressional Republic, the SCR, in general. As the leading faction within the Federation, they had demanded that the war be fought with much more rigor, lest they suffer a fate similar to that of the Lagoon.

Most explorers had turned away after it became clear that there were also no cities or other major legacies of interest left by the natives, who had apparently never left their planet. The wreckage of their defensive fleet did not reveal much that was new. The battle must have been fought with frightening determination. The only thing they were certain of was the aquatic nature of the annihilated species, for the only relics of their civilization were found beneath the surface, deep in the ocean trenches.

The colonists who remained led a meager life, with long waits for supplies, since hardly anyone wanted to travel to a system where a few hundred scientists were chasing a lost cause. Accordingly, there was little investor interest in local research, from which not much was expected.

All this changed sixty years later with the Harbingen disaster. The destruction of the Harbinger biosphere overnight left over a million people homeless who had been holding out in the AI government's planned colonist fleet or living scattered around the system at the time of the attack. After a long back and forth within the Federation, in which the Council had not been able to agree on a quick solution, the refugee fleet, with the *Oberon* at its head, had unceremoniously left for Lagunia to claim for itself what no one else had: A world without much living space, without significant resources and without good connections to the rest of humanity.

Under intergalactic law, Lagunia still had no recognized status as a Federation colony, but no one bothered to argue with the traumatized survivors of the greatest catastrophe of the Click War about whether they were allowed to settle on an insignificant ball of water, especially since the Harbingers still had a small fleet that, while not comparable to that of a Core World, was more powerful than what could be mustered by most of the fringe worlds.

The *Oberon*, which represented most of the power of the

Harbinger fleet—or what was left of it—was fortunately located at the outer jump point, while Dev accelerated the *Bitch* to entry speed and headed for the outer atmospheric layers of Lagunia according to the angle given by the HUD. Spaceport Control, which could operate with only twenty satellites and had no orbital platforms, had not even sent him an exact flight vector to follow. Only upon their approach to Atlantis did he receive precise altitude and angle information, so he had an exact course to land.

"A floating island," Aura said in amazement behind him. "Somebody peel me an egg!"

"No, we're not going ashore!" Willy snapped at them.

"I didn't say I wanted to go ashore, you fat old fuck!"

"Don't call me old, you little—"

"Guys! Really now?" Jezzy wailed, before continuing, "We almost got killed by a psychopath and we're lucky Dozer is still breathing!" She sniffed peevishly.

"I just don't want her to think about shopping again right away!" the flight engineer insisted.

Ahead of them, Atlantis grew into a dark green carpet with ugly gray blobs scattered across it. Dev had read somewhere that most of Lagunia the "houses" were actually colonist transporters that had simply been parked on the thrusters and then converted into living and working space. They grew out of the land mass like pimples—he couldn't believe they were really densely grown algae carrying so much weight—and were connected by thin lines.

"Shopping? I bought a damn phase solder on Dunkelheim because our crappy converter in the mess hall is junk," Aura shot back. "You can eat lukewarm beans for the rest of the trip if you'd rather!"

"No phase solder is worth fifty credits! You must have had the handle gold-plated so that you—"

"Shut up, both of you!" Dev yelled at both of them

without turning around. "We're going to drop our passenger off, and then we're going to continue according to plan."

"Can't we just skip this mystery trip and go straight to delivering our newfound cargo?" Jezzy whined. "I don't like this place."

"This mystery trip is from one of my best brokers," he grumbled. "And if he says there's something there, there's something there! He's never steered me wrong before."

"What's it supposed to be? A farting whale that we sell to a zoo?" Willy snorted.

"Aquarium!" Aura corrected him.

"What?"

"Fish belong in aquariums! Land animals in zoos."

"Whales are not fish, they are mammals!"

"For a Dunkelheimer squarehead, you sure read a lot of children's encyclopedias!"

"You should have done it once, then you would have known that—"

"—they put whales in zoos? I'm impressed!"

"I swear to God," Dev hissed as tried to explain to the penetratingly annoying pilot software that he had no interest in the recommended autopilot, "if you don't stop right now—both of you!—I'll throw you out the airlock!"

He was answered by silence. He shook his head and steered them toward the only landing field of the "city," which consisted of a huge skyscraper—he had no idea how they had been able to land a colonist ship, let alone not sink the flog with its weight—and about a hundred conical colonist ferries that seemed to be connected by wooden bridges, so there were no real roads. There was something so exotic about the contrast between crude but efficient technology for space and simplistic, improvised elements that Dev marveled at.

As soon as they touched down, they were assigned a parking position between two old ion-field gliders and an atmosphere-capable liner. The two smaller fliers had to be from the large corporate ships in orbit, apparently searching for profitable asteroids in the system for competing mining companies.

When he reached his assigned position, he killed the thrusters and extended the exit ramp.

"I'm going to say goodbye to our cursed guest. Anyone who gets in a huff is welcome to stay!" Sullenly, he unbuckled his seat belt and trudged past them to the central corridor. The planet's gravity was about 0.6 G, making walking and breathing pleasantly easy. Each of his steps resonated slightly, as if he were bobbing up and down.

Their unwilling passenger, because of whom Dozer was still on dialysis in the infirmary trying to rid himself of the neurotoxin he had been injected with, was already standing in front of the floor hatch that led to the ramp. He was average height with an equally average hairstyle, matchstick-length with a shaven undercut, similar to a military cut, and his face was that of an insurance salesman, the kind you'd find on any Core or Fringe World: Shaved and smooth, eyes calm and a dark gray. If his crew hadn't panicked when they explained why they had to transport this guy, he wouldn't have believed he had incapacitated Dozer. Everything about this man was unremarkable and barely registered in his mind, not even the plain black clothing. And it was that, along with the knowledge of his abilities, that scared him.

He wordlessly went to the hatch control and pressed his hand on the panel to open it.

The stranger eyed him briefly, and when their eyes met, Dev winced inwardly. It was cold in the corridor.

"See you around," the man said neutrally.

"I don't think so."

He left and Dev took a few deep breaths before closing the hatch and returning to the bridge. The others were already in their cabins or hopefully doing maintenance as he had instructed them to do.

Only when he had made sure by means of the ship's sensors that the creepy guy was really gone, did he head to the spaceport administration office and present his claim authorization, which he had applied for and gotten approved in the Federation network two weeks ago. The formalities were completed quickly, a DNA print with his finger on a sensor, and the absentminded woman behind her desk nodded.

Her hair was ruffled by a fan circling high above her and had apparently replaced the air conditioner, which, judging by its degree of rust, seemed to have lost the battle against the omnipresent oxidation of a water planet a long time ago.

"Congratulations, you are now a registered archaeological prospector ship," the woman said in a bored voice.

"Thank you!" he replied, beaming.

He hadn't been lying. Jerry, his informant, had never been wrong, although this time he had been strangely excited and impatient. He had insisted several times that the *Quantum Bitch* not make any detours. Well, the liner with the twenty-two augmented corpses was basically on their route to Lagunia. This planet reeked of algae and salt, and the humidity was so brutal that beads of sweat poured from his every pore, but they were on to something big here, he could feel it.

She rolled her eyes and waved him out of her office. She had probably seen hundreds of fortune seekers come and go who had never found anything bigger than a clay vase. But then, they weren't Devlin Myers.

So, in an uplifted mood, he returned to the ship, which looked huge in its parking bay on the spaceport, although it seemed rather puny in space, at only thirty-five meters long. The wings were retracted, and so the *Bitch* looked like a mangled bird of prey with spotted plumage.

As soon as he was back on board, he paid Dozer a quick visit. The giant with the bald skull and chrome eyes was awake, but did not respond to any speech, so he decided to leave the mechanic alone and not incur his wrath. That could end badly.

On the bridge, he checked Jerry's coordinates one last time. They were four hundred miles west of Atlantis in a little-traveled area where there were no flogs, islands, or floating artificial habitats. Official traffic data showed half a dozen freighters cruising in the area. There was no topographic map of the ocean floor, because no such research missions had ever been funded. The only people interested in the bottom were the prospectors, but they didn't care much about scans for posterity, only their own profit. Genuine Lagoon legacies were coveted in the Federation and fetched a handsome price. Even larger research institutes and non-government organizations paid what they could to get their hands on artifacts or interesting sites. They did not have the money to maintain their own research fleets, but they were able to work with what others found for them. Thus, a whole slew of free ship owners had emerged who were either wanted in most systems and had no other place to go, or were willing to take the slim chance of finding something valuable as an opportunity to plunge into the ocean.

Losers and outlaws, Dev thought inwardly. He checked Jerry's coordinates one last time. The location was a lone red dot on a thoroughly blue map, somewhere in the middle of nowhere. It looked as good, or bad, as any other, but there was something there, and they would make money on it.

"Because if you don't, I'll pay you a visit, dear Jerry."

Half an hour later, they lifted off again. Using its maneuvering thrusters, the *Quantum Bitch* could operate effortlessly within atmosphere, even though fuel consumption went up. Normally, he would have used their ion-field glider, which was designed for atmospheric flight, but they didn't know how big the artifact they were about to find would be. So, in anticipation of the big prize, he accepted the risk of rapidly diminishing fuel reserves.

The flight lasted an hour—he didn't want to overdo it—during which they flew over two large freighters with towering Flettner rotors at an altitude of ten kilometers, as well as two floating habitats where smaller ships of other fortune hunters were moored. These habitats, according to his pre-trip research, were the main black-market centers they would surely visit later. He marked their positions on the map created by the ship's computer and focused again on the red dot that was their target.

"There's nothing here at all," Willy said, disappointed, as they finally hovered over the spot that corresponded to Jerry's coordinates.

"It's all happening underwater, isn't it?" Jezzy asked, who was glued to the windshield just like the flight engineer, blocking Dev's view. He let her have her way; at least they weren't arguing.

"After all, if something had been sticking out of the waves, it wouldn't be a secret," Aura agreed with her and, looking over Willy, tried to glimpse the ocean.

The deep blue seemed endless, stretching from horizon to horizon, where it joined the equally blue sky. Whitecaps danced with each other as far as the eye could see, forming pretty white blobs that looked like reflections of the fleecy clouds high above them.

"I'm going down. Aura, you come with me," Dev decided, rising from his pilot seat.

"All right."

"Willy, you're in command. Put us on the water as soon as we've submerged. With the helium tanks empty, we should have enough buoyancy, so we don't use up all our reaction mass by the time we get back."

"You got it."

The *Bitch*'s ion-field glider was located in its own hangar at the lower end of the ship. "Hangar" was a somewhat generous term for the square indentation in the segment forward of the propulsion nacelles that could be accessed by means of two armored flaps. Originally it had been a loading bay for vacuum containers, but Willy and Dozer had modified it so their ion-field glider, with its stubby wings and squat fuselage, fit snugly inside and could be held in place by four retaining clips. The small cockpit had seats for a pilot and copilot in addition to six bucket seats behind them. He gave Aura the pilot's seat, which she reacted to with a surprised look. Dev knew how much she liked flying and begrudged her the joy of diving underwater in a spaceship for the first time. He had done it a few times before, mostly to impress women or after a night of drinking to prove to someone that it was possible. Since these occasions had always been limited to proofs of feasibility at shallow depths, during the run-up to their flight to Lagunia he had had a high-performance pressure system installed for the equalization chambers between the two hulls, which should allow them to descend to even the deepest depths without crushing them like a tin can under a wrecking ball.

But he was nervous all the same, and he used his place in the copilot's seat to keep a close eye on the instruments and adjust them so they weren't caught unawares by anything that could send them into the afterlife.

"Your first dive," he said, after he was satisfied with the setup of his displays, and she released the retaining clips by means of an old-fashioned toggle switch, technology that prevailed in space travel to this day. There was nothing like the reassuring, tactile feel of a flipped switch instead of a simple display readout. "So, nice and slow; always keep your eye on the pressure gauge. The yellow arrow should stay in the transition zone between red and green, okay?"

"All right." Delighted, she nodded and licked her lips as the hangar doors swung open and the glider fell toward the water one hundred meters below. Aura pushed the nose down, and they glided like a kingfisher into the waves, diving into the glittering darkness of the ocean. Fish swirled away in a panic, thousands and thousands of them, which had been collected in a tightly packed school and were now scattering in a whirlwind of streamlined silver bodies.

"My goodness," he marveled, glad when she slowed down to admire the beauty of this underwater world. After all, the fish weren't everything. They also saw long tentacles of creatures that looked like a cross between crocodiles and squids, luminous, gelatinous creatures with bioluminescent wings that rolled gracefully through the water sparkling with sunlight.

"Everything is bursting with life here," Aura said fervently, as the throng fled before them, dissipating more and more. The brute force of their disturbance brought the water behind them to a boil.

"Yes, but I don't see any great treasure," Dev replied thoughtfully and checked the sensors. The sea here was only a hundred meters deep. He could already make out the coral covering the bottom with bright colors, swarmed by small exotic creatures. Everything seemed to be searching for food or protection from those for whom one was food—an overwhelming swarm of life, as only undisturbed evolution could produce.

Aura turned up the intensity of the front headlights, which immediately scared away about half of the animals and made the coral look paler. Some spots were darker than others, but they had unquestionably reached the sea floor.

"I thought Jerry was reliable?" she said.

"He is, actually. He's even given me a contact to sell the find to. He said something about a six-figure sum."

"Six figures? My ass!"

"Yes. But there's nothing here! Damn it!"

"Can you continue the coordinate point from the surface down as a line and throw it up on the HUD?"

"Yes." He tapped the appropriate commands on his forearm display. "But I don't see what..."

He fell silent when the heads-up display marked a point below them that was darker than the others; barely more than six or seven meters in diameter.

"Mmm. Shine a light in there. Maybe a cave?"

Aura steered them directly in front of the dark spot, so they hung three meters in front of it, which was full of suspended particles that refracted the light. The headlights turned forward.

"Brighter," he demanded and leaned forward. The two beams merged into a single one and quickly got lost in the darkness like a frayed column of laser light. "What is that?"

"Looks like a tunnel," Aura said, mirroring what he was thinking. "The walls appear to be smooth, and the sensors are now picking up a determinable depth of three hundred meters. I'd say we've found what your Jerry wanted to show us."

"Obviously," he agreed. "We're going down. With the wingspan, it should work if you fold in the wingtips. Hand over control to the pilot software or we'll bump into something."

"Boss, this is going to be inch work!"

"That's why you let the control computer do it!"

Aura obeyed his order, and they plunged into the eerie hole they had first thought was a shadow. As they slid into the depths amid their cone of light, the external pressure gauge kept changing and he looked at the smooth rock walls as they passed them. From the cold light of their headlights, they looked pale, almost fake, but the small grooves in them were regular.

"No way this is of natural origin," he muttered. "The Lagoon must have built it. The only question is what's at the end of the shaft."

They found out a full hour later, at a depth of six kilometers. Suddenly, they were inside a gigantic cavern, an ocean within an ocean. The bottom of this underwater cavern was over two thousand meters away, and whatever might be to the right and left it was much further away than the sensors were able to reach. There were no light sources here, so they opted to continue descending exactly along the marker line of Jerry's coordinates. Now and then the sensors beeped because they thought they saw other spacecraft, which were probably deep-sea creatures, but they never came closer than a hundred meters. One by one, they threw out light buoys that sank leisurely toward the bottom. Half a kilometer from the bottom, Aura stopped the thrusters.

He was about to order her to keep diving when he realized why she had stopped. The red light from the buoys revealed a jagged structure that looked like a giant saber of brown rock, broken at the top. On the other side, there was a shorter piece covered with small shells and algae swaying in a powerful underwater current.

"What's that?" he asked, swallowing hard.

"Whatever it is, the structure is huge. Maybe it was circular once, but then it must have been at least a kilometer in diameter," Aura said, realigning the spotlights so they could scan the right-hand arc. "See that there?"

"The algae?"

"I don't think it's algae."

Dev looked closer and had to admit she was right. Along with the many microbes and plants that had made the long-submerged structure their home, there were dark gray tubes or cables that emerged from the material and disappeared back into it elsewhere.

Wait a minute, he thought, and gave a short command to the onboard computer. Self-learning algorithms pieced together the structure from the sensor data, determined the presumed size, including the parts that had to be lying beneath the ocean bed, and then created a simulation of a possible original structure. It threw the result onto the HUD, creating a hologram of a giant ring with irregular nodes on the disk in front of them, flickering here and there in false colors where the computer had reached its prediction limits.

"My God," he said, "do you see what I see?"

"A hyperspace gate," Aura whispered with unusual reverence. "Shit, boss. What's the meaning of this?"

"I don't know. But we're definitely going to be rich."

7

"D o we really have to do this?" Valeska asked, her face contorting as if she had bitten into a lemon.

"We have to," Franc said, taking her hand and pulling her toward him before they reached the large wooden door to the ballroom. He straightened his wife's glittering earrings, which had twisted as they walked up the stairs.

"But we have nothing to show. There is no claim we can lay claim to, and we won't be assigned any of the free ones, anyway. It's always been that way up until now." She sighed, so disheartened that it almost hurt him physically. He patted her cheek and forced an encouraging smile.

She looked him straight in the eye as if to rebuke him. "Franc, there's a reason we've been coming here for a year, and they still won't even give us the tiniest piece of the West Sea to develop."

"The Harbingen club." He shook his head. "These people may be nationalists and nostalgic, but they are not fascists. Just because we don't have members—"

"Yes, Franc, that's exactly why!"

"Dear, I know we came here with high hopes, and so far it hasn't gone the way we thought it would—"

"*Not the way we thought it would?*" Valeska glared at him. "We were the most renowned xenologists in the Federation! We were showered with awards for our Click research! Then you said it would be a good idea if we went behind the edge of the universe and researched underwater for new knowledge."

"We were at an impasse," he said, defending himself. "You know that very well! The data on the Clicks is minimal, and despite hopes within Fleet to the contrary, we failed to capture any of them or even find enough remains to dissect them. That's not our fault. We needed something new. We're explorers, not theorists."

"I know that," she said more calmly, sighing again. "All I'm saying is that it's frustrating to keep coming here and leave empty-handed every time. We're researchers, just like you said, but to be that we have to do *research*. How are we supposed to do that without a research object? In the meantime, even the remains of an old Lagoon dome would be enough for me, just so I can occupy myself with something. Maybe—"

Franc was interrupted by his forearm display, which showed an incoming connection originating from orbit.

"Hmm."

"What is it?"

"Someone sent me a video file."

"Who?"

"No idea. The sender is unknown, but the signal source is in orbit."

"Because it goes through a satellite." Valeska waved it off. "Like everything here. Don't open the file. Probably phishing or a virus."

"Too late," he said, starting the thirty-second video.

It showed a clip of Atlantis's spaceport, including a time stamp from last Monday at midnight. A man in a dark coat stepped out from the shadows behind one of the floodlights and walked through a thick curtain of raindrops to a small ship taxiing into parking position. In the background was the spaceport control tower, measuring over twenty stories tall and built into the drive nacelle of a former colonist transporter. No lights burned in it.

The blackout, Franc thought, remembering the day the news feeds had been full of it, that there had been an unexplained power outage. It apparently hadn't affected the floodlights, which was strange. The man pulled his hat lower and walked toward the spacecraft, an orbital shuttle, where he stopped and waited until a ramp lowered from the stern and a figure emerged. Franc recognized the figure immediately. He knew it from mug shots that had flooded the entire planetary network for several days. It was a suspected terrorist from the Free Harbingen Society, which was blamed for the bombing of the Fleet freighter *Shelly.* Last Wednesday, it had fallen victim to an explosive device that may have been smuggled aboard Atlantis's spaceport.

The last five seconds of the video, which was slightly shaky, zoomed in and showed a tiny object being handed off. Then the man in the hat, rain pouring down its brim, raised his eyes and looked toward the camera.

"Oh, shit!" Franc exclaimed, and he covered his mouth with his hand for his vulgar language. *That's the governor's secretary!*

"What is it?" Valeska asked excitedly, trying to catch a glimpse of his forearm display, but Franc shoved the video file into the buffer. He grabbed her upper arms and looked her straight in the eye. "Honey, do you trust me?"

"What?"

"Do you trust me?" he repeated emphatically.

"Of course. Now will you tell me what—"

"Well, let's go to the reception."

She said nothing more and did not press him. He loved her more for it as he pulled her along by the hand and toward the heavy double door, which had been closed. The doorman was no longer positioned in front of it. He pressed his hand on the

DNA scanner next to it, which matched his DNA to the guest list, and after it let out a delicate buzz, pushed down the handle.

The banquet hall was already packed. The governor hosted a science reception once a year, and every self-respecting researcher on Lagunia attended. Originally, it was an event to bring together the planet's only significant revenue generator —the claiming of fortunes and the taxation of upscale artifacts —and policy makers. It now served something much simpler: The awarding of claims, designated sea areas where Lagoon legacies could only be excavated with a license.

Hundreds of scientists in suits and ballgowns crowded into the oval hall in front of a double staircase made of wood, or rather the thickened xylem of the local hard algae, which were classified as wood, on which the governor stood. Hartmut Gassel was a fleshy-faced man with an astonishingly slender body, which did not match his bloated head at all. With rosy cheeks and outstretched arms, he clearly enjoyed the role of patronizing host and was in the middle of his speech.

"... we always just laughed at. But, please, remember that history always takes several turns. We may be outsiders, but because of our outsider status, every school kid in the Federation knows us. Everyone has heard of Lagunia, the blue ball way out there. Everyone has heard of the *Oberon*, our Titan, the last of the Fleet..."

Franc stopped listening and instead pushed his way through the audience. He pulled Valeska's arm and pushed her behind him. Some colleagues muttered curses after them, others ignored them. Only when he arrived at the front and took two glasses of crystal champagne from a waiter's tray did he pause. He tipped the contents down his throat, one by one, and then handed them to his wife, who was completely confused. He paid no further attention to her, however, and instead stared up at the governor's secretary, who was standing next to his superior at the top of the stairs and letting his smug gaze wander over the crowd.

"... always a chance." Gassel continued his speech with a wicked smile. "And that's what Lagunia stands for. For opportunities. I remember the discovery of the data globe out in the South Bank. It was no longer functional, but it showed us what else there is to find in the future, if only we don't give up. Even though you come from all corners of the Federation, I can tell you that we Harbingers know how to keep at it, not give up. Even in seemingly difficult situations, hope always keeps us carrying the flame and..."

Franc scrolled through his contact directory until he found the ping address he was looking for and selected it. Then he sent off the video and quietly dictated a short message into the pinpoint microphone just above his wrist. Some of the surrounding guests raised their eyebrows when they saw that he was wearing his forearm display over his sleeve, which was considered rude in upscale circles, and was brazen enough to use it during the governor's speech.

He did not care.

"Franc!" Valeska hissed at him, just as he pressed the last button and pulled his sleeve over the flat computer. "What's wrong with you?"

"Just trust me, okay?"

"You just said that! But you're acting really strange!"

"Shh!" someone snapped at her from behind. Angry glances were leveled at them, and he made a few placating gestures while Valeska hastily placed the empty glasses on the tray of a passing waiter.

Applause broke out and they quickly joined in. The speech had apparently ended, and Governor Gassel nodded with satisfaction.

Like a damned king in front of his noble assembly, Franc thought and inwardly rolled his eyes. *King of the most unimportant province in the country.*

As the polite, rather than frenetic, applause quickly died down, Gassel raised his voice again. "My secretary, Paulsen, will now, according to tradition, present this year's claims, which have been discovered by our brave prospectors. We have received your bids and, as always, we have weighed them carefully before making our decision."

The assembled scientists were politely silent. The selections were not a given because everyone knew corruption was a rampant problem on Lagunia. The administrators involved were happy to leak information about the best claims for large sums of money, giving advantages to blindly bidding foundations, companies, and the bored rich. At the annual reading of the distributions, the claims were never presented in advance, but it was an open secret that the most promising were named last, with the top prize at the end.

"The first claim goes to Doctor Burnett and Professor Heuer," Secretary Paulsen announced in a strained voice and restrained applause followed. No one was interested in the "cheap" research areas. It took almost a quarter of an hour for the first cheers from individual scientists or whole groups to ring out, but Franc had no ears for them.

"Why are you so tense?" Valeska whispered under the cover of another chorus of celebratory researchers. "Our bid was ridiculously small. If we'd gotten it, we'd have gotten it a long time ago."

"No, I haven't given up hope yet," he insisted without looking at her. He knew that once he looked into her eyes, she would not let him go.

"What hope? Come on, Franc. Let's go home. We still have our plan B, remember?"

"Switch to the prospectors?" he snorted and scowled. "That's not only dangerous, it's like looking for the proverbial needle in a haystack!"

"New claims are found every year. Today there are over

fifty. So, there's a chance," she insisted. Her voice was soft now, which meant her patience would not last much longer.

"Fifty for a huge planet."

"All right, ladies and gentlemen," Paulsen said and struggled to smile. He looked like he was suffering from diarrhea and urgently needed to go to the bathroom. "The last claim of this year's goes to Franc and Valeska Bellinger."

An astonished murmur went through the crowd. There was no applause, as with the previous winners. This was probably in part due to the fact that he and Valeska did not make a sound. Franc struggled to compose himself and give a serene smile, as if he had expected nothing else, while his wife held a hand over her mouth, her eyes wide.

Even the governor blinked a few times in surprise before he cleared his throat and tried to salvage the situation by clapping his hands and encouraging the assembled scientists to join in.

"Congratulations to all our winners this year!" Gassel said with feigned enthusiasm. He did a much better job than Paulsen.

"Franc!" Valeska whispered harshly. "Explain this to me! Now!"

"Not here," he murmured casually, nodding to the surrounding colleagues who were congratulating them. There was recognition and surprise on their faces, along with a lot of envy. It should be fine with him, as long as he could get what he and his wife had earned and worked hard for—without having to give in to the unofficial pressure to join one of the Harbingen clubs, like all the other lickspittles who pretended to really care about the cause of the doomed Core World.

But you extorted your success, said a voice in the back of his head, which he quickly pushed aside. Sometimes you had to redefine the boundaries.

It took them a while to find their way to the terrace, from which a small staircase led down. He had chosen it as the easiest escape route, which in retrospect turned out to be naive. Everyone wanted to congratulate them, and maybe find out who they had bribed and how much it took to win the bid, so they had to keep up appearances and shake a few hands until their palms hurt.

There was no one on the terrace when they finally reached it, which was probably because, typical of Lagunia, it was extremely cold at night and all the officials who wanted to be squeezed preferred to stay inside.

"It has something to do with the video, doesn't it?" Valeska said immediately as the door closed behind them, shutting out all the noise of the festivities with a muffled thud.

It was replaced by the roar of the ocean in the distance and the whistle of the wind around the corners of the colony ship, which grew like a four-hundred-story monolith from the center of the corridor. Above them twinkled stars and the dappled band of the Milky Way that looked as if a giant had spilled a glass of milk on a black disk.

"I knew I could count on you," said a familiar voice. Franc wheeled around, startled. A figure detached itself from the shadows near a large vase of plants next to the door, printed from the same wood as the terrace glued to the composite of the former spaceship hull.

"Agent Schmidt." Valeska greeted the nondescript man wearing the coveralls of a city department mechanic. He stopped in front of them and parted his hair. "Figures you had something to do with this."

The agent of the Terran Information Agency, the TIA, humanity's civilian intelligence agency, shrugged noncommittally.

"It worked."

"What *exactly* is supposed to have worked?" she huffed, her eyes narrowing. Franc knew he was in for it as soon as they got back to their apartment, that much was certain.

"When we found out Secretary Paulsen was involved with the terrorists who blew up the *Shelly*, I was able to convince my superiors that we should not waste our informant's recordings," Schmidt said.

"So, you sent it to me. Not out of generosity, I didn't expect that much. What do you want?" Franc asked.

"The backers find, of course. The man on the video getting out of the spaceship, his name is Lennard Buchweiler, a Harbinger extremist and known as such. He makes his living, surprise, as a prospector."

"So what?"

"I recruited you after you arrived because I value your patience," Schmidt reminded him. "Since I am the one who has paid your living expenses on Lagunia since then, you should make sure it stays that way."

Franc frowned in displeasure.

"So," the agent continued, "four weeks ago, Buchweiler supposedly found the most important claim since Lagunia was discovered. But he didn't approach the governor with it. Instead, he sold the information to off-worlders. To which ones, we don't know, because we couldn't catch the courier. Supposedly, he got over five million credits for the information, at least that's what our netheads claim."

"But he's obligated to... the find," Valeska continued, but Schmidt raised a hand.

"Yes, but terrorists sometimes don't care much about regulations. Five million credits for a claim, that kind of money can only come from someone who is very, very rich, or from a company that has interest in something that hardly anyone else wants, except those deadbeats and idealists who are good at hoping and bad at calculating. That can only mean that someone or some faction from a Core World has his or her fingers in the pie."

"What kind of game, then?" Franc asked.

"That's the question. I don't think I need to point out that this is all very unusual. That's why I've given you what you need to get the appropriate claim from Paulsen. The TIA wants you to go to the site and investigate. Just do what you would normally do."

Franc was surprised. And suspicious. "That's it?"

"We are the bait in the trap," Valeska said, and the agent shrugged.

"You're paid well. We want to know who has a five million interest in a claim and why. You two are going to find out."

"Is there anything else we should know, other than we're out there on a limb?" Franc asked.

"Yes, there is something else. Officially, the claim was discovered by the crew of a free trader named *Quantum Bitch* and reported to the governor's office. They collected the two million credit reward."

"Wait a minute..." Valeska shook her head as if she hadn't heard him right. "Someone buys the coordinates of the location from a terrorist only to send someone there to *officially* discover it and get paid again? Not their money, sure, but then why the secrecy at all?"

"To protect their informant, of course."

"Buchweiler."

"Yes."

"But why all this?"

"We don't know. We also don't know much about the *Quantum Bitch* and its crew except that it has never been registered by Jump Control on a Core World," Schmidt said.

"Smugglers or pirates," Franc concluded.

"Most likely. They may have also had something to do with the StarVan NM 98-03 robbery. In any case, they are obviously the link between our terrorist and the mysterious buyers in the Federation Core. Our umbilical cord, so to speak. We want to find out where it runs. Any questions?" The agent didn't wait and said, "Good. Do your job."

He disappeared down the stairs and Valeska flared at Franc.

"We should never have taken this side job! I warned you about it!"

"I'm sorry. At the time, keeping our eyes and ears open in exchange for covering all our costs sounded like the only way to even survive here without embarrassing ourselves." Franc sighed and rubbed his temples. "My God. This is... I'm sorry, honey. I don't know what we're going to do now."

"We're going to get that claim and do our job. Have you looked at what was found there yet?"

"No, you?"

"Yes. You're going to freak out!"

OFFICE OF THE GOVERNOR, ATLANTIS, LAGUNIA

"You realize the TIA had a hand in this, don't you?" the man in the gray pinstripe suit said, leaning back with the pomposity of someone who rarely dealt with people who had more power than he did. Or never.

Hartmut Gassel grumbled in displeasure and lit a cigar so he wouldn't have to worry about what he was doing with his hands to avoid looking nervous. This guy had been making him uneasy since he first showed up at his office four weeks ago. He didn't even know his name. The fact that it now smelled of his own sweat because the air conditioning was on strike again, making loud rattling noises, was not embarrassing for a change, but satisfied him in a very banal way. Even though his guest showed no movement and didn't even seem to be sweating, he was sure the man was anything but comfortable in this environment.

Shouldn't have taken his shitty money, the frustrated governor thought, knowing that hadn't really been an option. Not on this shithole of a world.

"The TIA?" he asked, genuinely surprised. "What would they have to do with this? We're sitting here in what used to be the cockpit of a landing ferry turned into a ridiculously short skyscraper, floating on a stinking carpet of algae across a fucking ocean. Do you really think the idiots from the TIA are sniffing around here? That's ridiculous."

"Your secretary supports Harbinger extremists. Omega fanatics. We know you condone it, so don't waste my time," the stranger said, his androgynous face expressionless.

Gassel was a high-ranking politician by title only and didn't even try to compare himself to his Core-World or even Fringe-World counterparts, but he wasn't as stupid as he might appear to some. And that was why he stayed silent, even though the man's obvious accusation infuriated him.

Even then, the TIA doesn't care about some guy blowing up a ship on the last dirt planet.

His guest seemed to notice his anger and his eyes twitched briefly, or maybe it was just imagination, born of a desire for the guy to show some human emotion.

"Do you want me to put a stop to them? The two Bellingers, I mean?" Gassel asked, when the silence stretched too long for him to bear his nervousness any longer. He sucked on his cigar and enjoyed the bright glow reflecting against his hands and the dark flogwood tabletop. "I can have their boat blown up way out there, slip them a crewman, or just tie them up in port. They wouldn't have that claim anyway—"

"There's no need for that. We have a professional here on planet who will take care of that problem."

Gassel chose to ignore the obvious disdain for his person and abilities and leaned forward. "Then what do you want from me? Bellinger is one of your dogs after all, you don't fool me."

"A man named James Russ has obtained information about Buchweiler's discoveries and sold it to a smuggler named Devlin Myers. He is the captain and owner of the *Quantum Bitch*. We don't need to worry about Russ anymore, but we do need to worry about how he got this knowledge. Buchweiler must have been shadowed, and there's no faction that can get something like this past us except the TIA. So, what I want from you, Governor, is Buchweiler's records and all logs of traffic at the spaceport from the day before he found the claim and the week after," the stranger said flatly.

"What, are you crazy?" the governor blurted. "The logs are obviously held by the TIA guy you were talking about. If I hand over all the logs so you can cover up your courier, who they used to smuggle Buchweiler's finds out on the claim, the TIA will shove a fist so far up my ass I'll be able to suck on their fingers."

"You got five million credits."

"So what? I'm not going to get killed for this!"

"Would you like to return the five million? That's no problem."

Because then we'll *kill you,* the eyes of his guest seemed to say.

Gassel sucked again on his cigar to keep from gritting his teeth. *I really shouldn't have taken that fucking money! If I'd had any choice at all.*

"I'll take care of it," he growled, finally.

"Wonderful. We prefer to have no one at our backs, and no one but the TIA could have dug up the information on Buchweiler."

"Uh-huh."

"He was not a terrorist; did you know that?"

"No. Does it matter?"

The stranger looked thoughtful for a moment and then shrugged before rising.

"*Everything* plays a role, Mr. Gassel. The only question is always which one? When you have found the answer—"

"—I will share it with you first," the governor said.

"No. You will never see me again, or any of the rest of us."

Gassel swallowed against a sudden tightness in his throat. "Uh, okay."

"As long as you hold up your end of the bargain, of course."

The stranger in the gray pinstripe suit left the office and activated his transducer so he could speak without moving his lips or making any sound once his comlink gave him an encrypted link to their satellite in orbit. The authorities used their twenty-two artificial satellites, but his organization used the remaining eighty, which the planet's primitive sensors mistook for more debris from the battle between Clicks and Lagoon.

Clicks and Lagoon, he thought, snorting inwardly.

"So, was he compliant?" asked a cool voice in his head.

"He's going to struggle. Enough to get the agent's attention."

"Did you tweet appropriately to Paulsen's birdie?"

"Of course. If everything goes according to plan, our dirty dishes will wash each other until everything shines again," said the stranger, not without a hint of self-satisfaction.

"Very good. Keep Sirion on a short leash so he can pick up the sponge if it still doesn't shine in the end," commanded the voice that always gave the orders.

"Does it matter at all? The admiral will be arriving shortly."

"The chance of the TIA interfering with us now is highly unlikely. We made sure of that when we sent Sirion. Everything is going according to plan. As long as we remain precise and prudent—even on the last few centimeters—nothing will change. The Bellingers have to do their job first. Do you understand?"

"Of course. They will unravel the mystery for us, even if we already know the answers."

"No. We have reasonable suspicions, but our project has to

be based on facts. So, the Bellingers will have to do their work first."

"They will."

"Good. Now come back while you still can."

"I'm on my way."

8

The under city of Atlantis was just that, a city beneath the city that had eaten into the carpet of algae like a boil, drifting as a living, floating island across the endless ocean of Lagunia. Sirion knew that the woody part of the algae reached about fifty meters deep and was so dense that the walls of the many caverns were more like loose rock. The number of caverns where the poorest of the poor lived was hard to keep track of, and it had taken him several hours to get an approximate picture of the network: The farther out on the island, the smaller and farther in, the longer the tunnels between each cavern, some of which were so large that hundreds of improvised huts crowded inside together. The spacing was because many of the older caverns had collapsed where the weight of the "real" buildings on the surface had become too much.

Down here, it smelled of unwashed bodies and the fishy stench of seaweed and eelgrass, which was the staple food among the city's less privileged residents. It didn't cost anything, it wasn't harvested on a large scale after all, so anyone could cast their mended nets on the edge of the island and eat the stinky plants. They had good nutrient content and were healthier than the protein synthesizers.

Sirion deftly weaved through the crowds of one of the largest caverns he had yet found, trying to touch as few of the downtrodden figures as possible. He doubted even a fraction of them possessed IDs. Which meant they were not Harbingers, who were automatically issued IDs by the self-proclaimed military authority—the *Oberon*—that identified them as citizens of Harbingen and residing on Lagunia. This, in turn, meant that these people, who rarely saw the sunlight, had some reason to prefer trading in the slums of the Core and Rim Worlds for the slum of this even more underdeveloped world. Whether murderers, pirates, smugglers, outcasts, religious fringe groups, or pacifists, all would surely tell him long, emotional stories about why they had ended up here.

He was not interested in any of them.

At a small roadside pub—or rather a farce of one—he stopped and peeled himself out of the stream of shuffling passersby whose babbles echoed off the low cavernous ceiling. The counter was made of old surfboards and a corrugated tin roof above. The host was a teenager who might be just about drafting age. Small stools made of carved seaweed served as seating. They were all occupied, so he deftly squeezed himself between two of the patrons and tapped the counter with his index finger.

"Darfs'n?" the boy asked with the watered-down accent of Panjas that sounded like he was talking around a mouth full of porridge.

"Seen them before?" Sirion asked, showing him an analog photo of his targets.

"Nah."

Smart boy.

"I come through here often," he said with a warning tone, then dug out a credstick with fifty Lagunia shillings. He hadn't even had to spend a Sol credit to get it. The boy's eyes immediately lit up as he reconsidered the question. He probably had no idea who Franc and Valeska Bellinger were, but he wanted the money. At the same time, he understood that Sirion came here often, so he couldn't just make something up.

"Seh'n like Wissensschafteler, jo." The boy scratched his shaved scalp. "They sure know that in the governor's office."

Sirion narrowed his eyes.

"Uh, but you don't go there. The governor's penguin is often down here. To fuck, of course." The boy laughed and winked but fell silent when he received no reaction from Sirion. "Heuka cave. Best in the evening."

A patron on the right complained, and the teenager tried to reach for the credstick. Sirion let him have it and let himself get swallowed up again by the crowd, which rolled through the narrow alleys like an endless stream.

It was not difficult to find the cave with the strange name Heuka, as the first passerby explained to him with shining eyes, even if they were clotted with pus, that there would be "garamsten Weiber." In fact, early on, red lanterns sewn together from patches of cloth announced what it was all about. Warm lights burned in large tents held together by seaweed and old cables, and cast shadows clustered around each other. It smelled of sweat and other bodily fluids that created a mélange of sweetly nauseating scents. In most men, it seemed to awaken something like an archaic sex drive, something Sirion had never understood.

He had long since hacked into the colony's CoreNet by means of his blacklink and infiltrated one of his proven subroutines. While he was still en route to Lagunia, they had loaded the entire personnel file of the secretary of the governor into his head memory, including the obligatory DNA sample with which every official employee was genetically registered, just like in Fleet.

Using the chemsniffer, a small membrane in his nose, he was able to analyze and track complex olfactory traces. But in a low-ceilinged cave filled to capacity with the exhalations and excretions of too many people, even his high-powered olfactory senses had reached their limits. So, he had to keep stopping next to the tents, or even lifting the fabric to sniff and get a result. No one seemed to pay any attention to him, since the passersby were themselves trying to not be seen, and accordingly saw little.

Finally, he "smelled" Paulsen in one of the perimeter tents, which looked less dirty than those closer to what amounted to a path. He was lying on a sweat-stained mattress. A woman as naked as he, was lying in his arms and playing her exhausted smile convincingly.

"Leave us," he said, standing in the doorway.

"Oh, shit!" the secretary cursed, wincing and scrambling back like an animal until he slammed his head against a tent pole and sighed, dazed. The frightened prostitute's eyes widened, and she pulled the damp sheet up to cover herself.

"I'm only going to say it once."

She nodded quickly and ran past him. He didn't need to tell her that she had never seen him. She was ID-less, that much was certain, and she knew how the game worked.

"W-w-what do you want?" the secretary stammered, trying with difficulty to regain his composure. He squinted at the single blanket lying on the wooden floor beside the bed, but Sirion merely shook his head. Paulsen swallowed without giving it another glance. "Look, I-I have a problem, I know that. But if you want to go public, I have a better suggestion. I'll give you a claim. A really good one. Then I'll tell you who you can sell it to on the black market. These eggheads pay a crazy amount of money for the right to poke around on our ocean floor. Honest!"

Sirion remained silent and was still.

"How does one hundred thousand Lagunia shillings sound to you, huh?"

Like two thousand Sol credits.

"You don't want that? I'll find something better." Paulsen

managed to regain some of his controlled politician manner, but it was crumbling. "You must be an ambitious man if you found me here. That should be rewarded!"

Sirion pulled the photo of the Bellinger couple from his sleeve and took two steps toward the secretary, who yelped and tried to crawl away like a cornered dog.

"What? Oh... that's the Bellingers!"

"Where do I find them?" he asked coolly.

"N-not here. They got a claim and I'm sure they're th-th-there already."

"Where?"

"What do you mean *where*?"

"The claim. Where is it?"

"To the west. B-but you can't go there. Every claim is a restricted area and monitored by satellite," Paulsen stammered.

"What if there's an emergency?"

"Then help is requested at the nearest swim habitat."

"Who?" Sirion asked.

"The radio operator in the naval tower. He's responsible for everything within three hundred nautical miles."

"The frequency of accidents?"

"What?"

Sirion merely narrowed his eyes.

"Okay, okay, all right, man! It's dangerous out there! The storms are dangerous, and the Mandibles are dangerous bastards!" Paulsen hurried in reply. The lanky man swallowed hard and looked around for help, a look not only full of panic but also desperation.

Smarter than he looks. Sirion made some estimates based on his personality analysis and the politician's file, then made a decision. As he snapped the long monofilament knife from his right forearm holster, Paulsen cried out, his eyes wide in horror. But it was brief, mingling easily with the ecstatic exclamations of the punters all over the cavern.

Sirion merged with the shadow between the door and the heavy-duty shelf and set the protective shades of his eyes to black so that nothing reflected off him. He hid the burnished monofilament blade that protruded from under his wrist behind his back.

His victim came whistling through the door. Unsuspecting, he warbled a melody he had heard many times before and that evoked in him one of the few emotions that came close to something like emotion: Hate. It came in many versions and variations, but in the end it was always the same song: The anthem of Harbingen. A soaring beacon of driving sounds that translated into chords the arrogance and superiority of the former showcase Core World. Lagunia's many nationalist society members, who never really considered themselves Lagunians but Harbingers in exile, loved their anthem.

Young men, like his victim, especially loved the hard driving riffs of the heavy metal versions that catered to their aggression, which they could not relieve. Their enemy was the Clicks, no one hated them as much as the exiled Harbingers, but in a way, so was the Federation, because they were no longer conscripted for Fleet. It was clear to every citizen that the reasons were obvious: They didn't trust the Harbingers, who had abandoned their own planet in the face of doom to save their skins. But also, their fanatical nationalism caused uneasiness within the fleet. One probably wondered for whom they were really fighting; for the continuation of humanity or the glory of Harbingen? The fact that the Federation had wriggled out of a dispute with the survivors by simply not accepting Lagunia as an official colony, since the founding process had not been completed and the formalities had been delayed, further helped to weld the Harbingers together and isolate them from the rest of humanity.

"Firm stands the Harbingers' Watch, shield and sword of

unity," the young man sang, dragging the chair with one foot to his large desk with the holopanels and old displays. He had his hands full with several packets of ready-made food and a cup that smelled like artificial lemonade. "In the glory of our founding fathers, faithful, brave, true..."

Sirion waited until his victim dropped into the chair and sorted the crackling packets in front of him before stepping out of the shadows and approaching with silent steps. The top room of the control tower was noisy because it was glazed all around and one of Lagunia's infamous storms was whipping thick raindrops against it so that it banged and rustled.

"Looking up at the stars, hands fiiirm on the waf-fe. In the sight of sinister powers, beats Harbingen's—oh, what have we here?" The radio operator interrupted himself and leaned forward as a red dot lit up on the holopanel. Imitation potato chips crunched in his mouth. "A ship that shouldn't be there." He pressed a button. "SN-277 *Skippy*, this is Control. You are off course. Do you have an emergency?"

Sirion did not hear the response; presumably, it came directly into the radio operator's head via an implant.

"I see. I'll notify the sea rescue. Hold your course as long as you can and don't shut down your engines," the man said. "No, don't worry, I'll stay with you until rescue arrives on the scene. Keep calm."

The radio operator turned off the music with a snap of his fingers and pushed away his evening meal. With curt gestures, he zoomed in on the image in front of him and made a few purposeful, routine entries.

Sirion stood directly behind him and looked at the cable stretching from his temple to the armature and unceremoniously cut it.

"What?" the radio operator cried out, staggering in his chair. The shock of ejection caused him to immediately vomit all over the table. Sirion gave him no time and held the blade to his neck.

"Quiet."

"Oooh," the man groaned. His short blond hair shone palely in the green passive light of the control room. "W-who a-are you?"

"Death, I think," Sirion replied, bringing his left wrist to his mouth. With his teeth, he pulled a cable connector from a small recess between the tendons, uncoiled it from the guide in his forearm, and held it out to his victim. "Insert!"

"What?"

"Into your data socket."

"Listen, you can't do that. I have an emergency here! Whatever you want from me—money, information, anything —you can have it. But I *have* to help these people!"

"No."

"What, are you crazy?" The radio operator gulped. Sirion noticed it in a slight wobble of the blade. "Wait. Who sent you?"

"No one."

"For money, you let innocent people die out there?"

He shook his head, unseeing. "Not for money, because I want that."

"You are insane! You can't—"

"Last warning." He held the cable closer to the man's face. "Now."

With trembling hands, the radio operator took the connector and plugged it into his data jack, a small collection of holes of various sizes protruding from his skin.

The sequester software from Sirion's head memory loaded itself into the officer's brain without any measurable loss of time, then took over his few implants and swept away the firewalls like a storm sweeps away a pile of brushwood. The second-rate software was no match for the aggressive heuristics that attacked every interface simultaneously and mercilessly overwrote the original code. It was like a wildfire that could not be stopped and left only scorched earth behind. But as the radio operator's chin sank to his chest and saliva dripped in long threads onto his shirt, the next phase of the enemy takeover began. Sirion used the free space in the other brain to send an AI that was as illegal as it was sophisticated into the basal ganglia. The code changed to nerve impulses, a lean algorithm that effortlessly made the leap from code to organic stimulus-response patterns, revealing to him everything there was to find.

Through his umbilical cord, Sirion siphoned off the information he needed before pulling a thin transparent mesh from his pocket. He pushed the brain-dead man's head back until it flopped over the backrest and stared up at the ceiling with broken, widened eyes. Then he placed the net over his face until the tiny electrodes inside glowed faintly, and he unplugged himself from the hijacked brain. He plugged the freed cable connector into the appropriate contact under the net and waited patiently while it performed its scan, loading the complex data sequences into its subdermal memory.

On a Core World, he would never have gotten far with a ReFace network. Even many fringe worlds had programs in their public surveillance systems that immediately registered such use. On more restrictive worlds, one might be vaporized by a microwave laser from an orbital defense platform without warning, depending on where you were.

But here, even with this taboo technology, he could still do and not do everything that had led to the entire Federation fearing it and investing in surveillance algorithms in a panic. He felt no joy about this freedom, he didn't even know when he had last felt it, only the certainty that his next course of action had become much easier than it should have been.

He went through the ship directories looking for the owners and their ships that had arrived here in the last twenty-four hours. Franc and Valeska Bellinger had no reason to hide, so they were easy to find, at least that's what he *would* have thought. But of course, it wasn't *that* easy. He knew from

Paulsen that they had come here, but there was no trace of them in the embarkation and disembarkation directories.

Why not? he thought and reflected.

He was not surprised. Someone had paid a lot of money to hire him, so much that there was hardly any other hitman who would cost more. One didn't do that to eliminate one's wife or unloved mother-in-law from the cosmic equation. So much, so understandable. But what secret could be held by two highly paid researchers who led dull, monotonous lives marked by streaks of bad luck? They were hardly the sort of people who could erase themselves from the systems of even the most backwoods colony whenever they wanted to. So, they had outside help. Someone or some institution knew exactly what it was doing.

But who?

He pushed aside the empty human shell along with its chair and used rapid gestures to go further back in the directories and then sent a request to the main server of the shipping office in Atlantis. Using the dead man's authentication code—his name was apparently Georg Haiger—his digital request was automatically granted. There he researched further, found some entries about contactless purchases in the city, mostly daily necessities, and finally the feed message about their triumph in this year's claim award. Their account balance before and after the award, which took him a long time to retrieve, did not give rise to any suspicion that they had raised the necessary bribes themselves. They were therefore acting on behalf of a worthy opponent with influence.

His job just got a lot more exciting.

Finally, the ReFace net beeped, and he detached himself from the holodata to pull it from his victim's face. He carefully placed it on the table and heaved the body off the chair before locking the door and sitting himself inside. Only then did he hold the translucent mesh in both hands, took a deep breath in and out, and placed it on his own face. He plugged in the cord and gave the command through his head memory to activate himself. The pain began immediately as the nanonic filaments bored through his skin, gradually causing the mesh to sink into his epidermis like melting glue.

Sirion didn't scream as the process ran its course, and as soon as he could think clearly again, he called up the steady stream of transponder codes and radio messages coming in and did what he was particularly good at: Waiting for the right moment.

9

"A tunnel," Valeska said in amazement, looking at the topographical data returned by the depth probe.

Her chartered boat, a two-masted schooner with its sails reefed, held its position in the center of their claim with the small electric motor. Their captain, a red-haired woman with mahogany skin and bright eyes, was named Oxana Reuel and had won them over on the West Bank Habitat with her good reputation. Everyone they had asked had recommended Oxana and her schooner *Elvis*.

The woman walked around with her three crew members, Ute, Oliver, and Powell, scolding them or goading them to work faster. There was a lot to do. The floating habitat had to be programmed and cast out, the ship firmly anchored in case there was a storm, and the equipment brought on deck.

"Clearly a tunnel," Franc agreed with her. They were both bent over the plate-sized display, shielding it as best they could with a towel, otherwise the blazing sun would have robbed them of any possibility of making out anything.

"Do you think it was drilled by the prospectors?"

"How?"

"They could have found the cavity underneath with a resonance scanner, then put a drill on it and gained access," she reasoned aloud.

"There is no such drill on Lagunia, I'm sure of that. It would have to be a huge drill built for underwater use. When was the last time there was one of those?" he asked rhetorically.

"A few centuries ago, when our barbarian ancestors dug up organic matter that had decomposed into oil and made fire with it." Valeska rolled her eyes. "That's all right. So, no drill."

"No drill."

"A laser from orbit?"

"Possible, but unlikely. The water would disperse too much, and to create a beam with enough power that it would vaporize the water in the column before scattering became a factor and still reach so deep... no." Franc shook his head. "Not to mention, only orbital defense platforms have mounted laser weapons, and they certainly don't cut a diameter of six meters or more."

"That just leaves Lagoon." They glanced at each other, and she had to smile when she saw the gleam in his eyes. It was just like the old days.

"Drilled from the bottom up." Franc nodded and straightened. "Let's allow the deep probe map the cavern first. Once we have a 3-D model, we can plan further."

"Good, then we can make sure our lab is in place and the submersible is doing what it's supposed to."

Valeska turned and watched the small boat crew toss the large box containing the swimming habitat overboard. It was two meters long, about a meter wide, and made of programmable silicon. Shining on its surface was the small display through which they specified form and function. As soon as it touched the salt water, it began to unfold and expand. It would be a while before the habitat was in place, in the middle of the endless blue of the ocean, but they had time.

The contrast between the self-assembling silicon block, which changed shape on its own by means of nanonic processes and the two-masted wooden sailing boat on which they stood could not have been greater.

On Lagunia, as on many Federation colonies, it had become apparent that development on any world took time and started way down the technological scale. It was a cost-benefit question. Wood was plentiful on Lagunia, though there were no trees. The local algae, which became woody when it grew old and died, provided a seemingly endless supply of building material and people had known how to build ships for millennia. In addition, the wind basically blew all the time. Therefore, wood was the cheapest—and only—raw material for shipbuilding, and sails were the cheapest and most efficient propulsion technology. Wind was, after all, free and renewable.

"The crew are getting everything ready like you asked," Oxana said, who looked like a pirate going barefoot and wearing a red bandana, walking across the damp planks to them. She squinted at the display. "Anything yet?"

Valeska nodded. "The tunnel."

"Ah. But you already knew of that, didn't you?"

"Yes, but we have to re-explore everything. The data from the prospectors can only be relied on with great limitations."

"Like this?" The sailor seemed unconvinced and put her hands on her hips. Valeska wondered if she had been a prospector herself before becoming a charter captain for claim owners, but she lacked a vessel capable of diving. Therefore, Valeska opted for evasive politeness.

"Well, you have a different goal when you search the bottom of the ocean. You're keeping your eyes open for things that are not of natural origin, indicating legacies of the Lagoon."

"But so do you."

"No. We don't want to study the *what*, we want to study the *how*," she explained. "We're interested in the habitat of the Lagoon, the nature of their environment. Did they need to be near coral, in nutrient-rich water? Did they prefer it warm, near geysers, or cold, away from black smokers? What was the function of their buildings? For example, what was the function of this tunnel? From their remains we know that they had no eyes and probably communicated and observed by means of passive and active sonar. This would indicate they lived so far down that they didn't need sunlight. So why drill a shaft up to the bright, warm water?"

"Which creates more questions," Franc added, who was sitting next to a winch, taking off his shoes and upending them, splashing the deck with water. "How could they even use a drill, let alone develop one?"

"Uh," Oxana said when he paused.

"They were obviously aquatic creatures. For electronics-based technology—the only way we know of to get manual work done by machines—those aren't good conditions. Water and electricity don't get along so well, except for the bioelectrics of some marine animals, of course. But you don't run a drill with an electric eel. So, you wouldn't be able to invent electric current in the first place, and even if you did, which isn't likely, you'd do a high-voltage experiment under-water once and it would be the end of civilization."

"I see." The captain waved a thumb over the railing. "But there's been a tunnel bored."

"That's right. So, how did the Lagoon do it? That's what we want to know, and that's not the type of thing a prospector is interested in. She just wants to know if there's a natural reef down there, or a former Lagoon city that can make money."

"Okay, I admit that sounds more exciting than I thought." Oxana smiled broadly. "You two are really contagious, though. What exactly makes the claim here the top prize, anyway? Heard on the West Bank that it's supposed to be the best find in recent years. Up here, everything looks the same to the likes of us."

Valeska tapped her forearm display until she found what she was looking for, then held out her arm to the woman.

"Do you see that?"

"Pretty dark down there and lots of suspended particles. But if you mean the thing that looks like a partially eaten onion ring, then yes. What's it supposed to be?"

"We can't be sure, but it looks strikingly similar to one of our technologies," Valeska said pulling up a new image. "This is the Lagunia hyperspace gate, which is scheduled for completion tomorrow. The image is from today's newsfeed."

Oxana blinked as if she had something in her eye. "You think there's a hyperspace gate down there?"

"Yes. And that wouldn't only be the greatest find of the last few years, it would be the greatest find of the entire Federation since its inception!"

"Now do you understand why we are so impatient?" Franc asked, grinning like a little boy. Valeska's heart warmed to see him so happy again after such a long time. Maybe the hassle with the TIA and blackmailing the sleazy Paulsen had been worth it after all. "This hyperspace gate, if it was one, might give us clues as to why the Lagoon were destroyed and what made them inferior to the Clicks, if they could build such a thing."

"And why the Clicks haven't just hijacked the technology," Valeska added.

"All right. It'll take a few more hours, though," Oxana said. "Their equipment is already top notch, I must say, but it still takes time. We'll pull up the submersible ahead of time, and when it's ready, we'll report to West Bank Tower."

"Why do we have to report there?" Franc asked.

The captain frowned as she eyed him.

"You really haven't been out of Atlantis much, have you?" She raised a hand. "That was a rhetorical question. Every dive has to be registered with the nearest radio operator, for safety reasons."

"And because someone wants to hold out their hand in case something valuable is found, I suppose?" Valeska said, snorting in disgust.

"Well, you've got it figured out now."

SPACE STATION HIGHGARDEN, ORBIT AROUND JUPITER, SOL SYSTEM

The unknown man stood in front of the huge panorama window looking out on the eternal storms of Jupiter circling in brown-grey shaded rings. He wore his epithet with pride, since it meant his organization had managed to learn the internal designations of the TIA. As long as they called him the "unknown," he was doing his job well, not that he ever doubted it. Too much money and two decades of meticulous preparation had gone into the plan.

His plan.

Highgarden was the most advanced of Jupiter's fifty habitats that rotated around the gas giant like great space moths with their wings spread wide. The habitat was not a pretty sight. Hundreds of square kilometers of black sails sucked up Jupiter's radiation and converted it into energy to power the fusion cores at the bottom of the cone-shaped carbon structure. What mattered at Highgarden were the "inner values," vast parklands of exotic xenoplant life from all corners of the Terran Federation. Well, expansive for an artificial habitat that wasn't inside a hollowed-out asteroid.

It had been built as an exclusive retreat for those rich in influence or money, which really amounted to the same thing, where they could get away from the politics and banks that owned half the space stations around Jupiter. On the meadows and in the observation decks, contracts were still sealed by a handshake and information was exchanged over cigars and whiskey, completely without eavesdroppers because microphones and cameras were forbidden here. There were only two connections to the outside, and they were located in the two hangars at the top and bottom of the station's mothlike body.

The perfect environment for him. Until today.

"It's time," said a familiar voice behind him. "The ship is ready."

"What about the fleet?"

"Most are already on their way home, separated and using inconspicuous jump point routes. Everything is falling into place exactly as it should."

"Of course." The man lifted his chin slightly and took in the sight of Jupiter one last time: The storms, the shadows of the other stations in lower orbits, visible only as tiny black dots thanks to their giant sails, the flashes of the submersible probes that extracted helium and hydrogen from the atmosphere and transported them to the refineries in orbit around Ganymede and Calisto. He had felt at home here because of the privacy and the knowledge in the back of his mind that Jupiter and the entire Sol System was the cradle of his species, but he never went native. His stay had been a necessity to be close to the Senate—and, of course, to the sky fortress.

"How was your meeting with the Fleet admiral?"

"As expected."

"That's good," said his aide.

"The thing with the claim on Lagunia should not have happened," he said sternly.

"Yes. It seems the TIA has been tracking Buchweiler for longer than we thought. They were cleverer this time. But the error will be eliminated soon."

"See to it. Sending Sirion was a gamble I would have rather not taken."

"He never fails."

"His training cost us five million credits and his hardware another fifty. If he failed, we'd be bad investors. Which we're not."

"Yes. They're worried about Konrad Bradley." The aide made it sound like a statement. He was a quick study.

"I never worry. If I did, I wouldn't have been able to prepare any of what we are about to launch. What has to happen will happen. That's the way it's always been, and that's the way it will stay."

"Of course."

"A new chapter in the history of our people will begin shortly," said the stranger, turning away from the window. His aide-de-camp, immaculately dressed in the uniform that did not belong to them but still had to serve as a disguise as long as it was necessary, was faintly illuminated by Jupiter's reflections. He looked like a translucent ghost—what irony. "Of our species, rather."

"We are all ready." His aide bowed.

"Make sure Sirion completes his mission and then leaves the system for home," the stranger ordered sternly. "We don't want our own plans to be thwarted by our agents getting in each other's way."

10

There was a knock at the door.

"Come in," Konrad called, tugging his blue board divider into place before rising from his desk and pushing aside the cup of spiced ramen. The bulkhead moved aside, and his son entered. "Ah, Nicholas!"

"Captain?"

Konrad beckoned him over and walked around the desk to retrieve two glasses and a bottle of Harbinger Habicht from his display case. His youngest son relaxed as soon as the bulkhead closed and settled on the uncomfortable narrow couch in a corner of the commander's quarters. The ceilings were low, and the walls looked like crude trash compactors, but for Konrad this environment gave him a sense of security and steadiness.

"How was the pirate hunt?"

"Inexhaustible," Nicholas said, nodding gratefully as he accepted his glass and they toasted. "These people are quite crafty, Father. With some of them, I knew we'd caught them, but they know well how to make hard evidence disappear."

"Well, that's our lot as a pseudo-ranker." Konrad sniffed the black liquor and cooed contentedly before taking a sip.

"On the Core Worlds, a commander's reasonable suspicion is enough, and he gets to shoot the ship in question out of the vacuum."

"That kind of thing shouldn't be allowed."

"You're a good boy. Did you discover any clues about the missing people in your actions?" He hated this topic, knowing that no matter how hard he looked for them, he would not find them. But he owed it to the relatives and his people to keep a lookout anyway.

"No. A ship had coffins loaded, of all things, but it was bringing them in, not out. For whatever reason Lagunia loses residents who don't check out. We don't think we'll find it with the smugglers. There must be something else behind it."

"Yes." Konrad nodded, knowing they were both aware that the reasons were almost certainly extremely mundane: Harbinger preferred to live with Harbinger, but not at any price. A world stinking of algae without any infrastructure and minimal job offers probably represented the limit of what one was willing to endure for one's attachment to one's homeland. Nicholas knew that, too, of course. Nevertheless, he approached the mission with his characteristic seriousness and conscientiousness, and that honored him. "I just wonder why it's been piling up the last few months."

"The deviations from what is expected are not *that* great."

"You're right."

"Jason's coming here," Nicholas said, abruptly changing the subject.

"I know."

"You know?"

"Yes. Silly shared the delegation's officer manifest from the *Caesar* with me. I don't know what Admiral Augustus intends to do with him, but that's secondary. What matters is our plan alone." Konrad tried for an encouraging smile and gestured to his desk. "Would you like some noodles, too?"

"Our *illegal* plan," his youngest said, ignoring the question and placing his glass with its untouched contents on the flat glass table between them. "Father, I know something has to change, but are you really sure there is no other solution?"

Konrad thought for a moment and then shook his head.

"No, boy. Unfortunately, not. I've been around long enough to know what works and what doesn't." His expression went blank, as if he were looking into an invisible dimension that had opened between them. "You can follow orders and still be ostracized. You can make decisions that comply with the rules of engagement, and be demoted. You can follow your moral compass, and always be questioned whether you did the right thing. There is no right or wrong. There is only the result of your actions, and I—we, as officers—have a responsibility to give our crew a future. A future that does not consist of sailing wooden fishing boats across Lagunia's oceans and casting nets. We're *Harbingers*, damn it. We deserve better."

"Do we really?" Nicholas asked thoughtfully.

Konrad's anger rose inside him, but he waited and then let it go. Everyone had the right to question him, even his son.

"What's on your mind?"

"Omega," said his son. "Was it really right to give a machine the power to govern our world?"

"It made us the most powerful Core World. We have it to thank for the *Oberon* and all the things that kept us at the top of the Federation twenty years ago. Only the SCR could hold a candle to us."

"But look where we are now. What's left of it? We are a museum-ready ship from another era of warfare. We are a relic of a more brutal phase of war, obsolete and redundant."

"No!" Konrad said, more sharply than he intended. He took one last sip and sent the rest of the burning liquid down his throat. More quietly, he added, "We are not superfluous."

"I know that. But Fleet doesn't. They're relying on

maneuverability and speed, on their new hyperspace torpedoes that we couldn't even locate or intercept."

"The *Oberon* won't buckle from a few torpedo hits," Konrad grumbled stubbornly.

"I'm not talking about us fighting Fleet, either." Nicholas sighed and shook his head. "But you know how it goes, when we make an advance, sooner or later the Clicks develop it too. That's how it's been during all the wars through human history, and that's how it's been with the Clicks. You know very well that's the reason they built fifty-one hyperspace gates at the same time. If we want to take advantage of rapid fleet deployment, we have one shot. They've nearly driven the Federation economy into ruin to complete this mammoth project."

"And it will succeed. And we will play a role in that victory."

"I think you're being too optimistic, Father."

"A commander has to be optimistic. Besides, I refuse to believe that the only reason we are the only non-Core World that got a gate Core World was because we're farthest from the front lines and can operate here unnoticed."

"That would make sense, though. The probability that the Clicks have witnessed the construction of one of the many gates is close to one hundred percent. So, they know what we're doing. They've known since they attacked Kor and destroyed Harbingen. They wanted to prevent us from mastering gate technology, or at least delay it. But they don't know that we're aiming for a massive simultaneous strike of practically our entire forces on their home planet. And for that, our gate is essential. They'll launch the diversion from here to give the target gate enough time to be assembled."

"Why are you here, boy?" Konrad interrupted his son, examining him closely. "Do you have a guilty conscience?"

"I... I think so." Nicholas nodded and picked up the glass again. He looked into it but did not drink.

"I understand that, and it speaks to your character. It will take time for you to realize the realities of having your own command, but it will happen that way, and then you'll remember this moment and that you did what was necessary to give your crew a future. One way or another."

"I hope so."

"We can do it. The *Oberon* will be a flagship again, and when it is, the Lagoon fleet must be recognized as such. Then we will officially have our own world, which we will set up to take back Harbingen once the radiation levels have dropped far enough and we as a nation can afford to heal the biosphere. *That's* our goal, and it's worth it for that, even if it takes many generations after us to see the results." Konrad leaned forward and put a hand on his son's knee. "Always remember that, will you?"

"Your optimism..."

"Fleet management has always stonewalled us, yes. But Augustus has shown himself to be extremely agreeable in our correspondence so far. Perhaps even as an ally of our cause in the Admiralty. If he comes here and the proficiency check convinces him, then we have a good chance of succeeding. A *flagship*! What we have always been. Then we won't be passed over or ignored anymore."

"Wouldn't that be better?" Nicholas asked cautiously. "To be ignored? You know how we've been since—"

Konrad flicked his hand out and abruptly leaned back as if he had received an electric shock.

"I'm sorry, I was just—"

"It's okay."

The connector next to his desk beeped. Konrad stood and picked up the receiver. The cable swung lazily back and forth, and so did he. "Yes?"

"The admiral's flagship has jumped into the system and has sent a message. The rest of the fleet is arriving as well," he heard his XO say.

"Thank you."

"The memo says to stand by."

"Stand by?" Konrad said, surprised. "The plan was to have an officers' dinner on the *Oberon*. The preparations for that have been completed, haven't they?"

"Yes. That's what the memo says," his commander said impassively. "Shall I ask what is meant by that?"

"No." *I wonder if that's part of the review.* "Just send a formal confirmation and then we'll wait and see."

"I took the liberty of having a shuttle made ready. Just in case."

"Well done. I'll be on the bridge soon."

"Roger that." There was a *crack!* and the connection ended. Konrad hung up the phone and turned to his son. "Time for those pesky parade uniforms."

Half an hour later, he was walking through the corridors of his ship in the blue dress uniform of the Terran Fleet, on his way to the bridge. He deliberately did not take the elevators so he could see as many of his crew members as possible. He wanted them to know that this was serious, that they had to be on their best behavior. He made very brief stops, inquiring about the respective status of water supplies, radiator maintenance, and internal superconductor bundles. Except for a couple leaks in the potable water treatment system that were being repaired, everything seemed to be in good order.

Wherever he appeared, he was saluted, and curt "Admiral" was murmured. He tried to make as much small talk as possible without wasting too much time.

The *Oberon* was a veritable monster, a small flying city if you would, only densely packed with a maze of narrow corridors. Things got cramped near the crew quarters, which were located along the central axis and held one hundred sailors per compartment and assigned bunkbeds. Many of the men and women were only half-dressed and shuttled between the washrooms on one side of the aisle and the quarters on the other. Others were off duty, and he noticed through half-open doors that they were playing poker at tables, dressed in shorts and gray undershirts. Of course, he saw the liquor bottles, too, but he had once been a young cadet himself and who was he to pretend it wasn't right. What mattered was what they ended up doing. As long as they were still at a rank and age where they needed little sneak peeks to relax, so be it. So, he pretended not to notice and nodded as the noisy crowd parted in front of him.

Just before he reached the next ship segment with the hangars and air treatment, the lights went out in the corridor. Immediately, the red emergency lights came on. Konrad looked up and scowled. He looked down at his anachronistic wristwatch and grunted.

"Sorry, sir!" said a young ensign wearing orange engineering corps overalls, who was currently squatting at an open wall panel. "It'll be right back on, I promise."

"I should hope so."

"That fucking cable cancer!" cursed the technician, who had already disappeared halfway into the wall again, tools in hand.

Konrad shook his head and quickened his steps until he reached the next communicator. He pulled the handset from the wall and pressed "1" for the bridge. The DNA scanner in the handle automatically gave the clearance and shortly after he heard the voice of his XO.

"Sir?"

"Central corridor port, power is out from section C-51. I guess that affects the elevators as well?"

"Yes, we just registered the damage report."

"I'm not going to make it to the bow hangar in time to

receive the admiral like this," he growled. Sometimes it was hard to love the old lady.

"You could take a shuttle from the port hangar and fly it," Silly suggested. "Sir."

"Not a bad idea. Get everything ready, just like we planned, only without me."

"Roger that."

Konrad hung up the phone and hurried toward the hangar. His desire to walk through the ship, clear his head and meet his crew—which was always good for him to feel connected with them—had cost him dearly. He only had forty minutes left.

The double doors hissed open, and he had to blink a few times when he was surprised by loud hooting and hollering. The gigantic hall with the closed gates was full of sailors in orange coveralls standing around three large cargo shuttles. The center one had its side loading ramp extended, where Chief Engineer Karl Murphy stood waving placatingly. Many of his nearly two hundred subordinate engineers and technicians were openly waving liquor bottles and spilling a lot of it as they cheered and clapped.

"What's going on here?" Konrad shouted, registering with some satisfaction that his roar was still that of a lion, gray-haired or not. Immediately, silence fell, and the crowd began to move. Faces wheeled to look at him with looks of horror. "Alcohol on deck? You're on duty for crying out loud!"

"Stand at attention, you damned no-good screwheads!" Murphy yelled from the ramp of his shuttle. "Commander on deck!"

A murmur was followed by the clack of many heels, then they all stood still. Somewhere a bottle shattered on the floor.

"I need a shuttle, and I need it now," Konrad turned sternly to the lieutenant commander, who waved two sailors over, briefly instructed them, and then sent them to one of the catapults, visible as holes in the floor.

"Right away, sir!" shouted his chief engineer.

Konrad nodded and walked toward the shuttle. The pale crowd parted in front of him.

Before he reached the entrance—actually a hole in the floor through which part of the shuttle's hull could be seen, with a hatch leading inside—he turned around.

"You've had success, I take it?"

"Yes, sir!" Murphy grinned, which didn't happen very often.

"Then get to work. The admiral will be arriving soon, and I want the *Oberon* to be unrecognizable in two days, understand?"

"Yes, sir!" the sailors replied in chorus.

Konrad grabbed the access ladder. Below him, the shuttle whirred to life. He turned around again.

"Good job. Contraband is forbidden on this ship, so I don't want a drop of alcohol leaving this hangar!" he shouted, earning wide grins among his crew. "That's an order!"

Then he descended into the long passenger compartment of the shuttle. Two young officers sat in the seats for pilot and copilot, making final preparations for takeoff.

"Launch as soon as we're ready," he ordered and sat in one of the bucket seats. He strapped in and grabbed a communicator from the wall. He disliked talking over a wireless connection that was prone to both eavesdropping and interference, but they were not in combat, and this was a special situation. Again, he dialed 1.

"This is the XO."

"Silly, I'm on the shuttle."

"Very good, sir."

"Chief engie succeeded."

"That's good news. I guess his people didn't follow service procedures." Silly sounded sour.

"No."

"We should be disciplinary..."

"No, we shouldn't."

"You're too soft with them," she said, unusually opinionated for an official conversation.

"In two days, we will take part in the final battle against the Clicks and expect everything from them. They deserve a little room to move."

"Of course, sir."

"Is the admiral running late?"

"Unfortunately, no."

"Would be too good. Then we won't waste any more time." He hung up and sighed. He hated waiting and not being able to do anything to speed things up.

Soon, a whistle sounded through the shuttle.

"Stand by for catapult launch," the pilot said.

Konrad took a deep breath in and out as they were launched like a torpedo out of the fifty-meter tube into the vacuum. The brief 4 Gs felt as if an invisible fist was pressing him into the seat. It was hard to breathe. It was hard to believe that a very long time ago, as the pilot of an old Triton fighter, he had been able to handle double the Gs and had even enjoyed it.

The pilot turned them to starboard, between the stars and the reflections of the forty other ships in their small fleet, and shot along the hull of the *Oberon*, the Federation's newest Titan and, paradoxically, now one of the oldest warships still in service. The war against the Clicks was costing humanity a great deal of lives and material every year, and the shipyards of the Core Worlds were constantly producing at capacity to make up for the losses. The other forty-nine Titans, once the backbone of every fleet, had been so badly damaged that the cost of repairing them was no longer worth it. But not a single one had been destroyed. It was an inglorious end to a brute strategy that had once displayed the pride of human engineering.

The scars on the heavily armored hull of his ship almost

physically pained him. Long cracks and deep craters bore witness to the *Oberon*'s last great battle, the one it had not won.

"Not for long," he murmured, almost caressingly.

The decision to report the four hundred brand-new Predator drones as lost during a weapons testing accident, when in truth he had had Murphy sell them on the black market, had not been difficult for him. After his chief engineer had negotiated the deal in advance with the traders at Taurus Station in orbit around Artros, even less so. They were getting enough carbotanium, carbon, and xenonite for the hottest commodity from Federation forges to help the *Oberon* not only achieve full armor but also state-of-the-art radiators, faster superconductors, and internal hull stability to match any newly launched cruiser. In short, they would be able to meet even the most stringent Fleet suitability criteria. Overhauling the ship was hardly possible in two days, but it would become clear what was happening, and that was the most important thing for his plan with Augustus.

The *Oberon*'s place was at the front, as the flagship of its own recognized fleet and fringe world.

After a short flight, they landed in the VIP hangar at the bow, whose hatch was below the now-closed observation deck. The senior officers were already assembled, his XO at their head, who was walking past the two rows making final adjustments. His COB, Walter Borowski, was also there, perhaps the most important man on the ship, without whom nothing at all worked, as he was the senior NCO who coordinated and kept over seven thousand crew ranks under control. So, his title of Chief of the Boat was well justified. He was currently speaking to the Honor Guard Marines, twenty of whom, according to protocol, were in formation, wearing white uniforms, and unloaded rifles.

"... practice right now," Silly said just as the shuttle's ramp descended and Konrad got out.

"Commander on deck!" she shouted, and heels were knocked together. At the same time, the Marines turned their faces to look at him. The officers came to attention and looked straight ahead.

"At ease," he said, stepping out into the small hangar, which was packed with those present. The shuttle immediately turned for the return flight, even before he reached his senior officers, among them his son Nicholas, who was standing very far forward.

"All set?" he asked Silly.

"The visit can proceed, sir."

"Wonderful." Konrad went down the ranks, deliberately starting with the COB and the Marines, speaking to them in curt phrases and winking here and there at a badge or medal. Only then did he turn to the officers. He made sure they were all standing perfectly, and soon a high-pitched whistle sounded, announcing the admiral's arrival. He stood up front with his officers, right next to his XO, at attention.

The vice admiral's shuttle was an elongated cylinder with stubby wings that indicated limited atmospheric capability. The hull shone like polished marble and the bow thrusters glowed blue. The engines made little more than a low hum as the small craft pushed through the force field separating it from space and smoothly extended its landing struts. The pilot, if it wasn't pilot software, turned and with amazing precision brought the shuttle around so the side exit was positioned directly between the two rows of assembled crewmen— Konrad's officers and the double row of Marines. The hiss of hydraulics bleeding off rushed through the hangar and then the ramp extended from directly in front of the wings.

Vice Admiral Augustus Bretoni stood in his shining parade uniform and enameled ceremonial buttons, his hands clasped behind his back. On his head rested a peaked, dark blue cap with a gold emblem. There was something aristocratic about his tall figure and slightly bony face that commanded respect.

He came down the ramp at a measured pace, followed by four officers, all of whom were as finely dressed as their superior.

"Permission to come aboard?" Augustus asked, following protocol, standing just a few feet from Konrad on the final stretch of ramp.

"Permission granted," he replied.

"Atteeen-tion!" the COB shouted, and there was a *clack* as everyone present came to attention.

Smiling, the admiral moved closer until he stood in front of Konrad. He saluted and Augustus returned the salute.

"At ease."

Clothes rustled. No one "relaxed," but now they stood with their legs slightly apart and their hands behind their backs instead of at their sides.

"Welcome aboard, sir!" Konrad greeted the admiral and shook his hand. "May I introduce you to my XO, Commander Silvea Thurnau?"

"Pleased to meet you."

"Our COB Walter Borowski."

"Ah, the secret captain." Augustus winked and Borowski smiled kindly.

"Actually, I'm just the grievance box on two legs, sir."

"Commander Nicholas Bradley," Konrad continued, introducing his son. The admiral looked at him and nodded appreciatively.

"So young and already with the rank of commander."

"Yes, sir."

"You must have done an extraordinary job. As did your brother, by the way. He's done the entire Academy proud. Of course, he's only at the rank of lieutenant commander, but then he didn't have it easy in the Sol System."

Konrad gritted his teeth at this blatant dig and was glad his son was in control of himself.

"But I think it's good," the admiral continued, waving his hand. "Such a young face at the helm of such an aged ship is certainly good for the entire crew."

"Thank you, sir," Nicholas replied neutrally.

"What about your officers, Admiral?" Konrad pointed in the direction of the two men and two women still standing on the ramp.

"They will wait for me here."

"I don't understand. We expected twelve people according to the list for the dinner."

"Ah, I'm sorry, Captain. Presumably my XO failed to contact your XO. There's been a slight change of plans."

"A change of plans?"

"The joint dinner will take place on my ship, the *Caesar*. A true flagship is an appropriate place for an experienced captain such as yourself."

"This is—"

"I know, I know," Augustus interrupted him. "But I insist. You deserve it."

Konrad managed not to clench his hands into fists, but his jaw cracked slightly.

"Also, I may be needed as preparations for our jump the day after tomorrow are in full swing. I'm sure you understand. Your son is doing really well on my ship."

"Roger that, sir."

"Wonderful. But as you can see, I'm here. I couldn't pass up the opportunity to see this flying museum with my own eyes for once." Noticing all the sour looks, the admiral laughed harshly. "Just kidding! By God, you're all stiff. Relax. I'd be honored to get a tour of this impressive ship, Captain. I've never set foot on a real Titan before!"

"Of course," Konrad replied neutrally. He dismissed the honor guard with a wave of his hand. "Follow me, please."

11

"Next time I'll bring my own grub, too," Oxana complained, holding her stomach. The sailor was visibly seasick and once again took her leave to head to the toilet.

Franc looked after her pityingly until she disappeared through the narrow door and sounds of vomiting reached them in the lounge. Valeska screwed up her face.

"We should give her some of our supplies. Surely the whole shipment is spoiled," she said.

That morning, a small cargo drone had arrived with two weeks' worth of food meant for Oxana, Ute, Oliver, and Powell. Valeska had packed enough dry food in Atlantis to last several months. Nobody liked the stuff except her and Franc, but it was full of nutrients and was quick and easy to prepare. But food had never been a big issue for her. Unlike the sailors, who apparently made a point of eating well.

"Poor Oxi," said Ute, a short Harbinger woman with chalky white skin and watery eyes. She sat at the dining table with Oliver and Powell, both sturdy young men with shaved skulls, playing cards while Franc and Valeska went over the data from the deep probe at the holotable.

The floating habitat had proven to be a good investment. After a few hours it had finished assembling and offered them forty square meters of space. That didn't sound like much, but for a shelter that could independently maintain its position on the water by means of balancing jets and had been the size of a large cargo box when packed together, it wasn't bad. The crew slept in a small room with bunk beds and she and Franc had their own double bed in the study, which could be folded into the wall to provide enough space for desks that could also be folded out and their research equipment. There were also two wet rooms for showers and washing and two toilets, one of which was now occupied almost all the time. The "kitchen" consisted only of a recycler for organic waste, which was broken down by the recycling system into macro- and micronutrients and then processed for the synthesizer, and one for inorganic waste, which automatically went to repair the habitat. Outside, there was another jetty where Oxana's sailboat was moored and where a ladder could be used to board the small submersible.

"She just can't stand the storm," Powell grinned. As if confirming his statement, the wind howled loudly outside. The hurricane had been going for two hours now and had ruined their plan to start their first dive. "She should just admit it."

"Very funny, bonehead," Ute snapped at him. "If you start pissing out the back, I'll laugh at you too."

"Hey! We also ate the provisions from West Bank and none of us has the snappy Djiffar!"

"That's because she's the only one who ordered vegetarian," Oliver grumbled.

"A little quiet please," Valeska called out without looking away from the holoscreen. "We're looking at the scans of the cave right now."

"Actually, it's not a cave; it's much too big," Franc said. In fact, the area under the shaft was enormous. Many miles deep and wide with a lot of life and, of course, the huge, half-decayed ring structure. "This thing must be ancient!"

"It looks like it. But the algae and coral growth is minimal." Valeska frowned. "Looks like it decomposed and collapsed under the pressure and current abrasion, but that would take centuries with material that could hold such a structure stable. Why didn't the plants settle more densely there? It would be ideal for them."

"Too few nutrients in the current?" Franc suggested.

"Possibly. We have to get down there. One way or another."

"If it wasn't for this damn storm."

"We'll go anyway," she decided. "It's quiet down there."

"Can't," Ute said without looking up from her deck of cards. She played a card and Oliver grunted. "West Bank safety rules. No salvage operations above wind force eight."

"We're not planning on salvaging anything either!"

"You're a smart woman, aren't you? *Every* dive on Lagunia is a recovery at best."

"Not for us. We need to take a closer look and see if anything can be salvaged. Maybe some samples from this ring structure."

"You mean the hyperspace gate?" Powell asked, tossing a few game chips into the middle. Ute frowned.

Valeska snorted. "That's pure speculation. Prospectors like to brag to drive up the price of their found claim."

"Looks to me like that thing in orbit around Artros that the *Oberon* guards so jealously." Powell shrugged.

"A hyperspace gate is unlikely to be located on the ocean floor in a cave that has no access to the surface."

"Someone did."

"Try pushing an object several hundred meters in diameter through a six-meter-wide shaft," she retorted sharply. "You don't even have to have studied to find that absurd."

"It was obvious that now—"

"If they want to go down," Ute interrupted her comrade, "then let them go down. We were hired to do our job, not to give them legal advice."

"Whatever," Powell relented, shrugging. "But I can't drive this thing."

"I'll do it." All eyes turned to the door to the toilet, from which a pale Oxana emerged. She sniffed peevishly and went to the kitchen to take some medicine.

"You're not in any condition to pilot a submarine!" Franc objected. "You need to lie down and recuperate."

"Nah. The pills are already starting to kick in and I've never been good at loafing around in bed. A little work takes my mind off things."

"And the thing about the laws?" he asked.

She waved it off. "Oh, they're more like guidelines. You don't really think anyone controls what goes on out here, do you?"

Valeska gave her husband and then Powell a meaningful look. The latter pretended to be engrossed in his cards. Judging by his facial expression, he was about to lose.

"So, what are we waiting for? We have something to discover that is the envy of every other explorer on Lagunia!"

Franc sighed and nodded. "All right. Let's do it."

Oxana asked for five minutes to get the dive boat ready.

Valeska and Franc followed her outside onto the small jetty platform. Large waves submerged them every second creating foamy dunes that flashed in the darkness. They had to be quick to open the hatch to the submersible, climb in, and close it again so they weren't drowned in the cabin. It was risky, and it wasn't until they opened the door to go outside that they realized just how risky. First, the wind tore so hard at the silicon hatch that it slipped out of Valeska's hand and slammed violently against the outside wall. Then a wave slapped past them, flooding half the habitat. Ute, Oliver, and Powell cursed and jumped up from the table to deal with it.

They would probably curse them as soon as they were gone. Not entirely unjustified.

"Quick!" Valeska shouted against the howling storm and jumped to the round hatch in the platform to which the submersible was connected from below. She turned the wheel, yanked open the entrance, and shooed Franc inside. He stumbled slightly, and she looked over her shoulder and saw the next wave rushing toward her. It was at least six feet high. "Damn!"

Without further ado, she gave him a push, and he cursed before rushing past the ladder into the interior. She quickly followed him, ignoring the rungs, and slipping behind with one hand on the locking lever so her momentum and body weight ensured that the hatch above her was closed. It was a close call, because at the same time she heard the water rushing loudly above her.

"I hit my head!" Franc cursed, holding a small laceration on his forehead.

"Let me see." She looked at the bleeding spot and nodded. "It's okay, just press a tissue on it, it won't need stitches."

"For science, huh?" he grumbled.

"It's better than drowning out there."

"We should have just waited until tomorrow."

"We've waited for years, that's over now," she replied firmly, looking around the small cabin.

There was only one pilot's seat, where Oxana squatted and operated the many toggle switches and holoconsoles, and two bucket seats behind it, each with a touch display on pivoting arms that could be pulled in. One after the other, they took their seats, which was not easy as the submarine swayed violently back and forth. Valeska was somewhat relieved when she was finally seated, and her husband had fastened his seat belt and was trying to remove his wet clothes. The humidity in the cabin had risen considerably. This was not the right place to be claustrophobic. They were sitting in a tiny oval bubble made of metal with a hemisphere of glass toward the front and was lined on the inside with holding nets and lots of flashing lights that gave the impression that the walls were contracting.

"How long are we going to sit in here?" Franc asked, pressing a white cloth against his bleeding forehead.

"It'll take us about an hour to get down there. This baby, while among the best you can buy here on Lagunia, is still a century behind the hardware available on a Core World. In that respect, we have to slow down to meet the high pressure, and down there, it all depends on you," Oxana said, flipping a final switch and focusing on the controls.

A jolt went through the submersible, and they slid into the depths. In front of them, bubbles streamed over the windshield and a couple of fish scuttled away. There was almost complete darkness until Oxana turned on the headlights, but their light was quickly lost in the dark water.

The descent through the shaft was fascinating. Although Valeska had seen the images from the deep probe, it was something else to see with her own eyes and slide down it. There was no doubt about it: The tunnel was artificial, with even walls and spiral joints like a drill would leave behind.

"White as limestone," she murmured, ignoring her display. She had pushed it to the side.

"Coral deposits. But they would take a very long time to form such a thick layer," Franc said. "And why is it so far above the bottom?"

"Maybe it's an arc shape that has enough static strength."

"We could spend months just studying this phenomenon."

"I know. We'll just work our way from the most important to the least important," she suggested. "Not that any of this is unimportant."

"It's like a fair for you two, huh?" Oxana asked.

"More than that. And the main attraction is yet to come."

For the next half hour, none of them said anything; only

the depth gauge reported every hundred meters with a high-pitched *blip*. Vast numbers of fish and tentacled mollusks flashed through the cones of light from their headlamps, white creatures with strange, whimsical, and decidedly eerie shapes. Some of them were bioluminescent and emitted bluish clouds that first glowed and then gradually faded. It was as if they were gliding through a beautiful chamber of horrors.

Then the first spur of the destroyed ring structure came into view. At first, Valeska thought it was one of the large whalelike animals of which she had seen the tail fins, but it did not move. Like a curved hand with weathered skin, the dark brown structure bent before them in the light, pale as a shy amoeba.

When Oxana sneezed, Valeska started.

"Heavens!"

"I'm sorry." The captain sniffled and wiped her mouth and nose with the back of her hand. She thought she saw red blood on it.

"Is everything okay?"

"Yeah, I'm fine. Probably burst a vessel." The woman waved it off. "But that's an oshi."

"Yes. We need to get closer!" Spellbound, Valeska pulled the display toward her and looked at the data from the spectrograph mounted under the hull, which listed the composition of the structure. "See that, Franc?"

"Yes. Carbotanium, oxygen, nitrogen—those are the molecules in the water—and lots of composite. Metal mishmash, like we use for our starships. A hyperspace gate."

"Slow down, slow down," she admonished him. "We're scientists, and we don't get carried away with rash assumptions."

"There are coral deposits there, too." He pointed to his display, but she had already seen it: White lime that had settled on the brownish structure and seemed to lose even the last bit of color in the spotlight, as if it were dissolving in the light. "Quite a few, though. It hasn't been there long, I'd wager."

"We need to go deeper."

"All right. Nine hundred meters to the bottom," Oxana said in a strained voice and cleared her throat. Valeska hoped the medication was working, and that she wouldn't be plagued by another attack down here in the submarine. It would be rather inconvenient, since there was no toilet.

Again, the headlight was swallowed by the blackness, filled with floating particles. Life was increasingly rare here.

"The sonar is showing quite a bit. The prospectors had already pointed it out, but there's a lot there!" Franc's voice was filled with awe. "Wow!"

Valeska saw it too. Over one hundred contacts on the screen, ranging from two meters in diameter to thirty and were very jagged.

"Maybe a settlement? Finally, a settlement!"

In all the years the extinct Lagoon had been studied, no actual habitats of them had ever been found. They knew they existed, an intelligent aquatic species that had inexplicably made it into space had to have cities, but no one had figured out how and where they might have lived. So, she was not ashamed of her enthusiasm. But when they were fifty meters from the bottom and Oxana tilted the submersible and turned up the headlights to maximum, she was quickly disappointed.

What they saw below them was a debris field. Skeletons of rust-eaten composite that wasn't supposed to rust, parts that looked like wings torn apart by claws, and broken life support capsules. It was easy to guess that they had once been oval, typical of those of the Clicks.

"There must have been a battle here," Franc muttered. "It makes sense. The Clicks attacked Lagunia because Lagoon developed hyperspace gates. They did the exact same thing to us. When the Omega almost had a breakthrough, they attacked Harbingen with everything they had and destroyed the research moon Kor. I'd be willing to bet that the Lagoon had the same thing happen to them, except they had no colonies and were wiped out on their homeland. Damn Clicks!"

"We need samples. Samples from every single wreck lying here," Valeska decided, her mouth dry. It felt like someone had rubbed it with a dusty rag. Impatiently, she swallowed. "Material samples from the wrecks and one from the hyperspace gate. Maybe we'll find radiation residue and find out if the gate was ever activated."

"Down here? Hardly. Opening a hyperspace gate on a planet would be madness. Lagunia wouldn't even exist anymore."

"Since no hyperspace gate has ever been used—at least not in the presence of a human—we have no way of knowing!"

"But the gravitational waves—"

"Crashed out of orbit. I don't think it could have," she interrupted him. "Would probably have burned up."

"Or broken?" he said irritably.

"I'll just get closer, okay? Then we can drop the little scraper drones and they'll start collecting with their spatulas," Oxana suggested. "Everyone in agreement? Wonderful."

Valeska wanted to say something angry because she didn't like to be brushed off like a toddler just because someone couldn't stand conflict, but the woman was basically right. She and Franc were just too upset.

"Sorry," she said in his direction, and he smiled mildly.

"All good. We have all the time in the world, and we should take it. After so many years, it's understandable that we're impatient, but if there's one thing we should have learned, it's that patience and perseverance pay off," he said, reaching out to take her hand, which she squeezed tightly.

"Scrapers are out," Oxana announced, sneezing again. "My goodness."

"Are you sure you're okay?"

"Yes. When we get to the top, I'm going to demand a refund for that crap food from the West Bank!" The captain snorted glumly. The propulsion lights of the small round working drones whirred away ahead of them, approaching the bizarre shadows at the bottom of the sea. "Truly amazing, these nimble things. Where on Earth did you find them?"

"We had plenty of time to build up contacts in Atlantis," Valeska answered evasively. She preferred not to think about that sleazy agent Schmidt and his TIA. Whenever she did, she felt like a puppet on a string. She wanted this to be entirely *their* project. They deserved to finally get the academic recognition they deserved. Everyone had laughed at them for choosing Lagunia, but soon she hoped no one would be laughing anymore.

It took thirty minutes for the first data to arrive from the busy drones with their half-dozen grippers and tool arms. The computer stored them and processed them into graphs and composition tables.

Then Oxana began coughing. At first it only sounded like she was clearing her throat, then more and more like a damp wheeze, a roar in her bronchial tubes that startled Valeska.

"Oxana?" she shouted when the coughs didn't subside, and the seizure did not end. The entire back of the captain's chair shook violently.

Franc unbuckled his seat belt and rushed to her side. She did the same as she shook herself out of her shocked stupor. Clumsily, she fumbled with the buckles of Oxana's seat belts until the two of them managed to free her. Foam poured from the captain's mouth and blood ran in dark red threads from her nose.

"Damn, what's wrong with her?" Valeska cried, trying to get the foam out of Oxana's mouth with two fingers as she started to choke.

"She's seizing. I don't know what's wrong with her," her

husband replied helplessly. "Come on, let's get her on her side so she doesn't suffocate!"

Together they lifted Oxana out of the chair, placed her on the floor between their seats, and rolled her onto her side and watched as foam and blood flowed onto the gray composite.

Suddenly the seizure stopped. Instinctively, Valeska checked her pulse, but found none.

"Her heart's stopped!" she cried. Awkwardly, she turned Oxana onto her back and began CPR. "How many do I have to count to?"

"I don't know! I don't know!"

"I'm not a doctor, damn it!"

The beeps from the computers and the roar of the engines seemed to get louder and the cabin more cramped, while sweat dripped from Valeska's forehead, but she didn't stop, pressing again and again with overlapping hands until she realized Franc was pulling her shoulder. Her vision cleared between tears, and she saw Oxana's eyes staring blankly upward.

"She's dead! Stop it! She's dead!"

"B-but sh-she can't be d-dead!" she stammered. "Sh-she can't d-die of fucking food poisoning down here!"

"I-I don't know. But she's dead." Franc slumped and slammed his back against one of the seats. He didn't even seem to notice. He looked consternated at the body of their captain. "What are we going to do?"

"I... I..."

"We need to collect the scrapers and surface immediately. We have to inform West Bank and request rescue. Then we'll go to Atlantis—"

"No!" She was surprised by her own sharpness. "The scrapers need thirty minutes. When they get back with the data, we'll move up."

"But, Valeska—"

"No. If we go up now, it's all been for nothing! First of all, that won't make her live again, and second, we need to figure out how to navigate this submersible without panicking," she said, taking a few deep breaths in and out. "We're going to calm down now. Oxana is dead. We have to take her up, but to do that we have to have a clear head and not make any mistakes. Down here there's a hundred times the pressure from the surface. You don't do experiments here!"

"Yes," he replied sluggishly, his face as pale as lime. He puffed out his cheeks. "You're right, I guess."

"See if you can get a connection to the base and let Ute or the guys know what's going on. Tell them to inform the West Bank radio operator immediately that we have a medical emergency involving a fatality. I'll get on the controls and hope I can figure them out or find a program. As soon as the scrapers get back, we can surface."

"Okay, all right." Her husband still looked as if he had seen a ghost. She felt so sick herself she wanted to throw up. But they had to act now. Not act stupid. Act smart.

"After you get the message off, see if you can get the sonar on one of the screens so we can find the shaft that leads up."

TFS GIBRALTAR, HARBINGEN SYSTEM

The destroyer TFS *Gibraltar* leisurely passed the farthest point of Harbingen's gravity funnel, far from the last piece of debris from its destroyed moon Kor, which looked like a triangular sliver with frayed, jagged edges on the long sides. Harbingen was still beautiful with its inviting green landmass crisscrossed by a vascular network of brilliant blue rivers. Only the large brown circles showed that it was not nature that had been at work, but the destructive force of what had evolved: scars from Kor's fragments that had bombarded the former Core World, turning it into a hell of unyielding radiation.

Captain Toyohiro Akiyama often imagined what it must have been like to stand on the surface that fateful day twenty standard years ago, to watch as the sky began to burn to the chorus of blaring emergency sirens in the paradisiacal cities. The sight of gigantic fragments of moon igniting in the atmosphere, the heat storm created by the inconceivable friction, which cooked the many inhabitants after a few minutes. Had they panicked? Or were they silent in the face of such unimaginable forces too great to comprehend? Had the men, women, and children on the night side left their homes at the onset of the alarms and pointed upward with their neighbors, where the tremendous storm of lightning, explosions, and swarms of rockets turned night into day near the brightest moon? How had those who had found shelter in bunkers or basements reacted to the news that the *Oberon* had jumped away with the colony ships and that they were now defenseless against the sky that was literally falling on their heads? Had they cried knowing it would take several days for help to arrive and that it would make no difference because no Federation logistic effort would have been sufficient to evacuate that many millions of people from a dying world?

Toyohiro liked to imagine they had died with their chins up, as the Harbinger's reputation suggested.

Today, there was hardly a trace of the chaos that had shaken the entire Federation and spawned a completely new Fleet doctrine that day. Of course, there were the five large stains on Harbingen's surface that told of the terrible things that had happened, just like the debris of Kor still in orbit, from whose regolith a thin ring had formed around the planet. The remnants of the battle between the Federation and Click fleets also circled the green ball on the screen, distinguishable only as a sparkling halo.

Otherwise, there was nothing. The habitats and industrial stations, helium refineries and asteroid mines of the inner and outer systems, were still intact and visible on the scanners but devoid of any radiation. Along with Harbingen, the rest of the system had gradually died over the months and years. Without the industrial and cultural center, the space dwellers eventually left for promising fringe worlds that needed skilled workers, or Core Worlds where they still had relatives, and which promised a better life.

Captain Akiyama was already in his last week of duty in Harbingen, which consisted mostly of the same patrol flights over and over to protect the inner system from pirates who were up to mischief further out in the asteroid belts, plundering the stations and habitats left behind like vultures. Even today, they registered several incoming jumps each day at the outer jump point near the gas giant Artros, but none of the ships were foolish enough to approach Harbingen in search of the really big catches. Fleet saw to that. *He* saw to that. A boring job, he had to admit, but one that was necessary, and more importantly, one that would be over shortly when his relief arrived.

The very existence of the bloodsuckers infuriated him, but the governor, with his contacts in the Senate, made sure Fleet's mandate was limited to the inner system so no "resources were wasted." That the governorship still existed here at all was a bad legislative joke that stemmed from the fact that someone with connections didn't want to vacate his post. His office wasn't even here, but on the Senate floor.

"Captain, I think I have something."

It took Toyohiro a second to realize that Lieutenant Chay had spoken. It was quite possible this was the first time he had opened his mouth since they had arrived at this post.

"And what do you have, Lieutenant?" he asked, having returned from his inner reflections and straightened in his seat.

"The scanners only picked it up for a few microseconds, but there was a spike in the signal."

"A signal?" Toyohiro frowned. "Have you checked it out? There are no possible transmitters or receivers out here at all."

"I did, sir. But both I and the computer are sure it was there."

"What about the source?"

"On the remnant of Kor, on the side facing the planet."

Toyohiro slid forward in his seat until he was sitting on the edge and folded his hands in front of his mouth. "Anaish, get us closer to the signal source; we'll take a closer look. Duarte, reconfigure our drones in orbit accordingly."

He waited until the bridge crew was about to implement his orders, then turned to Lieutenant Chay. "Is there anything that gives the signal's origin away?"

"High data density, extremely short pulse." The young officer's fingers flew over the holobuttons on his console, then suddenly paused.

"What is it, Lieutenant?"

"The signal was too short to tell with one hundred percent certainty, but I think I found the target point."

"Spit it out already," he urged his officer.

"Omega."

"Impossible. The Palace of Unity has had no power supply for twenty years, and the same goes for the computer center at its heart. Omega is inactive, probably dead, if you can put it that way."

"I know, sir, and I didn't mean to imply otherwise, but the signal was directed at the palace."

"Are you quite sure?"

"As I said, there is no way to be completely sure, but the approximation is convincing and there are only ruins there. The palace is the only structure within twenty klicks that is over eighty percent intact."

"Captain!" Duarte shouted from her console. "I've moved one of our drones closer to Kor and it has sent an initial image."

"On screen."

On the large "window" at the front appeared a poorly resolved image of a rugged gray lunar surface with something like a fountain at its center.

"What's that? Looks like someone is digging in the dirt," he thought aloud.

"Should we send a hyperspace buoy to the jump point to report?" Anaish asked.

"No," Toyohiro ordered. *I'll be damned if I'm going to jeopardize my career over the possible discovery of brazen pirates, only to have to explain how the bastards were able to sneak past us. But someone is here, rummaging where the Federation doesn't want anyone rummaging...* Aloud he said, "We'll gather more information first and then act accordingly. Rushing ahead hasn't helped anyone yet."

"Sir," Chay objected, "The *Braxis* is already arriving in the system tomorrow for relief."

"I'm aware of that, Lieutenant. So, we're going to make sure Captain Crocker gets as much information as possible so we can respond accordingly—with us, if we have to."

Who's there? And what are they doing there? he wondered tensely. Who could be so brazen as to sneak into one of the strictest restricted areas of the Federation and rummage through the ruins from a time which most would have preferred to cover with the cloak of oblivion? And above all: Who could afford to do it?

12

"You know," Augustus said as they walked back to the small bow hangar, followed by the COB and Silly, "it's no secret that the Federation has a contentious relationship with you and your ship, Captain."

That was at least an understatement.

"I rather think they hate me," Konrad said candidly. It had been a long time since he had last opened his mind to this fact.

The admiral waved away his remark and stopped to face him. Silly and Borowski stood away at some distance. Ahead of them, the hydraulics of their visitor's sinfully expensive ferry vented with a loud hiss. Deck personnel in orange one-piece suits were pulling the charging cables for the rear batteries from their connectors and running them back to the brackets on the wall.

"I know it's unfair, but don't hold it against the civilians. Although, most citizens have served at arms during their military service, few of them know what it means to be a soldier. Who can blame them? They spend most of their time in simulated defense of their respective home worlds, endless drills in the muck of the foothills and old industrial wastelands. They learn how to dig trenches and dig in, how to use a laser carbine or a Gauss rifle. Hardly anyone joins Fleet because you need more prerequisites for our service than two healthy hands and feet. They don't understand what it means to command a ship, to have responsibility for thousands, or, in your case at the time, millions of people."

"I've come to terms with it," Konrad said stiffly. "With my guilt, too."

Augustus examined him closely and then nodded seriously.

"You're a good officer, Bradley. Real admiral material." There was no mockery in Bretoni's voice. "I know that, and I'm sure I can convince my colleagues in the Admiralty of the arguments that have led me to this conviction. You will not rot in this colony system without a sound, you have my word on that."

Konrad was truly surprised and blinked a few times, which did not happen often. He had not expected such a turn of events.

"Thank you, sir, that's... very kind."

Augustus smiled and patted him on the shoulder.

"We'll discuss everything else when we meet on my flagship, agreed?"

"Agreed."

"Good."

"Admiral?" It seemed strange to Konrad to address this much younger man in this way, even though Augustus radiated a charismatic aura of authority. But such was the current reality of Fleet.

"Yes?" The admiral, just about to leave, turned and looked at him. "Captain?"

"The *Oberon* is ready to go. We can do our part if you draft us for your Strike Group. A Titan is made to last a long time and tie up enemy forces. Just what you need."

Augustus smiled mildly but shook his head.

"I understand that, and I'm impressed with how you've

managed to fund the current modernization and upgrade work that's obviously being done. But Fleet doctrine has changed. We fight in rapidly adaptable formations and patterns. Speed and adaptation are our strengths and fitting a Titan into those tactics is nearly impossible. No offense." Augustus inclined his head. "You have other goals now, Captain. Restoring your reputation and that of your crew and compatriots. That should be your first priority, and I will support you in that. You have my word."

Konrad knew when to accept a gift and carry it home, so he simply nodded. His visitor had already brought him more kindness and promises than he had expected.

"Thank you, sir, and have a safe flight back."

"I'll see you tomorrow for the officers' dinner." With that, Augustus finally turned and walked to the shuttle ramp, where his four officers in parade uniforms were still standing and waiting.

Konrad remained there until the shuttle lifted off and pushed through the force field, and even as the massive, armored doors closed from the sides. Only when a deep rumble went through the hangar, followed by the hiss of the gate hydraulics, did he relax a bit and turn around.

"Meet in my quarters in thirty minutes."

The two Marines outside the door clicked their heels together as Konrad opened the door to greet his COB. Borowski cleared his throat and nodded formally. His ship's coveralls were bulging strangely on the front.

"Come on in, Chief."

"Thank you, sir." Borowski stepped over the threshold and Konrad turned to the two Marines. "You two are off for the rest of the watch."

They exchanged brief glances with each other, presumably

to see if the other feared Colonel Meyer more if they obeyed the order, or the ship's commander if they did not. Finally, they saluted. "Sir."

As they moved down the narrow hallway where the senior officers' quarters were located, he closed the door and went inside.

"Ha-ha!" Borowski said, pulling two bottles of schnapps from his coveralls. The old warhorse with the gray hair and tanned leather face looked uncharacteristically childlike. Even Silly had to grin, which seemed to cause her pain. Nicholas merely smirked, went to the glass case, and pulled out some glasses. "What do we have here? Uh, that looks like homebrew from the chief engie and his screw eaters."

"I should have you thrown in the brig for having contraband on you! And you're supposed to be a COB?" Konrad said, with mock sternness, waving in the direction of the liquor. "This one time I'll turn a blind eye and just confiscate the goods."

Borowski grinned and filled the glasses Nicholas had set on the small glass table, which was surrounded by the sofa group like a horseshoe.

"If that didn't go well!" the old man rejoiced, setting down the bottle.

"I must confess that I didn't expect so many positive signals from the admiral," Silly said, taking her glass and smelling the golden liquid. Somewhat disgusted, she screwed up her face and was about to drink when Nicholas put a hand on her arm.

"I think we should toast."

"Ah, a toast, yes." Borowski nodded. "We are in distinguished company, after all."

Konrad had considered his COB the greatest achievement of his own first command thirty years ago because he had been able to bring him with him from the *Cervigo* when his service as XO there was over. They had known each other for over forty years, and Borowski was the rock of the crew everyone could lean on and without whom nothing worked. They weren't just friends, they were family.

Three pairs of eyes locked on him, so he cleared his throat and raised his own glass.

"I prepared myself to fight for what we wanted to do. To be run as a flagship again, not in the Fleet reserve, but on active duty, seemed almost too lofty to be attainable." He lowered his voice a bit. "After everything. But we didn't give up, and I have you to thank for pushing and pushing. We had to cut some corners and go through some walls, pass through gray areas, and accept that we wouldn't be proud of all the actions we've taken, but now that the goal is within reach, I can say it was worth it!"

"We've been flogging off expensive military hardware that friends in Fleet leadership, of which there aren't many, have sent us on the black market to make improvements to our ship," Nicholas said, sighing. "I think this is more than a gray area."

"Even more important that we are through, and the *Oberon* will soon be as good as new." Silly glared at him, but he didn't pay her any mind.

"All of that is irrelevant as long as it works. None of us have found it easy, but we don't have to. We *need* to be flagship again." Konrad was louder now, and urgently looked them in the eye. "Not for our pride, not merely for our family here on board..." He paused before continuing, "For our country."

He saw their concerned looks, and all the joy disappeared from their faces. They nodded heavily. It hurt to wipe the smiles off their faces, but they needed to be reminded that all of this was more than small triumphs or the impression of beating up Fleet. They *were* the fleet, and that had to be clear to everyone.

"Harbingen is but a shadow of what it once was. Our homeland is contaminated and plowed under by toxic superstorms. It will be so for decades and centuries to come. Saving the planet will consume vast sums that we don't have, but in the future some generation will do it, and we are here to make sure they have the opportunity. It's not us who will again feel the earth of our homeland between our fingers, but those who come after us. Not us."

"Not us," repeated Silly, Nicholas, and Borowski.

"Not us." Konrad took a deep breath and raised his glass. "But we'll be damned if we're going to be melancholy about it. We have a chance to do some good, to lay the foundation for a better future. Harbingers don't let things get small. We're laughed at as the weeds in the Federation. I take that as a compliment. Weeds don't go away. Let's make sure everyone remembers that when Lagunia gets its own fleet, and we are the 51st of the Terran Federation again! Then Harbingen will once again be under our ship designation, not Lagunia."

"Hear, hear!" Borowski shouted, and they touched glasses. "You should have given that speech in the hangar, it would make the oranges work faster."

Silly choked and coughed.

"Does our association actually know about this?" Nicholas asked after he had enjoyed the first sip and a long sigh. "About our plan with the fleet, I mean?"

"I dropped hints about what we were up to at the last captain's meeting, and you probably won't be surprised to hear that the twenty whippersnappers spent half an hour banging their knuckles on the table," Konrad said proudly. "They know it without knowing it, and when the time comes, we will celebrate the result with them."

"When they're officially part of our fleet," Silly murmured, draining the rest of her glass in one go. "That sounds like we need a second drink!"

"What about the civilian fleet? There are, after all, nearly one hundred ships of more than two hundred tons mass with civilian registration permanently in the system," Nicholas asked as the tinkle of homebrew sounded in Silly's glass. "Not to mention more than twice that many unregistered."

"The many illegals are a problem, but we'll take care of them," Konrad assured him, gasping. Borowski's stuff tasted awful for all it looked like honey. "I realize they are vital to the survival of the planet and the stations around Artros, but we'll come up with something. Maybe we'll recruit them as soon as we have the authority to do so."

"The Senate won't like that," his XO said.

"Politicians never like anything unless they get money from it or secure their next four years," grumbled the COB.

Konrad smiled. "One thing at a time. First, we have our guest list to plan for the dinner with Admiral Augustus. This is going to be a historic evening for us, and that's why I want to get as many members as possible signed up for our entourage. I want the whole ship to know what will happen tomorrow."

"We already know that." Borowski grinned wolfishly over his glass. "There'll be lobster on the table, then Silly will hang over the toilet bowl all night because her insides will turn inside out."

"Be glad we're here in the captain's quarters and not somewhere else in the ship, *Chief Petty Officer,*" the XO growled humorlessly.

Konrad leaned back on the sofa and smiled contentedly, like a father watching his children. Warmth spread through him, not just from the schnapps that must have been distilled somewhere in the farthest engine rooms by the reactor crew where there were no inspections because no one understood anything about what they were doing there.

Tomorrow, then, he thought. *Tomorrow is finally the day. After all this time!*

13

"How are you going to tell him, Konrad?" Silly asked next to him in the shuttle. Her blue parade uniform with its colorful insignia and gold buttons was held together tightly at the collar with a stylized cross, the only sign of Harbingen they were displaying that evening just like him and his delegation. For festivities aboard ship, they normally donned the steel-gray uniforms of the Harbinger Colonial Fleet, but it was no longer formally recognized, so he had ordered them to switch to the official Fleet colors. The production 3-D printers had had their hands full converting the patterns assigned to them as reservists into solid, ironed fabric. Silly appeared uncomfortable in her getup, like a teenager condemned to wear a scratchy wool sweater when visiting family. And that's how the others seemed to feel, too. Borowski looked as if he had bitten into a lemon and Colonel Meyer's jaw muscles were tensing steadily. The aging Marine clearly hated every ounce of his white uniform. The Black Legion, the undisputed elite of armed Fleet personnel before Harbingen's demise, had been notorious not only for its harsh drill and love of implants, then banned on most Core Worlds and now on all, but also for its namesake black uniforms.

Chief Murphy acted as if none of this was any of his business, which was almost never the case with the usually gruff and painfully honest engineer, and was a red flag. Only his son, Nicholas, seemed composed and little challenged by dressing in what was perceived as a foreign uniform. His boy was not only a rule follower but also extremely pragmatic within that rule circle, which made him a perfect officer. Konrad could always be counted on as a commander not to overstep the bounds of his authority, while at the same time not giving in to them and able to improvise and listen to his subordinates within his scope of action.

"Captain?"

Konrad shook his head and inhaled before turning to Silly. The shuttle had just accelerated and went into a long, gradual turn that brought them under the *Oberon* and on course to the *Caesar*, which was only one of the tiny twinkling lights in the shining panorama of the stars.

"Sorry. What did you say?"

"How are you going to tell him? The admiral, I mean," his XO repeated, adjusting the cross covering her top uniform button. It was just one of many gestures among his officers that showed a degree of uncertainty that was not common among them. The perceived triumph of what they thought was a paved path toward their reintegration into Fleet as a flagship had given way to the typical wariness that every team experienced before the end of the game, when the lead was razor thin and only a few minutes remained on the clock.

"I will present the new performance data according to the chief's calculations and probably impress him with it. He has seen our overhaul work, but not what it really means for the *Oberon*'s combat readiness," he explained. "After that, I'll present our plan to him quite openly and ask for his support."

"That simple?" she asked.

"That simple. You know what I think of beating around the bush."

"No objections."

He turned to the rest of the officers in the small shuttle, who looked like ghosts in the green light. "Don't act like you're sitting on nails. We have a plan today and that's it. Our goal is not this or that, but to execute our plan to the best of our abilities. That's all soldiers like us have ever been able to do. Don't forget that."

He also glanced at Meyer's four Marines, who were serving as his bodyguard—a deliberate signal to Augustus. According to protocol, a four-man guard was reserved for Fleet commanders. The admiral, upon their arrival, would either take him for a vain, arrogant man who wanted to provoke him, or as a subliminal signal that gave him time to prepare for their conversation and its content—and he rated the man's knowledge of human nature high enough for that.

When the nine faces turned to him, he made an effort to look relaxed, and nodded. "None of you matter today, is that clear? I don't want you to bend, not even for a noble plan. We fight how we fight, not how others want us to fight. Understand?"

He made sure they all nodded, then sat back sniffing.

So, let's go into the lion's den, he thought and felt it absurd. Tomorrow the Terran Fleet would strike the decisive blow against the archenemy of mankind and bring death and destruction to the presumed home planet of the Clicks. "The battle to end all battles," as it was being called, and here he sat comfortably in his shuttle, decked out like a peacock in false colors, playing up a meeting with an admiral into a big deal. Something had to change, and soon.

Ten minutes later, their approach to the *Caesar* reminded them once again how much modernization the *Oberon* needed. The entire shuttle jerked violently when one of the maneuvering engines oversteered and the pilot had to shut it down and manually steer with the remaining ones—a process that the flagship's ferries handled automatically via the pilot software. They probably wouldn't have even noticed anything had happened.

"Fix this while we're gone," he ordered the female pilot and copilot. He kept the anger out of his voice, after all, it wasn't their fault. Just like him, they were simply working with what they had. Lagunia wasn't exactly known for being well connected to the Federation's supply network. For the past few years, their stockpile of spare parts had been steadily approaching zero. While this had led to Murphy's engineers and technicians getting better at improvising, any creativity, no matter how great, would ultimately have to be measured against the resources they had at their disposal.

The *Caesar* was a silver arrow that shimmered in the reflective light of the gas giant Artros, whose never-resting storm bands traced paths along the left edge of the cockpit. Konrad knew she had a hangar, albeit a small one, but they were not directed there, but to a smooth spot closer to the tail where four robotic arms extended to receive them. The pilot cursed a few times and seemed to have every possible issue navigating the shallow bulge of the airlock that opened between the robotic arms below two doors that moved aside. Finally, after a few short bursts from the remaining maneuvering thrusters, they were locked into place and immediately pulled the last meter and a half to the hull.

"Airlock pressurized and stable," the pilot announced, and Konrad squeezed her shoulder as he stood.

"Good job."

She merely nodded. He waited for his officers and the four Marines to line up before he went to the side door. The hatch slid open after a long hiss of the equalizing valves. The airlock was short and bright white, which caused him to blink violently. He stepped inside and waited for the outer door to open as well.

His son, Jason, was waiting for him.

Konrad swallowed and tensed.

"Jason," he said, wanting to get rid of a torrent of words and phrases, but they got lost somewhere between his heart and his mouth.

"Captain." His son nodded and saluted stiffly. He stood alone in the hallway with the low ceiling, which had long strips of lights set into it that made him look pale.

"Permission to come aboard?"

"Given in the name of the commander," Jason replied, not moving until Konrad reluctantly returned the salute.

"Like... it's beautiful..."

"The admiral has asked me to escort our guests to the officers' mess."

"I see." He looked inquiringly into his eldest son's face but found no emotion in it except cool control.

"Jason!" Behind him, Nicholas pushed past the four Marines and gave his brother an unusually enthusiastic hug. Only now did a smile appear on Jason's face.

"Hello, little brother! Or should I salute, *Commander?*"

"Woe!" Nicholas grinned, pushed his brother away from him by the shoulders and eyed him. "Well, you look good! Still the family blond in your hair, strong and in good shape. I guess Fleet Academy did you some good."

"And you the security." Jason pointed to the three crossed yellow swords on his brother's shoulder.

Nicholas pulled back a little. "I worked hard for it."

"I'm sure you did. Captain, if you and your entourage would follow me, please?"

Konrad motioned to the oldest to go ahead. The corridors were considerably narrower than those on the *Oberon*, just one of the many signs that the Federation was depleted after decades of war and that the boom in asteroid mining had waned. New mines could not be developed as quickly as ships were destroyed and new ones produced. The shipyards never stood still. Instead of communicators with earpieces and cables, there was a simple button with a small speaker every ten meters. Even with the latest generation of warships, there was still no wireless communication because the risk of interference was too great. Some things changed only in the details.

The *Caesar*'s officers' mess was a rectangular room with a long panel of gleaming aluminum in the center, retrofitted with gold trim at the corners. Konrad was sure that it was not the factory standard; after all, the decorations showed lion heads, the coat of arms of the admiral's family, supposedly dating back to the time of Venetian naval power.

There were twelve chairs—or rather seats—upholstered in dark imitation leather. On the walls hung copperplate portraits of great admirals such as Charles Duke Wellington, Georg Scharnhorst, Frederick Camacho, and Jeremy Brandt.

"There are place cards," Jason explained, pressing a button on the panel next to the door, and small holoimages illuminated at each seat, rotating to show name and rank. Konrad's was at one end of the panel, those of his five officers to his right.

"Thank you. Are you going to participate too?"

"Yes."

"Good, very good." He nodded, tugged on his uniform, which pinched and tweaked in several places, then stood behind his seat. Silly, seated next to him across the corner, let her gaze roam meaningfully between him and Jason, and barely shook her head as Murphy moved to take his seat. He grimaced and then stood behind the chair with his arms folded behind his back, as did the others.

The next ten minutes were filled with an uncomfortable silence that seemed to swell between the walls and make the air scarce.

When at last the door behind the other end of the table opened and Augustus entered, dressed in a shiny parade uniform that looked so casually perfect as if it were nothing special, it wouldn't have taken much for a relieved sigh to go through those waiting.

"Ah, Captain," the admiral said, gesturing to his seat. "Please take a seat."

Behind the admiral, equally immaculate officers streamed in and walked purposefully to their seats on the left. Their expressions were serious and controlled.

"I must apologize for not being able to escort you here myself," Augustus said, sitting gracefully. His voice was clearly audible, although they were separated by at least four meters. "Unfortunately, the final preparations for tomorrow's battle have become very time consuming, and every department demands my attention on a regular basis. But why am I explaining, you know what I'm talking about."

"Quite."

"I hope your son showed you a bit of the ship along the way, as I asked him to do?"

Konrad looked at Jason, who kept his eyes forward and didn't move.

"Of course. Thank you."

"Wonderful, quite wonderful. Ah." Again, the door opened and several young sailors in white livery entered with large trays of covered plates balanced on their arms, which they spread around the table. "Our supplies of fresh food will last until tomorrow. So, we should enjoy it."

"Fresh food?" Murphy gasped. The bearlike chief engineer leaned forward, wide-eyed, as one of the plates was set in front of him, and he peered under the lid. "My gosh."

"Excuse my chief," Konrad said, and gave a curt wave of his hand so Silly would stop scowling in the lieutenant commander's direction, which she did reluctantly. "We've been depending on our protein synthesizers for twenty years, and we don't see *real* food that's been grown on a planet that often."

"Don't worry," Augustus laughed. "I understand all too

well. I paid for the entire shipment out of my own pocket. Fleet switched to dry food many years ago. I wanted to give my officers something special before we went into battle."

"I hope they didn't misinterpret that as a last meal," Murphy chortled, wiggling his fingers impatiently as if he could barely stop himself from gorging on the food. Konrad had to admit that it smelled fantastic.

"Oh no, Lieutenant Commander, my entire crew knows that the Clicks have nothing on us." With a gallant wave, the admiral released the food, and the serving sailors pulled the lids off the plates with practiced ease. "Filet mignon with flambéed asparagus, and sesame-honey goat cheese."

Konrad sucked in the wonderful aroma of the food, which lay before him like a work of art, and picked up his knife and fork.

"Enjoy yourselves, dear guests. And we're in the officers' mess here, so if anyone still needs permission to speak freely, it is hereby granted for the rest of the evening."

"Shit, that smells brutal," Murphy shouted, and laughter rippled through the room. Some of the stiffness of the earlier encounter dissipated—at least as long as Konrad didn't look to his eldest son to the left, who was cutting his meat with accurate movements and beginning to eat.

"Your senior officers, I presume?" Augustus said between bites, gesturing with his knife to the side of the table with the *Oberon* crew.

"Yes." Konrad nodded and pointed to Borowski, who was inspecting his food like a scientist, as if he were dealing with an alien artifact. "You already know my COB. Next to him, Chief Engineer Karl Murphy, who has also already made a good impression. You also already know my son Nicholas, as well as my XO Silvea Thurnau." Last, he pointed to Colonel Meyer. The burly Marine with the angular face and serious eyes nodded to the admiral. "Colonel Meyer commands the Black Legion, our Marines."

"An entire legion aboard a single ship." Augustus shook his head. "That's really impressive. My detachment is just ten men. My bodyguards, who are really only there to keep order on the ship. The fact that you have housed a hundred times that number with you is simply unbelievable."

"The *Oberon* is large, and with its original mission description it had to have the capability for boarding action and support planetary invasions," Konrad explained. "Since we'd rather drop bombs than read casualty reports to the Senate, that's obviously no longer the case."

"I see." Augustus nodded thoughtfully and sighed. "Indeed, the conflict has become increasingly ugly. I wish it were otherwise. But if all goes well—and we can assume it will —this final offensive will end that."

"I certainly hope so." Konrad cut up the last asparagus spear and put it in his mouth. It was delicious. It wasn't that the flavor was particularly outstanding or intense, as protein synthesizers came with the best flavor enhancers Omega had produced before its annihilation. It was more the texture, the knowledge that this piece of green vegetable had *grown* under a *real* sun thanks to *real* rain. "Regarding the offensive, I'd still like to talk to you about it."

"Of course. Ask me anything you want, Captain."

"I've brought a compilation of the projected performance data that the *Oberon* will achieve by 1500 tomorrow, the time of the offensive, when seventy percent of the integration of the upgrades will have been achieved." He tapped his forearm display and waited for Augustus to nod. With a gesture, he threw the data onto the latter's small holoscreen. "As you can see, our acceleration values place no restriction on the speed and maneuverability of your fleet. In accordance with the issued doctrine for Iron Hammer, I have also calculated how the *Oberon* and its escort ships would most effectively fit into the planned pattern. If you consider the response time of our energy pattern cells—"

"But, Captain," Augustus interrupted him with a furrowed brow, "an *incorporation* of your ship, or rather your ships, would only be possible on such short notice if I activate Article 18, paragraph 4 of Fleet Order."

"Incorporation of an unassigned fleet unit due to time urgency in the context of special strategic or tactical circumstances," Konrad quoted. He had probably left out a few words the admiral would notice, but the meaning remained the same.

"But you don't have a fleet."

The sounds of eating on the right side, where the *Oberon* officers were seated, diminished until they finally faded away.

"I'm aware of that. I'm sure that with the new performance data, you'll realize that it makes the most sense for tomorrow's offense to—"

"—I recognize the *Oberon* as the flagship of a separate fleet and incorporate it into the battle plan. They would be under my command and would make an important contribution to the success of Iron Hammer. This would also mean that Lagunia would be recognized as a Fringe World and the Senate would have to deal with the matter afterward. Your hope is that in the joy of victory and your contribution to it, public opinion would be positively influenced and there might be little resistance in the Senate," Augustus summarized.

Konrad nodded. "Yes, sir."

"I'm afraid that's not possible."

There were murmurs to his right.

"Sir?"

"I can't fit you in, Captain."

"But why not? When you left us yesterday, you said: 'You will not rot in this colony system without a sound, you have my word for that.'" Konrad struggled to release the anger that was slowly but surely gaining the upper hand over his surprise.

"Yes, I did."

"And what happened to that?" he asked in a strained voice.

"I think you misunderstood me, Captain." Augustus set aside his silverware and interlaced his slender fingers in front of him on the table as if preparing to deliver a sermon. "I am here to honorably discharge you with full pay and a citation at Fleet Headquarters."

"*Dismissed?*" The word burst from Konrad.

"*Honorably,*" the admiral added, raising a forefinger.

"And my crew?"

"Well, I would have to negotiate that separately, but my goal would be to transition them into regular Fleet service, to the places where they are needed most."

"You can't separate my team!"

"Excuse me?"

"Captain," Jason said from the side, but Konrad ignored his son.

"My team has been working together for almost three decades. They are much more than just my crew. If you want to relieve me of Fleet duty, that's one thing, but the *Oberon* will not be scrapped, and my crew will not be spread throughout the Federation!"

"I'm afraid it's not within your authority as a reserve captain to make such a decision." Augustus's voice was not angry, but the casual politeness had given way to a certain coolness.

"That's why you brought my son here? To make the bad news more palatable to me?"

"A gesture of respect and—"

"Look at the performance data. The *Oberon* can still do her part. It's as powerful as a fleet of these new paper airplanes!"

"Captain," Silly whispered urgently before Augustus paused and nodded.

"What do you say we retire to my quarters, have a scotch,

and discuss this in private?" the admiral suggested. "I think that is a more appropriate setting for this conversation. In the meantime, my officers will show your people the ship."

Konrad straightened and nodded.

SKY FORTRESS, HIGH ORBIT
AROUND TERRA, SOL SYSTEM

"Come in," called Hannibal von Solheim, putting away the tablet on which he had been looking at the recent deployment of an orbital laser that vaporized a vehicle near Valparaiso, plus the related news reports in the media about the military's ruthlessness and the constant bickering in the Senate over the authority disputes between Fleet and the police.

"Fleet Admiral," his guest greeted him and approached his desk. Senator Rosin was a small man with a thick voice and drooping cheeks, watery piggy eyes, and a thin fringe of hair, but despite, or perhaps because of, his appearance, not a man to be underestimated. He looked around the barren room, free of any emotion, which seemed even larger than it was without all the trimmings that von Solheim had removed.

"Senator," he said, pointing to one of the two uncomfortable aluminum chairs in front of his desk. Rosin sat without a sign of protest and crossed his short legs. "What brings you to me?"

"Fourteen missions in twenty-four hours."

"Excuse me?"

"Fourteen times your orbital platforms have fired on

targets on the Earth's surface in the last twenty-four hours," Rosin elaborated, his cheeks wobbling like a Great Dane's as he shook his head. "One hundred and eighty fatalities so far and—"

"*Killed,*" von Solheim corrected the politician sternly. "We don't call terrorists *fatalities.*"

"At least twenty were uninvolved civilians."

"And that hurts me, believe it or not. Any collateral damage is something that weighs on us, but we cannot let that cause us to stop providing for our security and internal stability. We cannot allow dissidents and secessionists to hide among innocents. Laser weapons deployed from orbit are the most accurate tool we have."

"Every innocent life is one too many," the senator insisted. "And the pressure in the Senate is growing."

"Of course." Von Solheim pushed the tablet away from him, leaned back in his chair, and sighed. "So that's what this is all about: majority shifts. Is your caucus in turmoil? It hasn't been good times for progressives for a long time, I hear."

"There are rarely good times for politicians. We're either fighting for our influence or someone else's, and it's always in circles." Rosin shrugged.

"You can come to Fleet anytime." He eyed his guest disparagingly. "I'm sure it wouldn't do you any harm."

If the senator was offended by the provocation, he didn't let on.

"Progressives are aware that pacifism, which has been growing for years among civilians, is a problem, even if some media outlets want to portray it differently. Fleet must remain strong and capable of action—"

"Good." Von Solheim tapped the tablet in front of him. "Because I get daily reports of sabotaged ships in my fleet, bombs going off in ammunition depots, space stations, and ships, misdirected resupply shipments, and anti-war graffiti in wet cells and canteens. There are even cells that have tried to send digital leaflets throughout Dunkelheim's fleet." He leaned forward. "Senator, you're upset because we took action against terrorists on Earth—under SCR mandate, by the way! —but I'm dealing with the defense of our species against an enemy that has shown how far it would go to destroy us."

"The Clicks haven't done anything in years."

"The Clicks wiped out Harbingen. A humanitarian and economic disaster from which we still have not fully recovered."

"You may be right about that, but let's stick to your problem with the subversive elements within Fleet," Rosin suggested.

"You mean *our* problem."

The senator spread his hands in apparent surrender. "Of course. You know as well as I do that universal conscription is the problem. I know you haven't officially taken a position on the issue, but a statement from you would carry great weight in the public debate. People like your unpretentious and matter-of-fact manner, aversion to any pomp and waste."

"Stop buttering me up, Senator. What exactly do you want?"

"I'm serious about this. *Conscription is the problem.* Everyone *must* join the military unless they are tied to certain jobs in the military industry. At least two years. Detailed screening of possible pacifists who might become radicalized is virtually impossible. We have to find our way back to a professional military to prevent that."

"That may be true, but it doesn't solve our problem: we have too few soldiers. We're bleeding more than we have IVs." Von Solheim saw by the senator's expression that he would not let up, but his time was limited and his appetite for the conversation had long since run out, if it had ever existed. "Our offensive will change that; you can tell your faction. Soon this war will be over and then it will be the job of politicians like you to reorder the Terran Federation. But in order for you to be able to do that at all, me and my soldiers have to make sure it *can* happen. The only way to do that is through a final victory, and that is now within our grasp."

"I hope your optimism turns out to be the analytical skill you are said to have."

14

"Where is he?" Valeska asked, irritated, and wheeled to Franc to tell him to stop tapping his foot all the time. But in the middle of the turn, she noticed that it was she herself who kept bumping her bare big toe against the magnetic stopper of the habitat entrance.

Her husband shook his head and gave her a meaningful look. Before she uttered an indignant retort, her eyes wandered to Ute, Oliver, and Powell, who were standing around the stretched silicon box in which Oxana's frozen corpse lay.

Not very reverent, she thought, and sighed guiltily. After informing the West Bank Habitat radio operator on duty of the incident, a certain weight had fallen from her shoulders. After all, the police of a Core World and most of the outlying worlds would have launched investigations by default. In a fairly clear-cut case of food poisoning, the sharpest detectives might not be called into action, but a clear investigative process had to be followed, at least for the insurance companies. Here, on the other hand, the radio operator was much more interested in her request for a replacement. Not in why they didn't abort, or at least interrupt the mission, but instead suggesting "the best man for the job," who also happened to be ready to go at a moment's notice. She had wanted to cancel because his exuberance had sounded so strange, but then it had finally come to what she had been thinking: He wanted money for his placement. Since he was the radio operator and thus quite influential in the West Bank jurisdiction, she had agreed and sent him a paltry sum in Lagunia shillings—at least, the sum was paltry considering her new wealth.

"He'll come around," Franc muttered, looking over his shoulder at the three grieving expedition members. "I think they resent us just moving on."

"Maybe," she agreed and sighed again. She tried to untangle the knots in her shoulder muscles that had formed from the tension. "But they've decided to stay, and that means we have to move on. It's either this or it's not. Now that they've made up their minds, we're going to go through with it. Franc, there may be a hyperspace gate down there that wasn't built by us, but by aliens a few decades ago."

"Don't you think the Clicks would have grabbed the technology back then instead of just destroying it?"

"Who knows?" She considered and finally grunted in frustration. "Yeah, maybe. It doesn't make sense, but it looks like a hyperspace gate, and that's reason enough to analyze it in more detail. At least material samples to determine age and molecular composition. Don't tell me you're not curious yourself."

"Yes, I am, yes. But I don't want us to put one in front of the other."

"We'll do our best." A bright triad sounded from the speakers.

"Approach message," said a pleasant computer voice.

"That must be him!" Valeska almost cheered. The last twenty-four hours had been tense and silent. Far too quiet. Her relief that work could soon start again was almost boundless. She didn't want to wrack her brain anymore about how and why Oxana had died and whether they could have done anything. What had happened had happened, and there were more exciting research subjects waiting for her and Franc below the water than she had ever hoped for. Did that sound selfish?

She unlocked the door and pulled her foot back, so the hardened silicon hit the stopper and was instantly anchored. Immediately, drops of salty water hit her in the face, hard enough that it hurt a little. The latent smell of seaweed typical of Lagunia filled the habitat, but she paid it no mind, and shielded her eyes from the lights of the helicopter whose rotors whipped up the water in front of the jetty. Like a UFO, it hovered above the spray, approaching sideways until a dark something landed at her feet—a duffel bag—followed by a figure leaping deftly onto the swaying deck. Before she had time to even recognize her new boatman, the helicopter steered away and flew off into the windy night.

Valeska wiped the salt water from her face and blinked. In front of her stood a medium-sized man with short dark hair and even darker eyes. At first, they seemed to her somehow too deep and veiled at the same time, but it was only a brief impression, because his broad smile was winning and open.

"There you are! I am Valeska Bellinger, and this is my husband Franc Bellinger. I'm glad you could come so quickly!" she called over the dying noise of the helicopter and held out her hand. The boatman had sunk his right hand into his jacket pocket and was moving before he abruptly stopped and looked over her shoulder, presumably at Ute, Oliver, and Powell, from whom no more murmurs could be heard. She followed his gaze and saw the three of them looking at them with somber expressions.

"You're very welcome, Missus and Mister Bellinger." The new captain pulled his hand out of his pocket and shook hers, then Franc's. "My name is Sirion."

"Very good, very good. Your resume has already been sent to us by the radio operator at West Bank Habitat. It all looks very good," she replied, waving him inside so she could close the door again and shut out the unpleasant weather. Through the fine membranes of the lattice floor, the water that had washed in slowly drained.

"That's Ute, Oliver, and Powell there," Franc said, pointing to Oxana's crew, who limited themselves to simple nods and somber looks. "They were part of Ms. Reuel's crew and kindly agreed to stay on for the next few weeks despite the tragic circumstances."

"I understand," Sirion said, pursing his lips. Turning toward the three, he added, "I'm very sorry. This must not be easy for you."

An uncomfortable silence spread, which Valeska quickly tried to dispel.

"You seem to have been very busy the last few years. Would you mind if we tackle the first dive right away? You're familiar with the Triton, aren't you?"

"Of course, ma'am." Sirion nodded, sounding a little piqued. "And I'll be happy to take you and your husband down if you'd like to get going now. You've already sent me the data on the shaft."

He seemed almost *happy* and in no way indignant about the immediate deployment.

Valeska smiled broadly. "Wonderful! I've already brought in everything you'll need; we can leave right away. We'll show you your bunk later!"

She started moving and paused by the door when she noticed the boatman wasn't following her. "Are you coming?"

"What about your husband?" He looked at Franc. "Aren't you going to accompany us?"

"No, I'm staying up here. We've sunk a couple of signal barks and we want to see if Valeska can send up data in real time so we can speed up the analyses. The Triton's onboard computer doesn't have enough processing power to analyze the molecular scans."

"Ah, I see."

"Is that a problem?" Valeska asked, frowning.

"Oh, no, no problem!" Sirion set his bag down and shrugged. "It'll probably be less crowded, then."

"Yeah, right." She nodded impatiently and opened the door again.

Climbing into her seat on the submarine, she quickly pulled the console toward her and began testing the various software, the sensors, and manipulator arms that extended from a thick bundle under the hull, twisting and stretching as if they had been hibernating.

She was startled when Sirion came down the ladder and closed the hatch behind him, shutting out the spray and much of the noise of the sea. It became abruptly silent. She hadn't even said goodbye to Franc. For a moment, internal images appeared in her head of her twitching in her seat, foam pouring from her mouth.

It was an accident. She was sick. It won't happen again, she thought, and briefly closed her eyes while their new captain dropped into Oxana's former seat and looked at the controls and gauges.

"You didn't cheat on your resume, did you? You do know this model?" she asked pointedly, without looking up from her screen.

"Yes," he assured her, not turning around. Instead, he pressed a few buttons and two toggle switches before familiarizing himself with the touch displays. "This model has undergone some changes I'm not familiar with yet, but that's normal. Every captain adapts his Triton to his needs. The model was an out-of-the-box hit over a hundred years ago for underwater exploration on subcrustal oceans like Enceladus and Ganymede in the Sol System. Since then, it has been found in every Core system and some promising marginal worlds. Not because it was outstanding new technology, but because it was older and simpler. It is extremely robust and reliable, with a modular design that allows rapid adaptation to different environments and preferences. Not every moon is the same."

"Of course not. Different gravity, different composition of the medium..." Valeska waved it off and nodded with satisfaction as her systems gave the green light, completing the test run. *Don't talk so much! You're nervous, but there's no reason. He's shutting you down and you're doing your job!*

For the next thirty minutes, that's exactly what happened: Sirion piloted the small craft unerringly enough that she didn't notice any difference from Oxana and exhibited no visible nervousness as they descended into the dark shaft and quickly gained much depth. The subterranean ocean below did not elicit any response from it either, and so she grew calmer and calmer, finally losing herself in the scans of the large half-destroyed ring after launching the five sentinel spy drones she and Franc had retrofitted.

"Is that a—" Sirion continued.

"Maybe," she interrupted gruffly, "but we need to do more research to know for sure."

She eyed the image the drones were piecing together and saw a half-submerged ring structure, the bottom 20 percent of which had disappeared into the ocean floor. Part of the right arm was leaning against a large chalk-white mountain that was vaguely pyramid shaped. Where the ring should have been closed at its uppermost point was missing, so it looked more like an inverted hoop. But that was not what intrigued her most, after all, a salty ocean was merciless when it came to corrosion, decomposition and change in surface structure had been to be expected.

What she had not expected were the deep scars and craters that stretched across the gray material like the growth of an alien organism. She recognized kinds of marks from the many images and films of space battles between Fleet and the Clicks, when dozens and hundreds of destroyed starships slid through the vacuum and the cleanup began. In the headlights of the salvage ships, the hulls always looked the same. Holes from railgun shells, scratches from smaller close hits, long cuts where lasers had merely grazed the armor, and the characteristic craters from torpedo and missile impacts.

"Are you okay?"

"What?" she muttered absently.

"Is everything okay with you?"

"Y-yes, why?"

"You sounded like you'd seen a ghost," Sirion said, steering them toward the ring to where they had taken scans of the large debris field on their last visit.

"Maybe I have. Please fly to the right arm of the ring as seen from us."

"Roger that." He pulled the control stick to the right and the sub's headlights slid to the side until they landed on the eerie gray structure in the center. "What distance do you need?"

"Head for one of the craters." She pulled herself free of her straps and came to his side. She had forgotten the images of Oxana twitching where he now sat. Staring at the ring section as if transfixed, she reached out a hand to point to a dark, rosette-like area. "That one's big enough. Two meters is enough."

"Okay."

Gently and deftly, they slid forward until she was satisfied, jumped back to her seat, and extended the manipulators. The tiny knives and suction pipettes looked like thin threads in front of the impact crater, which measured at least ten meters across, illustrating once again how huge the ring structure was.

"It's a hyperspace gate, isn't it," Sirion said. "How does that get down here?"

"We don't know," she replied absently. "But we're here to find out."

He said something else, but she had stopped listening and instead carefully controlled the finely calibrated tools on the telescope arms. It was no easy task, requiring every ounce of dexterity if one didn't want to leave it to the computer, as any sensible person would. With tiny movements, she scraped off pieces of the blackened material, and a suction device automatically pulled it into the boat via a transparent tube. Various scanners and feelers slid across the surface like intrusive visitors, sending a huge stream of data to the computer, which she could only manage by sending most of it straight to Franc on the surface.

"The line is quite busy," Sirion remarked.

"Yes." *My God, why does he talk so much?*

"I would need to send out some smaller data packets, can I do that through the main connection?"

"What, why? No, I need it for the measurement data. I'm already handicapped! Why even bother?"

"I need to request an update to the control software. We're using too much oxygen, which is probably due to the extractor glands sucking water in the direction of travel and then sending it to the ventricular chambers on the right and left where—"

"Okay, okay, just put it on there, too, if it's really that small. Just make sure we stay in position until it's all done. After that, we'll take care of some of those cuts," Valeska said.

"Thank you."

After a long time, during which only the beeps of the systems and the hisses of the screws could be heard through the hull like an unsteady drone, they changed their position to look at one of the cuts. It was several dozen centimeters deep and ended in a baggy little crater. Apparently, the laser had hit a pipe and caused an explosion.

"I hope our targets won't look like this tomorrow," Sirion remarked.

"Excuse me?"

"The offensive tomorrow that the news feeds are full of. It relies completely on our strategic advantage of traveling through the hyperspace gates, which will all be turned on at the same time. We could have used the first one we had to give them no time, but instead we're putting all our eggs in one basket. I don't know if that's so wise."

"Fleet knows what it's doing."

"I'm sure." He nodded, unseeing. "I was just thinking, what if someone has tried this before?"

"I need to focus now, please."

"Of course."

Valeska turned back to the data streams, trying to figure out as much as she could on her own, though of course most of the work would be done by the quantum computers in the habitat. The residue on the ring surface was more than ninety and less than one hundred and twenty years old, if the onboard computer was not mistaken, which should not happen in a simple iridium survey. The fringes of the crater, where the hot plasma had burned tiny fissures into the maltreated material, looked like the complex grain of a tree and testified to the impact of a warhead torpedo. The center, with its thin indentation and basic conical shape, however, looked more like a kinetic missile *without* a warhead. Odd, but not mysterious. A secondary effect, perhaps, or two different impacts in the same place—she had seen greater coincidences.

It took them a little over four hours to examine and catalog a total of forty-seven instances of violence and destruction on the object and send the corresponding data up to Franc in the habitat. They were far from finished with the survey, but oxygen was running low and Sirion could not be persuaded to test the tolerance range of the life support system, at which point Valeska finally relented with a snort. The findings were fascinating. Although she knew, of course, like any other choice Lagunian, that the locals had been wiped out by a war with the Clicks, the greatest concentration of debris testifying to the battle or battles was in orbit. A few wrecks had sunk into the ocean, but most of them had burned up so badly during atmospheric entry that the materials had melted, or their shape had been deformed beyond recognition. This one was the largest relic of the Lagoon's lying within the atmosphere—by far. Not only that, but it had retained its basic shape, making it identifiable in principle, even if they still had to identify the residue of antimatter to say it was really a hyperspace gate. But she'd be damned if this wasn't a destroyed portal. Except, how had it survived the fall from orbit? And why had it been erected there in the first place? There was no natural jump point here that it could have used.

"Can't we go any faster?" she asked, tapping her armrests impatiently as she stared at the depth gauge display. Outside the cockpit window, the ever-same structure of the shaft slid past them.

"Sorry," Sirion replied. "The expansion tanks can't handle any more. This thing isn't exactly cutting-edge technology."

"You've said that before."

"Is your husband even awake?"

"Why?"

"It's five in the morning."

"Oh, yeah, he always worries and waits until I get back. He can't sleep anyway unless I'm lying next to him. After so many decades of marriage, I guess that's one of the unfortunate side effects of not having multiple partnerships," she explained, yawning loudly so that her jaw cracked.

"And the crew? What's their job this late at night anyway?"

"They've been asleep for a long time. They take every second we're not looking to lie down. 'It's a sailor thing,' they said." Valeska snorted. "But they're doing their jobs and taking care of the habitat, and that's all they have to do so we can focus on our job."

"I see." There was a tone in his voice that she didn't know how to interpret. He was probably just as tired as she was.

15

"Forty-four launch bays," boasted the *Caesar*'s COB, who introduced himself simply as Chief Jaloo. The lanky man, who was half a head shorter than Nicholas, was pointing to the tubes lined up along the gray composite wall. They reminded him of the *Oberon*'s torpedo bays, though they were slightly smaller. "When the Predators get catapulted out of there, there won't be a dry eye in the house."

"Mmm," Nicholas uttered, nodding impassively. He wished his father had not retired with the admiral, sparing him this "tour." But it was his duty to play the game, and so he listened patiently to the COB's smug explanations, asked a polite question here and there, and practiced composure. He would much rather have talked to Jason, whom he had not seen since he had left for Fleet Academy and missed very much. But apparently Augustus had taken it as a sign of courtesy to use Captain Konrad's eldest son as a tour guide for his XO, or as a hint of something he couldn't figure out. His father often told him how complex and intriguing things were in Fleet, which had been one of the reasons why he had decided against following his big brother. He liked the straightforward nature of his people and accepted that their culture and behavior could only be preserved so well because they stood apart, far from the hullabaloo of real fleet life.

"You still have the old hunters," the COB continued. "Perches, right?"

"Barracudas," Nicholas corrected the sergeant, not responding to the obvious provocation.

"Ah, yes. I'd almost forgotten."

"You served in the Barracuda days yourself, didn't you?"

"I was stationed on a cruiser, not a carrier."

"I see." The discussion was going nowhere anyway, even if he had pointed out to the man that twenty years ago there had been no maneuvers or battles without whole squadrons of Barracudas. As long as the guy got something out of taunting an officer and getting away with it, it was fine with him. Vanity never interested him much.

"The Predators' acceleration levels would crush any human pilot," Jaloo continued, waving him along. Together, they continued walking through the narrow, elongated room, which seemed almost eerily deserted. He was used to always being among people; after all, one was never alone on the *Oberon*, not even in the toilets.

"Next, I'll show you the gun batteries. The *Caesar* has the latest generation of Hyatt railguns on the D33 mounts. This allows them to pivot one hundred and eighty degrees, allowing for wide firing angles without the ship having to maneuver extensively to bring new targets under fire."

"I see."

The bulkhead before them automatically slid aside, and they stepped into a short corridor.

"You're probably wondering how we maintain the mounts, after all, there's a reason they only put in pivoting joints and not full mounts back in the days of Titans like the *Oberon*."

With robots, Nicholas thought, but said nothing.

"With robots. The little things are extremely efficient and

can operate on the hull and perform repairs or maintenance, even during a battle. And before you ask, because of the wireless ban inside the ship, we communicate with the bots via complex light signals. We're not allowed to radio you, but unlike the older models, we don't just program them with their mission. Instead, we have high-powered diodes distributed along the hull that allow us to change their programming on the fly." The COB paused and leaned over as if to share a secret. "You've already changed over, too, haven't you?"

"No," Nicholas replied. "In our case, the Corps of Engineers is tasked with doing the maintenance."

"Oh, I see. I really didn't know."

"No problem."

"And is there no resentment among the crew?"

"Why would there be resentment?"

"Because working in a vacuum is dangerous. Besides, I heard that all the ships of the reserve units were equipped with maintenance bots two years ago," Jaloo said with apparent interest, but his eyes sparkled belligerently. Nicholas considered ordering the NCO to spend the rest of the tour in silence, which he might have done, but he didn't want to make a scene, even if it was a minor one. His father had demanded they not make waves, so he would comply.

"My father's view is that robots are a weak link."

"Why is that? They operate independently and are thus not vulnerable to jamming technology. Is it okay, then, to still risk the lives of sailors?"

"Robots are not people. Only programmers can control and change them, and my father doesn't like that because it takes them out of our control." Nicholas added before the COB could say anything, "And I agree with him. So does the team."

"I understand. I didn't mean to offend you."

Yes, you did.

"Of course."

"Let me show you some of these little things. Maybe that will change your reluctance?"

"I doubt it. But go ahead with your tour." Nicholas emphasized the last word slightly, but the COB seemed either not to notice, or decided not to respond.

Behind the next bulkhead, they entered a two-story room with fixed heavy-duty shelves in which strange yellow shapes were magnetically attached. He barely made out any right angles, only curves, and not even hoses, but they had to be folded robots—dozens of them. In one corner of the room, a technician in an orange jumpsuit was kneeling in front of an open maintenance hatch. A cable protruded from his finger and disappeared somewhere behind the wall.

"This is our storage bay for the bots," Jaloo explained, waving at the technician, who didn't seem to notice him. "Ah, he's probably jacked in. Probably fixing one of the diodes right now."

Nicholas had to restrain himself from shuddering when he heard the words "jacked in." The idea that the engineers on the new ships were connecting to the systems via a direct interface through a data jack made him extremely uncomfortable.

"Are you all right?" the COB asked.

"Yes. I was just wondering what would happen if one of the systems shorted out while this man was directly connected to it."

Jaloo waved a hand. "The risks are minimal. Really minimal. The security measures are enormous."

"I think it's too dangerous. I'd rather take a little more time and do it manually than end up in the infirmary with a burned-out brain."

"We're not in combat. That's where the little yellow helpers come in."

"It's not right," Nicholas insisted before admonishing

himself and pointing to the bots on the shelves. "Magnetic load restraint. What happens if the reactor fails?"

"Emergency power from the batteries. But the walls are extra secure. The worst that could happen would be the destruction of all the robots, but the problem—for example, as a result of a fire—would not escape from this room."

"I see. What is the unemployment rate in the Core Worlds?"

The COB blinked in confusion. "Excuse me?"

"You heard me."

"I don't know. Something around two or three percent?"

"And how high is it on the rim worlds?"

"Higher."

Nicholas nodded. "Significantly higher. For every robot my father would use, he would have to lay off a crew member or more. My people no longer have a home, but they have a strong leader who will not abandon them. They have a job that matters. For the ship and for them."

"I know where you're going with this. Very noble, speaking of crew, how does your old man still manage to pay his people anyway? Lagunia isn't exactly rich, and as a reserve unit, the pay from the fleet isn't particularly high."

"Crews don't work for money."

"No salaries?"

"No."

"Not even you?"

"No."

"This really is noble. Like I said. Wow."

"I thought we were talking about robots." Nicholas didn't like the man's manner. Everything he said seemed to be different from what he thought—at least that was Nicholas's impression—and he didn't like it.

"Want to see one?" Jaloo asked, but he was already walking toward the closest shelf where, after a retinal scan, he pulled back on a control panel and waited for a buzz. One of the bots unfolded like a delicate work of art. The little yellow man—there was no other way he could describe him—rolled out of his compartment and landed on two spherical feet before straightening up completely. Everything about him was round: the small torso with its many flaps, the four arms, each with three joints and many-fingered manipulator hands, and the head, which consisted practically only of sensors.

"Has little maneuvering jets everywhere, this little guy. On the ship, he rolls around on his legs or on all fours depending on the location. Out on the hull, his feet become hands and he just climbs over the jets." The COB looked conspiratorially over his shoulder as if they were being watched. "You want to see something funny?"

"Of course," Nicholas replied politely, though he would have preferred to just walk out.

"Okay, we gave these units a few extras with the algorithms they set up for us." Jaloo chuckled. The only thing missing was a companionable poke in the side. He would have expected the admiral's leadership team to be stiffer and more rule obsessed. A chief did not allow himself any "jokes" with the inventory of his ship.

"Doesn't that violate Fleet regulations?" Nicholas asked rhetorically.

Jaloo stiffened a little. Not so much that it would have been immediately noticeable, but Nicholas had developed a good sense about people over his years of service, which hardly anyone believed him to have—which was entirely to his liking.

"It's harmless. What would you do if you were on your way to the bathroom and it was very urgent and one of the bots cut you off?" The COB winked.

"I would take a step back so he could get through."

Jaloo sighed. "All right. Others might kick at the bot. 'Out of the way, trash can.'" He laughed but stopped when he saw Nicholas' serious face. "Why don't you try it?"

"No, thank you."

"Oh, come on. It's just a little fun. We spent almost an hour coming up with the right heuristics."

"I said no, Master Chief Petty Officer," Nicholas repeated more sharply than intended.

"All right, all right." With a delay bordering on disrespect, the COB added a "sir."

This guy was hard to take and tested even his patience, yet he had always prided himself on his self-control.

"I'd like to go back to the mess hall," he suggested neutrally.

"Of course." Jaloo hesitated. "Can I ask you a more personal question, sir?"

He has recovered his manners, Nicholas thought, tensing and nodding. Relenting behavior was to be rewarded.

"Your brother is really a good officer."

"Thank you. But that's not a question."

"Yeah, I mean, you're younger than him and you have less service time, right?"

"That's correct. What are you getting at?"

"Your brother is below you in rank. Do you think things are stricter at the Academy in Sol?"

"You actually want to know if I was favored by my father to be commander of the *Oberon*, I suppose?" Nicholas was not surprised. He'd had to deal with these questions for a long time, except that hardly anyone asked them out loud and he almost respected the *Caesar*'s COB for having the guts to do so and not whisper behind closed doors.

"Well, there's a lot of talk, if I may speak frankly."

"You're already doing that. I perform my service as comprehensively and to the best of my ability, as I hope any other officer on the *Oberon* does. My evaluations were largely based on those of the senior officers, not my father. On our ship, it's performance that counts, not favoritism from above." Nicholas couldn't help but feel a little ashamed of the little dig. It was usually beneath him, and he did not want to repeat it. Not wanting to give this point any further attention, he added, "So you can assume it's a number of factors. Good performance, different superiors who were responsible for the promotion, different requirements, and, I readily admit, certainly less competition for the post in question. I realize that the *Oberon* cannot be compared to Fleet Academy when it comes to training new leaders."

I wonder if Jason asked him to ask me about it, he mused, glad to have answered in sufficient detail. He probably did it for his brother.

"Why didn't you leave?"

"Excuse me?"

"Your brother left Lagunia and the *Oberon*, but you didn't." Seeing Nicholas's narrowed eyes, he made a dismissive gesture. "I'm sure you can imagine that people are running their mouths about this. After all, your father is one of the... most famous commanders in Fleet. I just wanted to take the chance to get the truth from you, so I don't have to listen to the constant chatter. None of us really know what happened, after all. So, it's better to stick to the truth, and where are you more likely to get that than from the people involved?"

"Have you talked to my brother about this?"

"No, why?"

"Because you share the ship with him." Nicholas stuck his chin out. "Thanks for asking, Chief, but I think it's a family matter that's none of your business."

He felt a knot in his stomach that was about to burst. It had been a long time since he had felt it so intensely. It was time to leave this situation.

"I'd like to go back now."

"Is it because of your mother?"

Nicholas froze.

"We're leaving. Now." His voice was low and dangerous and vibrated like a battered tuning fork.

"Oh, I didn't mean to offend you, sir." The COB sounded

concerned, but there was a hint of scorn and triumph in his eyes.

"You're not, and now—"

"I just thought that maybe it wasn't true, that *you* were the reason your mother—"

The knot in his stomach burst and Nicholas was just able to scrape together his last shred of self-control to keep from knocking the chief down. Instead, his brain quickly shifted, and he translated his erupting rage into a violent kick at the robot standing motionless next to them.

"Angry comment. You pushed my buttons," the bot squealed as it was thrown backward by the force of the kick. There was a low hum, and the stored robots in the heavy-duty rack began to sway and shift slightly.

"Oh!" The COB was wide-eyed, but something in his voice was *wrong*.

Nicholas's anger went up in smoke when he realized with quick glances that the shelf was not sealed, and the bots' magnetic restraints failed. Half a dozen tumbled out of the compartment and crashed to the floor with a deafening *clang!* One of them appeared to short circuit and began to crackle. Electrical discharges ran across its spherical yellow hull and a tiny bolt of electricity discharged and struck the wall.

The technician, still linked, began to twitch as if he were having an epileptic seizure.

"Oh, damn!" exclaimed the COB, but Nicholas had already jumped past him and roughly shoved the chief aside. With one hand on the technician's collar and the other grabbing the back of his coveralls, he jerked the man away from the open wall panel. The cable tore from his finger and wriggled in the air.

Nicholas didn't wait and turned the sailor on his side, wiping the foam from his mouth and clearing his airway.

"Ejection shock!" Jaloo shouted, running to the communicator button next to the door. "This is the chief! Medics to the port maintenance room! What did you do, man?"

"He's breathing," Nicholas noted after putting an ear to the convulsing technician's mouth. "His pulse is still racing, but he's breathing on his own. How long until the paramedics get here?"

"Two minutes, maximum. Damn it, you have—"

"Put out the fire! Now!" The fire wasn't spreading, it was more of a smolder and sizzle inside the bot's hull, but he didn't have the stomach to deal with the guy while there was an emergency to manage. With the man's head resting on his knees, he lifted the technician's eyelids and checked the pupils. They raced right and left like panicked animals. "You're suffering from ejection shock. The paramedics are on their way. Try to breathe calmly and focus on me!"

A moment later, a door opened behind him, and two paramedics dressed in red rushed in. One set a small suitcase next to the injured man, the other shooed Nicholas aside.

"There was a short that may have transferred to some conductor in the wall that this man was directly linked to," he explained calmly. "I cleared his airway and stabilized his position so nothing would settle into his trachea. His pupils are dilated and reacting to light."

"Thank you," said the paramedic, recognizable as a doctor by the white-bordered red cross. She didn't look at him and spoke quickly to her colleague, who artfully reached into the case and applied some medical equipment to the patient's neck. "We'll take it from here. Please step back, sir."

Nicholas nodded, rose, and followed the request. His duty was done, now it was the paramedics' turn. Jaloo had extinguished the smoldering fire and was standing among the damaged bots. When their eyes met, he saw something in the COB's eyes that didn't belong there: composure and triumph. He didn't understand how that was possible, after all, a crew member was injured, but something was going on that he didn't understand.

"You provoked me," Nicholas stated calmly without breaking eye contact. "Why?"

"I was just asking questions." Jaloo shrugged and smiled innocently.

"I will report your disorderly conduct to your supervisor and ensure that you are subject to disciplinary action—"

"Take a look around, *sir*," the chief interrupted him, "when you get your head out of this, feel free to try to have me prosecuted for asking the wrong questions. But I suggest you come up with a good reason to give the admiral for damaging six maintenance bots and transferring a technician from his flagship to sickbay."

Nicholas straightened his shoulders and stretched his back.

TFS BRAXIS, HARBINGEN SYSTEM

"Crocker must have fucked up," Tony said confidently as they shuffled down the corridor toward the airlock.

Madalena shrugged and gripped her tool bag a little tighter. "I don't care."

"No?" Tony snorted. "The captain is just about the clumsiest officer in Fleet when it comes to the floor of the sky party. She stepped on someone's toes, I'll bet. And you know what?" The technician gave her a sideways glance and raised his eyelids.

She sighed. "I guess you're about to tell me."

"I don't care!" he chortled. "Because of you, I've been pulling double shifts for two weeks, and now I've got to hang around the old *Braxis* for four weeks fixing nitrogen lines when I'm not being abused as a plumber and cleaning the toilet bowls of our comrades' poop."

"There are worse things, Tony."

"Do you always have to be so melancholy?"

Madalena stopped and turned to face him. When he noticed he did likewise. Two sergeants passed them, talking in hushed tones. She waited until they were gone and considered pressing a finger to Tony's chest but thought it too theatrical. There was nothing theatrical about this.

"My oldest brother was killed here twenty years ago."

"He was a Harbinger? I didn't know that."

"No, he wasn't a Harbinger, but he was a lieutenant at the local academy. Fleet sponsored an exchange program between Dunkelheim and Harbingen back in the day. Our two worlds have always been close, culturally, not least because of the common language." Madalena couldn't remember the last time she'd spoken so much at one time, and judging by his expression, the same was true of Tony. "He was probably cooked before Kor's rubble hit."

"I'm sorry, I didn't know..."

"My older sister didn't make it into Fleet and was sent to Jarl to join the infantry, where she was drafted to join the assault forces of the Darelam offensive. She died from defensive fire from the Clicks, blown to bits by some kind of mortar shell or something—it sounded nicer in her commanding officer's letter of condolence than it probably was. A form letter. I couldn't even blame him. My parents both died at first contact, they were exploration officers, prospectors to be exact."

"Man," Tony muttered and signed, "this is hard stuff. I'm really sorry."

Madalena shrugged and looked down the corridor to the recess in the wall, where it went to the dorsal airlock. The tool bag in her right hand was heavy enough to make her shoulder tense.

"I can't help it."

"Don't you have a family anymore?"

"Yes, I do," she said, and her gaze went blank. "A little sister. Her name is Ulyana, she has red hair and the happiest laugh in the world."

Her face wanted to smile at the thought of Ulyana, but her heart would not allow it. Instead, she only saw what would happen to her in ten years, when she reached conscription age, and her innocence would end. She saw the car of the recruiting authority in front of their house in Omsk, all she had left of her parents. The two dapper men or women in their uniforms, meant to give a heroic impression.

"Madalena?" Tony asked, snapping her out of her musings. "Are you okay?"

"Yes. I just don't want—Oh." She waved it away with her left. "Let's not do that. If all goes well, I'm worrying for no reason."

"You should never worry, my grandma used to say," said her crewmate, trying to cover his uncertainty with feigned optimism. "If you can change something about the situation, then you don't need to worry. If you can't change anything about it, then you don't need to. It's as simple as that."

"I wish it was actually that easy." She gestured down the corridor. "We dock at the *Gibraltar* in less than an hour. If we haven't fixed the airlock's climate control by then, the captain will skin us alive."

"That sounds just like her." Together they walked on in their stained orange coveralls, accompanied by the hum of the engines that were ubiquitous in any warship. For many of them, there was something reassuring about it; Madalena thought it was merely habituation. "Why this stunt in the first place? Is Captain Akiyama trying to put on a formal ceremony? It's not like this isn't the last siding for disagreeable officers and their command."

"I don't know. Supposedly they found something here and want to start a joint operation."

Tony grabbed her by the shoulder, forcing her to stop. "What? Where did you get that?"

"Crew radio halt."

"That means it won't be boring, will it?" He grinned from ear to ear. Madalena didn't and shrugged again. "Man, you wouldn't even be excited about participating in Iron Hammer, would you?"

"No. Now let's work on the airlock." She shook her tool bag and her entire arm burned with the exertion. She would have preferred to just drop it, but instead she didn't let on.

"Captain," Crocker said, greeting her colleague Akiyama an hour later in the middle of the short airlock that connected TFS *Gibraltar* and TFS *Braxis* like two skyscrapers tilted on their sides in high orbit around Kor—or rather what was left of the former moon. They were alone, except for their aides, which was probably due to habit.

"Captain." Toyohiro Akiyama said, bowing, as was customary in his culture.

"Very traditional," Crocker said, nodding half in appreciation, half in amusement. "Our ships are identical in design; I probably would have found the briefing room next to your cabin the same way."

"I know, but what are we without traditions?"

"Why am I here? Not that I mind a little change, but I would have expected you to want to get out of here as soon as possible?"

"We've spotted something," he replied, pointing toward his end of the airlock. "If you'd like to follow me?"

"Of course. What have you discovered?" Crocker asked as they walked toward his ship.

"Maybe nothing, maybe everything. But unless I'm mistaken, we need to alert Fleet immediately."

"What? Then why didn't you do it in the first place? And what was it supposed to be anyway?"

"We have to make absolutely sure. If it's a false alarm, we won't be stuck here for just a few weeks, we'll be stuck here for *years*. Especially this close to Operation Iron Hammer."

"Us? Or you?"

"Believe me, it doesn't matter," Akiyama said just as they reached the *Gibraltar*'s passage.

"Now I'm curious," Crocker said.

At that moment, a short circuit in the automatic climate control system triggered a smoldering fire in a switching relay. That cut power to a cylinder the size of a man's forearm that had been sitting between two wiring harnesses for an hour behind a maintenance hatch for shipboard technicians. The small antimatter containment chamber lost its magnetic field and half a gram of antimatter trapped in the field reacted with the cylinder's matter in an unmeasurable amount of time. Both masses annihilated each other and destroyed everything around them.

The interconnected destroyers were torn to pieces before the crews could comprehend what was happening. A short-lived white flash made the cosmos glow, then there were only ultra-charged particles doing a diabolical dance, boiling in the vacuum before it cooled again among the newly created debris.

16

"Scotch, huh?" Konrad asked, raising the bulbous glass of amber liquid to his eyes. "I know it's sinfully expensive. Just like this ship."

Augustus eyed him over the rim of his own glass and leaned back on the sofa. The two of them were only separated by a meter or two, and yet a whole cosmos seemed to lie between them, in which Konrad found a great emptiness. The admiral came from the ancient nobility of Terra, closely intertwined with naval traditions for dozens of generations, first during the time of the Venetian Republic, which had been a major naval power for about a thousand years starting in the 7th century AD, then in the service of Italy and the EU, and finally of the United Nations and the Terran Federation that emerged from it and its colonies. The various arms of the House of Bretoni, actually *di Bretoni*, that were intertwined with the politics of the SCR could hardly be counted. Augustus's path to the top had certainly been marked out early on.

Konrad came from a family of vacuum engineers who had earned their money with hard field work at Harbingen's orbital shipyards. He had been the first and only one from the

Bradley ranks to join Fleet service, more out of rebellious rather than patriotic motives, and accordingly had not been able to rely on any helpful connections. Only much later did he realize that there was one glaring difference between Harbingen and his mother Earth and her political administration, the Solar Congressional Republic, that had finally made him Harbingen's ardent supporter after all: politics itself. Harbingen had been eyed suspiciously when it became the first Core World to hand over all the powers of the system and its cultural, social, and economic center to an AI, Omega.

A development of the colony's best programmers—before Omega's awakening still a rather inconsequential agricultural world—it had taken only a few decades to make Harbingen the technological leader of the Federation. The achievements in science, technology, and industry had quickly followed each other and prosperity, wellbeing, and satisfaction had quickly reached peak levels. That was probably why Harbinger, like him, had revered Omega while the rest of the Federation viewed it as a dangerous digital Trojan horse. Until the end.

"I see what you're implying, Captain." Augustus snapped him out of his thoughts, and Konrad sighed before lowering the glass, holding it in both hands, and looking his superior in the eye. "But there is no need for such teasing. Do I come from a wealthy family within the SCR? Yes, I do. Neither you nor I can deny or change our origins. Did my connections help me to make a career within Fleet? Of course. That's no secret, nor is it a crime, if I may say so. Nevertheless, I have earned this place, just as you have."

"I guess you did," Konrad replied neutrally, nodding.

"Scotch not to your taste?"

"I don't drink much. Especially not while I'm on duty."

"You see this as a service?"

"Isn't it?" he said.

"Maybe." Augustus seemed to consider and peered into

his glass before sipping it and placing it on the glass table in front of him. "I'll be honest with you, Captain. I think you're a good officer, with a past that resembles an impenetrable jungle. No one knows what exactly happened back then, not even yourself, if the reports are to be believed. If you ask me, it's no wonder, after all, you took your orders from an AI."

Konrad gritted his teeth.

"Your ship is old and doesn't fit in with Fleet's latest doctrine, but she's a proud mammoth of a starship, that's for sure." Augustus didn't seem to notice his reaction, which didn't surprise him.

"We agree on that."

"That's a fact. But the *Oberon* is still not the problem. It would certainly be possible to make one or two changes to the mission details to incorporate her into the battle plan."

Konrad swallowed and straightened a little. It looked as if the conversation would take a turn for the better after all, but he was far too experienced to be blinded by it.

"Now usually follows the *but*," he said, "and I think I know exactly what it sounds like."

"There are subtle reservations in Fleet management about reinstating her to active duty."

"I thought you were going to be honest with me?"

Augustus eyed him and smirked before nodding.

"They are not negotiable, Bradley. Not to Fleet management, not to the public."

"The public? Pah." Konrad waved it off. "When has the public ever won a battle? When has the public ever made a decision that brought the fortunes of war back to our side? When has the *public* ever had enough information to have any informed opinion at all?"

"Fleet is the sword and shield of humanity, Captain. Don't forget that. The *public* you are so angry about are the people we have sworn to defend," the admiral admonished him.

"They're more likely to be the taxpayers who help you get allocated such war-making resources as scotch whiskey," Konrad snapped.

"Careful, Captain," Augustus said in a low voice. "Do not mistake my courtesy for weakness."

"Courtesy? You come to our system to *do* us an *honor,* only to inform us that we are not allowed to participate in the most important operation ever undertaken by the Terran Fleet because I am a political risk. They joke about the *Oberon,* only to praise its fighting prowess in the next breath and then reveal to me that I am to be dismissed and my crew torn apart and divided up like damned plunder."

"Captain—"

"To add to the insult, you want to *honorably dismiss* me as if I was a vain peacock from Sol who cares about medals and fanfare. You always struck me as someone who acted wisely and prudently, I don't think you would hold the rank of vice admiral at your age if you didn't have excellent people skills and political savvy to fall back on. You knew exactly what to expect here with us, and you also knew that I would never agree to it because I don't care about ceremonial pomp. *Honorably discharge* a reserve officer? Surely there has never been such a thing, at least not with military honors. What was this supposed to be? The ultimate mockery of me and, by extension, my crew?"

"That's enough, Captain!" the younger man said in a stern voice, and Konrad reined himself in. His lips did not quiver, and in other respects he remained calm inside. The anger was there, held its place in his stomach, but it did not escape him, and everything he had said merely corresponded to what he was also thinking. At this point, it didn't matter how hard he tried to be politically astute. He had never been very good at that, and he wasn't going to beat someone like the admiral in his arena anyway. That he had tried confirmed, if anything, that he was annoyed with himself.

"I meant what I said," Augustus explained calmly. "I respect you enough not to throw you under the bus to Fleet leadership—and believe me, they wanted you out of the field once and for all. As long as the *Oberon* and its fleet exist in the hinterlands of Federation territory, the wound that the loss of Harbingen has inflicted on Federation flesh cannot heal. They realize that, and so do you."

Konrad remained silent.

"My concern was and is not to wield the axe, but to wield the quill and ink."

"You want me to go quietly so there's not a big fuss in public. And then you sell that internally within Fleet as your great achievement—a nice second stirrup for your next promotion if Operation Iron Hammer is successful. The problem virtually evaporates into the shadow of the big victory over the Clicks. An elegant solution, just the way you like it best."

"Now listen to me very carefully—"

"No, I don't think so," Konrad said in his piercing voice, and for a moment the admiral blinked, dumbfounded enough that he was at a loss for words. *That's the way a real commander talks, you vain peacock!* "I'm not a stirrup holder, and neither is my crew. Do you think the *Oberon* would allow itself to be cannibalized and dispersed among a fleet that, even in the face of the final blow against the enemy, has come here to play politics and carve out something for itself? We're Harbingers, in case you've forgotten." He tapped the lapel of his uniform, where Harbinger's motto was sewn in. *Juratis unitatis.* Committed to unity. "To you, those may only be words. To us out here, they mean everything."

He stood and set down his glass. As he did, some of the expensive scotch sloshed onto the tabletop.

"I think I know what the game is here. You had to come here because you're jumping into enemy territory from here, undetected by possible spies or the Clicks' long-range reconnaissance. It's your first mission as commander of an entire fleet, and all eyes are on you. You got the assignment and the deployment order because of your good connections, so now you have to deliver. You're nervous because you have only one chance to prove yourself. To fail would be to jeopardize the entirety of Operation Iron Hammer, and that would be the end of your career. More than that, but I guess that's all you care about. So, you set out to quickly and elegantly get rid of Kor's unloved traitor and get the most experienced people in his officer corps under your belt, so you'd have soldiers with real experience and foresight on board, instead of a bunch of lickspittles and yes-men."

"That's enough, Captain!" Augustus's well-controlled expression faltered and finally erupted, with flushed cheeks and trembling lips. "That's no way to behave toward a superior officer. I've reached out to you to get this over with in a well-meaning way, but if you don't give me a choice, so be it."

"What kind of choice? We never had one, or am I mistaken?" Konrad countered.

"This conversation is over. I hereby place—"

There was a beep at the door.

"What?" roared Augustus.

"Sir." It was the *Caesar*'s wiry XO with the mottled gray temples who came in and bowed. "Sorry to disturb you, but there's a delicate problem."

"What kind of incident is this?" Konrad asked trying to remain calm as he and Augustus followed the XO through the corridors.

"I'm not sure, sir, which is why I've instructed the Marines and officers present not to leave the scene," the commander replied without slowing his steps.

"Marines?"

"Yes, sir, there is a possible fatality. One of our technicians is on his way to sickbay and his condition is critical."

"And my son is supposed to have something to do with it?" Konrad asked, snorting. "That's out of the question."

"No, it's not."

"Excuse me?"

"We should first get an idea of the situation ourselves," Augustus suggested. He sounded calm, and a sideways glance revealed to Konrad that the admiral was probably not merely feigning calmness. What that meant remained to be seen, so he kept silent the rest of the way. After a few minutes—on the *Oberon* it would have been unthinkable to reach any place in that short a time—they reached the end of a corridor, on whose door was written as a hologram, Maintenance BB-01. It opened automatically as the XO approached and revealed two armed Marines with submachine guns held at the ready, the knobby COB of the *Caesar*, and his son Nicholas, looking serious with his hands clasped behind his back as if he had nothing to do with any of this. The background was a messy pile of yellow metal parts, half of which were covered in black soot.

"What's going on?" Augustus demanded, his voice imperious and precisely accented.

"Are you all right, son?" Konrad asked in Nicholas's direction, and he merely grimaced. So, he was in trouble. But why?

"Sir, the commander became very agitated and kicked one of the maintenance bots, which caused a chain reaction. As a result, Technician Louis suffered ejection shock," the COB replied stiffly, but his eyes sparkled.

"My question will be answered first by the officer present, Jaloo," the admiral reprimanded his senior NCO, turning his gaze to Nicholas. "So, Commander?"

"The chief petty officer was disrespectful to me, Admiral,"

Nicholas replied with his usual even manner of speech, which might strike those with less knowledge of human nature as stodgy. "However, that doesn't excuse me for getting carried away and kicking one of the maintenance bots. That is damage to Fleet property and can and should result in punishment at the commander's discretion under Article 18, Section 4b."

"I see," Augustus said, nodding thoughtfully as he looked at the half-empty shelf, behind which was a small pile of demolished robots. Konrad looked over his shoulder and Silly, Meyer, and the rest of the Marines were coming toward them.

"It's just fender bender, Commander," Augustus continued, waving it off. "I'm not going to punish a respected Fleet officer for letting his nerves get the best of him for once. I will, however, look at the sensor recordings and decide how disrespectful my chief's behavior was."

"Admiral, I..." the COB started, but shut his mouth at a gesture from his commander.

"Thank you, sir," Nicholas said, clearly relieved.

"However," the admiral raised a finger, "I heard that one of my technicians is in mortal danger. Is that correct, Chief?"

"Yes, sir, the damage to the bot caused other bots to fall off the shelves and damage a wall panel, which may have resulted in a short circuit that caused Technician Louis to eject. The medics have not yet been able to tell if he can be saved or if the brain damage is too severe." Konrad noticed a hostile gleam in the COB's eyes as he gave his son a sidelong glance.

"And why wasn't the shelf's load secured?" Konrad asked, pointing to the gray heavy-duty shelf. "It has a magnetic lock, doesn't it?"

"That is correct, Captain," the chief confirmed. "However, the power supply probably malfunctioned, or the power supply was interrupted due to Petty Officer Louis's repair work."

"A technician breaking the magnetic latch on a cargo rack

while doing repair work on a warship?" he asked incredulously, shaking his head. "Hardly."

The COB shrugged his shoulders. "Or a malfunction."

"This ship is brand new and supposedly the best that the Core World shipyards are currently churning out. How likely is it that such an important part of the ship would malfunction?"

"We don't know enough. But I do know that the commander was displeased when he found out about the connected crewman. He said something like, '*I was wondering what would happen if one of the systems shorted out while the man was hooked up to it.*' I don't want to imply anything, but—"

"You, shut up! One more thing, Admiral." Konrad looked around and nodded at Silly and Meyer, who arrived with their Marines. Only now did he notice that his son Jason was also with them. Seeing him in the *Caesar* uniform stung him every time. But that he was here at least explained why his two officers and the Marines had come. "If I may?"

Augustus nodded patronizingly.

"As unlikely as a malfunction is, why would it occur just when my son kicked one of those tin buckets? And I don't even want to know what your chief said to him to elicit a reaction out of him that I haven't seen since he was a young teenager."

"I don't know, but we'll find out, of course," the admiral replied. "It will take some time, though."

"Excuse me?"

"In accordance with Fleet regulations under Article 11, I am compelled to place Commander Nicholas Bradley under arrest until the incident is resolved and Petty Officer Louis's condition is determined."

"You can't be serious," Konrad snapped, his teeth grinding.

"Don't you think this is a situation to which Article 11 applies?" Augustus said, challenging him.

"I am of the opinion that my son was lured into a trap."

"I did what I did," Nicholas said. "And I'll take the consequences."

"Easy now, son."

"You'd better listen to him, *Captain*," the admiral hissed.

"Why? So, you can put him in the brig until you leave the system tomorrow? So, you can blackmail me with him? I knew you were shifty, but not *this* shifty!"

"Father, I—"

"No!" he interrupted his son, glaring at the *Caesar*'s commander.

"You should listen to him. This is my last act of kindness," Augustus growled.

"I'll dispense with your alleged *good nature*. The commander will come back to the *Oberon* with me, and he will come now."

"You are not in command here, and after this incident you never will be again." The admiral gestured to his two Marines, and they went to grab Nicholas.

Simultaneously, there was a rustle behind Konrad as the four Black Legion Marines from his honor guard drew their pistols and pointed them at the *Caesar* soldiers.

"Have you gone completely insane?" Augustus said, and for the first time there was something in his eyes that wasn't acted or rehearsed: horror. "Put down your weapons, now!"

None of the Harbinger Marines responded.

"We are leaving this ship, and my son is coming with me," Konrad insisted calmly.

"You want to mess with the entire crew of the *Caesar*? Have you gone completely insane?"

"For my son, I would. And for every single crew member who accompanied me here, too."

"This is insane!"

"No, Harbingen."

"Chief, get the Marines!" Augustus said to his COB, who gulped and slowly walked toward the door with his hands up.

"Bad idea," Meyer growled behind Konrad, and the little man stopped, looking back and forth between his commander and the colonel. "Sir?"

"We're leaving." Konrad kept his eyes on the admiral and beckoned for Nicholas to join him. "Come, Nicholas."

17

"You're not going anywhere!" Augustus hissed angrily, and his two Marines now raised their weapons in turn, but looked unsettled, glancing uneasily between their commander and the four Black Legionnaires who were bearing down on them.

"If you want to initiate a fight on your ship, go ahead," Konrad said calmly.

He wasn't in a good position, couldn't even threaten to shoot a hole in the hull, since his Marines' pistols were nowhere near powerful enough to puncture the ship's armor. It wouldn't be long before they were surrounded and outnumbered, and then they would no longer have an ace up their sleeve. But leaving his son behind as a pawn was altogether out of the question. "Or else you can accept a compromise: There are enough people in the Sol System who want to see me court-martialed. Now you have a valid reason that didn't exist before because I didn't violate any regulations. You let my companions go, my XO takes command of the *Oberon*, and Nicholas takes her post. The *Oberon* will take part in tomorrow's battle, and I will stay here."

"You want to play the hero and sacrifice yourself? Forget it!"

"Captain," Silly said from behind him, "with all due respect, you can forget it. We're not leaving this ship without you."

"The scumbags set up the commander," Meyer growled.

"You really plan every detail, don't you?" Konrad asked Augustus, snorting. "I should have known. What a disgusting game. But you made a mistake."

"*You're* making a mistake right now." The admiral's gaze encompassed them all. "I promise you that. Chief, go and put the COB and the chief engineer of the *Oberon* into the brig."

"Roger that, sir."

"Do you want me to shoot him?" Colonel Meyer asked.

"No," Konrad replied. "Because the admiral will let them both go with us to the shuttle."

Jaloo left, slowly at first, then ran through the door and he could hear him running down the corridor.

"Colonel? Door!"

A gunshot made everyone present cringe. Smoke came out of the door's control panel and the security bulkhead came down, locking them in.

"Disarm!" He pointed at the two rattled *Caesar* Marines. In the next moment each had a pistol in their face, while Meyer roughly snatched the weapons from their hands and handed them to Silly and Nicholas.

"I hope you have a good plan," Augustus said, who seemed to have regained his composure and again displayed an almost unbearable arrogance. "It's going to take more than four Marines and your colonel to threaten me on my ship."

"I'd take my chances."

"Too right," Meyer interjected.

"Besides, we still have the *Oberon*. Just one signal from us and you can deal with the full firepower of *my* ship."

"You really are a crazy old man, aren't you?" The admiral

shook his head. "First you let your entire home world go down without protection, and then you throw away the lives of nearly ten thousand sailors because you don't want to put your son through a criminal trial. Of all people, how can these people still follow you?"

"We never had a chance anyway, I understand that now. They came to finish us off and make political capital in the process, but I'd rather follow the exiles with my crew than throw them to Fleet leadership," Konrad said calmly.

"Even you wouldn't dare."

"You think?"

"Admiral," Jason spoke up for the first time, stepping up beside him, "is there no other solution? I know my brother and I can assure you that he would never willingly harm a member of Fleet. The COB's accusations are unfounded. At most, this was an accident."

"You are not in a position to view this situation neutrally and should recuse yourself," Augustus chided him. "The circumstance will soon be cleared up, and then it will be very uncomfortable for all of you. Because the way I see it, there are only empty threats here. The *Oberon* can't hear you, so put an end to this farce now."

Konrad chewed on his lower lip and thought. The admiral was right, of course. They were trapped in the *Caesar*'s belly, several decks away from their shuttle, which could easily be shot down if they made it off the ship at all. Of course, the *Oberon* would answer such a launch, he was sure, but that would leave them for dead. If only they could...

"The *Oberon* can't hear us, but it might be able to see us," Nicholas said abruptly.

"What did you say?"

"The injured technician I'll answer for was repairing a light-emitting diode—or its connection—that the *Caesar* can use to contact the maintenance bots on the hull. So, we could send a beacon to the *Oberon*."

"Like Morse code?" Silly asked, surprised.

"Yes."

Konrad studied Augustus's expression and found what he was looking for. Anger.

"That might work," he said. "Does anyone know how to operate a port with a data jack?"

He looked over his shoulder but, as expected, found only perplexed faces among his people.

"I'll do it," Jason said after a brief pause.

"Lieutenant Commander!" Augustus said harshly to Conrad's eldest son. "You won't. That's an order!"

"I'm sorry, sir, this thing is going to end badly, I realize that. I would court-martial my father too if I could, but my brother doesn't deserve that. If I don't, he too will be executed or, at best, shot by drop-pod onto a penal colony. I can't let that happen." Jason walked to the still-open panel and knelt in front of it.

"Last warning! Step back, Lieutenant Commander!" Augustus yelled. Sounds could be heard from behind the door, metallic scraping and banging, and soon after, a pure white flame appeared, slipping through the metal. "They're finished! All of them!"

"Thanks, kid," Konrad said toward Jason's back, but got no response. The Marines took off their uniform jackets and used them to gag the two *Caesar* prisoners, who they then used as cover to aim at the bulkhead, which was being cut open. "You know what you—"

"Yeah," his son growled and shoved a cable connector into the hole in his temple. "I hate what you've done to us, but I'm still a Harbinger."

"That's ridiculous! You're surely not relying on the hope that a bunch of blinking lights on our hull can explain the situation to the *Oberon*'s bridge crew?" Augustus snorted. "I will have you all executed! Once the mission begins tomorrow, field law will apply!"

"Shall I shut him up, Captain?" Meyer asked almost casually, prompting an indignant look from the admiral.

"No. I don't want to humiliate him; I want to keep you safe."

The bulkhead crashed to the floor with a *clang!* and a cloud of hot air slid toward them. On the other side of the opening knelt several of the *Caesar*'s Marines, more stood behind, and between the shoulders of the heavily armored figures was the triumphant figure of Chief Jaloo.

"That's it!" Augustus decided, and made an imperious gesture with his right hand. "I'll count to three. If you haven't surrendered by then, I'll have them open fire. One, two—"

A loud beep sounded and for a few breaths it was silent.

"Sir," a new voice said, and Konrad gulped. It was the XO of the *Caesar*. The kneeling Marines made way, and he saw the gray-faced commander standing at one of the communicator stations on the wall. He looked concerned. "The bridge reports that the *Oberon* has powered up its weapons systems and activated its targeting guidance."

"Powered up? What weapons?"

"All of them."

"How can that be?" Augustus asked, glaring first at Konrad, then at Jason, who was pulling the cable from his temple and standing with a somber expression. "What did you do?"

"I blinked three times briefly."

A snicker went through the Harbingers present and the admiral grew even angrier. "What is the meaning of this?"

"Harbingen's hymn ends with three short, successive notes, the first scan signals picked up by the prospector ship from their home world at the time," the XO explained tight-lipped.

"They're crazy! They're targeting a Fleet flagship! Give orders to target the *Oberon*. All weapons are enabled!"

"Sir, they're not targeting us, they're targeting the gate."

"If I see so much as a blink from that old barge, I want it destroyed." Augustus was beside himself.

"It won't work," Konrad said, shaking his head. "And you know it." He turned to Meyer and the Marines, who looked resolutely at their comrades from the *Caesar*. "We're going to the shuttle."

"Roger that, Captain." The colonel nodded and signaled to his men, whereupon they moved toward the wall of muzzles, which parted after a reluctant gesture from the admiral. Only then did Konrad address his officers—Nicholas and Jason included.

"Come."

There was an eerie silence as they cautiously made their way into the tightly packed hallway, accompanied by the angry glare from Augustus's eyes.

"You'll regret this, Bradley!" he shouted after him, but Konrad didn't turn, enduring the tension of not knowing if a shot, followed by many more, was about to follow. It only took the twitch of a single finger to trigger a bloodbath that would spread from this corridor to two fleets with enough firepower to wipe each other out and send a hurricane of hard radiation through the system.

As if in slow motion, their cocoon of uniforms moved through the forest of rifles and closed helmet visors, tracking every inch they walked down the corridor. Only after they had put a few yards between them did Meyer dare to quicken his steps, then they trotted toward the brig to retrieve Murphy and Walter.

"That escalated pretty quickly," Silly said next to him.

"The executioner's sentence was already pronounced before the admiral jumped into the system. All his talk was just a facade to lull us," he said contemptuously. "None of us would have agreed to that."

"Of course not. But where do we go from here? We can't

stay in Lagunia if we don't want to be visited by two fleets once Iron Hammer has succeeded."

"I know." He shook his head and waited as they stopped so Meyer could yell to a couple of *Caesar* crew members. "We have to go into exile, and we don't have much time to do it."

"That's not going to be easy to explain."

"I know. But we have to try, and then everyone can decide for themselves whether to join us or not. Everyone else will probably face relocation, which can only be a step up from the damn blue ball we've been trying to call home for twenty years."

"Amen," grumbled his XO.

They observed how seriously Augustus took his threats a few minutes later when they arrived in front of the entrance to the brig and two Marines had already maneuvered Murphy and Walter into the corridor. They quickly joined their comrades, walking close to each other. Without a word, they set off toward the shuttle.

The way there remained free of surprises or obstacles that could have delayed their progress, and so after a few minutes they were climbing through the airlock to their two excited pilots.

"What the hell was going on? The *Oberon* is targeting the damn hyperspace gate and has alerted us to stand by for evacuation under combat conditions!" the pilot shouted from her seat, madly flipping various toggle switches and holobuttons.

"It's gotten a little uncomfortable here. Take us back to the old lady!" Silly ordered as they quickly buckled into their seats and the hatch to the airlock was closed.

"Everybody in?" the copilot called out, looking over his shoulder for reassurance from eleven thumbs up. He faltered briefly at the sight of Jason.

"Murphy's missing!" someone shouted.

"What?" Konrad unlocked his harness. "What do you mean he's *missing*?"

"He was right behind me, last!" said Walter, excitedly. His COB was staring at the locked security bulkhead barring access to the airlock like a dark gray wall.

"Unlock!" Konrad ordered as he hammered ineffectually on the control panel. They became restless, but no one stood or began talking.

The next moment, the bulkhead moved aside, and through the porthole of the manually closed hatch Konrad saw the chief engie being dragged, legs kicking, through the outer door by two of the *Caesar*'s Marines, back onto the flagship.

"What a bloody mess!"

"They must have locked our side with a Fleet priority code and used it to lock him in as I climbed into the shuttle," Walter said somberly.

"Open!" Konrad shouted toward the cockpit, pressing his fists against the composite next to the porthole in frustration. Murphy was almost gone. He could see the engineer's mouth opening and closing as he struggled valiantly, but the Marines' servo-reinforced armor didn't give him a chance.

"Sir, we can't. Our systems are struggling to fend off the *Caesar*'s code. If we stay any longer, they will take control," the pilot said.

"We're not leaving anyone behind!" Konrad insisted.

He felt a hand on his shoulder, and he jerked his head around. He looked into Silly's face. "There's nothing we can do from here. Not now. We have to cast off!"

"Damn it!" he cursed, and before he could give her a reluctant nod, his XO was already waving him forward.

A jolt went through the shuttle, which presumably meant the pilots hadn't waited for the retaining clips to release them. In front of the windshield, the *Caesar*'s hull receded, and they slid off toward the twinkling stars.

I'll get you back, Murphy! he promised his chief engie in his mind.

UNKNOWN POSITION, OORT CLOUD, HARBINGEN SYSTEM

Asteroid DC-66412 was a two-kilometer diameter chunk of compacted regolith whose interior had been hollowed out and transformed into a network of squat passageways and claustrophobic caverns. From the outside, it was just another ugly gray lump of stone in the dense cloud of relics from the early formation of the Harbingen system. With its myriad brothers and sisters surrounding the central star like a sphere, far, far away from even the outermost planet, the ice giant Karl, even the highest resolution telescopes could not provide "real" images of DC-66412.

Deep in the heart of the converted asteroid was the control center, where three women and a man floated in blue neural tanks and controlled far more than just the major functions of this station.

"Chancellor," said Major Heines, jumping up from the only chair with a working console.

"Sit tight," the chancellor replied, extending a hand. "Do you have anything yet?"

"Yes." The officer in his black uniform nodded and ran his right hand over the neural cushion of his armrest, whereupon a holo-image appeared before them. It showed the unmistakable silhouette of Harbingen and the remains of Kor that had not fallen onto his home, the wreckage that hung like a sword of Damocles over the former paradise.

"I don't see anything," the chancellor said.

"That's right," the major said triumphantly, and he made a swiping motion with his index finger, whereupon the sliver moved back in its orbit and the image zoomed in on a flash of white that grew smaller and smaller, finally morphing into two destroyers linked together. Then time moved forward again, and he watched them both dissolve into the flash.

"Very good."

"May I ask something, Mr. Chancellor?"

"Of course."

"The destruction of the *Gibraltar* and the *Braxis* will raise questions with the Fleet. They'll investigate soon enough, especially since the *Gibraltar* is expected to be in the Desmoines System and then they'll find the debris."

"Don't worry, son," the chancellor replied. "It's far too late for that. No one will come here because they won't have time for that—and no ships. They're so bent on destroying the Clicks that their fight against us has long since been lost."

"But they're not fighting us at all. They don't even know about us."

The chancellor smiled. "And that's how you win the war before it's even started. Contact the other stations and shipyards, Major, the time is near."

"Of course, Herr Kanzler." Heines bowed his head deeply.

"Prepare my shuttle. And do you have news from the Cassiopeia system?"

"Yes. Admiral Green reports that everything is in place in case the Clicks show up."

"Very good. Everything is going as it should."

18

"Good work, Lieutenant Commander," Konrad said as he walked onto the large bridge of his ship, accompanied by Silly and his two sons. The Titan's control center was located deep in its heart, enclosed by a massive sphere of carbon and carbotanium. On three semi-circular tiers, a total of thirty officers and NCOs did their duty at the holoconsoles spread out before them. Each of them had their own communicator complete with earpiece and cable, through which they could directly reach their assigned section of the ship. Many things could be controlled from here, such as the security bulkheads, automatic fire suppression, life support, and individual weapons systems, but there were restrictions for security reasons in the spirit of a safeguarding separation of powers, so the section commanders had to decide many things themselves and be instructed accordingly.

The red light of combat illumination prevailed as he walked with his XO and sons to the commander's table, which stood across from the ranks of operators on a pedestal that glowed faintly reddish. The "table" was an old-fashioned battle map based on holotechnology, a flattened 3D image of the entire space surrounding the *Oberon*, fed in real time by the sensors. Different vector lines, sometimes dashed, sometimes solid, and flashing in different colors, indicated the actual and predicted thrust directions of the ships and objects with which they shared that space. Each dot had an identifier that could be touched to learn more about the corresponding body. The gas giant Artros was grayed out on the left edge so that it did not outshine the rest of the surrounding vacuum on the display.

Lieutenant Commander Frederick Daussel, a burly middle-aged officer with short-cropped nut-brown hair and a jutting chin, took a half-step back from the "command deck," as the crew called the table.

"Thank you, sir."

"I'm taking charge."

"Of course, sir."

"What's the situation?"

"The *Oberon* is in full combat readiness given the ongoing maintenance to overhaul our systems. That means eighty percent of weapon systems, no hull magnetization, and availability of seventy percent of fighter launch pads," Daussel said.

"You decided to target the hyperspace gate," Konrad stated as he tried to get a picture of the situation with his hands propped on the edge of the table.

"Yes, Captain. I knew something was wrong from the light signal on the port side of the *Caesar*. I didn't think it was a courtesy signal, since the admiral is not considered a Harbingen sympathizer, and repairs had previously been made to the diode. I thought it possible there was trouble but couldn't interpret the situation correctly and decided to break protocol, but not Fleet regulations."

"All we could do was test the systems in case the gate malfunctioned, and we didn't actively threaten any Federation ship," Silly summarized, nodding with satisfaction. "Well done, Daussel."

"Thank you, ma'am."

"Really good," Konrad agreed. "But now it's time to up the ante. Fire control, bring all starboard guns to bear on the *Caesar* and surrounding ships within range. Fighter squadrons on full alert."

"Roger that!" Lieutenant Bauer replied from a lower tier. His face seemed to glow red in the twilight of the bridge.

"Port guns remain locked on the hyperspace gate."

"Yes, sir."

"Captain, may I ask..." put in Daussel, startled.

"You may. The admiral had Chief Engie Murphy arrested, and I will not allow even one member of my crew to be kidnapped!" He turned to Nicholas. "Commander, I want you to work with the lieutenant commander"—he pointed at Jason without looking at him,—"to come up with a plan to collect as many citizens of Lagunia and the asteroid settlements as possible and get out of here as quickly as possible. I also want an estimate of how much time we have in case Augustus calls for immediate support."

"Roger that." Nicholas made his way to one of the two alcoves recessed into the walls between the tiers and the commander's podium where there were more stations with various display systems. Jason, however, did not follow him.

"You've been given an order, Lieutenant Commander!" said Silly sternly.

"I don't report to the captain," Jason replied stiffly. "Besides, I don't think I need to remind you that as an active-duty officer, I don't have to take orders from reserve officers. It's the other way around."

"This here's the *Oberon*, boy," the XO hissed. "And the captain—"

"Let it go," Konrad cut in without taking his eyes off the battle display. "The lieutenant commander is excused and shall be assigned quarters."

He waited until his son's footsteps moved away before his hands unclenched and he took a breath.

"Sir," Lieutenant Jung reported from communications, "incoming directional beam from the *Caesar*."

"Allow audio, entire bridge."

"Captain," Augustus's strained voice immediately rang out, "you've gotten yourself into something there's no escape from. No matter where you try to escape to, Fleet won't let you get away with that. You've got active weapons systems pointed at a sister ship, and that's a noose waiting for you. You know that. As a commander and officer, you should still have the decency to think beyond your own fate and not drag your crew into it."

"You did that," Konrad replied calmly. "When you tried to frame my son to put me under pressure."

"Your son is with you now."

"But my chief engineer isn't. You arrested a member of my crew without cause, and I won't have it."

"You'd risk open conflict between our two fleets for one man?" Augustus's snort echoed through the bridge. Several operators looked up from their consoles and exchanged glances. Konrad looked at them.

"I would risk everything for each of my eight thousand three hundred and fifteen crew members," he finally replied.

"Shut down your weapons and I will send Lieutenant Commander Murphy back to you, but only on the condition that you turn yourself in."

He still wants his political victory at home.

"What's your plan?" he asked defiantly. "Get help through the hyperspace gate? We'll destroy it before you've sent a single ship through."

"No, you won't," the admiral said. "You may be crazy and headstrong, but you hate the Clicks even more than me or anyone else does. You wouldn't destroy our only chance to beat the enemy once and for all. And that's why I'm going to send a courier out now to reach the gate in half an hour."

"And you would not activate the gate until the time specified in your orders."

"You are mistaken, Captain. This is well within my authority, because an engagement with your museum ship could inflict losses on my fleet that would jeopardize the success of the entire Operation Iron Hammer."

Damn it! Konrad cursed inwardly and exchanged a quick glance with Silly, who nodded in understanding. She knew the admiral was right, and so did he. He could not allow a victory for humanity over the Clicks to be jeopardized. But he couldn't leave Murphy behind either.

Augustus seemed to misunderstand his silence and continued, "Don't count on any breaks, Captain. I know about the firepower of the *Oberon*, every recruit at Fleet Academy knows the specifications of the last Titan inside and out. You would sell yourself dearly, I'm sure, but you have no chance of defeating Strike Group 2."

"And you have no chance of winning tomorrow unless you leave in full force. How will you explain to Fleet leadership that you thought it was more important to use intrigue to arrest a reserve captain than to lead Iron Hammer to success?" he countered. "My demand remains: Turn my man over to me and do it now. I'll give you ten minutes to arrange his transfer to the *Oberon*, and then we'll come back for him."

"You wouldn't..."

"I'd wreck the whole system to get one of my people back."

He ran his hand across his neck and Lieutenant Jung broke the connection with a nod. He gazed at the three ranks of his crew.

"That I have asked this only once before is because we've only been in a similar situation once before. If any of you are unwilling to violate Federation Fleet regulations, then you are

free to speak frankly now and leave your seat, without consequences. My job is to make decisions for this ship and all who
live on it. A captain is not someone who is omnipotent but is
controlled and restricted by the rules and laws of the Fleet.
That is not the case now. If anyone agrees with the admiral
that I am overstepping my bounds and should be relieved of
my command, let them speak now."

He waited as a tense silence descended over the bridge. At
the forward edge of the command deck, the countdown he
had given Augustus ran down in minutes and seconds.

When no one said anything, Silly smiled, stepped forward
and raised her voice: "All right, back to work! I want not even a
pin to sail through the vacuum unseen, and if even one
unscheduled discharge is registered on one of the admiral's
ships, I want to know about it! We're in full combat readiness,
so focus, if you please!"

Konrad nodded at her and exhaled a long, slow breath
before turning back to the situation on the holo-map below
him. Daussel stood on the right side and his XO on the left.

"What are our options?" Silly asked.

"The hyperspace gate is off-limits; we won't destroy it,"
Konrad said, his mouth open in frustration. "He knows we're
bluffing, and we know he knows it, which makes our threat
worthless."

"We should still keep it targeted, sir, just in case. The
admiral might still have doubts, and we can't aim the port
guns at Strike Group 2 anyway, based on the current position
of our two fleets," Daussel noted.

"Right."

"Sir, are we really ready to shoot this thing out?"

"The admiral should at least think that," Konrad said.
"XO, your assessment of the situation?"

"The enemy fleet has one battlecruiser, three heavy cruisers, seven light cruisers, ten carriers, two dozen destroyers, and
about two hundred corvettes. Our escort ships include two

Harbinger cruisers, two carriers, ten destroyers, and no corvettes since we transferred all of those to the civilian sector to boost the inner-system economy." She cast a reproachful glance at the lieutenant commander across the table, but he didn't seem to notice. "I don't need to remind you of the age of our fleet."

"Have our escort ships head to Lagunia to arrange evacuations in the shortest possible time. If there is an accident here and we have to leave the system, I want to take as many of them with us as possible," Konrad ordered.

"Understood, but that doesn't exactly increase our slim chances," she said.

"We have to build on the fact that he doesn't want to jeopardize the success of his mission tomorrow," he explained. "That's the best strategy we currently have."

"And what about Murphy?" Daussel asked.

"Order Colonel Meyer to have four boarding ferries ready. If it comes to that, we'll take fire and cripple the *Caesar* so he can have a clear field and get the chief engie out. Meanwhile, we'll do what we do best: draw fire and take plenty until everyone is back on board. After that, we pull out."

"It's a long way to Lagunia."

"But not to the jump point," Silly said. "We could shoot our way to the jump point and jump to the inner conjunction point, then we'd be in orbit around the planet within fifteen minutes."

"That's the way we do it. Lieutenant Commander, work it out with the colonel. XO, you work out the plans for the operational situation we discussed and coordinate with my son."

"Roger that."

"Roger that, sir."

For the next few minutes, it was silent except for the murmurs of the operators on the tiers opposite him. The bridge crew on duty was busy relaying a wide variety of orders and evaluating, assessing, and converting all real-time data from ordnance, engineering, and all internal systems into something that would be relayed to his command deck with as little delay or deviation as possible. It was the professionally calm busyness of a well-rehearsed team in the face of a battle where people always died, no matter how well it turned out.

With each minute that ticked away on the holographic chronometer, Konrad grew more tense and had to remind himself to relax his shoulders and exhale. He had meant what he said and would do the same for any crew member if he or she was wronged, but how many sailors was he willing to risk or even sacrifice to save just one? He had asked himself these questions many times without ever coming to a satisfactory answer. At some point, in a position of responsibility, one had to face the fact that there was not always a good solution for everything.

When there was only one minute left and the clock turned to 0:59, he thought the edge of the table would break under his fingers.

"Contact request from the *Caesar*," Jung reported, her voice carried by the invisible speakers behind Konrad.

Thank God, he thought, but outwardly displayed the composure expected of him. "Accept."

"Captain."

"Admiral."

"I'm not going to jeopardize humanity's victory in this war because of this crazy thing, and I'm not going to jeopardize your crew, who have been through too much already. But as a senior Fleet officer, I can't ignore what you've done either. My offer to resolve this predicament, which is your fault, is as follows," Augustus stated stiffly. "You will face a court-martial and custody on my ship. I will send a shuttle of Marines to arrest and transfer you. On that shuttle will be Lieutenant Commander Murphy, returning to the *Oberon*. Once he is aboard, you will surrender to my Marines and I will recommend to Fleet Command that the *Oberon* and all her crew, including the officer in command in your absence, not be prosecuted under Article 82, Section 3, taking your light signal from my ship as a direct order. If you agree, I suggest that we immediately begin to resolve this situation and come to our senses. For your protection, I have recorded this conversation and we can send a courier from your fleet to bring it to Sol. That's a better offer than you deserve, Captain, but I'm willing to take a step back so as not to jeopardize humanity's most important operation."

"I accept your terms."

A murmur went through the bridge, followed by indignant whispering.

"Good, I'm glad you've come to your senses. The ferry is ready." There was a short crackle indicating the end of the connection.

"Have you gone mad?" Silly asked, upset. She had run from her alcove, sheer horror in her eyes. "You can't do that!"

"Yes, I can, and you know it. There is no good solution to this situation. Augustus would do everything he could to avenge this humiliation, and he would take his anger out on all the Harbingers. So, he gets what he wants: My head and his operation tomorrow. Other than those two things, he has no interest in Lagunia or our people. If I don't, then a lot of innocent people will die," he calmly explained and stepped back from the table. "You're in command, XO."

"But Konrad!" she almost pleaded, coming within an arm's length of him. "I need you! The *Oberon* needs you! You *are* Harbingen!"

"If Harbingen could be projected onto one person, it would not be the dream we all share. I am the chance we have to finally change something for the better. You know as well as I do that I am the reason we are treated like lepers. I'm not merely giving the admiral what he wants, I'm giving us what we needed to shake off the shackles of the past." He paused then grabbed her by the shoulders to look her straight in the eye. "My final order is to put all weapons systems on standby."

He nodded to her one last time and left the podium for the exit, which was below the lowest rank of operators and guarded by two Marines. The entire bridge crew rose silently and saluted with concerned expressions. He casually returned their silent salute and left the bridge without another word.

He encountered hardly anyone in the corridors except groups of sailors wearing battle helmets running from station to station. He rode the elevator to the starboard hangar, where he was met by a hundred technicians, pilots, and other sailors who formed a tight semicircle in front of the two parked shuttles, which were in the huge hangar now clear of any fighters needing repair or maintenance.

He entered the silence and frowned.

"What does that mean?"

"We won't let you go," someone said, and there were murmurs of agreement.

"We're not letting our commander go!"

"We're not handing you over to that vain peacock!"

"Captain Bradley!" someone else shouted, and cheers went up.

"Brad-ley! Brad-ley! Brad-ley!"

Konrad felt emotion moisten his eyes, yet he raised his hands.

"Quiet!" he commanded, and silence abruptly fell.

"I am honored by your loyalty and encouragement," he said, the distant walls producing a faint echo. "For me, there has only ever been this ship, and by that I don't mean the composite of which it is built. I don't expect you to understand why I made the decision I did, but believe it's what's best for the *Oberon*. It has been an honor to serve with each and every one of you."

He wondered if he should have gone to Nicholas, but his youngest son would have just tried to stop him, so he decided to live with the pain and be strong. At least he had experience with that, and he would do everything he could to not make it any harder for his sons than it already was.

"Prepare for the arrival of the *Caesar* shuttle. That's an order!"

19

S irion hadn't even climbed out of the Triton's hatch when an excited Franc Bellinger appeared before him, apparently unfazed by the lashing rain.

"Where is she?" he called out against the roar of the storm. A wave washed over the small jetty and into the submarine's opening, where Sirion pointed with an outstretched thumb. Hastily, he ran past the explorer into the interior of the swimming habitat, as if to seek safety from the ever-present water, and looked over his shoulder. Franc was helping his wife out.

With two steps, he reached the converter of the satellite receiver, which appeared hastily attached as a black box on the wall and the small display indicated the connection was stable. He took his right index finger, flipped open the dome and held the magnetic connector to the port for manual firmware maintenance.

"What are you doing?" he heard Valeska's voice behind him.

"I checked to see if the connection to the West Bank was still there," he replied calmly, turning to look at her. She, like her husband, was standing there soaking wet and was aimed toward the table, which was in the middle of the room and lit from below. "You never know with a storm like this. If you knew what I've been through. Most..."

Valeska was already not paying attention to him and talking excitedly to Franc as they ran to the table and activated the holofield.

"You wouldn't believe what the data contained!"

"Let me get settled first and catch my breath..."

"This is a sensation, darling. Nothing less than a sensation! If we take this to the governor—"

"Franc!" she snapped at him, wiping the wet strands of hair from her face. Sirion heard the rest of her tirade with only one ear, as he looked toward the closed crew door to make sure it didn't open with someone complaining about the volume.

As a precaution, he casually shuffled over without the two scientists even noticing. They were so engrossed in their excited argument and impatience that they seemed to tune everything else out. They didn't notice that he connected to the door control panel and transferred a small DAEMON file that tampered with the simple unprotected software and permanently activated the electronic lock.

Only then did he fetch a towel and return to the Bellingers while he dried his hair, giving the appearance of half-interested casualness.

"So, what did we discover?" he asked in the middle of their argument, smiling broadly. Franc seemed to think he was interrupting to let her catch her breath and looked relieved.

"Iridium is not the right parameter for these layers," Valeska insisted, merely frowning at Sirion for the disturbance.

"I got just as far with the carbon determination. The muon detector on this little piece of junk is..."

"... all we have, and that's not enough."

"It's the best we can get on this planet!"

"Franc! If we go to the compartment feeds, they'll grab us by the balls, twist them a few times, and then pull them so hard that the milk squirts out of our eyes!" She tapped the data columns on the holodisplay, which at first glance was completely incomprehensible to Sirion.

"But we can't keep it to ourselves either!"

"Uh, sorry." Sirion put on a cautious smile. "May I ask what's wrong?"

"No!"

"Yes, you can," Franc said, who again seemed glad for the opportunity to breathe a sigh of relief. "The hyperspace gate you found down there, the data shows that the composition of the material is that of Click ships."

"What does that mean?" Now he was actually surprised.

"The destroyed gate was built by the Clicks and *not* by the Lagoon," the xeno-archaeologist explained.

"How can you know that? Just because of the similarity of the material?"

Now it was Valeska who shook her head and answered. "Yes. The Lagoon did space travel, but their materials were different and are still not fully explored to this day. The fact is that they managed to make certain noble gases react in such a way that hard materials could be formed with them."

"I thought noble gases didn't react?"

"Correct. But they did it somehow, and we're still not sure how. In any case, they must have been able to initiate and control complex nuclear reaction processes, similar to the Federation replicators, only much more advanced."

"If these Lagoon were so advanced, why were they destroyed by the Clicks?"

"Who knows? Maybe they weren't that advanced in weaponry."

"But," he objected, "I read that the Clicks built the hyper-space gates, and the feeds say they don't even have the technology to do it."

"Just because you don't build something doesn't mean you can't provide the technology to do it. After all, we could never have built nuclear weapons and still have nuclear power plants. You just have to enrich uranium far enough and know about plutonium to use nuclear fission to release energy; the same goes for nuclear weapons. But whether you really use both applications is more of a cultural question. The Chinese of Terra knew about black powder long before the Europeans did but did not think of using it as gunpowder, they preferred to build fireworks with it."

"Are you saying that the Clicks might not *want* to build hyperspace gates?" he asked, pretending to be puzzled. Not a word of it interested him, but he needed time while in his field of vision the data columns of the electronic sequester software told him how far along the takeover of the habitat software was. The system was relatively well protected for one from the civilian market, and thus no hurdle at all for his military software, but the amount of data was large enough to delay the algorithm a predicted ten minutes. Only then could he process all the records from the sensors and logs so no one would ever know of his presence.

"That's the subject of a lot of hypotheses right now, but it sure looks like it, yes. They know the jump points and use them to their advantage, just like we do. Certainly, they have already thought about whether it would be possible to create their own jump points—we saw that at the battle for Harbingen. So, it's not too farfetched to think they may have also been mulling over constant connections like what a gate would provide," Valeska explained. "Still, we must not indulge in hasty judgments. This gate being built by the Clicks would be strange indeed, and everything so far points to that, but—"

"Until we determine otherwise, we should focus on this piece," Franc interjected. "The consequences would be far-reaching! The Clicks have very well researched hyperspace gates and even had success with them decades ago. But we've never seen any on their end, and even remote reconnaissance hasn't found any evidence to that effect. Either they're better at hiding than we give them credit for, or they've sworn off the technology at some point."

"All speculation, and as such—"

"We wait until the AI sorts and analyzes the data, then we'll know more."

"What's missing?" Sirion said to prevent another outburst of argument and keep them talking so they wouldn't hear the continuing muffled pounding at the door to the crew room. The programmable silicon was apparently soundproofed. It was hard to make out, even to his upgraded ears, but he preferred to play it safe.

"The AI is currently trying to figure out what kind of weapons were responsible for the gate's destruction using the Fleet's publicly available databases," Valeska said absently.

Sirion threw the satellite link data stream into the left half of his field of view and saw the download stream the AI was currently using. He dismissed the idea of stopping it. He couldn't see how it would affect his job here. As the couple faced each other and discussed the data, a little more civilly now, he let his right hand wander to the camouflage holster of his monofilament knife, hidden in the pocket of his cargo pants. Before he pulled it out, something flashed before his eyes, distracting him briefly.

It was a priority message from the governor, which the habitat system attempted to automatically cast to every screen, speaker, holoscreen, and forearm display within range. He suppressed the command and looked at the message himself. Instead of a video, he saw a still image with the coat of arms of the governor's office and white lettering on a black background, read aloud by a computer-generated voice: "Planetary Alert. This is a personalized alert for: Bellinger, Valeska, Bellinger, Franc. You are requested to stand by for emergency evacuation to orbit. When you receive this message, move immediately toward the nearest primary habitat. Take minimal baggage and save the holocode sent along on your UDs."

The message played on a continuous loop while Sirion pondered its origin. Such priority messages were reserved for immediate disasters on most planets, for example, an asteroid impact, a coronal mass ejection that could lead to radiation damage, or an attack by the Clicks. However, apart from Harbingen, the Clicks had never specifically attacked a planet, but rather the strategic infrastructure in the systems, primarily orbital shipyards and zero-G factories. An exercise perhaps? That did happen on occasion and was even written into many constitutions as a right of the government due to the prolonged state of war.

For safety's sake, he sent a short message to his principals over the designated frequency to reassure himself that he was not dealing with an actual emergency and should get out of here immediately.

The answer came in less than two minutes. They had someone in the system who was not only standing by as a courier to confirm his success message and pass it on to Sol, but this courier was also one with authority.

Interesting.

"No immediate danger. The governor has been instructed by the *Oberon* to prepare the population of Lagunia for an emergency evacuation. Not an exercise, but apparently presentable as such should it not come to pass. The window of opportunity for your mission has shortened. Operation Iron Hammer is imminent. We expect a success report within the next thirty minutes."

Sirion thought about the message. The attack on the Clicks had been moved up a day? And all of a sudden? That was not possible, unless it had been planned that way from the beginning. Fleet's entire strike force could not be moved to another date with a snap of the fingers. So, the secrecy about the exact execution of the Admiralty's operation had been as successful as keeping the secret about when the hyperspace gates would actually be ready at the same time.

The fact that his principals had not known about it was the best proof of the excellent work of Fleet management. But why did they insist on seeing the Bellingers dead before then? It had to do with this sunken hyperspace gate, of course, but...

None of my business, he thought, clearing his gaze, whereupon the message disappeared, as did the priority alert from Atlantis.

"That can only mean one thing," Franc said just then, looking up from the holo-image. The greenish image of the gate segment spun between him and his wife like a broken wedding ring, columns of data running down its edges like tears.

Sirion was about to pull out the knife when he paused and joined them at the table instead.

"The hyperspace gate was activated. Just a few hours before it was destroyed," the xeno-archaeologist continued. "It was only after that that it was destroyed and crashed onto the planet."

"Yes. So, they had the technology, but then destroyed it themselves," Valeska agreed with him. "There's no doubt about the data: The holes and craters are from Click weapons; the AI is sure of that. But the questions don't stop there. If they came here to destroy Lagoon why was the hyperspace gate on *this* side? It would have to have been on theirs. This was where they would have come out at the jump point. The idea behind the technology is to keep the connection to the point open, so jumps can only be made from one direction and every second, isn't it?"

"Unless you bring an unassembled gate through the jump point. Parts with their own drives that can be jettisoned. Using maneuvering thrusters, it's then assembled, and multiple ships can get through at the same time. I would bet Fleet has something similar in mind. That's how *I* would do it," Franc said.

"But then it still doesn't make sense that they destroyed

their own gate. If it was the Lagoon, okay, but it was Clicks' weapons."

"Hmm. If they had lost the battle in orbit, I would have said that they didn't want to leave such technology behind, so they preferred to destroy it, as human armies have done since time immemorial—"

"But they didn't lose. The Clicks are still there, the Lagoon haven't been since the battle," Valeska said. She sighed, then looked up and looked urgently at her husband. "Wait. There's only one hyperspace gate we've ever found, *this one*. Not on or around a Click world, nor anywhere in an uninhabited or legacy-covered system, of which there were at least half a dozen. We've encountered only one intelligent species since we've been able to travel our section of the Milky Way, and it apparently had a hyperspace gate in operation decades ago—if only for a few hours."

"And then they destroyed it themselves."

"Yes. What if it was voluntary?"

"Voluntarily?" Franc said frowning. "You mean..."

"What if we hadn't dropped the first atomic bomb on Japan, but someone smart had said, this is too dangerous, destroy this thing?"

"But why would a hyperspace gate be dangerous?"

"Hyperspace sleep!" Valeska exclaimed, ruffling her wet hair. "Travel by jump requires each passenger to be awake during the jump. Those who sleep during transit never wake up. Some call it the ultimate mystery of manned spaceflight, but it is merely the greatest. The fact is, it's dangerous for humans to sleep while the spacecraft they're making jumps through hyperspace for an immeasurably short time."

"You think the Clicks have figured out that a permanent link through hyperspace makes for a new threat?" Franc asked, going pale.

"I don't know. That's just the first hypothesis I can think of based on this confusing data. The Clicks may be cruel and aggressive, but they are not stupid. And they would have never given up such a technological advantage without good reason, after all, they were already at war with us at the time and had managed to jump to a world that was beyond our territory. The logistics alone of getting all those ships past us here must have been enormous."

"But if that's the case, even if it's just a guess," Franc said excitedly, "we have to warn Fleet immediately! Tomorrow the attack will begin and all gates in the Federation will be activated!"

"It's just a hypothesis and—"

"Valeska!" he interrupted gruffly, "we *have* to warn them. We'd rather be wrong and embarrass ourselves than have a disaster happen where millions—"

"You're right." She nodded eagerly. "I'll try—"

Sirion felt the blood run over his hand as he pulled the blade out of the explorer's head, which he had jammed into his brain through the skin under his chin. Valeska froze in shock and let out a horrified scream as her husband crashed to the table. Her eyes widened with surprise as Sirion pulled the knife out.

He leapt effortlessly over the plate, which the holofield commented on with a brief flicker, and would have hit Valeska directly in the carotid artery had she not fallen to the side. She scrambled away, howling in panic, while he repositioned himself and followed her. She got to her feet and ran toward the exit, but she would not make it.

When she grabbed his duffel bag and threw it at him, he fought it off and nodded after she stopped. A few useless jerks at the door had been enough to make her stop, discouraged and trembling.

"Why?" she whimpered, "We don't have anything..."

"Mission," he said curtly, stalking her. "Nothing personal."

"Are you out of your mind? Fleet really needs to know what happened here before it—"

"Let Fleet burn, for my sake." It escaped him in a rare burst of emotion that surprised even himself.

"You are—"

She didn't get any further; at that moment he ran the monofilament blade over her neck. After a moment, her expression changed and she slumped to the ground. He was about to open the door and begin disposing of the bodies when he saw something flash in his field of vision before the command to the control panel.

An outgoing message.

What?

During their brief conversation, Valeska Bellinger had sent a message to a public communications satellite, an emergency call. Not a personalized one, but a standardized Level 1 distress call that space control would deal with. Somewhere, a computer whined. He wheeled around and saw via buoy control that a submersible buoy had shot out of its launch bay.

I wasn't attentive enough, he scolded himself. He remembered that after sending the message to his contact, he had forgotten to lock the system again for outgoing connections. Such carelessness was rare for him, but it was also the first time he had been in the field in a place that was capable of stirring emotions in him. He had now learned what that could mean.

"What was in the buoy?" he asked, but of course she could not answer. Her eyes were already broken. *Data about her discovery? The truth about the hyperspace gate down there?* Sirion paused for a moment, thinking. It didn't matter. He knew what his employers knew, and if they were right, no one would ever be able to find that buoy.

It took a little over ten minutes to dump the bodies in the water—the local predators wouldn't leave much of them—and sink the habitat before he sailed away in the boat, leaving behind glowing flames like a two-dimensional wallpaper against the pitch-black night. It took another two minutes for him to report his success to his contact, and a further two for him to receive confirmation, which included a warning that an emergency commando from one of the ships in the *Oberon* fleet had departed to investigate a call for help from his coordinates. The ship was the *Danube*, a light cruiser responsible for space control of Lagunia on those days it did not have a corresponding orbital station.

This is going to be complicated, he thought, as he steered the vessel out into the open ocean in the opposite direction of West Bank.

CASSIOPEIA SYSTEM, OUTER JUMP POINT

Rear Admiral Doreen Whitmore stood with her hands clasped behind her back on the bridge, deep in the heavily armored heart of her flagship TFS *Dragonmount*, watching on the main screen as the six pieces of the hyperspace gate were escorted from the inner to the outer jump point. Each of the pieces was larger than a Titan and looked like a scimitar to which someone had taped thick rolls of toilet paper. The attached thrusters were improvised, an obvious spur-of-the-moment solution to something that would have taken a lot of time, as was everything about Operation Iron Hammer that they were preparing here.

Whitmore's fleet was divided in two: One part guarded the inner jump point, from which they took the pieces to the outer one, near the gas giant Cepheus with its formidable asteroid rings. Cassiopeia, the system's temperate world, had turned out to be a disappointment for the colonization authorities and corporate conglomerates involved. The planet's resources were manageable, but the presumed lithium on its two moons was so puny that the marginal world was soon written off. At least until some tourism companies specialized in developing Cassiopeia as a resort destination. The Clicks had never shown much interest in attacking Cassiopeia, probably because there was very little industry and few military installations worth mentioning, apart from the fortified jump points and some listening posts. The perfect system, then, to fly the six pieces to Attila to be assembled once Vice Admiral Bretoni's Strike Group 2 arrived and took over.

Until then, Whitmore's task was to prepare everything for the final blow against the metal skulls—quite an easy one, if there weren't three imponderables: First, no one knew what the Clicks knew, or even suspected. Second, the aliens had not shown *no* interest and had repeatedly made spy flights, some with sub-light probes sighted in the Oort cloud. Third, and most disturbing to them, there were hundreds of independent ships in the rings of Cepheus, raiding the resources of the asteroids without official permission, putting them in close proximity to the outer jump point. Strictly speaking, Whitmore could have driven them away, but there had long been a certain acceptance in Fleet of the free miners and traders, at least half of whom were pirates or smugglers. Large-scale mining was too expensive out here, without the infrastructure of a Fringe World with space control, accommodations, and logistics companies. So, they tolerated this kind of shadow economy, which paid no taxes or permits, but at least provided foreign currency. After all, every bit counted in the war against the Clicks.

Her presence now was a problem, however, because she had to divide her fleet so the outer jump point was guarded not only against the aliens but also against overzealous ship owners who might want to grab some of the Federation's most advanced technology. She was now working with a three-part fleet of one hundred and twenty ships spread throughout the inner solar system, and at the jump points and in between, escorting the six pieces that seemed to take forever despite their powerful engines.

She waited with the *Dragonmount* and forty sister ships two hundred thousand kilometers from the jump point at the small listening post where a crew of three controlled Jump Control, at least in peacetime.

"Admiral, multiple contacts!" one of her specialists said, snapping her out of her thoughts.

"Switch on, scan! Transponder?"

"Negative, ma'am." The specialist paused for a moment. "Clicks! They're coming out of the jump point."

What timing; this can't be a coincidence, she thought, and calmly ordered, "Fleet alert! Initiate attack pattern Rommel. Lieutenant Xiua, watch for Fleet synchronicity."

Whitmore watched, not without pride, as her bridge crew calmly and professionally carried out their orders. Her frigates, destroyers and drone carriers immediately moved to attack the incoming ships with maximum aggression. Their only goal now was not to let any of the enemies escape. Not a single one. Otherwise, Iron Hammer would fail before the operation even began.

Over the rather calm tactical screen, the rear admiral watched as the first torpedo salvos moved toward the aliens and the two drone carriers ejected hundreds of Predators, which hurtled toward the enemy at acceleration levels of over 100 Gs, firing their first submunitions after only a few seconds and flooding space with electronic jamming fire. It was a satisfying sight, even if they were merely colored symbols that didn't come close to reflecting the energetic bursts in the space around them. But she didn't need the shouts of her bridge crew to see the Clicks were increasing in number, as was their defensive fire. Soon, the Clicks were equal to them in numbers, which was usually good for the Federation, since the human ships were faster and typically more heavily armed, while the Click spacecraft were much better armored but slow-moving.

"Order the escort to maximum acceleration toward the

jump point," she called out without taking her eyes off the battle chart. "Have them launch their torpedoes as soon as they are in effective range."

This is going to be close, she thought, as the number of alien craft doubled. With eighty ships now—no more seemed to be arriving—they outnumbered her fleet, but they were outnumbered at the jump point. Then the first pods that had dropped out of hyperspace started turning back and recharging their energy matrix cells.

"Stop those ships! Concentrate fire!" she ordered loudly, using her holobuttons to mark the appropriate targets. The fleet responded within seconds, but the enemy's defensive fire was still too dense. Two glistening explosions filled the vacuum where torpedoes broke through, but two other ships took the place of their annihilated sisters and shielded those fleeing.

We're not going to make it, Whitmore thought in horror.

"Ma'am. New contacts!" the specialist called out. This time he sounded excited.

"More from the jump point?" She leaned forward but could see no new radar reports.

"From the asteroid ring. They're free ship owners, ma'am, but they appear to be armed."

Illegal! The thought shrilled in Whitmore's head. She had spent several years hunting pirates, which usually amounted to chasing one or a handful of ships through a system and either arresting or destroying them. Occasionally, some were lightly armed, but on her screen, she saw over two hundred contacts, each launching torpedoes. The tactical software interpreted other flashes as railgun fire.

"My goodness," she gasped.

"They're attacking the Clicks," her specialist reported triumphantly, but she could see it for herself. While she was still trying to comprehend what was happening and what it meant—Fleet forces fighting side by side with a fivefold superiority of pirates—she saw that the aliens would not escape. She looked for relief within herself but found mostly horror and worry about what it meant.

20

"No, Dev!" Willy grumbled.

"Yes, Dev!" Devlin replied, spinning the shot glass to slam it open side down on the filthy table. "You got a better idea?"

"How about we *just ignore the message?*" suggested the bearlike flight engineer, his face contorted as if he had bitten into a lemon. "It can't be true that we're going to get into trouble just before we take off."

"No trouble." He shook his head. "Just picking someone up."

"Captain, Willy's right," Jezzy remarked, shoulders hunched. "That guy was really scary."

"And that's exactly why we shouldn't say *no.*"

"That's not what I'm saying. Just don't react," Willy corrected him immediately, and the muscles under his throat made his voice rattle so loudly that several other patrons of the seedy bar where they'd been boozing away their last Lagunia shillings for a few hours turned to look at them. "Then we can always talk our way out of it. With all this evacuation talk, it wouldn't be too hard, would it?"

"Do you really want to screw someone like that guy?" Dev

asked, looking around when Willy didn't immediately answer. Jezzy, as usual, looked as if she'd seen a ghost. Dozer merely stared absently at the damp tabletop, like a mountain with two eyes. Aura's expression darkened.

"I hate to say it," the energy node specialist said, blowing a strand of hair out of her face in annoyance, "but Jezzy and Willy are both right. Something's going on here right now. They want us to stand by to receive civilians, so maybe there is something to the evacuation number after all. What if there really is a disaster? Then we should use our launch slot and not coast across the ocean. Not to mention that we don't even have permission to do that."

"Who's going to stop us?" Dev asked, snatching the bottle of black herbal liquor away from Aura before she could pour herself more. "The one reserve ship in orbit? And in the middle of an evacuation operation? I hardly think so."

"Screw the *Danube*!" she said, "I don't want this guy on board."

Dev considered reading the whole message to them for the second time but decided against it.

"He'll stay in the mess hall, which we can lock from the bridge." Again, he looked around, then tapped the table so that little drops danced. "Let's go!"

The pub was under a former colonist transporter that had been placed far from the edge of the spaceport and was already overgrown with verdigris and mold. Green and brown patches stretched from the first floor, where the drive pods had been removed and the composite was sooty, to about the middle. It was an ugly sight that matched Atlantis' overall impression and blended perfectly with the stench of the ubiquitous algae.

To get to the *Quantum Bitch* they had to pass through a security gate consisting of a simple scanner embedded in the high barbed wire fence and guarded by two bored security men who looked like bloated dolls under their rain ponchos. It had been raining incessantly all night, but Dev liked the pleasant chill once he got soaked and it no longer mattered. Besides, the red and yellow lights of the spaceport, refracted through the veil of drops, looked almost romantic. If it hadn't been for the stench, of course.

Since they weren't armed and the two guys seemed to have little desire to interrupt their conversation and lift their faces out of their ponchos to do so, they were able to walk undisturbed along one of the tarred paths to the *Bitch*, which was standing like a tiny spider between two large towers of containers.

As soon as he unlocked the ship with his forearm display and they walked along the ramp into the belly, protected from the rain and wind, he began giving orders.

"Jezzy, reactor up. Willy, I want you to change our transponder code; take one from Fujima. Aura, come with me to the bridge. Dozer?" Of course, he got no answer, but he heard the augmented giant stomping along behind him. "Don't go near the mess hall or this ramp, understand?"

A mechanical rumble answered him. "Mmm."

As soon as he reached the end of the corridor, he swung through the narrow hatch to the bridge. Dev rubbed the water out of his hair and brushed off his leather jacket, which he threw carelessly into the corner before dropping into the pilot's seat. He flipped four toggle switches on the left panel simultaneously with his index finger and a familiar hum went through the entire ship and loud, colorful lights illuminated.

"All right, here we go. Aura? Do you have a course for me?"

"Don't rush me." Behind him, he heard the creak of the copilot's seat and mechanical clacks. "It's pretty far out, about four hundred miles."

"Then we should step up to the plate."

"We don't want to keep the gentleman waiting," she said laconically. A 3-D map of the lake area west of Atlantis appeared before him as a holoprojection and a red dot flashed even farther west of the West Bank Habitat. A dashed line connected their current parking position to the red flashing light and helped him manually control it with the sidestick. There were few worlds, even among the fringe worlds, that allowed manual steering within atmosphere, or even near planets, space settlements, or cargo routes. He decided to take advantage of this, since far too often he felt like a bird whose wings had been tied together.

He made a brief announcement before asking for departure clearance, didn't get it, but took off anyway. He didn't plan to visit this turd of a stinking world ever again. The fleets were busy elsewhere and would be jumping toward Click territory as early as tomorrow and finally finish the endless war. This meant that all they had to do was get rid of their stolen cargo and then hide somewhere. Who was going to look for them? One of those ancient ships from the Harbinger fleet? Besides, they had made so much money selling the claim that he didn't think they would ever be so lucky again in a place like this.

As soon as he turned off the tower's furious radio transmissions, he lowered the *Bitch*'s nose forward and adjusted the direction of flight, according to the vector superimposed on it. After one last look at the floating city and its lights, he gave the joystick a thousandth push of thrust, bringing it to four times the speed of sound. The sonic boom would likely wake half the city and make some people's ears ring, but all that mattered now was to get out of there as quickly as possible before the *Danube*, circling in orbit somewhere a few hundred miles above them, decided that the evacuation measures were not the only priority after all.

Around them, the lights of the many ships that had answered the capital's call seemed like the shimmering glow of fireflies heading for a light bulb—almost beautiful, so devoid of the stench and ubiquitous mold.

Water droplets smashed against the cockpit glass in rapid

succession, the staccato of their impacts creating a steady crackle. The onboard computer automatically projected an artificial sensor image onto the glass so that, after a brief flicker, it looked as if they were untouched by the rain. Although the veils were still visible under the dark clouds where the residual light amplification had enough photons to work with, the glass now appeared clear.

Like a speeding hawk, they shot along the flight vector in low-level flight as if they were riding it, until seven minutes later they had to reduce thrust to avoid becoming a kinetic projectile.

Their target was a wooden sloop less than twenty meters long. Its position lights blurred in the dense rain. Far in the background, something was burning on the water, breaking up into several individual fires that persisted.

"Uh, Dev?" Aura asked as he leaned forward to eye the lone figure standing at the front of the deck, sending a shiver down his spine.

"Yes?"

"We're being called."

"Put him through."

"Not from that one," she said, tapping him on the shoulder and pointing to the long-range scanner whose display he could only see out of the corner of his eye because he had leaned too far forward. On it was a blue triangle approaching the center of the display—the *Quantum Bitch*.

"Who the hell is that?"

"An atmospheric shuttle from the *Danube*," she replied in an I-you-told-you-so tone of voice.

"Son of a bitch!"

"Do you want me to put it through?"

"Yes," he growled.

"This is Lieutenant Florheim of SS2 of HMS *Danube*, you are in our area of operations. Abandon your course immediately to the southeast," a humorless voice said over the loudspeaker. Dev turned to Aura and pointed impatiently at the man on the boat. She nodded reluctantly.

"Hello, Lieutenant," he finally replied, looking briefly at the fire on the horizon. "We were called here because of an emergency and wanted to provide assistance according to the laws."

"Move away to the southeast. We have a detachment of Marines with us to make an arrest. This is your last warning."

The connection was broken as he steered the ship into a hair-raising turn, as if aborting his course, but instead he steered the *Bitch* backward and extended the ramp to the passenger lock with a flip of a toggle switch. It would be uncomfortable outside with churning seas and a brutal wind from the engines, but their passenger would be able to handle it, he was sure. And if he didn't? Well then, maybe their problem would be solved in another way.

"Shit, we're being targeted!" Aura shouted, upset.

"Come on, you son of a bitch," he growled, staring at the dorsal sensors, which merely showed lights and frothy spray.

"Let's leave him here, dammit!"

"No! What do you think he'll tell those damned Harbingers when they squeeze him, huh?" he yelled back. "'Oh, they're nice enough people, they just stole twenty-two bodies and they're responsible for the liner raid.'"

"They'll be looking for us anyway because we snatched away one of their suspects, not to mention the number on Atlantis!"

"There he is!" he boomed triumphantly as he saw a dark figure sprint up the ramp with amazing dexterity. Immediately he retracted the ramp and was already turning to put them on a course to the southeast.

"SS2 reporting!" Aura sounded breathless.

"*Jotunheim*," the lieutenant called over the radio, and the name matching the fake transponder code confused Dev for a moment. "Hold your position and prepare to be boarded. You have taken aboard a federally wanted felon."

"Sorry, Lieutenant, we were just trying to get a castaway—"

"You have five seconds before we open fire. Florheim out."

"Five seconds?" Aura snapped.

"That's enough!" Dev pushed the joystick, and the fusion thrusters spewed a kilometer-long plasma lance from their drive nacelles, boiling the sea beneath them and sending a colossal cloud of vaporized water skyward. Obscured by steam, he steered them into an orbital course, correcting it by hand to take advantage of a convenient low-hanging cloud formation as the first tungsten projectiles shot past them.

"They're shooting at us!"

"I noticed!" He shoved the joystick forward and dove under the cloud, causing the *Quantum Bitch* to creak and groan dangerously, then pulled back up and began rolling. Just before the maneuver was complete, an alarm he hadn't heard in a long time howled: they'd been hit; right wing, a superconductor, and a nitrogen tank.

He corrected the spin caused by the escaping gas and pulled to the right as the sensors informed him that their trigger-happy pursuer had pierced the cloud and was directly below them.

"They're gonna shoot us out of the fucking sky!"

She was right, he admitted to himself. The *Bitch* was a fast, maneuverable ship—in space. It was atmosphere-capable, but not designed to operate inside a gravity well with dense gases, unlike the armed shuttle they were fleeing. However well it flew, they would not be able to outrun it, especially since they had to maintain the correct course for an extended duration to get the right orbital angle. One did not simply fly in a straight line out of a massive gravity well, but rather like a marble in a funnel.

"Hold on," he said and turned them sideways, as if to

dodge to the left. That got them another volley of projectiles that maltreated their other wing, where the secondary energy nodes normally were, but not since the recent rebuild on his *Bitch*. Before the last hit was reported, he searched with his right hand for the illegally installed switch under the control panel and flipped it, so all power went out in one fell swoop.

The *Quantum Bitch* dropped like a stone from the sky, slowly at first, as acceleration and braking canceled each other out. Then they hung weightless in their harnesses for a few seconds like seaweed sliding back and forth in an invisible current. Then it went down, faster and faster, until he felt the three-point harness dig painfully against his shoulders and hips.

"Aaaaargghhh," Aura groaned, as the G forces hit them and squeezed the air out of her lungs. After a few heavy breaths, he flipped the switch again, and the power came back. But not the thrusters, so they continued to tumble like a moth made of lead. On the scanner, he looked at the image of the *Bitch* and its pursuer, which would soon be at the same altitude and continued to target them.

Again, he killed the power, then after two seconds he switched it on again. The rotational movement caused saliva to fly out of his mouth and the blood to rush to the left side of his body, making it increasingly difficult for him to breathe or even think. At the last moment—and he hoped he had estimated correctly—he ignited the thrusters to full power. The plasma lance of high-energy gas particles hit the SS2, less than half a mile away, in the tail and simply vaporized it. Now the shuttle plummeted, but their own fate was only slightly better.

The sudden acceleration, in one direction out of the unstable spin, knocked them into their seats at an angle and Dev felt something crack in his back that wasn't supposed to. Blood shot up his nose as his head thundered against the backrest and slid backward at an ugly angle from it. Aura merely gave a long, drawn-out whimper.

He barely managed to turn on the autopilot and send them on the programmed course to Taurus Station before he passed out.

When he awoke, a white sphere with four arms and a round head was sitting on his lap. Two of the arms ended in thick hypodermic needles that were stuck into the crooks of his arms, the others were dressing his head with a nanonic bandage. The medibot's face showed a broad smile under ridiculously large eyes.

"Hello, patient. You have suffered a moderate concussion, plus a fracture of the left posterior rib—"

"Yes, yes," he said in a distracted voice and blinked slowly. Through the cockpit window he saw nothing but blackness interspersed with glittering dots. "How long was I unconscious?"

"Eleven minutes. There were more important priority cases," the bot replied.

"Did someone die?"

"No. All patients are in stable condition."

"Can I get up?"

"Yes." The arms with the syringes retreated and the other two seemed to be done with bandaging. Deftly, the robot folded up the tools and climbed over to Aura, who wasn't bleeding but must have been hurt judging by her angry expression.

"Hey, how—"

"Just don't say anything, all right?"

Defensively, he raised his hands and carefully stood. He was dizzy and the metallic taste of painkillers was on his tongue.

"Sorry I saved us," he muttered, checking their course again.

They were apparently not being followed and would reach the inner jump point in a few minutes, which fortunately, was not guarded by Fleet ships—which surprised him a little. His shock that his original course had included jumping from the inner to the outer jump point to save a great deal of time had turned out to be unnecessary. But why?

With a gruff gesture, he called up the system overview and was surprised to find that almost all the military ships were at the hyperspace gate at the outer jump point, and in tight formation in front of the gate.

"What's going on there? That looks like they're about to jump."

"Would you rather stay here?" Aura asked.

"No! We'll jump. If they're busy, maybe they won't notice if we show up at their party."

"You're going to jump straight to the fleet? Are you crazy?"

"They're not going to shoot at a civilian ship. Especially not so close to a transit. Isn't the battle supposed to start tomorrow?"

"I don't know. Do you really think they're going to share their plans with the public? If they led us to believe it was tomorrow, it makes sense for it to start today."

"I'm going to go check on the others," he said and pointed to the console. "Execute jump on schedule."

She saluted ironically. He limped out of the cockpit and into the corridor. First, he went to the infirmary, a small squat room with a medical capsule and two treatment couches where Willy and Jezzy lay. The latter was unconscious and hooked to a ventilator. Willy, on the other hand—mostly metal and wires anyway—was awake and scowled at him. Was anyone on this ship ever in a good mood?

"Before you say anything," Dev said, raising a finger, "we're still alive!"

"Oh, thank you very much!" Willy grumbled, nodding to his right. "Best go check on your passenger. Dozer's already radioed that he's just got a bit of a headache, but we don't want this guy dead in the mess hall and have all this be for nothing. After all that and we want to get paid." The flight engineer tilted his head. "We are getting paid, aren't we?"

"Wake up Jezzy, we're about to jump!" Dev quickly slipped out and trudged to the mess hall, which was two doors down. He stopped in front of the control panel, which had a red light indicating a lockdown, he tensed and ran his hand over it and heard an ascending triad. The bulkhead opened upward, and he jumped violently to see the stranger standing directly in front of him on the other side and looked him in the eye. He was completely soaked yet seemed composed enough to make Dev clear his throat.

"Hello, uh, we're in orbit and about to jump."

Sirion merely nodded.

"We're on our way to Taurus Station. That's as far as we can take you, but then we're even, understand? We don't like to be blackmailed, and this"—he made a somewhat vague gesture—"we don't normally do this, even for friends."

"The Taurus Station is sufficient," Sirion replied neutrally.

Sufficient? What the hell does that mean? He should damn well say that we're even!

21

"You can't do that, Captain!" Murphy pleaded as he stumbled down the ramp of the shuttle, which stood between the open gates. The force field that protected the gigantic hangar from the pitch-black of space glittered blue. Two Marines from the *Caesar* pushed him rather roughly down toward the deck of the *Oberon* before grabbing Konrad by the arms.

Immediately, the surrounding technicians rushed forward and gathered in a semicircle around the scene like a barely controlled mob. But Konrad shook his head in their direction, whereupon the two Marines relaxed somewhat.

"I'm glad you're back on board, Chief," he replied, nodding to his chief engineer, now Silly's chief engineer.

"Sir, this—"

"Take good care of the Old Lady, that's an order."

Murphy, usually never at a loss for a cynical comment, nodded weakly and then he was out of sight as Konrad was led up the ramp into the belly of the shuttle. He didn't turn around and allowed himself to be pressed into one of the bucket seats, his head held high. Only now did the Marines, of whom there were two more behind the pilots, place a cortical jammer around his neck, a small device that, if he moved too hard or too fast, would cause him to feel dizzy, nauseous, and disoriented.

During the flight, he did not speak, did not take out his indignation at the treatment he was receiving from these soldiers who were only doing their duty. He merely closed his eyes. If Augustus wanted to humiliate him to boost his ego, so be it. It didn't matter much now anyway. All that mattered was that Silly got his ship and crew to safety, even if that meant following the exiles into the dark distance of the Milky Way. Any fate was preferable to him than simply being dissolved and forgotten, diluted in the ranks of the Federation Fleet, which would like to simply erase any memory of Harbingen, and the perceived shame associated with it.

When they arrived on the *Caesar*, he was taken directly to the bridge from the airlock, which, admittedly, surprised him. The command center of the flagship was a much more modern concept than the one that had been used in the construction of the *Oberon*. It had a huge holoscreen that gave the impression of looking out a window forward of the ship, even though they were deep inside, armored and magnetically shielded with redundant systems that could ensure they had power and oxygen for days even if the reactors and ammunition chambers were destroyed. Well-trained bridge officers with practical experience had become scarce after so many decades of war, and Fleet had become increasingly concerned about losing as few sailors as possible since they could produce more ships faster than they could train suitable personnel.

Augustus sat in a ridiculously opulent chair, surrounded by just six operators in reclining seats with virtual displays in front of them. Their hands were in feedback gloves, which they used to make inputs into their data consciousness. Images appeared in front of them via holography so the commander could see what they were doing. Nothing about this was reminiscent of the great hall on *Oberon* with its many uniformed people working as if in a small hive. It was absolutely silent, and at the center of it all was the admiral, who turned as they entered.

"Ah, Captain Bradley. So, we meet again," he said with no small amount of self-satisfaction in his voice.

Konrad did not reply.

"You know this is the end, Captain, don't you?"

He shrugged. "I'm an old man. I had to retire at some point."

Augustus smiled thinly. "It's the end of the *Oberon*, and you know it."

"I think you underestimate my team."

"No. You *overestimate* them. Their hope is probably that the *Oberon* can escape, join the exiles, or find a new start somewhere very far away." That smile again. "But now that you're here, let me tell you a secret: That's not going to happen. According to the operational plan, one-third of my fleet is serving as a reserve to protect the gate on this side. Headquarters felt that the fact that the Clicks have been here before to destroy the Lagoon might suggest that they still have undiscovered listening posts or something similar nearby. We don't want them to interfere with our plans at the last moment, so I can assure you that my instructions to the ships that stay behind do not include a free pass for the *Oberon*. No one is leaving this system."

Konrad clenched his jaw.

"You didn't think you were going to get away with that criminal act, did you, Captain?"

"If you say so."

"Harbingen must come to an end," Augustus continued. "You know that as well as I do. What happened back then was a disaster, a tragedy, and depending on who you ask, either you alone are to blame, or Omega is."

"As with every problem, you need someone to blame to get yourself off the hook."

"It's not that simple and you know it."

"I see. Then why do you think 'Harbingen must come to an end'?"

"Because shortly we will achieve that victory we have long dreamed of. A victory that will restore the Federation to a time of freedom and exploration, bringing us out of a depressing period of restrictions and deprivations. Everyone will see it that way and celebrate it, but not your people, am I right?"

"We've lost everything we fought for," Konrad snapped, and he immediately scolded himself for it when he saw Augustus nod.

"That's what I thought. What good is the victory everyone hoped for if a small nation of refugees will always remind us of what they lost?"

"So, you figured you'd just erase us from memory. That's what I thought."

The admiral eyed him and was about to say something when one of the operators raised his hand.

"Sir, there was an incident on Lagunia that was just trans-mitted to the *Oberon* via satellite," reported the young officer, whom Konrad only saw from behind.

"Unauthorized transit exit at the jump point!" shouted another.

"Identification?"

"Civilian ship, under thirty meters, no active weapons signatures."

"Follow up, keep preparations going."

He is listening to our radio, all inner-system radio, he thought. *That should not surprise me.*

"It's not relevant now," Augustus said to the first operator.

"It was an emergency message with IPV-8 encryption." The admiral stiffened. IPV-8 was the intra-Fleet code for the Terran Information Agency, the civilian intelligence agency that, by emergency laws, had to share all encryption codes with Fleet.

"The TIA has agents on Lagunia?"

"Yes, Admiral. Agent Schmidt has already confirmed the authenticity of the message. It comes from Valeska and Franc Bellinger, an explorer couple who—"

"What does it contain? We have a battle to initiate here!"

Konrad could see on the holoscreen how the huge hyperspace gate in front of them seemed to swell and several ships arranged themselves into a wedge formation in front of it. They were about to activate it.

"Just that they have an emergency and need to evacuate immediately. It was a standard emergency call. Agent Schmidt, however, feels it could be important."

"I see, and why?"

"Because a delegation from the *Danube* in orbit reported to the *Oberon* that they claimed to have seen a federally wanted assassin believed to be working for the syndicate at the location of the distress call, but was evacuated by a smuggler ship before they could catch him or rescue the couple. They were shot down and are being recovered."

"Then that's the way it is. Let Schmidt and the *Danube* take care of it." Augustus was indignant.

"The ship that just showed up at the jump point matches the signature of the ship reported by the *Danube*, sir," the operator said.

"We're not here to deal with syndicate criminals. Let the Harbingers take care of that." The admiral looked at the chronometer below the holoscreen. "Activate the gate!"

"They didn't think it was necessary to inform our fleet about the schedule, I suppose." Konrad hadn't really wanted to say anything, but in the end, he couldn't stop himself.

"The Admiralty decided that we were going to move up the schedule from the beginning, contrary to the official feeds. We had to inform the civilian agencies so appropriate arrangements could be made for civilian traffic and to keep the jump points clear—a logistic nightmare, if you ask me. But striking when even our population wasn't expecting it seemed safest. Even if the Clicks got wind of Iron Hammer, we'll still take them by surprise."

"But we're not a civilian fleet!"

Augustus shrugged his shoulders. "Reservists... It's almost the same thing."

"Gate energy matrix cells sixty percent charged," an operator announced, and the huge ring control capacitors, protruding like fat cheeks on the mighty ring, began to glow white as long radiators extended to dissipate the heat they generated.

Augustus, with a terse wave, ordered the Marines, "Take the captain into the brig."

UNKNOWN POSITION, OORT CLOUD, LAGUNIA SYSTEM

"These are unfavorable developments."

One of the two men in the dark room with the cold glowing display wiped aside the blurred camera image showing the scene on the bridge of the *Caesar*, which was already more than half an hour old.

"The Bellingers almost blurted out their find," the other voice replied. Only the glow of a lone cigar gave any light in the room, peeling an unmoving face out of the darkness.

"*Almost*, but not quite. Konrad Bradley is in control of the admiral, and that's all, so everything is going according to plan. The chancellor is on his way, isn't he?"

"Yes."

"Where do we go from here?"

"That remains to be seen. It depends on how well Bradley keeps his crew under control. Even when he tells them to do something they resist with every cell. Though, we might be surprised. These Omegans won't make a difference, that's for sure."

"Are you sure? The *Oberon* has already proven to be extremely unruly and resolute in the past," the smoker said.

"Not the *Oberon*, she's just an old Titan, Bradley. It's

Captain Bradley who made her the unpredictable beast she is today. His XO is a minor minion who panics without a master."

"People who panic can be dangerous."

"Himself, perhaps. Not us anymore. We'll be out of the shadows soon enough, finally, after so many years. No one will ever change that. Not even the *Oberon*."

The smoker growled, took another drag on his cigar, and clicked his tongue disparagingly. "*He* should have known that sending Sirion here was a risk. This could still end badly. We need Bradley. In fact, we need every single Harbinger."

"*He's* the one who makes the decisions, and there's good reason for that, you should remember that. Otherwise, you sound like an Omegan. Speaking of *Omegans*, remember, those are Harbingers out there, but they're not the same as us." There was a brief pause in which they were both silent. "I'm sure Sirion had no alternative. After all, you don't get the railgun out of the closet when you go sparrow hunting."

"Do you naval types really *always* have to unpack railgun metaphors?" the smoker snorted, blowing out a thick cloud of smoke.

"A tungsten cone fired from a railgun works only with force, without its own propulsion..."

"So, the picture hardly fits our agent."

"... but at the same time is highly accurate, especially due to its speed. If it penetrates the hull of its target, depending on the armor, it may simply exit the other side and continue flying endlessly."

"And what is that supposed to tell me now?" the smoker asked. "That Sirion can no longer be captured?"

"His main purpose has long since been fulfilled. On Lagunia. *He* will have calculated everything else. Perhaps he sees Sirion as a kind of Plan B for the admiral—without his knowledge, of course."

"He always has a plan B; I think we can agree on that."

"We need a simple solution from Bradley, nothing more. Either he will give it to us, or we will find another way. The basis of either is that he never commands the *Oberon* again. I think that should be achievable, so don't worry about it."

Another long glow from the cigar. The accompanying face appeared orange in the darkness. "We should have briefed the admiral further so he could make fewer mistakes. I doubt he'll do what's necessary when it starts."

"He will. Bretoni is a smarter man than those who see him only as a vain, career-obsessed peacock who loves to stride across the Senate marble. If he didn't have principles above his emotions, he wouldn't be working for us, would he? He'll see the greater reason in everything when the time comes, if he doesn't already."

"I hope you're right."

22

"He *what*?" Nicholas almost shouted. He stood hunched over the command deck, staring angrily at the XO.

"You heard me, Commander," Silly said coolly. Her upper lip twitched slightly, betraying the emotions she was struggling to hold back.

"And here we have them, the two stones that once every ten years become glowing lava," Jason commented about the surreal scene. It was very quiet on the bridge of the *Oberon*. The air almost crackled. He had rarely seen his brother so uncontrolled, at least in front of others. They had spent all their time together as children and teenagers, so he knew how Nicholas really felt inside.

"The captain has made a decision and I have to respect it," the new commander continued, and although Jason despised her—she was nothing but a failed Fleet lapdog with no backbone of her own—he had to admit that her self-control was amazing. After all, she had nothing in her life but the great "admiral" in whose shadow she had always felt so at ease. Now her protection was swimming away and everyone here knew she would be overwhelmed with command, herself included. But at least she didn't let it show.

"That's... that's..." Nicholas gasped and pushed himself away from the command table, which made all their faces glow chalky white in the darkness of the bridge. Frustrated, his brother clenched his hands into fists and collected himself, as if waking from a dream and only now realizing where he was. "Request to be relieved of bridge duty."

"Rejected," Silly replied immediately and took a deep breath. Her voice was softer now, if that was at all possible in a woman who always sounded like two pieces of sandpaper rubbing together. More quietly, she added, "I need an experienced officer like you on the bridge."

Nicholas said nothing, and Jason expected the XO—no, the commander—to turn her gaze on him at any moment to throw him into the brig, or at least from the *Oberon*'s control center, but she didn't, ignoring him instead as if he were a ghost. He knew she didn't like him, and he wondered if she tolerated him because he was the son of the man she saw as a fatherly mentor.

"XO!" someone shouted from the ranks, and no one seemed to notice he was using the wrong rank designation.

"Speak!"

"The jump gate has been activated! Full charge of energy pattern cells in three minutes!"

"Holodisplay!" Silly commanded, and a huge three-dimensional image of nearby space was projected over the command deck, with the jump gate in the center. Before the giant ring, waited much of Strike Group 2, with the *Caesar* at the center of the dense, flattened arrow formation. About a third of the fleet, however, had hung back, forming a fan between the arrow and the *Oberon*, whose escort ships were on the starboard side facing away.

"That looks strange," Daussel observed. The lieutenant commander pointed to the fan of Terran ships facing them.

"That looks like the admiral doesn't plan on jumping with

his entire Strike Group," Silly opined, sucking in her lower lip. "If that was ever the plan in the first place."

"Charge at eighty percent!" came shouts from the ranks.

"Do you think Augustus won't keep his promise?" Daussel asked.

"He will," Jason said, "but in his own way."

"What's odd is something else entirely," Nicholas said calmly. "The admiral's fleet is positioned defensively. It doesn't fit the mission profile. He's trying to hide it with the implied triangle, but when the tip pulls back with short maneuvers, it becomes a dented crescent, defensive."

Every eye at the table turned to him, then back to Jason—except Silly's.

"He sees himself as a man of honor, but he's also a politician at heart, as is everyone who has made it to the Admiralty," Jason explained. "From his point of view, he's kept the appointment, but he hasn't promised to leave any chaperones for us."

"All right. I want full combat readiness," decided the involuntary commander.

"But, Commander, we have talked to the admiral—" Daussel started to object, but she silenced him with a raised finger.

"Maybe so. I don't plan to open fire either, but if someone puts a fleet in front of us, I'm not going to sit on my hands. Besides, given the occasion—the start of a Fleet operation into enemy territory—we have the right under the rules to go into combat readiness. After all, those ships there are, aren't they?"

"Jump gate active. Terminus is powering up!" one of the operators shouted, their eyes lowered to the holodisplay, which was deceptively convincing, as if they were looking out into real space. The light on the bridge changed from cool white to dark red.

Four hundred thousand kilometers away, the massive ring of

Lagunia's hyperspace gate hung in the vacuum. In the background, the silhouette of the gas giant Artros with its brown-red cloud bands was displayed like a two-dimensional wallpaper. Miles of radiators grew out of the six thickened jaws that clamped onto the structure like anachronistic calipers. They glowed cherry red as, in the circle between them, the twinkle of stars in the darkness was replaced by a flash of white that immediately faded. The light from distant suns began to rotate and bulge inward as high-energy particles formed a flux and dissipated in a burst of hard gamma rays. Then there was only blackness, so all-encompassing and perfect that all the sensors on the human ships sounded the alarm, hovering like ants in front of the structure.

No one had known what the passage would look like, since it had only been produced mathematically and in simulations but had never been observed. Every eye that looked at a display or holo-representation at that moment saw nothing less than perfect darkness, an indescribable depth that was more than the mere absence of photons.

"What happened?" Silly demanded. "Didn't it work?"

"The gate isn't reporting any malfunctions," Daussel said, typing away on a holo-keypad on his side of the table, reading off data.

"But shouldn't there be—" The commander stopped herself, because anything else probably would have sounded strange. But Jason knew what she wanted to say: Shouldn't there be a glow? A blue window that looked like a rippled water surface? Or a dark green undertow? This oppressive blackness, in which every bit of light was lost, was so unnatural and unsettling that even an explosion would have been preferable to him.

"Strike Group 2 is moving!"

Jason watched as the admiral's arrow formation began moving toward the subspace terminus, a sight of perfection as hundreds of ships advanced simultaneously in a flawless pattern. They were arranged to fly through the ring without course corrections and come out the other side—or so Fleet's scientists surmised—in exactly the same way. The intense exhaust flares cut through the vacuum and grew into longer and longer tails.

For some time, no one said anything until Nicholas cleared his throat and spoke up. "Our overseers are still here."

"What about combat readiness?" Silly asked. There was a faint gleam in her eyes, and Jason suspected that the reason lay hidden in every other crew member of the *Oberon* and its accompanying fleet: The pain of not being part of the most important operation of this war, when late revenge was taken on humanity's archenemy and its home system would be reduced to rubble. No one had more reason than the Harbingers to want to bring fire and death down on the Clicks, and yet they were the ones who had to stay behind, and watch others fulfill the fate reserved for them.

Jason had never understood this fanaticism and had breathed a real sigh of relief for the first time when he had left Lagunia and the *Oberon*. Their shared past was the cement of this crew but at same time the straitjacket from which they could not escape without losing their footing. Would this connection dissolve and disappear as soon as their nemesis was brought to its knees?

"We're having problems with the weapons systems," replied Lieutenant Bauer at Fire Control.

"What do you mean?" Silly asked somberly.

"We can control the various weapons systems but get no feedback on their function. All the indicators are yellow."

"Commander!" shouted an older female NCO of the highest rank who didn't know Jason. She sounded horrified. "Activity in the jump gate!"

"Activity? What kind of activity?" demanded Daussel.

"Refresh display, damn it!" Silly braced her fists on the command deck until finally the holodisplay flickered and after a lag generated a simulated real-time image: The circle in the ring was as black as ever, but now something shimmered inside it. A faint glint, no, several, many, and it became more. At first, Jason thought the twinkling stars had returned, but then the shimmer became stronger, denser.

It came closer.

"Anyone have any idea what we're looking at?" the commander asked.

Before anyone could answer someone yelled, "Enemy contacts!"

"Twelve thousand contacts! Number increasing!"

"Strike Group 2 breaking formation!"

"Energy spikes in the gate's energy pattern cells!"

"What kind of contacts? Identify!" Silly interrupted the many shouts, trying to keep order. Face pale, she asked the question that had immediately occurred to them all: "Clicks?"

"Negative! Unknown signatures!"

The first explosions blossomed among the leading edge of the admiral's fleet.

23

"Shit, what is that?" Dev yelled at no one in particular. He jerked the *Quantum Bitch* hard to starboard to avoid a huge ship that had abruptly shot out of the activated hyperspace gate as if it had materialized directly in front of them. All the warning indicators on the instruments and the holodisplays frantically flashed red.

"Shouldn't our ships be *flying* in?" Jezzy asked in a strained voice.

"It's the Clicks!" Willy said firmly.

"No Clicks!" Dev growled, turning on all the military systems the *Quantum Bitch* possessed. Normally, he would never have done this in such close proximity to Fleet ships—or *any* ships, for that matter—but now it was a matter of sheer survival. Hell, everyone could know they had illegal weapons and jammers, as long as they got out of this in one piece.

As the *Bitch* raced through the oncoming fleet, its fusion tail blazing and its maneuvering thrusters firing again and again, chaos erupted all around them.

Whoever the attackers were, of which his scanners had already picked up over a hundred of various sizes and more were appearing, they wasted no time. They fired with missiles whose engines flickered strangely and showed no plasma flares but seemed to absorb the darkness of space itself. Their weapons spewed swarms of flashing ammunition into space, flooding it with metal. For a few moments, the admiral's Strike Group seemed completely caught off guard and unresponsive, after all, they were in a waiting position right in front of the gate and were now suddenly surrounded by enemies from nowhere.

But then they returned fire and chaos turned to pure madness. Whole swarms of missiles raced toward each other, only to explode because of the short distances. Kinetic projectiles shredded everything in their path until something stood in their way that was heavily armored enough not to shatter immediately. Those with explosives approached the enemy to detonate near them, vaporizing everything around them. X-rays and laser beams, highly focused pulses of radiation invisible to the eye, probed for sensitive systems like sensors and antennae to melt. From the flanks of the carrier ships, dozens of Predator drones were simultaneously catapulted from their launch pads at two-second intervals, and shortly thereafter aligned themselves against the unknown invaders, only to be immediately shot down or begin firing.

Sensors were operating at reduced power as the entire surrounding space boiled with hard radiation and was flooded with minute debris that reflected off radar and lidar and made for hundreds of tiny fractals on screens. A unified image was hard to generate because it was just a random jumble of ships hammering each other with everything they had. Nothing about this battle was elegant or strategic; it was a brutal slaughter. They slammed into each other without caution at such short distances that Dev could see ships and muzzle flashes with the naked eye through the cockpit window.

The *Quantum Bitch* launched decoys. Tiny, heated cylinders that shot off from their launch tubes with cold gas jets, mimicking the flight vectors and radar reflections of missiles.

However, due to the incessant proximity alarms of the completely overloaded pilot software, the supply was exhausted after less than a minute. The jammers also fired everywhere at once and yet into nothing, since there were far too many targets for them to even identify.

A laser, judging by its wavelength in the electromagnetic spectrum X-rays, briefly swept over the *Bitch*, but with such intensity that half of the dorsal sensor clusters failed.

"Shit! Damn it!" Dev cursed, dodging a stray kinetic projectile, a trundling missile with a massive iron head whose targeting computer had apparently been fried by the omnipresent radiation.

"We're almost blind!" Jezzy yelled.

"Thanks, I noticed!" he shot back.

There was a *bang!* and another warning light popped on somewhere. He had no idea where or what it meant, just a part of his brain noticing a tiny change in the confusion of red flashing lights.

"Uh, Captain?" Something in Willy's voice was unfamiliar enough that Dev immediately wheeled around in his seat, only to be painfully reminded of his seat belt. He turned his head until it cracked and saw that Aura's left leg was missing. Blood spurted from the stump, which she stared at in disbelief, her face pale, before she began to scream. He noticed the blood was flowing unnaturally down and up at the same time, directly toward two holes barely larger than a golf ball, but just as round and sharply defined. If not for the red spots around them, he wouldn't have even recognized them.

"Railgun!" said Willy, unbuckling his seat belt to rip a medikit off the wall and come to his comrade's aid.

"Jezzy, seal it up!" Dev ordered, turning back to the controls. The air was already getting thinner.

The pilot software incessantly tossed his ship back and forth, as it attempted to dodge projectiles it could see— missiles—and those it thought it could identify from registered muzzle flashes from surrounding ships, but which it could not see because they had no propulsion of their own— railguns. Like a half-blind cripple, the *Quantum Bitch* staggered along the edge of the battle, along the outer reaches of madness, and Dev gave them no more than a few minutes before they had to extend their radiator, simply because of the many heated particles in space all around, which kept heating them up.

Dry-mouthed, he licked his lips, which felt like running sandpaper over an open wound, then came up with a plan just crazy enough that it might work.

"Boss, why are we flying toward the ring?" Jezzy shouted from behind him. Her voice had once again taken on the sound of a badly tuned violin that had been stroked too hard by its player. Somewhere above and behind him he heard her sealing the small hole the stray railgun round had punched in his ship.

"Shouldn't we get out of here, man?" Willy asked. The wet smacking sounds coming from his direction sent a shiver down Dev's spine. He silently prayed to himself that Aura survived and didn't lose too much blood before the medikit did its work. She had stopped screaming, so the analgesics were obviously working.

"Not a chance," he replied curtly, pushing the ship at full thrust under a ship that had sprung from the massive darkness of the event horizon, which spread across several kilometers inside the ring. Even the pale static discharges along the monstrous structure seemed garish and intrusive in comparison.

The *Quantum Bitch*, aided by the pilot software, dodged thorny attachments and antennae that stabbed out of hyperspace and from the hull of the colossus like daggers into normal space. There were so many of them that Dev thought he had run into the spines of an interstellar hedgehog.

"What the hell is that?" he muttered, turning on the real-time sensor data still coming in from the crippled eyes on his beloved *Bitch*. The image they pieced together on the holo-screen made his blood run cold. The "ship" was several hundred meters long, possibly half a kilometer. Its bow section was curved forward like the nose of a cold-blooded horse, and dozens of gleaming metal lances jutted from it into the void as if to impale everything in its path. The hull was dull gray, but not uniformly dark, and littered with bulges. The middle section and the stern were more bulbous, giving the ship an insect-like feel, as if a Gothic artist had cast a particularly sinister-looking scarab in metal.

Whoever had built this monstrosity, humanity had obviously never encountered them before, because Dev knew all kinds of ship types, human or Click made, and this one was certainly not one of them. Dark green plasma lances erupted from massive cannons that protruded from small flaps, and he could already see himself and his crew ending up as gas in a vacuum, but the shots raced past them, presumably blending in with the rest of the battle.

Relieved at this fortunate twist of fate, he jerked the *Quantum Bitch* to port and sped toward the left edge of the hyperspace gate, where one of the thicker sections that looked like an oversized brake shoe was visible.

"The first ones are throwing in the towel!" announced Jezzy, and Dev's gaze darted to a display on his left, which showed processed real-time images of the battle as captured by the aft telescopes at maximum magnification. Sure enough, ten percent or more of the admiral's ships were extending their radiators, huge heat dissipation panels, some longer than the hull of the spacecraft in question. Like black solar cells, they grew longer and longer, stretching far into the vacuum to radiate the excess heat from within. For them, the battle was over. In most battles, the radiators going out meant that so many systems had failed and that the ship was so badly damaged that it was often considered a loss and the sailors died from heatstroke. Each captain waited as long as he could because once the panels were out, it also meant that the armor was exposed, and with it the unprotected systems. It was a point of no return, like a bug lying on its back with no way of getting back on its feet.

The alien invaders immediately fired at the radiators. The thin, sensitive diverters instantly dissolved into clouds of shrapnel and turned into sparkling geysers of composite. Horrified, Dev stared at the screen and watched as small areas of the affected ships began to glow cherry red. In his mind, soldiers were running through the corridors, sweaty and skin reddened. They shrieked in agony as they were cooked in their own skin from the increasingly rapid buildup of heat inside their ship. Water pipes expanded and burst, releasing fountains of bubbling liquid into the corridors, and anyone who came in contact with it was scalded until their flesh began to slough away. It had to be a grisly death for the men and women out there.

The war between the Federation and the Clicks was bitter and brutal, but even so, it had never before happened that the enemy's ships, which were at their end, were targeted like this. There was no treaty, no agreement, but every sentient being seemed to know what fate they didn't want to inflict on any other sailor, and putting enemy radiators under fire was one of them. Affected starships were no longer able to fire, and most were also unable to maneuver. They posed no danger, not even indirectly, because they could not be salvaged and repaired, at least not in most cases. Of course, it happened that shrapnel or stray bullets would hit a radiator here and there, sealing the fate of the crew, but never with such obvious intent.

The silence grew heavy in the cockpit and Dev had to swallow several times before he could turn away and cut the thrust. They were dangerously close to the ring, and the systems were suffering from the jumping static discharges, against which their electrical shields fought like a firewall of conductor cables.

He ignored another warning light and yanked the *Bitch* upward while applying maximum counterthrust, so the little ship lined up. Then he shut down the thrusters and, despite his trembling hands, delicately adjusted the maneuvering thrusters until, a little roughly due to the many system failures, they approached the bottom of the wide gap between the two parts of the ring's brake shoe. His hair stood on end all over his body and he felt the tingle of the static on his skin, as if ants were walking across it. The thickening in the ring had looked small from a distance, but up close it was huge; a chunk split down the middle, fifty meters square. Through the cockpit window he could see welded composite honeycombs and insulated cables.

A slight jolt went through the *Bitch*, and the magnetic retaining clips were triggered. The charge equalization between the ring and the ship happened immediately, and equilibrium was established, which instantly calmed the corresponding warning indicator and elicited a sigh from Dev.

The windshield now faced the battle, which looked strange to the naked eye, like a distant shower of comets without tails, except that the glowing chunks didn't appear to move while they flashed and flickered around them. It was almost beautiful and graceful the way they covered the stars, far away and yet so much closer than anything else. Five thousand kilometers to the nearest ship was not even worth mentioning in cosmic terms. To the sensors it was as if something was being held directly in front of their eyes. But to the human eye, which was useless out here, everything was happening so far away that all that remained was the beauty of the distant light show. But this beauty had a flaw, namely the images of men and women in Dev's head, boiling in their own fluids and perishing miserably.

"Any ideas what just happened?" Aura gasped. He turned

and looked into her pale face. She looked composed, calmed by the cocktail of drugs that had taken over her nervous system. On the stump of her leg, the medikit clung like a white octopus whose tentacles had crawled up her leg and attached themselves to her. Her foot and the rest of her lower leg were nowhere to be seen, except for the blood that stained half the cockpit red, so Willy had probably already taken it away.

"I don't know," he admitted dryly. "But those aren't Clicks. Shouldn't this damn gate have a safety mechanism that a stable connection must be confirmed by both sides?"

"That's what the feeds said," she grumbled. "But they also didn't say the offensive would start today."

"Maybe the other side confirmed the connection," Jezzy said. "Surely the gate parts that jumped to the endpoint and assembled there should have Fleet code confirmation automation for Iron Hammer."

Aura rolled her eyes. "Again, *that's what the feeds said!*"

"Whoever or whatever this is, I've never seen this kind of spacecraft before. They look like they were welded together in a junkyard."

"Then I don't think they'd shoot up that vain peacock of an admiral's fleet," Dev said gloomily. "I wish the forward tele-scopes were working. One of the plasma lances fried them when we were more than a hundred meters away!"

"Why don't you send a Seeker out so we can see and hear more," Willy suggested.

Dev waved it off. "It would get shot down."

"Maybe, but it has a good radiation shield, and maybe then we'll know when we can get out of here. Anyway, we can't see if the ring is still active. The charge balancing idea was clever. The downside is that only our well-shielded, passive systems still work. In any case, we can't measure anything going on in the gate itself with this."

"You're right," he admitted and pressed the launch button for one of the reconnaissance drones.

The Seeker was a spherical mini-ship about the size of a soccer ball and radar-deflecting hull. It wasn't particularly fast, but hard to track as long as it was traveling at the speed of the launch catapult and didn't have to launch its mini jet.

It left its launch shaft and raced toward the distant gleam.

"Let's wait for the bad news then," Willy grumbled.

"Quite the optimist!"

"If you saw something today that might make me optimistic, send it over!"

Dev reluctantly kept silent.

"Take Aura to the infirmary," he finally instructed Willy. "We're not going anywhere for now anyway."

"But—"

"Right now! I want her in a med pod. The better care she gets now, the easier it will be to clone her a new leg."

"Thanks, boss," Aura croaked. "If you do need me, I'm—"

"Being well taken care of in sickbay," he interrupted her and waited until the two limped out of the cockpit.

Jezzy, meanwhile, had finished caulking the damaged area and was bent over the instruments beside him. Her expression was feverish as she gazed through the window at the battle before them, which looked deceptively distant.

"The first probe data is coming in." She pointed to the main screen.

"Way too much interference. The damn vacuum is crackling with radiating particles," he said. There was no visual data since the spy probe had no optical sensors on board. Instead, it only collected passive incoming signals, of which there were normally a lot, like automatic transponder beacons and radio traffic, but now such a multitude that no clear picture emerged. Here and there, scraps of unencrypted radio messages could be heard, mainly from civilian ships that had actually wanted to witness the departure of Strike Group 2 and were now accelerating in panicked flight toward Lagunia.

"Did you hear that?" Jezzy asked.

"What, the static noise?"

"No! There was something about Bradley being arrested."

"Bradley like the *Oberon Bradley*?"

"Yes. Then I guess Fleet has—"

"Fuck Fleet. Look at that one!" He pointed to a large spot on the schematic of the battle that was approaching their position, even though it was the object farthest away from them.

"That must be the *Oberon*."

"Yes! And I know what they're up to!"

"What?" Jezzy asked, and she twisted her mouth into a grimace.

"I wouldn't bet on it, but I know what I would do if I were them. They're the only ship that wasn't built to maneuver quickly and outsmart enemy ships with rapid acceleration patterns. The *Oberon* was built solely to take the longest beating possible without striking sail. She's not a precision tool, she's a hammer, and we're sitting right on the anvil here."

"Oh you—"

"Yes! Get them both back from the infirmary. Tell them to buckle up! And tell our guest that—"

"We need to get on that ship," a new voice said, and they wheeled around at the same time—Dev as far as his seat belt would allow. Sirion stood in the doorway to the cockpit, his face expressionless.

"How do you—*what* are you talking about?"

"The *Oberon*. We need to get on the *Oberon*."

"You can't."

"Make it happen." Sirion turned on his heel and left.

"Shit!" Dev pounded on the controls. "Shit, shit, shit! We're not going to—"

"We *can't*," Jezzy corrected him, and only now did he see that she had tried to power up the engines, but they were not responding.

"Oh no."

UNKNOWN POSITION, OORT CLOUD, LAGUNIA SYSTEM

"What did we do?"

"What it takes."

"This is going differently than we thought," the smoker said as they watched the battle ignite on the display.

"Only marginally," the other replied, though he had to work hard to sound as composed as ever.

"There are so many."

"There are enough."

"I would like to remind you that our ships have left the shipyards. There is no turning back."

"That thing coming out of hyperspace destroyed Lagunia. They must have been technologically superior to us if Bellinger is to be believed. Did you think we'd only have to deal with a couple small sloops?"

"No, but that looks like a glimpse of hell."

"That's what the Lagoon called it, too, I guess."

"This one won't take," the smoker muttered. His cigar hadn't glowed for quite a while.

"The *Oberon*'s escort fleet is evacuating, sit tight."

"And where are they going to go?"

"That's not our decision. They knew that scenario had a high probability, with all its consequences."

"That one"—the smoker pointed vehemently at the display flickering with explosions—"is big enough that even *he* can't estimate the consequences. We've opened Pandora's box."

"Strictly speaking, the Federation did," he reminded his compatriot.

"The thing with the oldest Bradley son, that was a mistake."

"A mistake?"

"He behaved differently than expected. A miscalculation."

"That's just a detail." He turned to the smoker and froze the image. "The darkness is here now, and it's not going away anytime soon. I understand you're scared; you won't be alone in that. But this dark force"—he gestured to the image in front of them without looking—"is the best thing that could have happened to humanity, mark my words."

"What about the Clicks?" the smoker wanted to know.

"What about them? Who knows what the metal skulls are up to or will do? For me, only one thing is certain: They are a lot wiser than we are, but powerless against what has come here to our galaxy. If they are skilled, they may be able to use it to their advantage."

"And would that be a good thing?" The mockery in his voice echoed heavily through the narrow room.

"When I look at the state of the Federation, I don't think it could get any worse than it is, even under Click rule."

"We agree on that." For the first time, the front of the cigar glowed red again. "Shall we send our ships?"

"Not yet." He pointed to the hyperspace gate in the center of the display, which looked blurry and distorted in the still image. "Jason Bradley might turn out to be valuable after all. Let's give him some time."

24

"Forward flak has reached full power!"

"Railguns at maximum output!"

"Molecular bond generators at seventy percent capacity!"

Commander Silvea "Silly" Thurnau looked up from the command deck toward the operators, who looked like ghostly faces at their stations. Since it was dark, so as not to offer any distractions, the sailors' features were illuminated only by their displays, which looked downright garish, unlike modern holoscreens.

"That's enough," she decided, nodding to no one in particular.

"Well, now we're lying here like a beached whale," Jason said. "I suggest we pick a strategic target and—"

"Noted," she interrupted the young officer. She wanted to throw him off the bridge, but he was still the old man's eldest son, so she did not give up hope that there was something of his father in him. Konrad, at least, seemed to think so, otherwise he would have refused this ungrateful fellow's entry onto the *Oberon*. That would have been an affront to Admiral Augustus, of course, but such rudeness on the part of reserve units was commonplace; after all, many of the second-class soldiers didn't know any better and weren't exactly highly qualified when it came to protocol. "But we're holding position."

"But—"

"We already have a strategic target." Her eyes fell on the command table, which separated them like a rectangle of pure light on which red, green, and yellow dots shifted back and forth in real time, lighting up briefly and dying out here and there. An out-of-control orgy of destruction in a vacuum, broken down to three colors and simple symbols.

"We can't save him!" The lieutenant commander's voice had a sharp tone. Silly swallowed her anger and calmly raised her eyes. She was in command now, and the lump in her throat at this responsibility would not go away just because she let her anger run wild. Apart from the fact that this rage had, to a large extent, nothing to do with Jason Bradley.

"We can and we will," she replied coolly.

"They seem to have forgotten what they owe to him. What *we all* owe him."

"How could you even agree to this demand by the admiral?" Nicholas asked, who had been uncomfortably silent until now. His eyes were sparkling with emotions that were being held back with difficulty. She had never seen him so upset, and she sympathized with every bit of it.

"Surely you don't expect me to disobey an order from your father." Silly watched the tactical overview as the ships of her escort fleet set off at full thrust to flee the battle. The Fleet butts from the admiral's Strike Group would grumble about the "cowardly reservists," but they always did anyway. The flag officers would joke about the frontline officers, the frontline officers would joke about the staff officers, the NCOs would joke about the officers, and the active Fleet personnel were united in looking down on the reservists. So let them blaspheme all they wanted, her priority was to save what was left of Harbingen and get as many civilians to safety as possible.

She had positioned the *Oberon* to shield the bulk of the ships from the seemingly indiscriminate formation of enemies. It didn't give her many options, but it bought them time. Nicholas seemed to want to say something else, but she shook her head. "Not now!"

She turned to Daussel. "Design me a deployment pattern that will get us into CQB with the *Caesar* once our fleet is outside the red threat area." The lieutenant commander nodded.

"You want to go to close combat distance with the flagship?" Jason Bradley gasped like a choking fish. "Are you insane? May I remind you that the Federation ships are not our enemy, those damn aliens are?"

"Discipline on deck!" his younger brother said sternly, and they exchanged a long look.

Finally, Jason narrowed his eyes and squeezed out, "Yes, Commander."

Silly nodded to Konrad's younger son, but he did not respond. Instead, he studied the tactical map between them.

"Four hundred ships and counting." He voiced what had been troubling her for several minutes. Whoever the alien invaders were with their strangely indifferent space cruisers, their numbers were large enough to cause real problems for the Strike Group, even if they hadn't been caught cold and already reported five percent losses before the slaughter even started. The reason had been that, due to the so-called mass ejection effect, when transferred through a stable hyperspace link, any incoming object materialized from subspace at near-relativistic speed. Fleet had been informed of the corresponding information of the research and development department, however, not on *this* side. On the contrary, the instructions had been to turn forty-five degrees to port or starboard immediately after transit to avoid colliding with following ships and ending up as a volatile gas cloud. The invaders either hadn't expected so much traffic in front of the gate, or they didn't care. In any case, the first ten ships had turned the leading edge of the admiral's formation into spreading spheres of debris before anyone understood what had even happened. Now they knew. Instead of taking the fight to the enemy's home, they had been caught by surprise, at that point furthest from the planned front line of Operation Iron Hammer.

"Enemy fire is still concentrated on the center of Admiral Augustus's fleet," Lieutenant Feugers called out.

"We're holding position." She had understood what the lieutenant was trying to say, after all, she could read the positions herself in front of her. The crew was anxious to join in the frontline fighting.

Currently, they were to the relative west of the flattened formation of the fleet in front of the jump gate. The billowing red battle area on the command table, showing that area where the density of active weapons systems was so high that sensors were unable to generate a real-time image, was called the CQB, close quarter battle, zone, where ships engaged each other with short-range weapons and evasive maneuvers were impossible. No captain ever voluntarily entered a CQB situation because close defenses had little to no time to react to projectiles. However, the forward half of Augustus's Strike Group 2 was in CQB, and the red zone was pushing further and further into the formation. She had to acknowledge that she was impressed. In a fleet even slightly less disciplined, it would have broken up long ago.

The *Caesar* seemed to hover like a fixed star amid the cone of cruisers and destroyers, firing volleys of missiles and torpedoes at regular intervals, but had not yet launched any Predators, while the escort ships had long since thrown every single drone into the fray.

Straining, Silly tried to tune out the muffled conversations, the whir of computer systems, and the occasional vibration as a missile overcame the *Oberon*'s defenses and exploded or shattered on the fifteen-meter-thick armor of carbon and mono-bonded carbotanium. She had to understand how the attackers were proceeding. What looked like a chaotic raid might be allowing them to act effectively.

Konrad always did. *Every move follows a consideration and every consideration in Fleet combat is based on a huge nothing called space,* he had once said.

Space is empty, she reminded herself. *How many moves can you make there?*

She rubbed her temples and looked at the *Oberon* on the holomap, which hovered as a schematic bar of green light at the edge of the battlefield, trying to *sense* the actual situation in her mind's eye.

The *Oberon* was heavily armored enough that kinetic missiles could strike dozens of times per minute, and it would still take hours for enough small craters in the carbon to become a breach, and yet her armor began much farther out. Over one thousand Votan anti-aircraft guns on the starboard side fired their shells into space at a rate of sixty rounds per minute each, forming a shield of exploding shrapnel charges five thousand kilometers away. The steady, hemispherical cloud of tungsten fragments amid the bright explosions was virtually impenetrable to missiles and torpedoes. Only railgun shells managed to penetrate the flexible shield here and there, but those were mostly intercepted by the short-range defenses; small rotary cannons that spat out thousands of computer-controlled rounds per minute to shred the hard-to-locate iron cones.

Even farther out than the wall of shell explosions, which at the moment were not even at half the possible density, about five thousand more kilometers away were the first ships of Strike Group 2. These were mainly smaller corvettes and gunboats constantly launching guided missiles that were heading toward the denser areas of fighting at ludicrous acceleration rates of 100 Gs and more. Three thousand kilometers away, the first ships of the sinister invaders *flowed* through a tangle of missiles and unpowered projectiles. She could think of no better word to describe their movements. Although they looked crude and misshapen, they seemed to float gracefully through the vacuum, with no visible plasma jets to indicate maneuvering. Instead, they looked as if they were sucking the darkness into the large funnels at their tails. Silly had never seen anything like it, not even in the conspiracy feeds about supposed secret Fleet projects.

Judging from the initial sensor data, they were firing something like plasma lances at shorter ranges and guided missiles at longer ones. They didn't seem to be particularly accurate on the one hand, but on the other they didn't show any susceptibility to jamming attacks. This was a very different kind of battle compared to the ones they were familiar with when fighting the Clicks. Not two fleets warring at three distances like two jousting knights racing past each other, hoping to throw their opponent out of the saddle. Due to the unusual situation at the gate, something happened that she had never experienced in forty years of service: Two factions forced into close range from one moment to the next. Accordingly, chaos seethed at the center of the inferno that had swallowed half the Strike Group. The admiral's ships, flying neatly into position, were swarmed by the glowing plasma trails of their missiles, which had barely enough time to reach their maximum acceleration before they were either intercepted by plasma lances, smashed against stray debris, or slammed into their targets, adding more metal shards to the madness. Thrusters of Predator drones—by now over six thousand of the unmanned fighters were in use—buzzed seemingly erratically among the warships, which appeared stolid in contrast, firing their submunitions in all directions. Faster than any human pilot could have done, they dodged missiles, scattered electronic jamming fire, and threw out reflector foils before fading away in short-lived fireballs.

Every so often, small suns would awaken for a few seconds, hot balls of plasma that expanded rapidly and dissipated just as quickly when a ship's reactor overheated, or a munitions chamber was hit. Some of these suns, however, were more durable, glowing for a while like red dwarfs before melting into patchy embers when enemies targeted extended radiator panels.

Augustus's fleet wavered. The forward third was down over 60 percent. Muzzle flashes ebbed, and fountains of vented atmosphere occurred on more and more warships where entire compartments were decompressed to put out fires. Silly knew that these geysers of breathable air contained not only debris but also the bodies of hapless sailors. But she didn't follow that eerie thought and instead concentrated, eyelids closed, on what her inner eye was making of the holoscreen's schematic representation.

The admiral's formation was basically nothing more than a sharpened hollow cone with his flagship and two carriers in the middle. It was easy to blame this choice on Augustus's self-absorption or even cowardice, but she would not make the mistake of underestimating him again. The alien ships, on the other hand, were like a storm, trying to destroy the cone by force rather than precision. Not a single drop seemed to have a trajectory that was related to the others. The only common point connecting them was their source: the hyperspace gate.

With the admiral, however, it was different. He maintained order by staying alive and protecting the *Caesar*. That was also the reason why his overrun Strike Group had not yet broken apart. Only now did it occur to her that she had not seen any of the enemy ships explode from strafing. The tactical map had recorded failures on the alien side, where radar and lidar signatures had disappeared, but as far as she could remember, all these incidents had been high-speed collisions.

She opened her eyes and looked at the formation again.

Konrad's sons were talking with each other, but she ignored their voices until she heard only distant bubbling in a calm sea.

"Daussel, what is the status of our escort fleet?" she finally asked when she realized what the admiral was up to. It was amazing what vanity could do.

"Sixty percent are already outside the danger zone. The others will follow in a few minutes," the lieutenant commander replied calmly.

Silly nodded and tapped her finger on one of the green dots at the end of Augustus's formation and lettering appeared: TFS *Garibaldi*. "Lieutenant Alkad, set course for the *Garibaldi*."

"Ma'am, our escort ships are—"

"When in doubt, armed and time plays for them," Daussel said, waving it off.

"May I ask what you have in mind?" Nicholas asked, looking first at her, then at the tactical holomap. Before she could answer, his older brother beat her to it.

"Augustus may have been caught off guard, but he is no longer." Jason pointed to the half-entangled hollow cone that was Strike Group 2. "The back half of his ships are accelerating. Slowly, so it isn't clear to the eye, but they'll wrap around the inside of their sister ships that are being raked in the front, like a second, fresh skin. That way he can keep the enemy tied up in front as long as possible without being heckled."

"And that opens the cocoon for us," Silly added, her eyes fixed on the *Caesar*. But instead of seeing the admiral's flagship in the green dot with the gold star, she merely saw a place where her commander was being held in captivity. "Commander Bradley, inform Colonel Meyer to stand by for the rescue of our captain."

"Ma'am, may I make a comment?" Jason asked, and she gave him a cool look. She knew all too well that he was just being polite so as not to give her a reason to order him off the bridge.

"Speak."

"The gate is still active and more enemy ships are jumping into the system. The Strike Group won't be able to get through to it, but the *Oberon* might be able to hold out long enough to cut a swath and destroy the gate before things get worse."

"The system is doomed," she said. "It doesn't matter how much more their superiority grows. But there is a difference for your father. If we don't get him out of this ship's brig fast enough, he'll die along with your beloved admiral, and I won't let that happen. Once we have him on board, we'll deal with the evacuation of the civilians in the habitats of Artros."

"Comm—*Captain*," Nicholas said, "my brother is right. If we don't stem the influx of invaders, it will be nearly impossible to escape the system via any of the jump points."

"I gave an order," she replied gruffly, steeling herself inwardly. "Alkad! Full combat thrust!"

25

"Dozer, cut the redundancy systems to the radiators!" Dev ordered angrily over the ship's internal radio, pushing himself out of his pilot's chair. Immediately he began to float, and the initial push he had given himself off his armrests sent him upward far too quickly, causing him to bash his head on one of the overhead fittings. The artificial gravity had failed, which meant that the output of the three fusion reactors at the heart of the ship had dropped below fifty percent. But they were still working, at least at reduced efficiency, or life support would have long since gone out and they would eventually suffocate or freeze to death, depending on which system failed first. The energy potential of the hyperspace gate with its gigantic power consumption was much higher than that of the *Quantum Bitch*, which ensured that because of the successive failures of their surge protection, one component after the other would give up the ghost, which one was a pure gamble. Dev had never been averse to games of chance, but on the condition that there was something to be won and he could cheat. After all, any game was more fun if you could influence your own chances of winning in your favor. Here and now, however, there were no chances, except those of a quick death.

"Willy, how are things in the infirmary? Do you have any juice left?" He rubbed the growing bump on his head and shimmied, not very skillfully, along the ceiling to the exit in the direction of the corridor.

"The treatment is still working," came the reply via the button in Dev's right ear. "The stem cell extraction has already gone through; she's just waking up."

"Get her stabilized and then unplug her. After that, immediately get her into one of the escape pods with you!"

"In there, we're going to—"

"Have your own surge protection. This buys you a few minutes. As soon as you register a critical overload, you'll disengage. With the catapult power, you should make it to Taurus Station."

"Boss—"

"Can't you do something without talking back for once, fucking Willy? Last time I checked, *I was* still captain of the *Bitch!*" he grumbled, dodging a dark object that crossed his trajectory. When he realized it was Aura's foot still in a shoe, along with the lower leg shredded below the knee, he winced. The uncontrolled impulse of his body made him collide with the wall again and gave him painful bruises on his elbow and hip.

"We'll hurry," Willy assured him over the radio, apparently misinterpreting his groan.

"Radiators disconnected," Dozer reported unemotionally.

"Good. Jezzy? Release the magnetic docking ports!"

"System not responding!" the fusion engineer replied on the verge of hysteria. Dev's skin on his arms tingled uncomfortably, and a glance down showed him that all the hair on them was standing on end. Here and there it began to pinch.

"What about the keel phalanx?" he asked, thinking while Jezzy, as expected, lectured him on how crazy his idea was. The phalanx was one of two close-in defense guns his ship was equipped with. They called the lower one the keel phalanx because it could reach beyond the depression that housed their airlock and extendable ramp for planetary landings. In cross section from a distance, this looked like the keel of an archaic sailing ship.

"I'd rather shoot our country guns into dust than turn the *Bitch* into an electric chair. Now get on with it!"

Jezzy didn't answer this time, so he hoped she would just shut up and carry out his order. Too frantic to be satisfied about it, he shimmied down to the maintenance hatch in the corridor, through which he could turn off the onboard computer. Just possessing such a hidden shutdown device was enough to secure a one-way ticket to a penal colony on most Core Worlds. This was no wonder, since the pilot software combined all the automated safety features that made safe and efficient piloting of a starship possible in the first place. A human alone, no matter how many implants he was fitted with, was hopelessly inferior to any machine when it came to keeping an eye on numerous factors at the same time and interpreting them quickly and rationally on a permanent basis. Now, however, their only salvation lay in doing something that the onboard computer would immediately stop, because it would most likely lead to their death.

Dev released the flap with a long tap on the hidden DNA scanner, which looked like the indentation of a sticky rivet. It buzzed, and he was able to release the square panel above the baseboard with a quick press and pull it up. He found the switch behind six colored cables sitting on gray metal guides.

"What are you doing?" said a voice, and he winced violently.

"Shit, man!" he cursed and swallowed when he saw Sirion hovering above him on the ceiling like a flying demon. The guy's dark pupils seemed to rotate like black holes in the whites of his eyes, sucking up the light of the entire corridor.

"What are you going to do?" Sirion asked calmly.

"Save this ship!" He flipped the switch. Nothing happened. He had expected an alarm, maybe beeping, something that signaled to him that from now on their minutes were numbered. There was nothing. His skin still felt like it was crackling, but aching rather than tingling now, and the first hairs lifted. "Dozer, are the redundancies off?"

"Yes," came the curt reply.

"Jezzy! Radiators out!"

"Captain! Dev! If we—"

"—don't do it, we'll get grilled! Now do it!"

"*Fuck!*" That was enough confirmation for him.

"They're killing us." From Sirion's mouth it sounded more like an interesting observation than a fearful remark. Was this guy maybe not human at all, but a new kind of robot?

"Yes, but not until later."

"Explain." Dev saw a hand of the never-smiling man move to his hip. The movement looked casual, so it almost escaped him. He couldn't see a weapon, but remembered that even Dozer had been outgunned by him, and didn't want to bet that Sirion didn't know how to hide his murder tools.

"The radiators are crisscrossed by a network of electron matrix cells that use heat pumps to release the potential energy injected into them as thermal energy to the vacuum. Right now, we're being grilled by electric current, which I want to release to friggin' space before it gets to that point."

"I understand." Sirion nodded. "How long will we survive without radiators?"

"It depends. We need to get away from the ring until the discharges stop jumping out at us. Getting here saved our asses, now it's killing us. If we accelerate too hard, the heat radiation from the fusion reactors will cook us in less than half an hour because we haven't deployed the diverters in a long time."

"Can we make it to the *Oberon*?"

"I already told you we're not going to *Oberon*, for crying out loud!" Dev's fear of the taciturn fellow paled before his panic-fed anger and concern for ship and crew. "What the hell do you want with that old bastard anyway?"

Sirion's face hardened even more, if that was even possible. His eyes narrowed and his jaw muscles stood out clearly enough to make Dev swallow. He could hardly save his crew if he let this psychopath cut him open because he couldn't control his emotions.

The guy destroyed an entire research habitat, and probably turned the entire crew into fish food, he recalled, and instinctively backed away, which caused him to bump hard against the deck and sail in Sirion's direction from the renewed momentum before he could grab a panel handle.

"I have one final target in this system and it's on the *Oberon*."

"Target? You want to kill someone else? In case you haven't noticed: Those zombie ships are taking care of that for you right now!"

"No."

"It's the fucking apocalypse out there, man! Fuck your murderousness! I should have let you rot on Lagunia!" Dev snapped as anger took over again.

"I would gain no benefit from killing you and your crew. I am not familiar with the flight pattern of this model ship, but I have a similar one in my neurosoft that should suffice. Considering the fact that extremely special circumstances prevail, I would prefer you be at the helm. If that is not possible, I will end our cooperation now."

"Cooperation? What cooperation? You're forcing us to become accomplices in your sick shit. But I won't be intimidated far enough to put the *Quantum Bitch* and my people into the heart of an out-of-control space battle without radiators!"

"You're all about money." Sirion nodded, as if surprised by

347

his own surprise at this fact. Then he pulled something from a previously unseen pocket on his chest and Dev tensed, ready to flee. But it was a small credstick that the dark-eyed fellow with the strangely over-correct Dunkelheim accent delivered in his direction with a quick shove. Dev caught it and the wireless connector in his palm reported a fortune stored on it: twenty-five million Sol credits including the decryption pattern. They were unregistered.

He blinked a few times and then looked up at his unwelcome guest.

"Who the hell are you?" he breathed.

"Are you flying to the *Oberon*?" Sirion asked.

"It's a trick."

"I'm not interested in money. Time is short. Make up your mind before I count to three. One—"

"Okay, okay!" Dev raised his hands defensively and immediately went into an uncontrolled spin from his careless movement, which was only caught when a frighteningly strong, and cold, hand grabbed his shoulder and steadied him. A shiver ran through him that did not come from the statically charged air.

"Just answer me one question," he growled, though the rushing blood in his ears warned him and everything in him screamed to shut up. "Why?"

To his surprise, Sirion did not kill him on the spot, nor did he simply turn away. Instead, something happened that he had not thought possible with the sinister man: A brief flicker, almost something like an emotion, came over his eyes, even if it was indistinct.

"I will kill Captain Konrad Bradley for murdering my mother." Sirion's mouth narrowed until it was barely visible. "Sarah Mantell. Before he dies under my hands, he will remember her name."

"Sarah Mantell?" Dev muttered, irritated. "Who—"

"You should return to the cockpit now."

26

Konrad walked quietly among the four Marines who had closed around him and were escorting him through the corridors of the *Caesar* toward the brig, machine guns held ready. All were tall men who towered over him by half a head or more. Their state-of-the-art full-body suits of nanonic memory fabric made them look like dancers in spandex suits, much more delicate and agile than the heavy powered armor of his own Black Legion Marines. Their slender appearance, however, did not tempt him to make the mistake of dismissing them as lanky or weak. Speed and precision could be more deadly than brute strength and force.

Again and again, the deck vibrated beneath his feet as launch pads were activated. The flagship shook several times, but not hard enough to indicate an impact, so they were obviously in the most-protected area of the ship since the surprise attack had occurred. He himself would have accelerated his ship forward and imposed it to shield as much of his fleet's firepower as possible and buy them time to assess the situation and adjust the battle pattern accordingly. But the *Oberon* was a Titan and the *Caesar* a heavy cruiser, to that extent the admiral's tactical decision was correct. Maintaining the chain of command was now the most important link in a long, tense chain that could not be allowed to break.

Thousands of questions clamored at once in his mind for attention: Who had attacked them? How could someone use the gate network who was not authorized? How did they know the codes? How had the top-secret program been exposed? Why hadn't anyone warned them? What were the attackers up to and did the Clicks have anything to do with them? What was the status of the *Oberon* and its fleet? His sons?

He banished all these questions deep into his mind, reluctant to waste time and energy on things he didn't know the answers to and had no way of getting. His current assignment was to be a prisoner; after all, he was here by his own choice. There was no use driving himself crazy and hoping for a miracle that would lead him to the only place in this universe where he needed to be now, the place of his duty, the bridge of the *Oberon*.

Silly will make it. It's time she realized her potential, he thought, smiling faintly.

"What are you grinning at, Grandpa?" one of the Marines asked from behind him, jabbing the pommel of his submachine gun into his back.

"Handcuffing a *grandpa* must require some very special Fleet training," Konrad said calmly.

"Reprimanding recalcitrant reservists is standard repertoire," the faceless voice countered.

"I understand you're afraid, son. We don't know who's attacking us right now and what their goal is, and that's always a bad sign for a battle. However, there's nothing we can do about it, so calm is the best advisor."

"Scared? Pah!" the Marine sneered. "Last time I checked, it was *you* hiding in the ass end of Federation territory like a rat."

"I do what I have to do to protect my people," Konrad replied. "That's my job. What's yours?"

"My job?"

"Yes."

"My fucking job is to get a coward and traitor like you into the brig, man!"

"That sounds like a very easy task. At many points in my service, I would have envied you that. How easy do you think it is to decide whether to sacrifice eight thousand crew members and twenty million colonists to go down *honorably*, or to get your crew and those twenty million colonists to safety and accept not throwing yourself into the hopeless but heroic battle with everything you have?" Konrad felt something inside him loosen, as if he was actually talking to himself to find acceptance with everything that had brought him to this point. At least his officers and crew were now rid of the stigma that had clung to him all these years. Was this the liberation he had always wanted for them and himself?

Peace spread through him, and it was followed by a touch of joy.

"What are you grinning at now?" grumbled the Marine. "You do know you're facing execution, don't you?"

"Who could ever have hoped for more, son?" Konrad said.

"I—what?"

"Leave the captain alone already, Lombardi!" said one of the other Marines from the front. He wore the insignia of a sergeant and was probably the one in charge. His accent sounded like the typical over-correct English with a British twist that almost certainly identified him as an Earthman.

"Captain? Tsss! He's a traitor!"

"Traitor to the reserve," chuckled another behind him.

"Until he's legally convicted, he's a captain in Fleet under arrest; nothing more, nothing less," the sergeant said. "You damn pudding heads should have paid more attention in training. You know this man from the feeds, huh?"

"Yes, he—"

"Bullshit! Have you ever been interviewed by any of the networks, Captain?"

"No," Konrad said. They turned a corner and got into an elevator. Like participants in a well-rehearsed choreography, they positioned themselves in their X shape, facing the door.

"Do you understand now, Specialist Lombardi?"

When Lombardi didn't answer, Konrad filled the silence.

"Every feed follows a narrative that sells well. Revelations, sensations, catastrophes. Balance, amplify what people are outraged about—in other words, what's being talked about. None of these *editors* were there when my home planet went down, and neither were you, Specialist Lombardi. I don't judge you because you make decisions based on the information you've received. What else could you do? That's exactly what happened to me twenty years ago when I was called upon to make a decision in a matter of minutes that affected millions of lives. If—"

"We don't have much time," the sergeant interrupted him after glancing at his forearm display. "In-ship warning." The man turned to Konrad and eyed him. "Your *Oberon* has just set a course for us."

"Hm," he said softly.

He had hoped that Silly would obey his order and had firmly believed she would. To disobey him was not really her style. This could only mean that something had changed to bring her to this decision, which was certainly difficult for her. He wondered if the battle was really that bad.

"We're fighting fucking aliens, and these traitors have nothing better to do than attack us?" Lombardi grumbled. A moment later, a violent blow to Konrad's back threw him forward. He tried to catch himself with his leg stretched forward, but the lack of balance due to his bound hands ruined the attempt and he crashed between the front two Marines and his head hit the elevator doors.

Stars danced before his eyes and he heard angry voices, far

away and indistinct. Briefly, his vision went black. When it cleared and the sound returned to normal, he was being held up and there was a face directly in front of him eyeing his forehead.

"Now we get to detour to sickbay, Lombardi!" the sergeant said, placing Konrad back into the middle of the four Marines. "Touch him again and there'll be disciplinary action."

"Man, his people—"

"Or I'll talk to the COB!"

"It's all right," Konrad said, blinking to clear his gaze. The young Marine was frightened, and young men with power, be it even a quantern, were prone to hormonal overreactions. Ironically, he recognized himself as a young fighter pilot in this Lombardi. Always with his head through the wall and following every impulse. How he had gotten his pilot's license was beyond him. "If a laceration and a young man's anger would kill me, I wouldn't be—"

That was as far as he got. A hollow *plonk!* sounded at the same time a hole the size of a child's head appeared in the elevator door and in the stomach of one of the Marines behind him, who stared down at himself in disbelief. Blood poured from the wound and ran down his body in streams. He slumped and a shrill alarm went through the ship.

"Jupiter!" the sergeant cursed, thrust his weapon into the hand of one of his shocked comrades, and leaped to the Marine, who was staring at the ceiling with blank eyes. Blood bubbled and welled up over his glistening lips. Konrad also knelt beside him and grabbed the specialist's shoulders to roll him onto his side. Immediately, bright blood poured from his mouth, and he sucked in a gasping breath.

"The bleeding must be stopped," he said loudly over the alarm. The red emergency lights of the stopped elevator created a ghostly twilight that visually amplified the emergency and created a sense of unease all its own.

"I realize that, man," the sergeant murmured, baring his teeth. "Unfortunately, there's no medikit here! Gonzo, see if you can connect to the bridge."

"Give me your gun," Konrad said, and the sergeant looked at him as if he had lost his mind. But he maintained eye contact and held out his cuffed hands. "He doesn't have much time."

He was a little surprised when the sergeant actually reached back and snatched the machine pistol with the long round barrel out of his comrade's hands.

Konrad grabbed the gun, set it to maximum fire rate and checked the digital ammunition display, which read 500. He aimed at the rear cabin wall and pulled the trigger. It wasn't particularly loud, no louder than the alarm, except for the protesting screech of the composite tearing open behind Lombardi's head. The struts and cables behind it began to smoke, but he didn't let go and watched the ammunition gauge drop rapidly. A red light warned of impending over-heating as it reached 100. He ignored that, too, until it was almost to 0 and the submachine gun began to vibrate. Then he held the left side diagonally across Lombardi's wound, through which he could see the grimy floor. The overheated battery, an elongated object the size of a cigar box, glowed cherry red, was ejected, and flew hissing into the hole in the Marine's stomach.

Konrad threw the gun away and started to continue, but the sergeant realized what he was doing and grabbed the battery with gloved hands, which hissed and spread the heat over the suit, which visibly lit up. Then he moved it along the edges of the wound, which crackled and gave off a sickening smell of burnt flesh that rose to the ceiling with thick smoke.

Lombardi screamed like mad during the improvised cauterization, but that meant his airways were clear, which Konrad took as a good sign.

"Won't save him but might be enough to stabilize him in

the infirmary until the destroyed organs can be cloned," he said, nodding at Lombardi. "You'll be fine, son."

The sergeant gave Lombardi a long disparaging look after he threw away the battery, which had cooled enough that it no longer glowed. The specialist's bleeding had decreased noticeably but not stopped.

"Thank you."

Konrad merely nodded. The elevator started moving again, screeching menacingly.

"You'll get in the brig anyway," the Marine said gravely.

"I'm here by my own choice and I'm wearing these handcuffs by my own choice." To emphasize his statement, he raised his bloodied hands and wiggled the metallic shackles so that they rattled.

27

"Seventy klicks!"

"Full acceleration achieved!"

"Bring us alongside!" Silly ordered; her eyes raised. The *Oberon* had crossed the rear lines of Augustus's fleet's formation after the ships had, as expected, pushed farther and farther forward, opening the hollow cone from behind. The first enemy had come into range and fired whole swarms of strange, erratic missiles at them, though most of these were destroyed in their flak shield. The rest were neutralized by the short-range defenses. After directing hundreds of missile salvos in response for over ten minutes, she had soon come to realize that there was no point. As if by magic, the missiles had failed to pick up any target bearing, as if the eerie ships from hyperspace did not exist. Some managed random hits because the projectiles had flown into the path of individual targets and so had done corresponding damage, unless they were intercepted. But the hit rate was less than five percent, making it a waste. They had more success with the railguns, but their range was limited and not particularly effective at the current engagement distance, so she had reluctantly agreed with Nicholas and ceased all offensive fire.

The *Caesar* now lay like a lone fish in a pond with a storm raging on its shores. Explosions and plasma coronas made the black space glitter and sparkle among dazzling flashes of lightning. But inside the formation, a deceptive calm prevailed, except for an increasing number of driftless projectiles piercing the screen of the fleet's nonstop close-in defenses. The *Caesar* was hit several times and was losing atmosphere at short intervals, visible on the telescopic images as short-lived gas geysers shooting from the hull before being sealed.

"Ten minutes until we're in range," Lieutenant Alkad announced.

"Where is Colonel Meyer?" Silly asked no one in particular. Daussel picked up his handset from the command table and pressed some keys.

"I see," he said before hanging up and looking at her. "The colonel selected himself to command the liberation operation."

"Excuse me?" She narrowed her eyes and pointed at his communicator. "Order him not to do that. He is responsible for the entire Black Legion! The forty Marines on the boarding party can't be led by one lieutenant!"

"He said you would say that. They already had to come down and stop him from getting on one of the two ferries. That was the only way to stop him, he said."

"Son of a bitch!"

In her mind, she played through the scenarios. With their current course, they would be sufficiently close to the *Caesar* to intercept any possible missile attacks on the two boarding shuttles before they could accelerate enough. But railguns would be lethal at such close range, and would not be able to neutralize them. That left her only two options: Either she ordered the firing of the flagship's gun batteries, or she could hope that Augustus feared she might order the destruction of his ship if he destroyed her boarding shuttles, which meant he would do nothing. After all, he could assume that he and his crew were in no immediate danger as long as Konrad Bradley was on board with him.

This was a bad position for Silly to be in, and she was well aware of it. Accordingly, she was frustrated by Meyer's decision to participate in the mission himself. The possibility that all the Marines would die in this operation was simply too high and reminded her once again of the high price she was willing to pay to get the captain back.

There is no time for such questions now. I have to show determination, she reminded herself and straightened her shoulders.

"Adjust flak shield," she ordered as the red dotted line of her defensive screen of shells came too close to the allied ships of Strike Group 2.

"Captain," Jason said, "we can still drop the Marines and continue toward the gate."

"Once we slow down, it will take too much time to accelerate again. The Strike Group's formation will be broken by then, and the *Caesar* will be history, too," she explained, hoping she sounded as confident as the old man with her choice of words and tone of voice.

"That's why we can't slow down! The only chance we have of stopping this madness is if we fly full speed toward the gate!"

"This *madness* cannot be stopped!" she said more harshly than intended. How she wished she had the old man's cool head. "Whoever these invaders are, their electronic jamming is far superior to ours. We haven't gotten a single bearing and they're getting more and more."

"What if we do both?" Nicholas asked, and all eyes at the table turned to him.

"Both?"

"We could stay at full speed and launch the boarding shuttles at the right moment."

Daussel shook his head. "Impossible. That would require

maximum thrust from the port maneuvering thrusters on the ferries over several minutes."

"Which would only be possible if they used up the entire cold gas supply. If at all," Silly said.

"Granted." Nicholas nodded, but continued, "That's why I suggest a close-range catapult launch."

"You can only do that with impact ferries," she objected. "And those are one-way operations, as you know, Bradley."

"That's true, but it solves two problems for us: We'd have to get closer to the *Caesar*, depriving them of reaction time when they could fire on the ferries. At the same time, we launch at full speed, start the rescue operation, and attack the gate at the same time."

"That still leaves the third problem: The ferries become unusable once they have penetrated the hull of the target," Daussel insisted.

"Meyer is resourceful. With forty of the Black Legion, he can take control of the *Caesar*'s ferries and come back with them. With forty Black Legionnaires, he could take over the whole ship." Nicholas pointed to the admiral's flagship on the holoscreen, a tiny line next to the large silhouette of the *Oberon*. The image looked like a whale trying to swallow a sardine from behind.

"Even that won't do any good if we're in the middle of the battle, in a dubious attempt to cut off the enemy's reinforcements. Worst-case scenario, we won't be around to recover him and your father."

"I love my father, but we cannot throw away the lives of all the people of Lagunia and our fleet for the chance to bring him back." Nicholas was almost pleading now, which unsettled her. "That would mean the end of Harbingen and the beginning of a debt so great that we would never be able to live with it."

"Your father had to make a difficult decision before, and it turned out in the end—" she said, but Nicholas stopped her.

"That was something else. Dad chose to save as many as possible. We can't save Lagunia, I understand that, but we can buy them time so as many Harbingers as possible can escape via the inner jump point. To do that, we have to not only tie up the enemy's forces here but also cut off their reinforcements if we're going to have any chance at all."

"And risk losing your father," she added.

"Yes." His voice lowered to a whisper that weighed heavier than a mountain. "I know."

Silly rubbed her temples.

"Captain," Jason started.

"Quiet!" she snapped at him and closed her eyes. *Damn it, Konrad! Why aren't you here? What do you want me to do? I can't let you be sentenced to death in a politically motivated show trial in the Sol System.* She sighed. *But I can't pay for your rescue with the blood of innocent people either.*

"Make it so," she finally murmured.

"Excuse me?"

"Full speed ahead on the hyperspace gate!" she said, louder. "Let Meyer know he has five minutes to relocate himself and his people into the impact shuttles! We'll destroy the gate and then turn back to collect him. If he doesn't have our captain with him, I'll rip his stubborn skull right off his shoulders!"

Nicholas sighed in relief. Jason looked confused then even more incredulous. She didn't care. Konrad's youngest was right, even if she didn't like it. But wasn't that exactly the job of a good commander? To weigh things and remain open to better assessments and ideas than her own?

A good captain is a level-headed facilitator, not a dictator. A good captain knows how to use his resources purposefully and effectively, and his resources are his officers, noncommissioned officers, and enlisted ranks, she recalled the old man saying on a particularly grim day after their escape from Harbingen. They had been sitting in his cabin discussing it over a scotch and she had asked him why he had not court-martialed a number of protesting senior officers after they had refused to carry out orders, citing service regulations—although service regulations had not been on their side, as it later turned out. Again, of course, Konrad had proved to have the better foresight: Today, one of those officers was Daussel, who stood next to her and was one of the captain's most ardent supporters.

"Don't stare at me like two bug-eyed cadets! Get ready for CQB! All stations! I want everyone who doesn't have a direct assignment in an emergency seat! Lieutenant Jung, permanent broadcast to all allied ships in our flight path; tell them to give us some damn room! Share our plan with anyone who will listen; we're destroying the gate. Anyone who won't help us, at least don't stand in our way. Lieutenant Bauer, fire at your discretion, but don't waste time once the path is clear. Concentrate all weapons systems on the gate. Keep everyone else as busy as we can with our enemies. No missiles, railguns only."

"Aye, ma'am!"

"Yes, ma'am!"

"Let's welcome these scumbags to Harbingen!"

Cheers started and Silly straightened her shoulders in satisfaction. The decision was made. What result it brought, fate had yet to show. At least they would not have to wait long.

FRAGMENT OF THE MOON KOR, HARBINGEN SYSTEM

Roger raised his right arm, which was encased in a clunky mining spacesuit that shielded him from the fierce radiation on the sun side of Kor's debris and gazed at the stars. Around him, Kor's surface looked like the landscape of the Terran moon, drab gray with craters, larger and smaller rocks, and the hints of mountains—except for the gigantic telescope protruding from a fifty-by-fifty-meter floor hatch not a hundred paces away. It looked like an oversized flashlight surrounded by toothpicks, as tall as a skyscraper and the result of over fifteen years of work and many billions of credits, finally seeing the light of the stars six hours ago.

"What are you doing?" Frederick asked beside him. His voice was scratchy over the radio and echoed in Roger's helmet.

"You're about to see." He pressed a button on his overlaid forearm display, and a hologram settled over the sparkling black sky like the window to an alien world. It zoomed in several times before pausing on a point guarded by two dozen warships, between which a large transport materialized out of nowhere.

Jumps looked great, Roger thought, *like a ship hurtling out of nowhere into the present at insane speed and slowing to zero. So fast the eye couldn't keep up.* More transporters followed, joining the long caravan of glowing exhaust flares flying toward the system's outer jump point. Also approaching from much farther out, from the Oort cloud, were ships with larger and heavier dimensions, undetectable to the sensors of Kor's close-range surveillance system, into which he had latched on. They were still too distant and would take several weeks to detect because of the long distance.

"Somehow it makes me nervous that the sleeper ships take so long to reach Bohr," Frederick said. He had positioned himself behind Roger so he could look over his shoulder at approximately the right angle to see what his friend was looking at. "It's like we're doing a bank robbery in slow motion while the clock keeps turning normally for the police."

"I know what you mean. But the chancellor knows what he's doing. I've heard that Fleet is busy with Iron Hammer, and they're going to give the Clicks a run for their money. I don't think there's a better time for us."

"Just look at that jump point up there," Frederick changed the subject. "There are already hundreds of ships arriving from the rim worlds. I never knew there were so many of us."

"That's because the TF is only interested in the Core Worlds." Roger snorted. "And yet our ancestors were more emigration-friendly than we thought. At least with the Omega takeover."

"Do you think our course is the right one?"

"What do you mean?"

"I don't want to say we're doing the wrong thing, that's not what I mean." Frederick pointed to the giant telescope, next to which they felt like ants at the foot of Mount Everest. "Will it do what we want it to do? Everything hinges on this thing, which is pretty crazy when I look at what's going on out there and the risks involved. If Fleet gets wind of it, there won't be any mercy for us."

"We don't need their mercy." Roger nudged his friend in his side. "Come on, we'd better make sure everything goes smoothly. The maintenance flaps aren't far off. Then maybe we can do our part to make it show us what it's supposed to do."

28

Colonel Ludwig Meyer pulled his lips back from the hard foam mouthpiece that fixed his two rows of teeth together and grinned at his Marines, exposing the white foam. The N7 pre-armor they wore made them look like beefy Space Marines from a martial action fantasy, with bulky shoulder plates that housed much of their ammunition supplies. The joints in their legs, arms and hands were chunky thickenings that protected servo motors that gave them their superhuman strength and outstanding zero-G combat capabilities. Nothing about them was aesthetic. On the contrary, from a distance they could have been mistaken for bugs locked in a box-which is why the Black Legion was readily disparaged in the Federation as bug people. But Meyer knew this kind of mockery merely served to cover up an all too uncomfortable insecurity. Their equipment might be outdated by current Fleet standards, where speed and precision were all that mattered, but the training of Terran Marines had also become increasingly faster and more precise during the war. To ensure that enough soldiers were ready for the front lines, basic training had been streamlined, and as early as their second year, graduates were sent off for specialized advanced training in their respective areas of operation like engineering, communications, heavy weapons, zero G, planetary operations, security, and many others. His recruits needed twice the training time and went through each area until he was satisfied with their results—and that was a good thing.

The mass catapult demagnetized their *Puma*-class impact shuttle, and a violent jolt went through the cramped cabin. Not for the first time, he wondered what the safety harness that secured him at the shoulders, hips, and thighs to the magnetic bar at his back was for anyway, except to make the flight even more uncomfortable. He, along with Lieutenant Zumwalt and Chief Petty Officer Freud, were at the rear of the cabin. The rest of his twenty Marines in Puma 1 were split into two rows to the right and left, close together, with a narrow corridor between them that ended at the front in a wall that wasn't actually a wall, displaying a large, red, flashing explosive hazard symbol.

"Hoo-ra, black furs!" he shouted mumbling past his mouthpiece. "Finally, we don't have to sit on our hands and kick some fish ass!"

"Hoo-ra!" the Legionnaires replied, and their roar resounded so loudly in the cabin that the audio filters on his helmet system cut out.

"All right, launch in five seconds. Helmets closed!" ordered the lieutenant.

He nodded to her and closed his visor by voice command. It flipped down from the top to the chin bar, and a short hiss announced that he was now breathing the filtered air of his suit. From the inside, everything looked the same as before, as if he could still see normally without two inches of carbotanium in front of his face. The artificial image on the inside was generated from a near real-time image from the high-resolution sensor band around his forehead section. The latency was so low that the human mind could not consciously perceive it, but there had been repeated cases of kinetosis since the introduction of the N7. Marines had complained of nausea, dizziness, and headaches, but only in the first few months of training inside the armor; they were Marines, after all, not stubble-hoppers.

A red light on the cabin ceiling lit up, giving them about a second's warning, then the mass catapult accelerated them to 6 Gs before they were even shot out of the muzzle on the starboard side of the *Oberon*. They would cover the five-kilometer distance to the *Caesar* in just over thirteen seconds, little time for close range defense, but still time.

Meyer tried not to think about it while the ferry jerked and vibrated like a bucking animal. Something had probably broken. He didn't care. As a Marine in the age of space travel, one was used to being locked in a tin can and at the mercy of the engineers and their machines until it was finally their turn. It wasn't a good feeling, he had to admit to himself, but one that you either learned to live with or you didn't.

"Drop successful, Puma 1," came the message from the *Oberon*.

"Roger that," he grunted against the violent forces of acceleration, almost unable to push any sound past his lips. He felt woozy despite the amphetamine cocktail in his blood, and even his titanium-coated bones—it had been legal and affordable in his day—and powerful muscles didn't save him from the sixfold weight of his body pressing against the back of his servo armor as if a giant had kicked him and then left his foot on his chest.

He counted eight seconds and was preparing for impact when he heard a string of one or two dozen bangs, as if a series of bolts had flown out of the deck at high pressure in quick succession. Immediately, a high-pitched roar began, and dust and bright steam from the air conditioning system streamed furiously toward finger-thick holes in the ceiling and floor. They had been fired upon.

That son of a bitch! he growled inwardly, checking the vital signs of his Legionnaires at the left edge of his vision. No one had been hit.

Two seconds left.

"Defensive fire. Puma 2 destroyed," the *Oberon* reported, and Meyer clenched his teeth tighter than the hard acceleration forces could manage.

Then came the impact. The heavily armored tip of the impact shuttle rammed itself ten meters deep into the *Caesar's* hull like a giant kinetic missile, fast enough to penetrate armor and composite walls, but not fast enough to leave a crater or be destroyed itself—except for the penetrator tip.

There was a *click*, and the safety harnesses went up and settled into place. He was free. He was the first to sprint for the front wall, which exploded at the same moment and flew outward to clear the passage into the admiral's flagship.

Twenty Legionnaires lost before they could lift a finger. Shot down by our own people, he raged. *Half the troops for the mission. Worse odds, but still good enough.*

Meyer charged through the smoking breach and leaped over several feet of crumpled ship debris and twitching cables into a debris-strewn corridor. Thunderous currents of air told him that the hole the one-time ferry was in was not tight and they were losing atmosphere. Safety bulkheads had already been lowered to the right and left, which was certainly convenient for the defenders.

"*Oberon*, total loss of twenty Legionnaires. I guess the rules of engagement have changed with that?" he asked over his encrypted channel to their mothership, but he got only static in response.

Jammers, of course.

The rules of engagement, which he himself had drawn up and agreed upon with the commander, stipulated that they use non-lethal force to free their captain, unless they were forced to do otherwise in order to achieve their mission objective. The whole Bradley thing had escalated so much that it didn't matter to a court-martial how much further they went. But those on the ship were still Federation citizens, soldiers and humans, and thus not the primary enemy.

But now they had killed his Legionnaires, apparently without making the same considerations as he had. That made him angry. Not a good situation, but one he could live with. Some others soon would not, because he had prepared for both cases.

After securing the small section of corridor with Freud and Zumwalt and seeing that they were not being fired upon by any self-propelled grenades or the like, he waved to the rest of the waiting Marines to follow.

"We're sticking with rubber bullets in forearm barrels. Main armament, change to carbines." He carried out his own order by extending one hand upward and the weapon mount from his back pressed the grip of the heavy Gauss rifle into his palms in response. Through his gloves, the gun connected to the automatic aiming device in his computer, which in turn connected to his neural stratum via a network of artificial synapses, allowing him to react more quickly. The Gauss carbine unfolded and extended to full length, which was about an arm's length, since it was the shortened version with the bulky barrel. He flashed the schematic of the *Caesar* into his HUD and considered it briefly. They had had two models available for the, very short, planning: The heavy battlecruiser of the previous series and the auxiliary cruiser of the current series. Neither was the exact model of the *Caesar*, but they were what they had. As reservists they didn't have much insight into secret Fleet data. So, the brig was either port or starboard below the crew quarters and above the electron matrix nodes.

"Zumwalt, you take Second Platoon and advance to position Beta. First Platoon, with me, Position Alpha." He pointed to the security bulkhead in front of him. "Open it!"

Two of his Legionnaires stepped up to his right and left and, with fluid motions, applied the carbines, which immediately barked away, chasing a barrage of tungsten cones at near-relativistic velocities toward the bulkhead. As they did so, they moved their weapons up and to the side until they had described a perfect square and the cut piece of armor steel crashed to the corridor floor, smoking.

"Advance!"

The first resistance came after the first turn in front of the elevators. Four Marines had entrenched themselves there, waiting with the barrels of their modern laser rifles, their bodies hidden behind the corners of two recesses. Meyer and his Legionnaires didn't need to pretend they could hide anywhere in their clunky armor, which made whirring servo noises with each step. He could not help but imagine an analogy: medieval crossbowmen in cuirasses facing modern infantrymen of the 20th century. At first glance, an unequal duel, but crossbow bolts were able to pierce all later armor, which was used less and less in favor of mobility, while a chemically powered pistol could not penetrate armor common at the time. They were the crossbowmen, and he was willing to bet they had an advantage their counterparts didn't know about.

"I'm giving you five seconds to lay down your weapons. We're going to get our captain whether you like it or not," he boomed at full volume over his suit speakers. It would hurt their ears but that was fine with him. "Even though your admiral has my soldiers on his conscience, I'm giving you five seconds out of respect and decorum among Marines."

As if to emphasize his words, his Legionnaires brought their carbines to bear around him, so that he looked like a fir tree combed forward.

"Do not take another step! You are trespassing on the flagship of Strike Group 2. Lay down your weapons. You will be court-martialed, and—"

"Twenty percent," Meyer ordered over his platoon's radio, and a storm of Gaussian projectiles swept through the short corridor. Wall panels were shredded, straggling projectiles chopped flying debris into smaller and smaller pieces, then the screams began. Two laser lances dislodged from their barrels and streaked across them, but the pulses were too short to seriously harm them. His own armor was hit, glowed red briefly and redirected the heat over his boots into the ground, which began to smoke slightly.

He gestured and his men moved forward. The *Caesar's* Marines lay with tattered legs to the right and left of the elevator doors. They weren't screaming, so it seemed their ridiculous spandex suits had an internal med system. He ordered his medic to tend to the wounds while four others pried open the right-hand door by pressing their hands into the gap and, aided by the engines of their armor, tugged at it until it opened.

Meyer, meanwhile, stepped in front of one of the amputees and pointed. "The brig you're taking Captain Bradley to, where is that?"

When the man, faceless behind his slim helmet, did not answer, Meyer pressed the barrel of his Gauss carbine to his forehead.

"Twenty of my people are dead because of you. So, I'm only going to ask once."

"Two decks down to the left. Second door on the right," the Marine gasped.

Port side, then. They got lucky. He tried to reach Zumwalt, but nothing but static answered him. The lieutenant would figure it out and find the hangar by himself.

Meyer looked at the Marine and nodded. "I'm sure your comrades are on their way."

He saw the man's helmet move imperceptibly toward the laser rifle to his right.

"Leave it." With that, he turned away and walked to the open elevator shaft, which was vertical, not multidirectional. Three decks down he saw the roof of the elevator, gleaming in the light of his helmet lamps. He jumped and broke through the metal with his half-ton weight, only to land hunched over in the car like a force of nature. Two of his specialists landed next to him and were about to open the doors when they noticed a gaping head-sized hole in the left one and the right one was wide open. They were standing in a pool of blood that was still fresh enough that it was only clotted at the edges. The trail continued outside the elevator into a short hallway identical in construction to the one above, ending in another corridor.

And they were staring at weapons. At least a half-dozen Marines crouched behind massive shields with submachine guns and laser rifles drawn, designed for combat in narrow ship corridors like these.

"Shit," he cursed and moved to the left behind the elevator's control panel to safety. His Legionnaires did the same on the other side. They didn't really have cover, at most only partial cover.

"Surrender!" said a loud, commanding voice. "This is Commander Pyrgorates, XO of the *Caesar*. What you are doing here is treason! End this madness here and now, before more Fleet men and women have to die."

"Reservists, you mean," Meyer grumbled to himself, dialing Jules and Hoffman in his display, who were in the cabin with him. Via direct line, he said, "We've got some breaking to do, I guess. The brig is to the left. I need a tunnel, so we don't have to go through these fellows."

The two nodded, positioned their Gauss carbines slightly to the left, and squeezed the trigger in continuous fire. The Marines' response was immediate, showing either their tension or their determination. The black-painted carbotanium of their armor spat sparks and soon glowed red in an attempt to disperse and absorb the heat of the laser beams. But after a couple seconds the rain of shredded wall debris was dense enough to give them at least visual cover and a little scattering. They took advantage of this to make changes in position. Meyer waved upward and sprinted out of the cabin, keeping tight to the left and using the ultrasonic sensors on his neck to spot the hole Jules and Hoffman had torn in the wall. It led to a storage room containing now shattered crates, the remains of which he simply knocked aside or ran through. The inside of a ship wasn't particularly well armored, except for some safety-related areas like the reactor, the bridge, or life support, so it didn't surprise him that the next hole in the wall opposite was already created. It was not cleanly cut out like the first, but still perforated enough for him to hold his carbine in front of his chest and break through. Behind it was the outer corridor, three decks below where their impact shuttle now sat.

To his right, he saw the *Caesar*'s Marines engaged in a fire-fight with his men in the elevator. The ones in the "rear" swung around to face him, but several Legionnaires had already followed him.

"Fire at will," he growled, and they wasted no time. To hell with restraint, none was being shown by the other Marines, after all.

Meyer jerked forward slightly and turned reflexively. He saw a small group of people firing at him. Small caliber. The ineffective projectiles shattered against his armor like firecrackers. The aiming focus scanned three Marines, two of whom were carrying a wounded man. The third was firing at him, frantically running backward, with Captain Konrad Bradley crouching behind him.

"Thunder case! Hold position!" he ordered his Legionnaires.

He jerked up his carbine and sent three volleys into the

wall lining a meter in front of the Marine firing at him, shielding Bradley. Then he ran and fired again to keep the cloud of dust and composite close. He magnetized his boots and accelerated, fast enough to keep running along the undamaged left wall, shouldering his carbine smoothly as he did so. Entering the cloud, he peered into the jerky scene from a distorted angle, grabbed the man's weapon, and snapped it in two accompanied by the screech servos. He headbutted his opponent to the ground and simultaneously fired rubber bullets from forearm cannons at the other two Marines, who had dropped their comrade but were already reeling back from the impacts. Not enough to hurt them or keep them busy for long, but enough to grab Bradley and spin around him like a shield.

"We've come to rescue you, sir," he said over the helmet speakers.

"Cease fire!" Bradley ordered in his typically deep, raspy voice, which even now sounded as calm as the natural center of a storm.

"Sir?"

"Cease fire, Colonel."

"Cease fire! Order of the old man!" Meyer relayed the order on the team radio, and immediately the weapons fell silent. Only theirs at first, he could still hear the rattle of the submachine guns and the high-pitched beeping of the laser rifles with their high-capacity batteries. But even that lasted only a few seconds before silence fell.

"Drop your weapons! Medic!" the *Caesar*'s XO yelled somewhere in the sea of smoke and metal dust.

"Do it, Colonel." Bradley nodded and gestured curtly for him to let go of the Marine—a sergeant. Meyer hadn't even noticed that he had grabbed the guy again and turned him to block the shots of the two other Marines who had since stood. He obeyed, and the sergeant seemed undecided about what to do. He kept looking between the captain and him. "I appreciate your loyalty, but this is not the way."

"But, sir, this Augustus just wants you..."

"It doesn't matter what the admiral wants. *I* don't want innocent soldiers to die or the future of our people to become even more uncertain because of me. I think I know what Fleet leadership ordered Bretoni to do and what he made of it. My remaining here would be the only way to protect the *Oberon* in that case."

"Understood, sir," he said reluctantly.

"How bad is it out there?"

Meyer ejected the magazine from his Gauss carbine, and those of his internal suit weapons also fell clacking from their receptacles.

"Bad. Looks like this battle can't be won."

"I see."

"The XO will kill me if I come back without you."

Bradley smiled humorlessly. "She'll get over it. She's a good commander, she just doesn't know it yet. But so is every first command."

It remained quiet for a while as both sides determined whether the ceasefire was real or merely a feint by the other side.

"Commander Pyrgorates," Konrad finally called out. "Have my people pull out. I'm staying here. Enough blood has been shed."

"On our side," Meyer growled, and the captain nodded sadly. At that moment, he looked as if a burden greater than the universe weighed on his shoulders.

"Remember the unofficial motto of the Harbinger Fleet, Colonel."

"Duty is heavier than a stone, death lighter than a feather."

Again, Bradley nodded. "This is more than martial talk."

"Unarmed!" Pyrgorates shouted after a brief pause, during which he no doubt must have spoken to the admiral.

Konrad sighed with relief.

"Go, Colonel. Mourn for our dead but keep fighting for the living."

Meyer sensed that the old man was telling him more than his spoken words suggested, but at that moment he couldn't say exactly what it was. Only that it was serious and important enough to him that he disappear from this ship.

29

"Approaching the top of formation!" Lieutenant Alkad reported. Silly watched the tactical display. Of the sixty ships that had originally formed the cover, just twenty-five were still fighting. Thirty were completely lost and five were extending their radiators, which meant they would burn up shortly. Augustus's Strike Group was beginning to waver on the flanks, and the first enemy ships had broken through toward the flagship and the two carriers, which were throwing their last Predator drones at them.

"Focus forward railguns on marked targets!" she ordered, simultaneously tapping those red dots closest to those allies currently deploying their radiators. "Full fire pattern!"

On each of the *Oberon*'s forward bow bulges, fifty heavy railguns swung toward their new targets. Twenty-meter-long, counterrotating magnetic rails raced past each other in the massive tubes, accelerating the conical, fifteen-centimeter-long tungsten bolts to a fraction of the speed of light. The extreme pressure difference between the muzzle and the vacuum formed two hundred massive, if short-lived, plasma clouds that projected dozens of meters into space, making the forward section of the *Oberon* look as if it were lit by a forest fire. Since they were already in CQB and the flight time of the bullets was in the single-digit-seconds, the impacts occurred almost immediately.

Subdued cheers erupted on the bridge as several miniature suns appeared on the screen where reactors had lost integrity or enemy munitions depots had been hit. Some ships were so badly punctured that by the third and fourth waves they had veered off course and their plasma fire broke over the radiators of the overheated Terran ships.

"Keep it up!" Silly looked at the thrust indicator, which was approaching ninety-five percent, the maximum she had authorized.

"Ma'am, we need to focus on the goal. Twelve more klicks," Daussel said.

"As soon as we open fire on the gate, we'll have nothing to keep the entire fleet of hundreds of damn alien ships from beating on us."

"We have the flak shield."

"We've already had that. I won't use it while allied ships are in range."

"She's right. What good is the destruction of the gate if we have dozens of allied ships on our conscience for it," Nicholas said and Daussel sniffed glumly.

"Augustus shot down our Marines, just like that."

"Not just like that," Jason said. "After all, there were two impact shuttles racing toward his ship."

"Maybe you should share that justification with the colonel when he gets back here."

"Maybe you shouldn't take your frustration out on the crews of those ships who are fighting the invaders just like we are and have already lost hundreds, if not thousands, of comrades," Jason shot back.

"Whose side are you on, anyway? Would you rather go back to your beloved admiral?"

"He is not *my beloved admiral!* I am where my brother is,

and I am not justifying what is being done here. I am merely of the opinion that in foggy waters we should not make rash decisions that—"

"Quiet!" Silly yelled. "We don't have time for this. Unless it's absolutely necessary, I won't use the flak shield because it might put Terran ships in danger. It's bad enough when we can't protect them from losing their radiators."

By now, the eerie alien spacecraft with their deformed hulls and superstructures were arranged in a loose cloud, dented along the front where the admiral's formation had held. The tactical overview gave the impression of an arrow that had struck a cushion, but she knew it was really the other way around: the cloud had broken over the arrow, which had not moved an inch, but had lost much of its tip and plumage, while the cloud itself had grown.

The *Oberon* raced with glowing drive nacelles further and further toward the gate, which became increasingly larger on the sensors. With it, the eerie darkness that reigned within also drew closer, making Silly's hair stand on end. That she was here to destroy it all helped, though.

"Concentrate fire on the gate!"

What looked like a dense melee on the tactical holoscreen was a massacre of distant glittering dots surrounded by fast flashes and shooting stars in the dark cold space. As the *Oberon* left the dense spire of Terran defenders behind and plunged into the sphere of more than nine hundred invaders, there was still a vast expanse of nothing, dense with hard radiation that pushed even the well-shielded sensors on the hull to the limits of their functionality. Pieces of debris ranging from the size of small cars to tiny grains of dust smashed against the armor of the last Titan, and swarms of flickering missiles, bucking back and forth on their course, approached simultaneously from all sides. Plasma lances dispelled the darkness and cut a path through the vacuum, finding their center in the *Oberon*, impossible to intercept. Each impact ate away a few centimeters of the magnetized armor of the battleship, leaving first small, then deeper and deeper craters.

"Ma'am!" Daussel said as the first rockets hit, ripping whole chunks out of the mono-bonded carbon and hurling them into space. Again and again, they were jolted and had to hold on.

"No breaches!" reported Warrant Officer Treut.

"Continue to concentrate fire."

Volley after volley of missiles left the *Oberon*'s several hundred launch bays, located on each side of the ship in the gaps between the upper and lower hull sections. From the forward torpedo bays, fifty antimatter torpedoes per minute joined them. Slower than their smaller kinetic brethren, they took advantage of the protection provided by the massive swarm of guided missiles descending on the gate like a swarm of bees.

The enemy tried to block the attack, firing at the projectiles with everything they had and positioning themselves to deal with the onslaught.

On the screen, Silly watched in frustration as first a few, then more failures were displayed as her ship pumped more and more firepower into space and the impacts became more frequent and more violent. She looked at the formations and clicked her tongue.

"Raise the flak shield!" she finally ordered, and Daussel immediately gave an impatient wave in the direction of the operators in the ranks.

The starboard and port anti-aircraft guns swung out of their recesses, aligned, and began releasing their fragmentation shells. Ten long breaths later, Silly saw the familiar continuous flicker of explosions five klicks away, quickly mingled with much larger flowers of fire as the missiles aimed at her were shredded. She allowed herself a brief moment of relief. They were still getting pummeled by hundreds of plasma lances, but they would be able to take them for a while longer.

"Ma'am!" The voice belonged to Lieutenant Alkad. "I've got a ship coming at us! It's racing right through our missile salvos!"

"Then shoot it down!"

"Ma'am, it's a clipper with a Federation signature."

Silly stared at the picture and had to let Alkad mark the corresponding spaceship before she saw it herself. The *Oberon*'s onboard computer seemed sure it knew it.

"It's those smugglers the *Danube* tried to pin down!"

"Yes, ma'am, shall we intercept?"

"No. They won't survive anyway, and we're not here to play police, we're here to destroy the gate."

"Captain," Daussel said, and she was already preparing for the next objection.

"Yes?"

"The *Caesar* is accelerating."

"The *Caesar*?" she repeated, incredulously, lowering her eyes to the command table. Sure enough, the admiral's damaged flagship was picking up speed as if to follow the *Oberon*. "Did the son of a bitch finally grow some balls?"

"I don't know, but the carriers are staying behind."

"They're too slow anyway. But that makes it easier for us to get back, as long as he doesn't kill himself. He's probably too cowardly for that." Silly waved it off and ordered every railgun with a clear shot to engage in the attack on the gate. That would distract the enemy even less, but the failure rate of the guided weapons was simply too high. Although it didn't look like the invaders' weapons would be particularly accurate, their sheer numbers were worrisome. Again and again, the deck shook beneath their feet and new damage reports jumped onto the screen. It wasn't until the first explosions were seen on the ring structure that she nodded to herself and clenched her hands into fists.

"Alkad, how long will it take us to turn around and return

to the *Caesar*?" she asked, looking anxiously at the situation on the screen.

"Ten minutes, possibly less if the *Caesar* continues to accelerate toward us."

"Lieutenant Bauer, as soon as it's clear the hyperspace link in the gate will be broken, notify Alkad directly. Turn at your own discretion! We have no time to lose!" Silly could see they had stirred up a hornet's nest, and the noose was tightening around them. They might not have ten minutes before the situation became critical, and all hell broke loose. Behind them, the first ships were already beginning to move into position to take their retreat under fire, making it even more difficult to return to the already collapsing formation of Strike Group 2.

The old lady can take it, she told herself, and watched as more and more explosions appeared on the ring. It was the railguns that did the work. The missiles were almost entirely intercepted, despite their sheer numbers. But at least that meant fewer tungsten bolts were being hit by accident. *Keep going, just keep going!*

LOW ORBIT AROUND ARTROS, LAGUNIA SYSTEM

As the giant hyperspace gate lost its structural integrity and began to break into ragged pieces, exactly eighty-four ion engines came to life in the shadow of Artros. They emerged from an energetic slumber that had lasted years for some ships, while it had been only a few weeks for others that joined later. Although they were relatively close together, in the midst of one of the gas giant's fourteen ice rings, they did not look particularly impressive.

The fleets of invaders and defenders were still busy destroying each other, and the bulk of the battle was steadily shifting toward Lagunia, where evacuation efforts were in full swing. They would not be able to save everyone until the outsiders got there, but that did not concern the secret flotilla.

The eighty-four *StarVan*-class liners were leisurely pushed by their engines toward the outer jump point, from which the debris of the gate was slowly moving away. A pilot and copilot were in each ship, piloting one thousand souls in the passenger compartment and two thousand tons of cargo in the cargo deck below. They possessed neither armor nor armament, but they would not need them once they reached the jump point in less than an hour and began their erratic jump sequence to Harbingen.

Despite the shorter route, none of the ships would take a path across any of the fifty Core Worlds, knowing full well that a similar picture would prevail there as it did here, albeit with considerably more opposition from the defenders. After all, the Core Worlds were known for protecting their wealth, armed to the teeth in the middle of an all-out war.

The passive scanners of the foremost ship reported no incoming radar or lidar scans, so they initiated their jump preparations after a short pause, so as not to waste precious minutes upon arrival at their destination. After all, what they had waited years for would not tolerate any delay once it was within reach.

30

"Now you've lost it, boss!" Jezzy yelled over the roar of the engines, which reverberated through the cockpit via vibration and burst nitrogen lines.

Dev did not answer. What could he have said? He could agree with her, sure, but that would only make her more hysterical. He could also tell her that he'd rather take a 5 percent chance of survival—which was very optimistic—than none at all with a second grin in his throat.

Thinking of Sirion made him feel even worse. He knew the killer was sitting somewhere behind him in the cockpit, closely watching what was going on. And he was aware that Jezzy was not aware of what that meant.

Since the *Oberon* had, as expected, started to attack the ring with all guns, there had been only one way out for them: To fly directly into the eye of the storm. But as is so common with storms, the center was behind a nasty wall of wind, and in this case, lots of hail. The shower of missiles that awaited them was denser than Jezzy's mighty mop of hair and caused the *Quantum Bitch*'s warning systems to go completely haywire. The entire cockpit flashed, but unlike before, there were no more shades of green or yellow, only red. Lots and lots of red.

He had to turn off the control software for good because it kept interfering with his controls, so it was entirely up to him to push the thrust lever all the way forward and fly right into the missiles.

Once he had entered what he thought was the best course and saw the vector in front of him on the HUD, so he only had to follow it, he closed his eyes, expecting his ship to immediately explode. Instead, nothing of the sort happened. They were shaken as if caught in a hurricane, but he was still breathing and could perceive the shaking and Jezzy's screams, so he was either in hell or alive.

He snapped his eyes open and saw green lances of frayed light crashing into the missiles, causing them to explode en masse, some closer than he would have liked, but he wasn't going to argue with fate when it was being so kind to him. The invaders scared the hell out of him, but right now they had paradoxically saved their lives. That didn't mean they were off the hook, only that they had worked their way into the second circle of hell.

Like a fly in a wind tunnel, he continued to push the *Quantum Bitch* forward, dodging left and right when the proximity alarm whined, and diving under a volley of torpedoes that, fortunately, didn't lock on to them but steadily continued toward the hyperspace gate. Due to their insane speed, he saw them merely as brief blue flashes outside the window before they, too, passed. His reactions were no more than the vain imaginings of a human brain that was far removed from any actual reaction times in this chaos. Only computers were still playing in this league, and even they were begging for mercy.

But it felt good and right to do *something*, if only to dodge erratically in all directions and be able to say he had done his best. For a few minutes he thought he had succeeded because he was still breathing, and his body allowed itself the luxury of flooding him with a stimulating and euphoric hormone cocktail that elicited the whooping screams of a madman.

Then came the railgun bolts. Unlike the missiles, they were an invisible swarm, much closer and followed by the next volley. The *Bitch*'s sensors, nowhere near as finely tuned as the best systems available in Fleet, didn't even register them. He couldn't see them either, but he could see what they were doing: From one moment to the next, there were a dozen holes in his ship, five of them in the cockpit, two in the windshield. The escaping atmosphere roared so loudly that his ears rang until the first objects flew against the holes, briefly plugging them and providing deceptive silence.

"Seal it!" he yelled, unbuckling his seat belt and pointing at Sirion, who was sitting in Willy's seat. "Right flap under the faucet with the red cross on it. GO! Jezzy! Disk!"

She did not answer but nodded and rushed to the right flap with the supply of sealing foam and monomats. No blood was flying around, so no one had been hit. At least here.

"Willy? Dozer? Are you guys still in one piece?"

"Yes, boss, but the infirmary has six new windows," Willy shouted, though barely audible because of the static.

"A reactor has failed. Shut down." Dozer sounded the same as always. So, either he was dying or not a hair on his head had been touched.

Dev shut down the emergency cockpit power supply so the two remaining fusion reactors could direct all their power output into the engines and ripped the breathing masks from their holders above the door to the corridor.

"Hey!" he shouted, tossing the first to Jezzy and the second to Sirion after both had turned to face him. Then he returned to his pilot's seat and winced when a fat hole suddenly appeared in the headrest. He looked down at himself and noticed that the fabric in the crook of the arm of his overalls was shredded.

"Fuck, another!"

Back in his seat, his mouth was dry as desert sand, but he forced himself to retake controls and he found himself on a direct collision course with the nose of the *Oberon*, visible to the naked eye ahead of them—a shadow three hundred meters wide and only eight hundred meters away.

Panicked, he pressed down on the joystick and barely avoided being smashed. Another breath later, the Titan hurtled over them, and they slid below the phalanx of grenade launchers that flooded the space with their shrapnel, enveloping the Titan in a distant sphere of explosions and splinters.

Then the *Oberon* was gone, too, and life support reported that the atmospheric loss was weakening. It was at 30 percent and no longer breathable, but the pressure had stabilized. With the mask over his mouth and nose, he turned to Jezzy— and reluctantly to Sirion—and gave them each a thumbs up before pointing it at the *Caesar*, which was approaching them even faster than the *Oberon* had just done.

"What the hell? Are they all going to kill each other today?"

At the word *kill*, he thought of Sirion and his threat if Dev did not take him to *Oberon*.

Fuck it! If I do this, we're dead anyway!

Meyer ran down the corridor to the rise and fall of his own breath, the sound rushing in his helmet like the surf of a distant ocean. His hands were empty, both physically—his weapons were empty—and figuratively. His mood was appropriately grim. No one from his platoon had commented on the situation, although he could almost physically sense what was going on in their minds. The same thoughts that plagued him: twenty comrades lost, the return to the *Oberon* uncertain and difficult—perhaps they would be shot down as they abandoned ship—and the primary objective of their mission not achieved. If he confronted the XO, she would rip his head off as she had promised, and he couldn't even blame her. But the old man's order had been clear and there was nothing he could do about that. It only made things worse. He would have loved to tear the whole ship apart from the inside out, but that would have suited a frustrated child far better than a Black Legion colonel. So, just like his Legionnaires, he kept silent, accepted his fate, and did as he was ordered.

The starboard hangar was one deck below and astonishingly still had a shuttle, which Zumwalt and her platoon had already made ready by the time they arrived.

"The captain's not coming?" she asked over the radio, and he shook his head.

"Personal order: Return to the *Oberon*. He specifically wanted it that way."

"Do you have the video footage from their helmet cam?"

Meyer, proud of his lieutenant's restraint, nodded.

"Good, the shuttle is ready."

"Everybody, get in there!"

Zumwalt and Meyer waited while their twenty Legionnaires boarded through the open door in a disciplined and orderly manner. It would be very crowded but leaving even one N7 behind was out of the question. The passage to the hangar was directly connected to the door in the corridor by some sort of micro airlock, so the hangar was probably an emergency bay that opened and pushed the shuttle out.

"I didn't think they'd let us go so easily," Zumwalt said, looking around cautiously. Even she didn't doubt that they were monitored at every turn by cameras and sensors.

"Their XO promised us safe conduct to the shuttle," he said, leaving out his own response that he hadn't expected it himself. These people here were as vain as they were vindictive, it seemed. Why had they stopped now? What did the word from someone who wasn't above trying to trap a captain's son during an officer's visit just so he could bust his father count for? "Here we are anyway, so let's get out of here."

"The captain's not coming, but he made sure we got away." The lieutenant nodded and patted the last Legionnaire on the back.

"Otherwise, we'd die here with him," Meyer muttered, following her into the shuttle.

The *Oberon* was still four klicks away from the hyperspace gate when the first shield around an antimatter containment chamber of the ring structure burst, sending a bright white flash into the surrounding space. A wave of highly charged particles followed, racing up and down the electromagnetic spectrum as they took anything that got too close with them. This included dozens of Invader ships, which veered off at the last moment but could not escape the rapidly spreading annihilation front. It was delayed satisfaction for Silly to have at least indirectly caused further damage to the enemy. When the radiation wave hit the *Oberon*, a few warning symbols lit up on the holoscreen, similar to when they flew very close fly-by maneuvers on gas giants or a central star, but nothing the old lady couldn't handle.

They were already in a hard turn, now firing from several thousand guns simultaneously at anything without a Federation signature and had become the focus of enemy fire. The remaining half of Augustus's once-mighty fleet had changed course and was in the process of forming a hard-accelerating ball around its flagship, but her own firepower had visibly suffered. The missile stores must have been used up too quickly, even if they had had little effect anyway.

"Ma'am! We won't be able to approach the *Caesar* sideways," Lieutenant Alkad shouted from navigation. "She's accelerating too fast and will pass us before we—"

Silly tightened her hands around the edge of the command table, and the dim red lighting on the bridge seemed to grow more intense and darker with her anger. She did not immediately answer and blocked out Daussel and Nicholas, who were discussing the situation.

Instead, she looked at the *Caesar* on the tactical display and the *Oberon*, which was turning ponderously. The barely noticeable pauses in the loading of the real-time display reinforced the effect that her Titan appeared extremely sluggish.

What are you up to, you son of a bitch? Why are you accelerating so hard? Where are you going? She looked toward the gate, which had mostly turned into volatile gases, except for a few surprisingly resilient pieces of debris that were now tumbling through space and would soon clog the jump point once the gravitational conjunction zone recaptured them.

Conjunction zone, she thought, running her fingers over the virtual buttons and controls at her disposal. She blanked out all the ships except the *Caesar* and displayed the jump point, a five-kilometer-wide area behind them at an angle, into the far edge of which the *Caesar* had almost flown.

Jump points were natural phenomena that they had learned to exploit technologically, but still a gamble each time they were used, becoming smaller the closer they got to the gravitational center. The admiral knew he could not win the battle, and he also understood that he could not reach the center of the conjunction zone. That meant he was taking a risk. All at once she understood the formation of his fleet, which was why she had recklessly plunged forward instead of retreating to buy time to adjust to the new enemy and protect his ships from collision. He had made a decision early, and she had helped him make it succeed.

He wanted to jump!

"Pawn! Fire on the *Caesar*'s thrusters! Now!"

"Captain?" Daussel asked, looking at her in shock.

"She's right!" Nicholas said, his face pale, his gaze fixed rigidly on the tactical display. "He wants to jump!"

"Everything you've got!" Silly's voice almost broke.

"Captain, we still have countless requests from civilian ships asking for emergency docking permission," Lieutenant Jung called out, but she barely heard him through the veil of her excitement. "We are their only chance—"

"Whoever makes it, makes it!" she barked. "If we have to jump, we jump right behind the *Caesar*. Whoever isn't on board by then stays behind!"

"This is Captain Devlin Myers, I repeat, requesting docking clearance! Our life support is failing, and I've had to shut down our last reactor!" Dev shouted into his microphone once more. He turned to Sirion to prove to him that he was doing everything in his power, but the creepy guy wasn't there.

They were only eight hundred meters from the *Oberon*, which had suddenly stopped accelerating and was attempting a massive braking thrust.

"Energy radiation is increasing!" Jezzy warned.

"What?"

"They're charging their damn electron matrix cells!" she said, on the verge of panic.

"But we're too far out!"

"We are inside the conjunction zone, at the very edge," she said. On the screen, the *Caesar*'s symbol disappeared. "The *Oberon* is going to jump after it at any moment!"

"Fucking Fleet fuckers!" Dev pounded on his armrests so hard his fists ached. If the Titan jumped, there was a fifty-fifty chance they would even survive the jump intact and not be shredded by the hyperspace tides. Any injured soldiers on board who were heavily sedated enough to sleep or were in an induced coma would never wake up again if they could not be wakened before the transit, even if it succeeded. The worst, however, would be the gravitational waves that, in creating the subspace bubble around the ship, were likely to shake everything within a five-hundred-meter radius hard enough that no molecule would remain next to another. This was also the reason why jump points were monitored by space control and transit permits were left to complex organizational programs.

"We can't go back. We're out of power!" he cursed and did the only thing he could do, he used up the last of his cold gas supplies and fired the aft maneuvering thrusters simultaneously at full output, hoping they would at least make it into the battleship's subspace bubble before disappearing into the void of hyperspace. He didn't want to die, and he certainly didn't want his crew to die. Thanks to Sirion's disappearance, not by his knife or a piano string, he didn't much prefer a tidal wave.

Seven hundred meters. Six hundred and fifty. Six hundred. Five hundred and fifty, he counted along and closed his eyes. *Come on, come on.* "Stand by for transit!" he broadcast over the ship's radio and snapped his eyes open again. The ship ahead of them got bigger. If they were wrong and it didn't jump after all, they would crash into the hull, because they couldn't brake now. They simply had no more juice and breathed the last oxygen through their masks.

EPILOGUE

"They're gone!" Nicholas announced redundantly. "They jumped!"

Silly did not answer and instead stared at the missing icon on her tactical display. The *Caesar* had disappeared. Just like that. The admiral had duped her like a damned cadet. How had she not seen it? Why hadn't she been able to believe he would sacrifice his entire fleet just to save his ass? She should have known.

The rest of Strike Group 2 did not even attempt to reach the jump point because the cloud of enemy ships had long since closed on them. They fought on without regard to casualties. As far as she could see, no more radiators were extended, and they simply fired until the onboard computers took over because the crews were cooked. Eventually, the ships would burn up.

"Alkad, plot a course to Earth with the least number of jumps," she ordered.

"Ma'am?" Daussel asked. "What are we going to do?"

"We follow the *Caesar*," she growled.

"Captain!" Nicholas walked around the command deck. "We can't just let our fleet—"

"Silence!" she barked. "I have already made the mistake of letting you persuade me once. Now, not only are Colonel Meyer and twenty of our Legionnaires gone, but our commander and twenty other Legionnaires are dead. I'm not going to let him get away with it, and we're no help to our fleet anyway. Or how should we get out of this situation, huh?"

She pointed to the holoscreen, which showed the *Oberon* in the middle of a sphere of red dots. As if to emphasize her point, the *Oberon* was then jolted by several impacts and the image flickered for a few moments.

"They only have one chance now anyway." She turned away from Nicholas, who was staring, pale faced, at the tactical display and joined the silence on the bridge. "Young, open a fleetwide channel and broadcast to ship's internal speakers."

"Open!" reported the lieutenant from communications.

"This is Acting Captain Thurnau," she said in a firm voice. She involuntarily clasped her hands behind her back as the old man would have done. "We have destroyed the hyperspace gate, but the enemies are numerous. We do not know who they are, but their intentions are very clear. The admiral's flagship has fled the system with Captain Bradley aboard and we will follow to retrieve him. My previous order remains in effect: Evacuate as many civilians from Lagunia and the system's space stations as possible. Exit the system via the inner jump point. *Do not* attempt to approach the outer jump point. The invaders do not take prisoners. Stay together if possible and do not risk anything. Evacuate only if your ship will not be put at too great a risk. We need everyone. We need *you*. We won't forget you and we will come back when we have our commander back. Duty is heavier than a stone, death lighter than a feather. *Oberon* out."

"Course set!" shouted Lieutenant Alkad.

"Transit alarm!" Silly ordered immediately and waited for the blaring alarm to go off, reminding every crew member not to fall asleep or, preferably, not to even close their eyes lest they end up a brain-dead husk on the other side, not that she believed anyone was asleep right now. After three breaths of thinking of Konrad and making him a silent promise, she said aloud, "Jump!"

"Damn it!" Dev shouted as the *Oberon* lit up, stretching and spinning like an illusion—which was probably a hallucination in his brain—for an immeasurably short period. It disappeared.

The *Quantum Bitch*, just now swooping down on the former pride of Harbingen, hurtled into suddenly empty space, which soon filled with all manner of projectiles, causing the alerts to explode even further. A reminder that a brutal battle was still raging.

Dev took no time cursing every deity he had ever heard of and sent them downward at maximum acceleration the damaged reactors were able to produce, diving under missiles and then ripping the *Bitch* to the left, under the Invader fleet. They were still being fired upon, though with the disappearance of the two most powerful ships and the collapse of Strike Group 2, enemy fire visibly divided among many small targets, which scattered amid the inferno like a startled flock of sheep.

So, he took advantage of his ship's tininess compared to the rest of the battle participants and continued to tease it against the direction of flight of the enemy fleet. As if asleep, he instructed his frighteningly silent crew to get oxygen and continue sealing any leaks, to secure the heat pumps and to kindly ignore the shrill warning signals of the reactors. With reckless maneuvers, he circled one of the eerie Invader colossi whose green projectiles licked at him but miraculously missed, continued his madness, and then shot between two more starships into a massive debris field where the first of Admiral

Bretoni's ships had been destroyed, their remains now mingled with those of the hyperspace gate.

That's how far the battle has shifted, he thought. *They want to go to Lagunia, for sure.*

Dev followed his first impulse as they flew between a large piece of hull with half the inscription of a ship's name and a shredded reactor core and shut down the engine and all active scanners after releasing a fusion mine. It exploded three clicks behind them. They then suddenly tumbled weightlessly among the debris—hopefully no longer recognizable as a ship, but just one of many victims of this unequal struggle.

"Dev!" Jezzy shouted, her voice distorted by the respirator.

"Huh?" he said dejectedly as it dawned on him that his survival instincts had not brought them to a particularly better place. At worst, the aliens would come looking for them and vaporize them. At best, they would slowly suffocate or freeze to death out here.

"Before you turned off the scanners, I saw something else," she said, sending the appropriate data to his screen.

"What is it? Another fleet of those bastards?"

"No, according to the preliminary signature check, these are *StarVan*-class liners. Eighty-four of them, to be exact. And they're coming right at us."

"I'm guessing to the jump point, to be exact."

"What are they doing? Have they gone crazy?"

"No idea," Dev muttered, calculating their speed and the distance between the civilian ships and the jump point, which was less than fifty klicks away from them. "Hmmm."

AFTERWORD

Dear Reader,

The Last Battleship continues, of course. I am aware (as mentioned in the preface) that there are many loose threads, especially with regard to the background conspirators alluded to in this volume. But I promise: In Volume 2, you'll see the puzzle pieces all fall into place. If you enjoyed this first volume, I would greatly appreciate a starred rating at the end of this e-book or a short review on Amazon. That's the best way to help authors like me continue to write exciting books in the future. If you'd like to contact me directly, you can do so at joshua@joshuatcalvert.com I answer every email!

If you subscribe to my newsletter, I'll regularly chat a bit out of the sewing box—about me, writing, and the great themes of science fiction. Plus, as a thank you, you'll receive my e-book *Rift: The Transition* exclusively and for free: www.joshuat-calvert.com

Best regards,
  Joshua T. Calvert

Made in the USA
Monee, IL
13 August 2023